Restless in L.A.

To Jen)
Aren't we all a ?"
little "Restless in LA ?"
Lots of love,
Robin

A Novel

Robin Finn

Restless in L.A.
Copyright © 2016 Robin Finn
All rights reserved.

ISBN: (ebook) 978-0-9976212-7-3
(print) 978-1-945910-03-6

Inkspell Publishing
5764 Woodbine Ave.
Pinckney, MI 48169

Edited By Rie Langdon
Cover art By Najla Qamber

DEDICATION

To Michael
Without you, I wouldn't have dared.

ROBIN FINN

Come to me now
And lay your hands over me
Even if it's a lie
Say it will be alright
And I shall believe.

-Sheryl Crow, *I Shall Believe*

PROLOGUE

I didn't mean to friend him. I don't even like Facebook. Other people's perfect lives annoy me and put me in a bad mood. I have this fantasy of starting "Real Book," an online site where people post their truths: my husband and I haven't had sex in weeks, my daughter got a D on her math test, my son is irritating the hell out of me with his bad attitude, whatever. I just think it would be funny. But I digress.

It wasn't my intention to friend him. I know: *The road to hell is paved with good intentions*. But I'm not claiming my intentions were good. Or bad. I didn't really have any intentions. Or, if I did, they were subconscious, which seems to be a theme of this whole fucked-up story.

So I typed his name into the search bar and took a drag from my cigarette. The kids were at school and the small room at the back of the house, which doubled as my office, was quiet except for the ticking of the Lucite clock my life coach accidentally left behind after our last session. She'd left it on the shelf, wedged between my collection of kid art: lumps of clay splashed in rainbow colors, pencil drawings of our family, painted picture frames with various toddler faces poking out, and a little round Buddha statue with man boobs and an overstuffed sack across his back. The lady in Chinatown told me he signified abundance. I told her I was looking for creativity but she said he signified that too, so I bought him for twelve bucks. When I got home and placed him on the shelf next to the kid art, I noticed the sticker at the bottom read $10. So much for abundance.

I pushed aside the linen curtains in my office and morning light streamed in from the open window. It was that lazy morning light, the kind that illuminated the white specks of lint that clung to my black Target yoga pants. The kind that showed finger smudges on my laptop screen and reminded me that the *E* on the keyboard was nearly worn off. The spine was still white but the horizontal lines were missing. A slight breeze blew in the room and sent cigarette smoke in a wave across my desk. The ash was getting longer and, although my nail polish was pale, I could see it was chipped. I needed a manicure.

It had been twenty years since I'd seen him. Let sleeping dogs lie, I told myself. But I was curious. I wondered what he looked like. Was he gorgeous in that middle-aged sort of way—kind of Richard Gere in *Pretty Woman?* Or had he gone hipster with tattoos and black-rimmed glasses? I waved the smoke out of my face and ashed into the Dixie cup on my desk. I noticed water stains on my yoga pants. Someone once told me to add laundry detergent *before* putting the clothes in the washer but no thank you. I couldn't handle standing at the washing machine with a basket full of dirty laundry, just waiting for the detergent to emulsify or whatever. Patience was never my virtue.

I took another drag from my cigarette. The Lucite clock tick-tick-ticked. Fuck it. I hit *Enter.*

CHAPTER 1: THREE DAYS EARLIER

The psychiatrist said every family has a barometer child, the child around whom the family revolves, and ours was seven-year-old Ryan. Not like we didn't know this. Not like our other kids didn't constantly point this out. Ever since Ryan was little, he'd been moody, impulsive, temperamental, and physical. It was kind of a weird relief when, earlier this year, he was officially diagnosed with severe ADHD, anxiety, and features of ASD/AS. This meant he had Attention Deficit Hyperactivity Disorder and Generalized Anxiety Disorder and displayed signs of an Autism Spectrum Disorder/Asperger's Syndrome. It was a lot to grasp. I knew he struggled. But there was a part of me that hoped he'd outgrow it. That we'd wake up one day and everything would be fine. He would be fine. My husband Jason used this magical thinking all the time. *Ignore it and it will go away* was his motto. He said Ryan was just "sensitive." But in my heart, I knew something was wrong.

The psychiatrist prescribed a cocktail of a stimulant, an anti-depressant, and a mood stabilizer for Ryan. The potential side effects I read scared the hell out of me: sleep problems, irritability, suicidal thinking, heart problems, and this condition where his skin could burn off from the inside. Jesus, I thought. Really? My son is seven years old; am I really going to do this? I thought about my other kids, twelve-year-old Natalie and five-year-old Ben; would I do this to them? But the doctor said parents who didn't believe in medicating their kids didn't have kids who required medication. Maybe. But it was still hard.

I was a moronic optimist. Some people say doing the same thing over and over again and expecting a different result is the definition of insanity. I call it moronic optimism. To me, it's a life skill. So when Ryan started the cocktail, I thought maybe this year would be different, smoother. But just weeks into second grade, things got rocky. One day at recess, Ryan's best friend Trevor told him he needed a break. He said they should put their friendship on hold. They're in second grade—clearly Trevor had been coached. But his mom, Cyndi, never said a word.

Cyndi and I were friends. Or, at least I thought we were. She knew how hard Ryan worked, how hard we all worked. I helped her out when she had meetings or her sitter cancelled or her husband was out of town. I didn't mind. Ryan had so few friends and I was grateful for her son. Then suddenly, after three years, their friendship was over. And, apparently, so was ours. When I saw Cyndi at Back to School night a few weeks later, she walked right past me. I stopped her and said, "Hi! I've left you a few mess—" but before I could finish she took off, saying, "I've been so busy." We haven't spoken since.

The worst part is, there's nothing I can do. I tried to tell Ryan he has to move on but he can be like a dog with a bone—once he sinks his teeth into something, he won't let go. The doctor calls it perseverating. I call it heartbreaking.

***

"Mom," Ryan said over his dinner. "Do you think Trevor

forgot about me?" He was eating a giant bowl of spaghetti and forking it up at lightning speed. About half made it into his mouth and the rest splattered onto his blue basketball shorts. "Do you think I'll still get invited?"

"You get what you get and you don't get upset!" Ben shouted through his missing front teeth.

"Shut up, baby Ben! Mind your own business!" Ryan reached over and whacked his brother on the wrist with his fork.

"Ouch! I hate you!" Ben shrieked.

"You're a baby!"

"Ben, mind your own business. Ryan, let's talk about this later." I grabbed Ryan's chair and pushed it away from Ben. "Use your fork properly or I'll take it." I kept my voice steady and gripped the back of Ryan's chair, noticing that his chewed-up cuticles looked like a war zone.

Just as the boys turned back to dinner, Natalie entered the kitchen. Ben held up his wrist indicating where Ryan had poked him and Nat immediately ripped into him. "Oh my god, Ryan, you hurt him again? What's wrong with you?"

"Shut up! I hate you! Mind your own business— MOM!" Ryan barked.

"Mom!" Natalie yelled. "Ryan told me to shut up!"

"Everyone calm down!" I stared at each of my children. "Let's have a nice dinner!"

"That's it?" Natalie said, holding up her hands in frustration. "Why does he," she pointed to Ryan, "always get away with it?"

"Natalie! We were calming down until you walked in." I crossed my arms and faced her. She wore knee-high plaid socks with purple Converse sneakers. After a long day at school, her denim shorts and One Direction T-shirt were immaculate. Purple clips pinned back her perfectly coiffed brown hair. It was hard to believe that she and the two boys were related; neither of them cared about their appearance and Natalie never left the house without a shower and a swath of Bath & Body Works Raspberry Melon lotion applied to both arms.

"Me? Are you kidding? It's him! It's always him!"

Ryan jumped up and smacked his chair into the table with such force that his bowl of spaghetti overturned and red sauce and pasta strings exploded everywhere. "I'm not going to school tomorrow!" he shouted. "Natalie hates me! Everyone hates me! It's ALWAYS my fault!"

"Ryan, wait—" but before I could finish, he stormed out of the kitchen, the stomp of his sneakers echoing across the hardwood floors.

"Are you happy now?" I asked Natalie. I bent down and picked the bowl off the floor, wiping the red sauce into half moons, and blotting them up, spot by spot. I didn't want to unleash my frustration at my daughter, even though it needed to be unleashed. There was no one to blame. Except, of course, myself. I clutched the sponge and kept blotting. Was the medication cocktail making things better, or worse?

"I'll help you, Mommy." Ben said, grabbing a paper towel.

Natalie stood frozen, watching. "Mom, I didn't mean to—"

"I know." I stacked the dishes in the sink and left them there. "Do me a favor, when you're done eating, get Ben ready for bed, okay?"

I walked toward the sound of feet whacking into wall and tried not to overreact and blame everything on the medication. It helped, it did, but it was a deal with the devil. All the drugs had side effects, some of which intensified the problems they were supposed to fix. Anxiety meds could make him more anxious and ADHD meds could make him more aggressive. And some days it was impossible to tell. Was he hungry? Tired? Anxious? Or was his latest meltdown due to "rebound" side effects from the drugs that were supposed to help?

"What's going on, Ry?" I opened his door. Ryan lay

facedown on his bed, his sneakers kicking the dark blue wall.

"I hate Natalie—and Ben too!"

I sat down on his plaid comforter and laid my hand gently on his leg.

"They never get in trouble at school."

"That's not true." I sighed. "Did you get in trouble today?"

"Trevor hates me," he said, wiping his eyes with the back of his hand. "He's never gonna be my friend again." He buried his head in his navy fleece blanket. I strained my ears to hear him. "When we were at recess, he had the ball and it was my turn and he wouldn't give it to me. So I grabbed it—it was my turn!—and I pushed him. But I didn't mean it!"

"Did he fall down?" I asked gently.

He lifted his head and nodded. His angry scowl and tear-stained cheeks masked the pain and frustration that had become the hallmarks of his life. "I got benched for a week. No one's going to play with me now! The coach called me a *bad sport* in front of the whole class!"

I studied my son in his T-shirt and basketball shorts, his sneakers still smacking the wall. He was seven years old with red-rimmed eyes, a clenched jaw, hands balled into fists, and cuticles bitten to the quick. The shame he felt was a dagger in his heart and in mine, too. I grabbed the hilt with both hands and tried to pull it out.

"You made a mistake, " I said, rubbing his shin. "You are *not* a bad kid. You made a bad choice—that's it. Remember what the doctor said, 'Good kid, bad choice.'" I lifted the blanket and tried to make eye contact but it was hard, so hard to get him to look at me. I met his gaze long enough to see tears in his eyes and the rage that lay beneath. Is that what boys do to pain and hurt, I wondered, turn it into anger? Natalie would have been beside herself had she been singled out like that. But not Ryan. His angry eyes told a different story, the story of

9

how much he hated himself, hated being different. And he was smart enough to know how very different he was.

"You're a good boy," I said, stroking his back. "You've always been good."

"Nuh uh!" He cocked his leg and kicked the wall so hard his framed poster of Luke Skywalker shook. "Trevor doesn't think I'm good! He hates me! He didn't even invite me to his birthday party! And Cyndi doesn't think I'm good!" He slammed his fist into the bed, strangling a hoarse, hiccupping sound as he fought back tears. "She could've invited me! She's the mom!"

But I knew that didn't make a difference. Mom or not, experience taught me that when it came to hyperactive, impulsive kids, most parents pointed fingers before they walked in your moccasins or whatever the expression was.

I leaned over and kissed Ryan's head, letting my lips rest in his silky little-boy hair.

"You're doing the best you can, Ry. Everyone makes mistakes. Sometimes people forget that...even grown-ups."

I wished I could suck out his pain like snake venom. I heard Ben calling my name but I didn't answer. I rubbed Ryan's back, feeling his body cuddle into mine, pouring in the antidote as best I could. Just before he drifted off, I nudged him and he changed into his pajamas and crawled under the covers.

"I love you," I said. He nodded and snuggled into his pillow. I turned off the light and stood in the darkness. Some things I just couldn't fix. No matter how hard I tried.

***

Natalie was working on her laptop at the kitchen table. I sat down next to her, hoping to talk but she was deep in concentration, clicking through photos of me.

"Ben's in bed," she said, without looking up.

"What are you doing?" I asked, peering over her shoulder.

"I'm making an iMovie for your birthday; Dad thought it was a great idea. I'm calling it: *Alex Hoffman: Then and Now*. It's going to be a slideshow of your whole life—isn't that great?" She re-clipped the barrettes that pinned back her dark hair.

This had to be the hundredth iMovie Natalie made in her young life. She spent hours online, selecting images and downloading music, but I had to admit they were masterpieces. She used graphics and transitions and even inserted video clips. I told my husband it was the modern version of scrap-booking.

"Sounds terrific," I said, lying through my teeth. I wasn't excited about my fortieth birthday. It had been a crappy year and I wanted to usher in my forties quietly. But the kids had pitched a backyard "fiesta" with surprising teamwork, arms around each other, all three pleading desperately. I couldn't turn them down.

"Dad emailed me a bunch of pictures of you," she said, "but they're all recent." She pulled up a few photos and then glanced sideways at the phone sitting at her elbow. "To show how old you really are, I need pictures of you from college and, you know, from when you were young."

"Sure, Nat," I said.

"I know there's a lot of old albums in the garage... Please, Mom." She pressed her cheek against her folded hands and made her best sad-dog face. "The movie won't be good without historical photos."

Historical photos? Who was this kid? "Okay, okay, I'll look." I winced at both the *when you were young* and the thought of the dreaded hellhole that was our garage.

Our garage was a wasteland of unfinished business. Baby books half written in; plastic boxes filled with clothes Ryan outgrew that Ben would never wear; broken toys needing to be glued, screwed, or thrown away; boxes from my parents filled with mementos; and unmarked paint cans in need of labeling and storage in a cupboard. The garage was a long-term bone of contention between Jason and me. I wanted him to tackle it—clean out the cupboards, put hooks in the walls, move stuff into the rafters—but he never had time. I hated being reminded of things left undone so I avoided going out there like the plague. It stressed me out just to open the door.

"Go to bed," I said, leaning in to give Nat a hug that she quickly shrugged off before I hurried down the hall to say goodnight to my Benny boy.

He was asleep with *Danny and the Dinosaur* rising and falling on his Spiderman pajama top. I leaned over and kissed my little boy, noticing the smudges of spaghetti sauce on his face. When was the last time I sat with him while he took a bath? The last time I helped him brush his teeth? He was happy, I knew, but I was sorry. There just weren't enough hours in the day. I kissed him on the forehead and went into the bathroom to clean up and turn off the light.

I stooped over to lift the wet towels off the floor and caught a glimpse of myself in the large vanity mirror. At nearly forty, I was the definition of skinny-fat. After three kids, I was small but with cellulite pockets collecting on my thighs and butt—my saddlebags, I thought grimly. Maybe if I went to the gym more than three times a year I'd firm up? That was the thing with skinny-fat, you could pull off "skinny" in clothes—I had a waist, not-too-saggy breasts, smallish tummy pooch—but naked, well, that was another story. Varicose veins had begun popping up on my thighs and there was a layer of cottage cheese along my backside. Maybe it wasn't so bad that Jason got home long after I'd retreated under the covers in my gray sweats with the over-loose elastic waistband? My straight brown hair—the grays were well camouflaged by blonde highlights—still came down past my shoulders but the ophthalmologist had recently suggested Botox for my forehead. Fabulous confidence booster that was. I avoided looking too closely in the mirror but consoled myself with the thought I'd recently bought a good concealer.

"Might as well get it over with," I muttered to myself as I closed the door and headed toward the garage. I flipped on the fluorescent lights, took two steps inside, and looked around. In a dusty corner, partially hidden by the garage door tracks, was the white cardboard box I'd inherited from my parents when they'd moved to a condo a few years ago. It was still sealed and labeled ALEX HOFFMAN in black Sharpie pen, followed by our address. I climbed over Jason's golf clubs, through duffel bags of ski clothes, broken beach umbrellas, and other potential deathtraps, and approached the box.

Peeling off the tape, I opened the top flaps. Inside was a treasure trove of pictures that had fallen out of the old-style, gummy-glue pages of the ancient albums my mom had salvaged. I grabbed a handful of pictures and sorted through them. They were all jumbled in time: my graduation from UCLA, sitting on a Big Wheel in a pink party dress, at a resort in Hawaii with Jason on our first trip together. God, that was a great trip—the volcano hike and the ocean views and endless hours playing backgammon over martinis. Natalie will be thrilled, I thought, as something at the bottom of the box caught my eye.

My heart pounded. Pink tulips danced on a pale blue background. The corners were frayed and part of a heart-shaped leaf had worn off but it was unmistakably the journal I'd kept during my junior year abroad. My hands trembled as I lifted it out and thumbed through the pages. Suddenly, something fluttered to the ground. I bent down and my hand jerked back as if stung. There he stood, in front of the Thames River wearing jeans, a T-shirt, and a black leather jacket...Matt Daniels.

I remembered the day vividly: Matt and I played a game of Ultimate Frisbee in Hyde Park and then headed over to our favorite pub to celebrate. Afterward, we walked hand-in-hand along the Thames. The sun was setting and the light had turned a rich shade of yellow-gold. I stopped at a bench to take out my camera and positioned him in front of the river with the light behind my shoulder. His green eyes gleamed playfully.

***

"You should be very proud of yourself today, Mr. Captain-of-the-Winning-Ultimate-Frisbee-Team," I teased.

"Oh, I am, I am," he agreed, nodding his head and pushing his unruly black hair out of his eyes. "What do you think would be a fitting victory prize?" he asked with a wink.

"Try to keep your dirty mind in check while I take the picture," I said, attempting to focus on the foreground. "The light is perfect and you look adorable."

I framed him standing along the river's edge. The wind ruffled his hair and he reached up and brushed it off his forehead before flashing me a smile. At six feet tall, he was built like a runner, with muscular legs and calves, and arms that could carry me up two flights of stairs when I over-optimistically consumed one too many pints of Guinness. His dark, wavy black hair, straight nose, stubbly cheeks, and full-lipped mouth—always a mischievous grin playing at the edge—formed an incredibly attractive picture, but what completed the package and made him nearly irresistible, were his eyes. Those piercing green eyes stunned me and left me unprepared and breathless. I was an over-achieving college junior from UCLA studying literature in London on an honors scholarship and Matt was a twenty-five-year-old budding filmmaker who'd left New York for a job with a British production company. We'd literally bumped into each other on a London street the day I'd first registered for classes and had been inseparable ever since.

"Say cheese," I joked and snapped the photo. I'd just

set the camera down when he lunged at me, knocking me off balance and pinning me to the bench.

"I'll say anything if you let me take you to bed," he quipped, biting my neck and sliding his cold hands under my sweater.

"Get off me." I craned my neck to the side, frantically surveying the path for onlookers but flushed with heat from the feel of him against me.

"Alex," he moaned, taking my hand and rubbing it up and down the button fly of his faded Levis. "I've been watching your ass in those jeans all afternoon and I want a piece of it...bed be damned." He lifted up his head, his hair smelling faintly of Drakkar cologne and freshly cut grass, and glanced around. "No one's around for miles," he added hopefully.

"We're in public!" I hugged my jacket around me. "People might see..."

He got up and hopped behind the bench, away from the lamplights.

"Come here," he gestured, daring me with a rise of his eyebrows.

My feet followed as if by rote. Kissing me, we slid down onto the gravel. He stretched out on top of me, quieting my nervous opposition by sliding his tongue between my lips. His large, warm hands slipped inside my black sweater and underneath my bra, teasing my nipples mercilessly. I squirmed against him, breathing heavily and swatting playfully at his hands.

With one quick movement he unfastened the four buttons of his fly and pressed my hand against his swollen bulge.

"Feel me," he said, looking directly into my eyes, emboldening me with his gaze.

He was a hypnotist, and under his spell, I did things I'd never done before, never even dreamed of doing. I was a "nice" girl, no public hand jobs and certainly not sex. But there I was, huddled in a dark corner of a park, with my lover lying on top of me and my underwear soaked between my legs.

I can't believe I'm doing this, I thought to myself, but I couldn't resist. He raised himself up while I unzipped my jeans. I watched myself wrangle them down below my thighs as if I was someone else. I kept thinking this wasn't really happening, even though I knew it was. He shrugged off his jacket, lowered his pants, and covered our backsides as best he could. The jeans pushed low across my thighs, constricted the width my legs could open but he was undeterred. Using his knees, he pushed apart my legs. I wiggled to dislodge a stone stuck beneath my back as he grabbed my hips and entered me hard. I squeezed my eyes shut and bit down on my lower lip to keep from moaning and attracting the attention of any passersby.

"Hey," he said. "Don't go anywhere." He ran his hand along my forehead and brushed aside my bangs.

"I can't believe we're—"

"Sshh," he said. "Open your eyes and watch." He leaned up, making some space between our bodies.

"I...oh—"

I'd lost the power of speech. I did as he said and lowered my gaze, watching him slide in and out of me. Pleasure emanated out from the satisfying ache between my legs, all the way to my toes, my head, my whole body. His musky scent mingled with the cold air and his mouth pressed against mine while he kissed me over and over and quietly murmured, "You taste so good," and, "I love to make you come," until I turned my face away to gasp and squeal. He pulled up my sweater and reached behind me to unsnap my bra with one quick flick of his finger. His mouth was warm on my breasts as he bit and teased me, which only intensified the sweet throbbing between my legs. I was going to come so hard with the gravel crushed into my back and blades of grass prickling my cheeks, and Matt leaning over me, pushing so deep inside me that I wanted to cry out. Nothing I'd ever experienced prepared me for how free I felt—how reckless and bold—to let him take me like that, in the open air, listening to his dirty talk, watching him slide in and out of me, knees forced apart, bare bottom resting on twigs and pebbles.

"Hold on to me," I gasped, digging my fingers into his hips. He crushed me close against him while my body shook with a tingling sensation that made my toes curl. He quickened his pace and raised his head skyward, pumping into me vigorously. I watched his face in the fading light, his eyes lost in concentration, a rebellious lock of dark hair falling over his forehead. The heat rose again inside me but I'd already let myself go. I couldn't bear it again. "Oh, Matt, go," I begged as he moved in urgent rhythm. He came with a barely stifled groan and collapsed on top of me. We lay there for a while, satisfied and spent, panting and chuckling. I could feel my cheeks burn.

"I love it when you blush," he said, propping himself up on an elbow and looking at me as I lay in the grass next to him. His jeans were pulled up but unbuttoned at the top. I could see the happy trail leading from his navel downward.

"Why?" I asked, feeling embarrassed and knowing my flushed cheeks gave me away. "Because you make me do things any nice girl should be ashamed of?" I got up and brushed small pebbles off my legs as I wiggled back into my jeans.

"No. Because you look like you've been caught doing something naughty. It turns me on," he said, flashing his green eyes and looking sexy and self-satisfied—the cat that ate the canary.

"Oh my god! I better get out of here before you decide you want another go." I jumped up and re-fastened my bra, smoothing down my sweater and shaking out crumpled leaves from my hair.

Matt got up and stood behind me, brushing dirt off the back of my open jacket. He turned me around to face him and tucked a wayward strand of long, brown hair behind my ear. For a moment, we stood staring at each other. Then he broke into a wide smile that traveled up from his lips to his eyes, as if a light had been turned on from the inside and couldn't help but illuminate his face.

"You drive me wild," he said, with a shake of his head. "Every time I look at you I want to eat you up," he half-roared, taking my face in his hands and planting a hard kiss on my already swollen lips.

"I think you already did," I teased, zipping up my jacket and darting up the path toward the street.

***

I gazed at the picture: the leather jacket, the dark green shirt, the jeans he wore...I remembered the texture of the denim in my hand, the feel of the pebbles pressed hard against my back, and the look on his face, dark against the sky, his green eyes staring into mine, sparkling with amusement and pleasure.

The sound of Jason's car broke the reverie. I grabbed the pictures, dashed into the house, and ran to my office. I slid the photo of Matt inside the back cover of the journal and shoved the whole thing into an overstuffed desk drawer. I was standing in the dining room stacking up "historical photos" for Natalie when Jason walked in.

RESTLESS IN L.A.
Mommy Musings. Stupid Confessions. Life.
Posted by Anonymous

The Middle of the Night

Last night, I woke up in the middle of the night, went into the kitchen, and made myself a cup of coffee in a silver to-go mug. I grabbed a jacket and closed the front door softly so as not to wake any of my three children or my husband in his Armani boxer shorts, legs curled around a white pillow sham.

It seemed like I should have somewhere to go, someone to meet, some pressing need to fulfill. I couldn't decide if I should head out of L.A. or go by the all-night gay lounge in North Hollywood where I could watch two guys make out. I wanted to see where I'd end up, if I'd end up anywhere at all.

Yesterday, I stopped by the Back-to-School Parent Breakfast and made myself a tall cup of Starbucks and shoved a pre-made egg sandwich on seven-grain bread into the pocket of my jacket and left. I didn't stay for sign-in or icebreakers or speeches. I just grabbed some breakfast and took off. I had this weird urge to blurt out that I'd masturbated that morning, that I'd gotten out my old vibrator and closed my eyes, and had three massive orgasms before 8:15. But I didn't. Tell anyone, that is.

So where did I end up in the middle of the night? I walked past the neighbors' houses and wondered if everyone was tucked into their beds, their legs wrapped around overstuffed pillow shams, their mouths making soft shushing sounds as they dreamed about doughnuts or horses or whatever. Then I went home.

ROBIN FINN

CHAPTER 2: THREE DAYS EARLIER
PART II: *WHEN WILL THIS DAY EVER END?*

"Hi hon," Jason said, giving me a quick peck on the cheek and heading toward the kitchen. "Anything to eat?"

He dropped his jacket, briefcase, and gym bag on the counter, loosened his tie, and opened the oversized stainless steel fridge, searching for a snack.

I put the evening's foray into the garage out of my mind and pointed to the left. "There's a cut-up rotisserie chicken in Tupperware on the upper shelf and a plate of spaghetti waiting for you on the counter." He turned to me and smiled, his blue eyes crinkling in the corners.

"I can't believe it's Friday," he said, rooting around the shelves. "I've got a ton of shit to do this weekend." He grabbed a container of Parmesan cheese and a bottle of Stella Artois beer and sat down at the kitchen island to nibble. "So, how you doing, hon?"

"I'll heat it up for you." I placed his plate in the microwave before I pulled up a barstool and sat down across from him. He'd unbuttoned the top two buttons of his still-pressed white dress shirt.

"What's up?' he asked, popping open his beer.

"Ryan had a tough night. He's so upset by the whole Trevor birthday thing. You know I called Cyndi three times and I even tried to talk to her at Back to Sch—"

"Forget about it." He squeezed my hand and took a sip of beer. "He'll get over it."

"Jason, I think we need to talk about other options...for school."

"Alex, he's fine. What about that meeting we had last year with the principal and the teacher and all those people? I thought Ryan was getting some kind of personalized plan for education or whatever they called it."

"You mean the IEP? Jesus, honey, you're a lawyer. I don't know why you can't remember this stuff. It's called an *individualized education plan* and yeah, it's supposed to help the teachers work with him. But it doesn't help him with friends. And I don't think it's working, anyway."

Jason got up and grabbed his plate. "The doctor said the whole cocktail thing takes time, Al. Let's see how it goes, okay? I think you worry about him too much." He sat down, tucked a napkin into his shirt, and looked at me. "Speaking of meds, you're still taking the Klonopin, right?"

"Haha."

"I'm serious. Are you?"

"Yes, Jason, I'm still taking the Klonopin. What's your point?" "I'm just saying..." He picked up his fork and skewered the spaghetti, twirling the hair-like strands in a perfect loop around the tines and placing the whole bite flawlessly into his mouth.

"You're just saying what? This is not about me. Or the Klonopin. And you know it."

I moved the bottle of beer from one side of his plate to the other so I could glare at my husband unobstructed. "This is about Ryan. I don't know how you can say I worry about him too much. Have you looked at his fingers lately? His cuticles are completely destroyed and if I try to spend a second with Ben, our ignored third child, he has a meltdown, and Natalie's always on her phone…" I crossed my arms and faced him. "We need more balance in our lives—"

"Shit, Alex, don't start that again. I keep telling you it's temporary."

"Temporary? It's been like this forever." I reached over and unconsciously handed him another napkin.

"Thanks," he said. "What about Maria? Can't she come another day?"

"That's not the answer." I grabbed the sponge off the marble counter and scrubbed at a spot of red sauce. "Maria's not me. She's not you."

His phone, seated at the edge of his plate, vibrated. I stopped scrubbing and stared at him. He glanced down and back up at me. "Just one second." I watched him text at lightning speed. His eyebrows knit together and I noticed the dimples sitting astride his neatly trimmed dark blond goatee, the same dimples Ryan had.

He stuffed the phone into his pocket and shot me a quick smile before reaching for my hand. "Look, hon, I know this is hard but it's for us, for our family."

"But we need to *be* a family. You promised you'd make more time." The sauce was leeching into the marble countertop. I pulled my hand away and leaned into it, buffing harder to get the stain off.

"I'm trying, Al. There's fires to be put out everywhere and I'm juggling a thousand things and, with all these balls up in the air, I can't afford to blink and—will you please stop that scrubbing?"

I put the sponge down. "I'm juggling and putting out fires, too, Jason, but you've got a support team. Around here, there's only me."

"We've been over this. I can't be your support team. Not now." He pushed away his plate. "Once I get this merger teed up then, I swear, it's gonna be smooth sailing…"

Jason had spent the last two years spearheading a major merger of his law firm with a number of smaller firms. The creation of this mega-firm required long hours and little vacation but it was an enormous opportunity to play in the big leagues. I got it: bigger firm, bigger clients, bigger salaries and the lifestyle that went with it, but I couldn't help wonder where it all ended. It felt like forever since I'd seen him in the typical L.A. weekend wear of ripped jeans, faded T-shirt, and flip-flops, his dark blond hair hidden under a baseball cap. These days, he seemed always to be in a suit and tie, deftly navigating the issues and egos of the other attorneys with whom he had to deal to get the job done. I knew he was good at it. Smart, detail-oriented, and tenacious, Jason was adept at getting what he wanted. This particular endeavor—a marriage of decidedly different firms, both in tenor and size—required the use of all his skills to push the merger through. I knew he loved the challenge.

"This sounds familiar," I sighed. "You don't hear me."

"I hear you, okay? I said I'm trying." I could tell he was getting angry by the way he spoke each word individually: *I. Said. I'm. Trying.* As if clear enunciation could win the point. He wasn't one to yell. He was forceful in a quiet way. I was more the yeller.

"Ryan and I—we're like invisible," I said. "He never gets invited anywhere and I have to stand there and watch all the other kids go off on play dates, and the moms? I swear they whisper about us."

"Who cares? They don't know anything about our life; they don't know how hard he tries. Fuck 'em, Al."

"Easy for you to say. If I was at work all day, I wouldn't care, either."

He reached out and grabbed my hand. "I do care...you sure you don't want more Maria? Maybe she could take him to some of those doctor's app—"

"She's not you, Jason. You're the only one who knows what it's like for me and when you're not here, I'm alone.

That's why I keep talking about balance—are you listening?" He had taken out his phone and was quickly skimming through a text.

He shoved it back into his pocket and looked up. "Yes, I'm listening—balance. I got it. I'll check my schedule and see if I can take an afternoon off, next week maybe, okay?"

"You promise?" I asked. I couldn't let it go.

"Yes." He picked up the sponge from where it rested between us and tossed it neatly into the sink, signifying an end to the conversation. His face softened as he reached under me and pulled my barstool closer to his. "I don't want to fight with you." He bent his head underneath my hair and nuzzled my neck. "The deal's so close now, I swear. We're almost there."

"Okay, okay," I said, giving in to the feel of his chin against my collar bone, "but I'm serious. I need you. We all do."

"Okay," he whispered into my hair, "I'll do my best."

I got up, stuck the dishes in the sink, and switched off the kitchen lights. He pushed in his stool and walked over to the counter to pick up his briefcase. He caught my arm before I walked away, and kissed me on the cheek.

"I promise," he said.

RESTLESS IN L.A.
Mommy Musings. Stupid Confessions. Life.
Posted by Anonymous

Don't Look Back

I think it's better to live in the present and not dwell on one's younger years. Personally, I find all it does is make me long for something I can never have—the past. A time when I was younger, tighter, had smoother skin, less lines, less worries. When I look at pictures of my kids as infants, I remember how easy it seemed, when wipe warming and breast pumping were my biggest concerns. I know it's trite but true: little kids, little problems; bigger kids, bigger problems.

I never imagined it was going to be this hard. And I thought I'd be a whole lot better at it than I turned out to be. Every time I look at baby pictures, I see my own life whizzing by and I ask myself, how am I doing? I guess my answer depends on the day. Frankly, I'm considering going out to the garage and burning the damn baby albums. While I'm out there, I'd like to burn down the whole fucking garage and everything in it. Who needs memorabilia? It just brings me down, way down, and reminds me that the years are ticking by while I drive an SUV around a hamster wheel.

CHAPTER 3: MONDAY MORNING

The journal sat in the desk all weekend burning a hole in the drawer. I could still feel it smoldering Monday morning when I got dressed and ready for my appointment with Lark.

I'd been seeing my life coach Lark for about six months, shortly after my internist prescribed Klonopin for anxiety. The doctor told me I needed better coping skills and wrote down the names of three local therapists on her prescription pad. Of course, I never called. But my best friend Laurie kept after me. I told her I went to enough therapy appointments, thank you very much. Still, it was no surprise when, two weeks later, Laurie stopped by my house to announce she'd met this "amazing" life coach in her Pilates class. She hadn't even stepped inside the front door before her excitement got the better of her.

"You're never going to believe this but I found the perfect person for you to talk to," Laurie gushed. "She's a life coach and her name's Lark, you know, like the bird." She flapped her arms up and down, cocked her head to one side, and smiled at me wide-eyed so I wouldn't mistake the connection.

"Life coach?" I asked, rolling my eyes. "Gimme a

break. Aren't life coaches wannabe therapists who smoke a lot of pot?" I took her by the wrist and pulled her inside. "Stop flapping your arms and come in, you nut." I shut the door and laughed. "You look like a fitness freak high on Red Bull."

"Just meet her. She's got great energy and she's so intuitive," Laurie talked at a rapid-fire pace. "She even knew I was going to approach her about you. When I told her I had a friend in need—you won't believe this—she just nodded and said, 'I know.' Isn't that incredible?" She suddenly noticed my dish-filled sink and added, "Wow, you really need to clean up around here." Scratching at my marble countertop with her pink, manicured nail, she added, "Well, what do you think?"

I grabbed the sponge off the kitchen table and began to wipe. "I love that you think about me and you're right, I could use someone to talk to but—"

"Oh, come on," she said, pulling out a barstool and plopping her well-sculpted backside onto it. "Even you, the great cynic, have to admit it's a pretty amazing coincidence." She kept talking as I scrubbed a pile of hardened corn flakes off the counter. "There we were in Corkscrew position when I noticed this beautiful quote on her water bottle, something about the caterpillar turning into a butterfly and I had this feeling. So I talked to her after class and she told me she 'assists people in their transformations' and I just knew!"

She reached into her bag and pulled out a purple business card with a large green butterfly on it. "Look Al, I try not to bug you—not about your refusal to do Pilates or spinning or anything with me, not about the fact that you're still wearing your stained Target yoga pants that you've had, for what? Six years? Not even about the fact that you are way overdue to get your roots done." She lifted up one of my highlighted strands of blond and shook her head. "I know you've got a lot on your plate but...I worry about you." She pressed the card into my reluctant hand and squeezed with both of hers. "A life coach could be just what you need. Promise me you'll call."

Since then, Lark knocked on my door every Monday. She entered my house carrying a colorful hobo handbag filled with the spiritual accoutrements she needed to hold a safe space, and greeted me with a quick hug, whispering, "heart to heart," as she positioned the left side of her chest against mine. We'd go into my office where she'd light her funky patchouli candle set in a handmade wooden frame with images of dancing pregnant women carved on it—her spirit guides, she called them—and call in the light. She usually sat Indian-style in my beat-up former nursing glider while I sat across from her in a tan leather desk chair.

Dressed in jewel-toned yoga pants with a matching T-shirt, her red hair piled in a messy knot on top of her head, Lark would clasp me by the hands and say, "Beloved Spirit, we ask for your assistance in guiding Alex Hoffman along her journey," or some other quasi-religious thing like that. Then she'd close her eyes for our five-minute peace meditation while I thought about all the shit I had to do that week and peeked through my lids at her trim yet curvaceous earth-mother body. She had the most amazing posture I'd ever seen. When we were finally done communing with the Divine or whatever we were supposed to be doing, she'd sit up straight, elbows on her knees—her left arm was tattooed in black Chinese symbols that meant, "Happiness and sorrow are neighbors"—and listen patiently to every word I said.

It took a while but I'd gotten used to her spiritual jargon. During our sessions, she asked pointed questions to support my uncovering my inner knowing. She viewed her job as a compassionate listener, while I looked inside for my own authentic truth. I didn't always know what she was talking about but I did feel better every time she came. And although it seemed strange and rather weird, she ended each session with what she called a goddess embrace, wrapping her arms firmly around me, crushing her large breasts against my chest, and cradling me full-on for an entire minute while whispering into my ear, "Give what you can, take what you need," as her red, curly hair flew around my face. The heart-to-heart hug was quick and light but the goddess embrace was another thing entirely— it definitely took some getting used to, particularly because she didn't believe in deodorant.

Lark wouldn't accept any set fee for our sessions. She just asked that I give her something of value so we remained in balance. Whether or not I believed in her spiritual sayings, I had to admit she was pretty intuitive. After all, it was Lark who encouraged me to create a blog and start writing again, and when I balked, it was her idea to set it up anonymously. She didn't care what I wrote, she said, she just wanted me to have a sacred space to share my feelings. No one but her even knew I had a blog, and even she didn't know it was called, *RESTLESS IN L.A.* This morning, I almost had a panic attack when she asked about it.

"I think I told you," I hedged. "I write about parenthood and mommy musings and, you know, shit like that."

"You told me what you write about, Alex, but this is a different question. I want to know what writing is about *for you*?" she asked.

"Oh. I don't know." I wondered if this was one of her trick questions. "Well, it's a way for me to let out my feelings. And since it's anonymous and there's no way to identify me, I feel kind of free to say how I really feel and I, well...I don't have to feel embarrassed."

"Are you embarrassed by your feelings?"

"No. It's not that. It's just that I don't want anyone to know how I feel. It's private. You know. I have a public side and a private side. Doesn't everyone?" I brushed cereal crumbs off my shirt.

"Who do you share your private side with?" she asked,

leaning forward so we were practically nose to nose. I noticed the crinkles at the corners of her brown eyes and the light freckles scattered across her cheeks. She scooted so close to the edge of her seat that I was afraid she might fall off the glider altogether.

I considered her question. "My best friend Laurie. And Jason, of course."

"Have you told Jason about the blog? Or that you're writing again?" she asked.

My heart constricted. Just to hear the words hurt. "No," I said.

"Would you like to share it with him?"

When I was holed up in the office, Jason assumed I was working on projects for the PTA since I'd volunteered a few times last year. He never asked what I was doing but when he was home, he tried to be a team player. He'd hang out with the kids and try to keep them occupied. He wanted me to be happy and upbeat.

"I could tell him...but I don't want to," I said, shifting in my seat. "First of all, he's busy. He's preparing for this merger and he's hardly around and when he is, I want to talk about important things, like Ryan and the kids. The blog is nothing special. It's just me letting off steam."

"Okay, Alex, I'm going to do it," she said, nodding to herself as if she'd come to some big decision. Her lips formed a small O and she exhaled in a loud whooshing sound. "It's generally against my policy, but I'm going to share something with you. I see an image of a book, Alex. It's your book. I'm getting a message that it's time for you to stop hiding and claim yourself as the writer you are." She squinted her eyes as she leaned forward and squeezed my hands. "You are ready." Her dark purple top, purple yoga pants, and tattooed arm lent her the aura of some kind of modern-day shaman.

I was taken aback. I'd shared with Lark my passion for reading and writing, but I never told her about my dreams of becoming a novelist. She'd encouraged me to start the blog and it felt good to share the mommy frustrations I posted about. But it was another thing to out myself as a writer. There was no way I was ready for that and, maybe I'd never be. I liked being *RESTLESS IN L.A.*

"I—I don't know. There was a time when I thought I was a writer but that was a long time ago, like a million years. I don't think I have a book in me anymore."

"Well, I see it as clearly as if it's already happened. I encourage you to keep going." She smiled. "I want you to post an authentic truth on your blog this week, something that has heart and meaning for you."

Heart and meaning? I thought about the journal hidden in the desk. "Um, okay," I said. I must have looked confused because she reached over and grabbed my hands.

"Always be definite with the Infinite," she said, giving me a squeeze.

"Huh?" I asked.

She leaned forward, looked directly in my eyes, and spoke in a voice two octaves lower than the singsong one she usually used. "It means, Alex, you need to know what you want if you plan on getting it."

So I sat at my desk and thought about an authentic truth I could mine for my blog—something with "heart and meaning" as Lark had commanded, but nothing came. Between the call of the journal buried in the drawer to my left and the unanswered questions I'd tried for years, decades even, to ignore, there was no way I could write. I lit a Marlboro Light and inhaled, trying to clear the clutter in my head. My curiosity burned. What ever happened to Matt? When had he come back to the States? Was he married? Had he missed me? I promised myself not to search for him online. And for the whole weekend I didn't. But today was a Monday. I was alone in the house and the Facebook icon winked at me from the computer. Before I knew what happened, Matt Daniels was staring at me from the screen.

RESTLESS IN L.A.
Mommy Musings. Stupid Confessions. Life.
Posted by Anonymous

Groundhog Fucking Day

Why does my life sometimes feel like a sick version of the movie *Groundhog Day*, where I make lunches, take my kids to school, do laundry, shop for meals, pick up my kids, help with homework, drive carpool, make dinner, make lunches for the next day, go to sleep and wake up and do the whole thing over again? My coping mechanism of late has been sneaking off to 7-Eleven to buy Marlboro Lights (my cigarette brand of choice since high school) and smoking a few before the kids get home. I know smoking is bad for me and I shouldn't do it and, of course, my husband would totally kill me if he found out, but somehow it appeals to the rebel in me and calms my nerves. This is unfortunate because, even though I douse myself in Febreze, my youngest child has the nose of a bloodhound and can smell a neighbor opening a can of tuna two houses down. Like high school, this forces me to come up with outlandish excuses of why Mommy smells like smoke but is not actually smoking. For example: the handyman was here and was smoking in the backyard; Mommy was in line at the car wash and someone in front of her was smoking; that isn't smoke you smell on me, it's gasoline/oven cleaner/Formula 409. Oh, the joys of parenthood. I can't even light up in my own back yard.

CHAPTER 4: RANDOM FRIENDERS

He looked exactly the same. If it were possible, I'd swear he hadn't aged at all. I looked behind me. Of course no one was home: it was the middle of a Monday morning. I was really getting paranoid. I took another drag of my cigarette and clicked on the photo.

His profile picture had a white mat around it like an old-fashioned Polaroid. He was smiling, his green eyes hidden behind sunglasses. There was one other photo, two boys in bathing suits standing on a beach. His hometown was listed as New York, NY. Twenty years later and I'd found him with only a few keystrokes. I clicked on the Photos button but a box popped up on screen:

Matt only shares some information publicly. If you know Matt, send him a friend request.

My finger froze above the *Send* button. It was one thing to lurk on Facebook but it was another to friend him. A friend request would generate a message that I wanted to connect. And I didn't. Want to connect, that is. I always thought there was something weird (and maybe a little pathetic) about being a random friender, one of those people who just popped out of the ether after twenty years to say, *Hi! We haven't talked in decades but let's be friends on Facebook!* I know it's a national pastime but, to me, it was just a no. If we weren't close enough to meet for lunch, we didn't need to be friends online, which made what happened next all the more devastating. As I stared at the screen lost in thought...the little gray box changed before my eyes from

Send friend request?

to

Friend request sent.

Wait! What? No. No. No. How did that happen? My mutinous, right pointer finger twitched slightly. I searched for a cancel friend request button but I had no idea how it worked. Would he still see it? *Shit.* I thought about sending him a message to say I hadn't meant to friend him, but that would only make me look creepier and more pathetic. Maybe his account was dormant? Maybe he had a personal assistant who checked Facebook for him and didn't accept friend requests? I dropped my cigarette into the Dixie cup, logged off the computer, and wildly sprayed Febreze around the room before I bolted.

I should deactivate my Facebook account! Who needed more people to keep up with and more ways to complicate my life? Argh. I grabbed my keys and headed out to do my supermarket-drycleaner-pharmacy errands but couldn't shake the miserably embarrassed feeling so I called Laurie. She was in the midst of her own million-errand marathon but we managed to squeeze in a good car call.

"Hey Laur, it's me, can you talk?"

"Yeah, for a minute. I just dropped off Sasha's lunch, which she forgot for the second time this week, and now I'm late for the trainer—what's up?"

"Oh, just that I'm a moron," I said, trying to speak above the loud hum of the air conditioner. "Remember how I told you about the journal and Matt Daniels?" I was nearly shouting. "Well, I looked him up on Facebook this morning and I friended him—by accident."

"You what? You friended him? Hold on—" I heard her switching to her earpiece. "Wow! I thought you had that weird policy about not friending people you haven't seen in five years or whatever asinine system you came up with—"

"Exactly! It was a bizarre mistake. My finger hit the button before I even knew what happened—it was like possessed," I said in a rush. "I was lurking, fine, but I haven't seen the guy in twenty years. He's going to be totally creeped out that I friended him." I turned down the A/C so I could hear her better.

"No he won't," she said. "People do it all the time. Not you, Alex, I know. But people." She paused for a moment and asked, "So? Is he still hot?"

"I don't know…" I remembered his profile picture. He looked exactly the same.

"What do you mean, *you don't know?*"

"Honestly? It looked like he hadn't changed a bit but I couldn't be sure. There was only one picture and he was wearing sunglasses and then that box popped up that said only friends could see his profile and, boom!—I friended him." My hands tightened around the steering wheel. "I feel like a loser."

"C'mon," she laughed. "This happens all the time, trust me. Haven't you heard about Infidelity 2.0? They were talking about it on *Couples Therapy*—"

Oh shit, I thought. But it was too late. Laurie had this thing for what I called therapy TV. She loved any show that featured a doctor, therapist, or counselor of any kind, and there were tons of them. One of her favorites was a VH-1 series called *Couples Therapy* where *celebrity* couples went into group counseling with this hip therapist, Dr.

Jenn, with two n's. Laurie was hooked. And there was no interrupting her once she decided she needed to share an insight from one of the latest episodes.

"One of the couples, they were like college sweethearts and the husband—I think he was a comedian or something—found his seventh-grade, summer-camp girlfriend on some online camp connection site. Soon he was emailing her every day and talking to her on the phone and planning secret visits—"

She barely stopped for breath. I glanced at the rearview mirror and waited.

"Their marriage was in the toilet until Dr. Jenn demanded he cut off Internet access immediately. And she was serious. This is no joke, Alex. Online flirtations are a national epidemic." She was so excited I could practically feel her pulse rising. "Everyone and their grandma is hooking up online with old flames."

Laurie Rankin was my best friend so I endured her maniacal obsession with therapeutic television. She was a psych major in college and her interest in human behavior clearly continued, even though she'd given up psychology years ago to sell jewelry online. She made hand-stamped, silver medallions customized with children's names, pet initials, or qualities such as "Joy" or "Inspire." She'd given me half a dozen necklaces over the years but my favorite was a sterling silver disc stamped "BFF" on one side with our initials on the other.

We met our senior year at UCLA when we were both tutoring for the athletics department. We helped this struggling basketball star get off academic probation and been best friends ever since. She and her husband Evan were godparents to our kids. And we were hers. She was like a sister to me so I tolerated her twin obsessions: working out—she had a fat-free body to die for—and following her shows.

"Relax, Laur," I said. "If you recall, my beloved grandma died years ago and I'm not 'hooking up' with anyone, online or anywhere else. The whole friend thing was a total mistake."

"You know," she continued, without taking a breath, "Internet communication with an ex is considered a violation in most marriages. Are you going to tell Jason?"

"Tell Jason? About what? Are you quoting Dr. Jenn now?" I looked in the rear mirror and watched the guy behind me bouncing up and down to whatever was on the radio.

"Are going to tell him about the accidental friending?" Then she dropped the bomb. "My therapist said that married people who, you know, find an old photograph or a diary or whatever, and then do an online search for their old flame risk opening up 'Pandora's Box.'"

"Wait, what? Laurie! Did you discuss me with your therapist?" Sometimes her love of all things therapeutic drove me nuts. I could just picture her spending her whole session analyzing me with her shrink.

"I just mentioned that you found your old journal and were considering a search—that's it. She knew all about the 'reconnecting with old loves online' epidemic, of course, she's a professional! Plus, she saw that episode of *Couples Therapy*. Anyway, she said it's more dangerous than starting something new because, with an ex, there's already something to build on." Laurie had the weirdest therapist. They were like BFFs who sat around sharing insights.

"It was a mistake!"

"Well," she continued, clearly on a roll, "are you going to tell Lark?"

"You're killing me," I grumbled into the speaker. "I just saw her this morning before it even happened and no, it's so insignificant, I wasn't even going to bother."

But Laurie was a bulldog when she had a point to make and the car was the worst place for an intense discussion. She couldn't hear me trying to break in while she was talking and, with Laurie, there were almost no pauses in the conversation long enough to effectively interrupt.

"Oh, don't be naïve," she said, with a snort. "That's what they all say until the emails become voicemails become text messages and the next thing you know, you're holed up in some cheesy motel in Santa Monica."

"All right," I said. "If you'll let it go, I'll talk about it with Lark. Sheesh—you're worse than my kids. But you can forget Jason. He's exhausted and half the time, he falls asleep when I'm midsentence." I took a quick breath and continued before she could jump in. "Honestly you're making much ado about nothing. I doubt Matt will even remember me."

"Really? From what you said, it was pretty hot and heavy."

"Yeah, and another lifetime ago."

"Well, I guess we'll see. Just remember, there's a reason they call it an epidemic."

"An epidemic?"

"Jeez, Al, have you been paying attention to anything I've said? Infidelity 2.0—it's an epidemic. I think you better start binge watching *Couples Therapy*, like, pronto."

"Okay, okay, I get it. By the way, are you still hooked on *The Housewives of Orange County*?"

"Goodbye, Al. Just don't say I didn't warn you."

"You warned me, you warned me," I said with a laugh.

RESTLESS IN L.A.
Mommy Musings. Stupid Confessions. Life.
Posted by Anonymous

Secret Blogger

I have to confess that no one in my real life knows I'm a blogger. I can't tell anyone because, if I did, they might ask what my blog was about. Or worse—they might want to read it. And that just can't happen. I'd be beyond mortified if anyone who knew me knew how I really felt about all the people I can't stand and their perfect children, and the crazy ways I fantasize about getting the hell out of my life, and how much I hate going to the grocery store. Plus, I think if my loved ones read my blog, they'd be concerned. Very concerned. Better to post anonymously.

ROBIN FINN

CHAPTER 5: PERCOLATING

How long was the coach going to keep at it? The man was either a saint or a nut, depending on how you looked at it. Nine seven-year olds chased a soccer ball, their cleats connecting more with each other's shins than with the white and black leather of the ball. I sat at the soccer field on a waterproof blanket watching Ryan play a scrimmage game while Maria took Ben and Natalie for burgers.

This was Ryan's second season of soccer. Some games, he was on fire but then there were the times when he'd get tired and suddenly run off the field, throw himself down on the sidelines, and wail, "No one's passing to me. They never do! This sucks!" Jason thought Ryan should forego team sports but I disagreed. Ryan *needed* to be a part of a team, even if he was inconsistent. The other parents shook their heads at me and made faces. When I told Jason, he'd go into his, *Oh, Alex, the only one judging yourself is you* lecture. But if his sage-like counsel was so accurate, why did I overhear two moms discuss that our losses were due to "that difficult kid" on the team? I tried not to let it get to me. But it did.

That afternoon, I saw a line of blue and green folding chairs set up to the right of the field. I set my chair off to the left, my mind rifling through the aisles of the local supermarket to come up with dinner. Jason was rarely home to eat with us but he usually slid under the covers before I was completely unconscious. He'd undress, hang his clothes over the edge of the chaise, and lay down next to me. Some nights, he'd whisper my name and if I was awake, he'd pull me over to him and kiss me and we'd have sex. As tired as he was, Jason was still pretty interested in sex. Never more than a few weeks went by without him making the effort. Sometimes I pretended to be asleep but other times, I responded and did my best. He knew what I liked and was conscientious about it, but somehow, when we were done, I had this uncomfortable feeling of wanting more. Of what? I couldn't be sure. It wasn't an orgasm. I often had one; he took pains to make sure. It was something else, something I couldn't articulate. But the feeling made me anxious and kept me from falling asleep. I'd lie next to him, staring at the ceiling, listening to the sounds of his rhythmic breathing, and wondering what I'd forgotten to do that day. The Klonopin was supposed to help. But sometimes it just didn't.

My purse vibrated. I unzipped it and pulled out the phone. There was an email...from Facebook.

Alex Hoffman is now friends with Matt Daniels.

My pulse raced. I craned my neck and looked behind me. Why was I being so weird? No one knew I'd become "friends" with my old boyfriend. No one cared, anyway. My phone vibrated again. It was another email from Facebook.

New Message from Matt Daniels.

Underneath, I could see the first line and an arrow to view the rest:

--Hey Alex >

It was the first communication between us in twenty years. I stared at my cell phone, slowly scanning my Inbox from bottom to top, making myself wait. There was an email from Ryan's teacher wanting to discuss the math homework followed by an email from GoldStar offering discount Clipper tickets. There were two reminders from the public library that I owed $3.72 in overdue book charges followed by a chain email Laurie had sent, entitled *FORWARD TO ALL THE ANGELS IN YOUR LIFE* and listing the similarities between angels and girlfriends.

I hit the arrow with my pointer finger. Up popped a miniature profile picture of Matt in sunglasses, his name listed alongside it in blue. Below was the message.

Hey Alex
It's been a long time. How are you?
Matt

I re-read it twice. I wasn't sure what I'd expected— some folksy message detailing everything that had gone on in his life over the last twenty years? His resume? Well, at least he didn't seem to think I was a stalker/loser/bored housewife/pathetic random friender. I clicked on it and was re-directed to the message screen.

Hi Matt,
I am well. I live in L.A., have three kids, and recently started a blog about the many aspects of life that drive me crazy. I'm on Klonopin, see a life coach, and spend half the week driving carpool and the other half taking my middle son to therapy appointments. My ophthalmologist recently suggested Botox and I drink three cups of coffee before eight just to get through the day. How are you?

Better not to go with truthful. Keep it breezy and upbeat:

Hey Matt,
Nice to hear from you! I am well. I live in L.A. with my husband and three spirited kids who keep me busy. All is well. You? Working on anything great? I see your name occasionally.
Alex

He must have been online because his reply came swift and painful:

What? No novel?

Now I really felt like a loser.

Not yet. Still percolating—

More pain:

I'm surprised.

Yes, I know, I'm pathetic. Best to try to keep the focus on him:

Tell me about you- how's work? Family?

I couldn't exactly admit that I'd lurked on his Facebook page and saw the photo of his boys. He replied in a beat:

Live in NYC with my wife and two boys. Started a project in L.A. several months ago. Funny, huh? We should catch up when I'm in town. Gotta run into a meeting. Great to hear from you.

He had a project in L.A.? We should catch up when he's in town? And the worst—he was surprised I didn't have a novel. I'll be damned; I guess he remembered me after all.

***

"Go on," Lark said. She rocked back and forth in my glider, smiling at me. I hadn't seen her in a week and couldn't help but notice how her pale skin gleamed. She had a very natural look and barely wore any makeup but this morning, I'd swear she'd just come from a facial. I supposed that was what happened when you did yoga every day, drank kale juice, and meditated all the time.

"Well, um…there's been something on my mind lately, something I wanted to bring up." I'd promised Laurie I'd tell her.

"Would you like to talk about it?"

One thing I knew about Lark was that she was totally nonjudgmental. Her only goal was to support me in my unfoldment, as she called it.

"I friended an old boyfriend on Facebook and it turned out he started a project in L.A. and I haven't seen him in twenty years. When we were younger—years ago—we had this, this, thing, and it was really intense and I—I—" I stopped abruptly, not knowing what to say.

"Come out of hiding, Alex," she said, her pale lips carefully enunciating each word.

"What?" I asked, startled.

"Ask your question."

"Um, okay. I wanted to know if you thought it was wrong to look up an old boyfriend. Online, I mean."

"Wrong? What do you mean, 'wrong?'"

"Oh, I don't know, it's stupid. Forget I mentioned it." I felt myself blush. Why did I promise Laurie I'd bring this up? It was nothing but a dumb diversion from my life.

"I don't think it's stupid. Was this someone important?" she asked, as she rocked slowly back and forth in the glider.

"It was so long ago, Lark. It was honestly a lifetime ago. I think I'm just bored. I feel so…so unsettled all the time and I think I'm looking for something to do other than mommy stuff. Maybe I should take a class or something. I like origami…" I lifted my hand to my mouth and began to chew on a fingernail.

She leaned in and held my gaze. We sat still for a moment. I couldn't think of anything to add. I felt like I was stumbling over my words. I realized I was biting my nails and dropped my hand into my lap, waiting. Finally Lark nodded at me.

"Destiny meets us at the point of action, Alex."

Destiny? What destiny? My destiny was to pick up the kids at three o'clock and drive to a zillion places before six, after which time I'd make dinner, get Ben to bed, and spend the evening arguing with Ryan over homework while Natalie scowled at me for giving him all my time and attention. That destiny?

"I'm not sure what you mean."

"Look, Alex, there's action and there's feedback. You have to *do* something if you want feedback. If you feel unsettled, maybe you should try something different this week and see how it feels?"

Different? Like driving a different route to school or trying a new drycleaner? Why did she always speak in riddles?

"Like what?" I asked.

"Just think about it. You'll know when the opportunity presents itself."

Well, that was a Lark-like answer if ever there was one. If her internal GPS was wired directly into the heart of the Universe, mine was tuned to Mr. Magoo. I could barely see where I was going but I hoped for the best.

I leaned in for our session-ending goddess hug. Her giant boobs felt like two squishy pillows as she gripped me for dear life and whispered for me to give what I can and take what I need. I was pretty sure what I needed couldn't be found between her boob-pillows but I held on tightly nonetheless.

RESTLESS IN L.A.
Mommy Musings. Stupid Confessions. Life.
Posted by Anonymous

Market Phobia

Any large market is my most hated enemy and merely exists to suck my soul dry. When a trip to Costco is absolutely unavoidable, I practice deep breathing in the car on the way over. By the time I get my cart and head toward the back of the store, somewhere between the bakery items and the meat section, I feel my heart racing. My palms get sweaty around the refrigerator section with the boxes of yogurt and jumbo cartons of milk and by the time I maneuver over to the enormous plastic containers of chicken soup and chopped chicken salad, I am totally losing my shit.

I'm ready to have a major breakdown when I hit the hot stand with the rotisserie chicken and it is only because of the blast of freezing cold air from that damn refrigerated room stuffed with boxes of fancy lettuce, asparagus spears, and colored pepper trios that I don't stand in the middle of the store and let out a primal scream. Somehow the drop in temperature in that icebox helps me hold it together for the next forty-five minutes which is all I need to grab some bananas, and as many bottles of Smoking Loon Cabernet as will fit into my already overstuffed cart and get to the checkout.

If the lines are really long, I start doing yoga breaths and using positive self-talk like, "It's okay, you have all the skills you need to make it through this Costco line." If that doesn't work, I concentrate on who I'd want to have a fantasy date with that week. On my latest Costco outing, I was deciding between George Clooney and Owen Wilson. "Come on, focus on George (or Owen). Where are you going on this date? What are you wearing?' I stand there in the checkout line talking to myself like a crazy person, breathing deeply in through the nose out through the mouth until I can get the fuck out of Costco.

CHAPTER 6: AUTOPILOT

I jumped every time my phone vibrated but there was nothing new from Matt. I couldn't help but laugh at how I'd overreacted to the accidental friending. He sent me a nice note, we said hello, and that was that. Back to life as usual.

Natalie's twelve-year checkup was scheduled that morning at nine-thirty so she got to sleep for an extra hour. I thought this would put her in a good mood but I couldn't be sure. One minute, she was a sweet and loving child and the next, already a grumpy adolescent. Either way, I couldn't seem to get my timing right. If I scheduled a date for the two of us, she spent it scowling and texting, and when I was busy with one of the boys, she suddenly had something pressing she wanted to talk about. Between the endless appointments, practices, and rehearsals, I tried to find quality time for each of the kids, but it wasn't easy.

"Mom, hey, Mom! What are you thinking about?" she asked as we waited in the doctor's office for her name to be called.

"Nothing much, Nat, what are you thinking about?" I input her dance rehearsal schedule into my phone's calendar and quickly checked Facebook. There were no new messages.

"You never want to spend any time with me," she said with a scowl.

"What?" I asked, looking up into her hazel eyes. "I spend, like, all day every day with you. I love to be with you." I stopped typing and reached for her hand. "You and I stayed up late this weekend and had a Scrabble tournament. And what about last night? We didn't finish watching *Legally Blonde* until ten o'clock."

"Yeah, well, *they* are always around—"

"*They* being your brothers?" I asked.

"Yes, Mom. I can't believe there was a time when it was only you, me, and Dad and you had to go have more kids. I don't know why you were so desperate to have Ryan or Ben. They're so immature and—"

"Nat, please, give me a break."

Whenever the kids and I shared a nice moment, whether it was playing Scrabble or shopping at the mall, the next day, it was lost in their score keeping. It was as if all three of my children had inner calculators that tallied up the moments they spent with me against the hours, minutes, and seconds I spent with their siblings. No matter how much fun we had, the outcome was always the same: *I was cheated! My sibling (usually Ryan) got more time/attention/love than I did.* Maybe that was just the nature of having multiple kids but the constant competition drained me.

After the appointment, Natalie and I stopped at Starbucks for a vanilla tea and a blueberry muffin. We talked about her friends and she caught me up on the latest drama from her favorite TV show. She smiled and waved fairly enthusiastically as I pulled away from the school. I was rushing to Target to get a jumbo box of paper towels for Ben's classroom and a black leotard and white tights for Natalie's dance class when the phone vibrated. I looked down and almost crashed the car.

New Message from Matt Daniels.

I scrolled down.

Hey Alex,
Looks like I am going to be in L.A. next weekend.
Any chance you're available for dinner Saturday night?
Matt

Matt Daniels was coming to Los Angeles? And he wanted to have dinner? I clicked on my turn signal and looked for a space to pull over. Ever since he'd mentioned a project in L.A., I wondered what it would be like to see him again. How weird. We hadn't seen each other in two decades. Not to mention that I didn't tell Jason that we'd connected online. But, really, there was nothing to tell. Although if we were going to have dinner, I obviously needed to say something. I could just drop it in casual conversation, "Hey hon, I re-connected with some old friends from my London days. Remember Matt? I mentioned him to you once." I doubted it would even register.

I pulled behind a beat-up minivan and scanned my calendar. Jason was leaving Friday for a golf weekend with his uncle in Palm Springs. I was on my own Saturday night—the same night Matt was in town. Usually, Jason and I went out for dinner on Saturdays or, if he was busy, Laurie and I grabbed a chick flick. We were planning a girls' night but I knew she'd understand. I also knew she wouldn't approve.

I'm making too much out of this, I thought. But, as I sat there mulling it over, a weird phenomenon occurred. It first happened a few weeks ago, the day my pointer finger pressed *Send* to the prompt about the friend request: I autopiloted. My body took action while my brain was still thinking. While I contemplated Matt's message and my calendar and Jason's trip and my hands gripped the sides of my phone, I autopiloted again. This time, it was my thumbs. Shit. What did I write?

Hey Matt:
Saturday night is great. Look forward to catching up.
Where and when? Just need to tell the sitter.
Alex

I guess I was meeting him. What was I going to wear? What were we going to talk about? What was it going to be like? I shook my head but I'd already sent the message. I might as well see what happens. I could always cancel later if I chickened out.

***

Jason was working late so I attempted to get homework done, reading logs signed, lunches made, and our dinner of defrosted chicken fried rice and salad prepared, served, and cleaned up before nine so I could get the kids to bed at a reasonable hour. On a good night, dealing with the kids was challenging, but tonight I was edgier than usual. I struggled with my patience, trying not to lose my temper through our nighttime routine. Keeping my cell phone zipped away, I still jumped at each buzz audible through the ink-stained leather of my purse. During kitchen cleanup, Natalie yelled at Ryan for not clearing the table fast enough, pointing accusingly to the food-encrusted plates and silverware yet to be brought to the counter.

"Do you think he could hurry it up?" She turned to me, exasperation visible all over her face.

"Nat, give him a break, " I replied trying to remain calm. *Breathe,* I told myself, *in and out, in and out.* I didn't get much out of the meditation Lark and I did but I had to admit I liked the cleansing breaths she'd taught me. You are a vessel of clear, white light, I told myself uselessly. "And you," I exhorted Ryan, "move it!"

54

Ryan rolled his eyes heavenward and continued clearing the table at the pace of our ninety-year-old neighbor down the street with the broken hip. Natalie's self-righteous indignation was bubbling over while Ryan kept moving in slow motion, gleefully waiting for the dam to burst. Ben, the World's Slowest Eater, had at least a dozen pieces of rice stuck to his Buzz Lightyear T-shirt and I could see some grains trapped on his left elbow and the back of his arm.

"Ben, get in the shower right now. You have rice all over your clothes and your body."

Ryan jumped on this and began to run madly around the table, waving his arms and singing at the top of his lungs about Ben's eating habits, "Ben's a messy butt! His head's like a coconut!"

"Stop it!" Ben screamed and stamped his foot.

Ryan started to bash the table with his fork. "Ben's a butt! Ben's a butt!"

"Ryan, that's enough." I used my sternest voice but Ryan was over the edge. He continued to bash the table and scream at Ben. The meds had definitely left his system and he was wired and irritable. I tried to talk him down but Natalie cut me off.

"Leave him alone, you obnoxious brat!" she shouted, holding the extendable spout of the kitchen faucet.

"Ben's a stupid dummy! He looks like a grossed-out mummy!" Ryan ran around the table and began poking Ben in the ribs.

"Stop it!" Ben shrieked, his face screwed up in angry defiance and his small fists clenched with rage.

It wasn't Ryan's fault that the rebound coming down from the meds made him even more hyperactive and volatile, but I had to protect Ben. The doctor warned that stimulants caused irritability "going in and coming out." Since Ryan took the medication every day at breakfast and it wore off around dinnertime, family meals were riotous at best. I had a sudden vision of Natalie turning the spout on

Ryan and flooding my kitchen with water, leftover chicken fried rice, and the floating remains of my three kids, who were about to pulverize each other. Breathe in and breathe out, imagine yourself filled with clear white light—oh shut up!

I separated the boys, threatening to send them to their rooms for the rest of the night when I heard buzzing from my purse on the kitchen counter. Ryan needed an intense incentive to control himself and I had just the ticket.

"I am going to the bathroom and I want this kitchen cleaned up. *Anyone fighting or causing fights will not be playing Wii or watching TV for the entire week. Now get this kitchen cleaned up.*" I looked at Ryan and added, "I mean it. *No screens all week.* You got it?"

"Yes, Mom! I got it!" He grabbed the broom resting in the corner and began furiously sweeping.

I picked up the phone. It was a message from Facebook. I dashed out of the kitchen and into my room, locked the door, and hoped for a moment of peace. I scrolled down and there was a note from Matt.

8 pm Saturday, Katsuya Hollywood?
I'll make the reservation.
Look forward to seeing you.

It was done. We were going to meet. I responded quickly:

Sounds great! See you then!

What day was it? We were meeting on Saturday. Could I get my roots done by then?

I returned to the kitchen, packed up the lunch boxes, and hustled everybody off the TV and into the bathroom for tooth brushing. Finally, I ushered the kids into their bedrooms. Natalie gave me a nod as she put on her headphones to listen to the bedtime playlist she'd made on her iPod. That was her way of telling me there'd be no pillow talk tonight. Being the mom of a tweenager was a constant process of leaning in and being pushed out. I understood even though I could see my little girl peeking through.

When I got to Ryan's room, he was lying over the covers, banging his dirty feet into the wall. I apprised him from the doorway. He looked so much like Jason, with his dark blond hair and blue eyes. "Good night, sweetie," I said, with as much patience as I could muster. "I want you to take a shower tomorrow, okay?"

"I can't sleep," he complained. "I never can. I hate school. Do I have to go?"

"Oh honey," I said as I sat at the edge of his bed and rubbed his back. "Tomorrow's a fresh day. Try to sleep, buddy."

He suddenly kicked the bed so hard that the wall shook and his framed Luke Skywalker poster crashed to the floor. I jumped at the sound and smacked my knee against the side of his bedframe. "Stop it!" I shouted, grabbing my knee and pulling it into my chest until the pain subsided. I hobbled over to the poster and leaned it against the wall. I was going to have a nasty bruise in the morning.

"I'm sorry, Mommy! I didn't mean to!" Ryan looked stricken. "You're mad at me!"

"I'm not mad. It was an accident."

"My teacher's always mad at me," he said, tearing up. "I'm the only one who gets in trouble! I always call out—I try not to but I forget!—and I get all these checkmarks next to my name and all the kids make faces…"

God, this kid is tortured, I thought to myself as I leaned down and stroked his cheek. He smelled like mint toothpaste and Tide and tube socks—the smell of a little boy. "Everybody gets in trouble sometimes," I told him, feeling the baby-soft smoothness of his skin. "It'll get better. I promise." He squeezed his eyes shut as I talked. "I love you, Ry-Ry," I used the toddler nickname I hadn't called him in years.

He reached up and threw his arms around me, squeezing me so tightly he nearly knocked the wind out of me. His bear hugs were famous in our family and they were as rare as they were precious. I squeezed him back, inhaling the toothpaste smell, pressing my cheek against his hair and feeling the muscles in my arms strain to lock him in.

"I love you, too," he said, letting go.

I hobbled down the hall to Ben's room thinking that I needed to meet with Ryan's teacher—again. He just didn't get it. We had talked about accommodations and ADHD and positive reinforcement. What were all the stupid checkmarks going to do except make him feel worse than he already did?

Ben was sleepy but asked if I'd walk around the room and check for monsters. I opened the closet doors and looked underneath the bed and then gave him the all clear. He clung to my arm and begged mercilessly for me to read to him but I was too tired and anxious to be off-duty. I pried my arm out of his grip, smoothed back his hair and kissed him on the cheek, promising we'd read together tomorrow. I replaced the dirty Sponge Bob T-shirt he'd laid out for the next day with a clean striped polo and made my way to the office.

When would Jason be home? I stared at the oversized bulletin board suspended over my desk. Birthday invitations, school calendars, and permission slips were pinned randomly all over the board. I have to input all this into my calendar, I told myself. I plunked down in the swivel chair and laid my head in my hands. Something was bothering me. What was it? I wrapped my fingers in my hair and rested my face in my hands. Ryan had talked about his feelings. He went to sleep pretty easily. Natalie and Ben were safely in their beds. Jason would be home soon. So what was it?

The fact was I had unfinished business. I had put this

away for twenty years: Matt and my year in England…I'd tried not to think about him over the last two decades; I'd trained myself not to go there. Nothing good came of looking back and I wasn't the kind of person who lived in the rearview mirror. It was a long time ago and I was a different person then. I had an incredible experience and then it ended. Period. The End. But I couldn't help rifling through the desk until I found the journal. Flipping through it, I turned to a page in the front.

November 12

I've been living at Matt's for three days. We came back to his flat Friday after my 8 am class and now it's Sunday evening. He just went to pick up some Indian food for dinner. I can't believe I haven't opened a book all weekend. I've got a report due next week and, for the first time in my life, I can't concentrate. One of my professors even made a comment about "staying focused", and I swear he was looking at me. Me! Not focused! Ha! But Matt is so totally distracting. He gets me to do things—crazy things—and I feel like this can't be me but it is. I don't know exactly what's happening between us but I know I like it. He makes me feel like I'm someone different, someone sexy and adventurous. Saturday night, he took me to my first rave at this huge warehouse on the outskirts of London…

I remembered the rave vividly. It was the only one I'd ever been to. Matt did my makeup and picked out my clothes and we'd gotten totally wrecked before we'd even arrived. It was a wild night of sex, drugs, and music. I sighed and closed my eyes to relive it.

***

"Hand me your black eyeliner. I want to make your eyes more dramatic," Matt said as I sat on a stool in his bathroom while he carefully applied a silver shadow to my eyelids. I blinked a few times.

"Hold still," he said. "I'm going for drama but not *Eyes Without A Face*."

"*Eye's without A Face*? The Billy Idol song? Oh, I remember *Rebel Yell*. That was the best album—"

"No silly, not the Billy Idol song," he stopped and looked at me. "Have you never seen the horror film, *Eyes Without a Face*?"

"Um, no, I don't think so."

"Okay, we definitely have to put that on the list. It's this crazy 1960s French-Italian horror film directed by Georges Franju, the guy was a genius—"

"What's it about?" I loved to listen to him describe films and architecture and art, any subject about which he was passionate. His hands would gesture wildly back and forth as he explained the arc of a story or the shape of a building, and he grimaced in mock dismay whenever he discovered I hadn't seen whatever he was describing. His list of *essential* movies, buildings, and art exhibits he had to show me was already a mile long.

"It's about this crazy madman doctor," he said, waving his arm about still holding the black eyeliner. "He kidnaps innocent girls and tries to transplant their faces onto his daughter to make her beautiful. It's a horror film so, needless to say, things don't work out too well for her. But it's a great film, really odd and ghastly, but haunting and lyrical too. Anyway, the hollow-eyed look's not exactly what I'm going for tonight so hold still."

"Gee, that's reassuring," I teased. "So you're the madman doctor?"

Matt flat-ironed my brown hair, powdered my cheeks and face until I looked like a native Londoner, and applied dark red lipstick to my lips. I kept giggling but the seriousness with which he approached his work gave me a sense of what he must be like professionally: very detailed and exacting.

"First of all, you don't need anyone to make you beautiful because you already are," he answered, turning me toward the mirror. "Secondly, you can't be one of those innocent girls because, let's face it, you're no innocent—at least not if I can help it." He winked and then bent down and kissed me on the collarbone. "And lastly, the *Rebel Yell* album sucked." He pulled me over and kissed me on the lips. "Now put on some more of this," he added and tossed me a silver tube of Revlon Super Lustrous lipstick, Black Cherry.

I looked in the mirror and barely recognized myself. Heavy black eyeliner ringed my hazel eyes, my lips were covered in dark red lipstick, and I wore no blush and an excess of powder. Matt, who was also in charge of wardrobe that night, had chosen a short black skirt, tight white T-shirt, and black, high-heel boots from among the stuff I'd brought with me. Putting on small silver hoop earrings and a black leather jacket, I thought I resembled a rocker-vampire but Matt, of course, thought I looked sexy. He was wearing his standard dark jeans and black boots, but he'd added a bright red button-down shirt. His friend Floyd stopped by and dropped off a tiny Xeroxed map to the warehouse where the rave was being held and a mysterious brown lunch bag. For some reason, when I came out of the bathroom, Floyd looked oddly surprised to see me. It wasn't anything he said but I noticed a look pass between him and Matt. Matt just shrugged and pushed him out the door.

"What was that about?" I asked.

"What?"

"The look."

"What are you talking about?" Matt asked, dropping the mysterious brown bag onto the farm table in his kitchen.

"Are you denying that Floyd gave you a look?"

"Oh…" Matt trailed off. "He was just surprised to see you, I guess."

"Why? I met him at your place, like, weeks ago. Didn't he recognize me?"

"No, he recognized you. It's just that…" He actually seemed lost for words. "I don't usually—I haven't—it's been a long time since I've…dated anyone."

"What? I met that model you went out with and that girl you'd been seeing from work and—"

"No, I know…but that wasn't dating,…those were just…"

"Yes?" I raised my eyebrows and enjoyed the sight of Matt—for once—off kilter.

"Flings."

"Oh, so he was surprised to see that I'm still around? Is that what you're trying to say?"

"I don't know why he was surprised," he said, recovering himself and handing me the brown bag off the table. "And, honestly, I don't give a shit. Now look inside."

I peeked into the bag and lifted out a small, blue Thermos and a sandwich-size Ziploc bag with some pills in it.

"You have two options," Matt said, "either one of which will significantly increase your enjoyment of your first rave: number one, some Ecstasy, the rave drug of choice these days, and number two, Floyd's own home-brewed mushroom tea. What's your poison?" he asked sweetly, placing them both on the table.

"Poison? Hmm…what do you suggest? Mushroom tea?"

"That's a psychedelic, Alex, made from mushrooms. Or we can try some Ex if you want. It just kind of heightens the rave experience."

He was so casual about it. All I'd ever done was smoke pot but he made it seem so no-big-deal. I remembered an article I'd read recently about how poorly produced

Ecstasy fried some Harvard kid's brain, so I opted for the tea, thinking, at least it's natural. Matt poured us both a mug, diluting mine with a cup of water. We sat at his kitchen table drinking it warm out of two *I heart London* mugs. Shroom tea? Sounded cool, tasted like shit.

"Floyd tends to make a pretty strong brew so I added some water to yours," Matt said matter-of-factly. "I want you to have fun, not hallucinate melting faces all night."

"Aak," I cried, swallowing the bitter concoction. "Now you tell me? Melting faces doesn't sound fun…besides, if we're just having a 'fling', how do I know you won't dump me when I'm in some drug-induced stupor…"

"Don't worry, I made yours just right," he said, taking the mug out of my hand and placing it into the sink. "And besides, who said anything about this being a fling? Now let's get out of here, you vixen."

And off we went. Matt hailed a cab and gave the driver directions. I didn't know where we were headed; it was way out of town. Finally the cab pulled up in front of an enormous warehouse in what looked like an industrial park. Matt paid the fare and we got out. At this point, I noticed everything seemed to be sparkling. Matt's red shirt was so crisp and bright, it glowed. I leaned into him and felt his incredibly soft and smooth skin. I ran my hand across his cheek.

"Mmmmm," I commented.

"How you feeling?" he asked, smiling at me. He'd never looked more gorgeous—dark hair, intense green eyes, beautiful bone structure. I just stared at him, dumbstruck.

"You okay?" he asked again, taking my hand as we waited at the entrance.

"Mmm, I feel great," I said, looking at all the shiny people entering the warehouse.

The rest of the night passed in a blur. Some skinny guy in a green shirt holding an old-fashioned cigar box wandered my way. When I approached, he flipped open the lid to reveal pills of different colors and shapes resembling candy.

"What's your pleasure?' the skinny guy asked, his green shirt blinking at me.

"Hmm, let's see," I answered, reaching in to choose a candy-colored orange capsule that seemed to pulsate in my hand.

"Uh, uh," said Matt, suddenly appearing at my side and covering my hand with his own. "I can't take my eyes off you for one second. The last thing you need is an upper. Come here." He pulled me over to the back of the warehouse and waved the skinny guy away. "You're going to love this."

Behind him was a huge blow-up jumper castle, the kind rented for children's birthday parties, filled with glittering revelers defying gravity. I unzipped my boots, crawled inside, and jumped wildly to the techno beat that pervaded the space. I watched the faces of the other jumpers nearby lit up with laughter, their eyes and teeth glowing in the dark space. Suddenly I heard sirens and the place seemed to dissolve into a mass of screaming and running. I knew raves were illegal, but I didn't realize British police, or bobbies, as they were called, would bother to break them up. Matt grabbed my hand and pulled me out of the jumper castle. I somehow managed to nab my boots and rushed toward an exit followed by hordes of other ravers. Am I going to be arrested? I thought fleetingly. This is hilarious.

We ran outside into the alley behind the warehouse and wedged ourselves between the back wall of the building and a tall wooden fence. From our hiding place, we peeked around the corner and watched scores of people stream out the back door. I laughed as I zipped up my boots thinking that their faces resembled cartoon characters. Finally, we watched the bobbies leave the building. They marched out, swept their lights up and down the alleyway, and then wrapped a heavy metal chain around the door. As they drove off, lights still ablaze, Matt and I exchanged glances.

"So, how'd you like your first rave?" he asked, eyes alight. "I can't believe your luck. I went to a half a dozen before the cops actually broke one up. I can't believe you got all that action your first time."

"It was amazing," I giggled as I pulled his face closer to mine. "Did you know I can see in the dark? I can see your eyes sparkling. I can't believe I never noticed that before. Do they always do that?" I asked, my 'shroom high still going strong.

"Only when they look at you," he answered. He put his arms around my waist and backed me up against the brick wall of the building. I stared into his hungry eyes and felt him fingering the sides of my skirt, rubbing my hips. My heart pounded inside my shirt. I could hear the whooshing sounds of traffic on the nearby road and the distant voices of revelers getting into cars. Our mouths met in a rush of desire. His silky tongue devoured me and I moved my head to the side to maneuver closer to him, to crush my mouth harder to his. He pulled open my leather jacket and ran his hands along the sides of my T-shirt, his thumbs tracing the outline of my breasts and then down along the length of my skirt. I moaned softly.

"What do you want?" he whispered. He loved to hear me say it.

"I want to feel you inside me," I panted in his ear. In a frenzy, he pushed me against the side of the building and lifted my skirt. He held me against the wall and I was lost in the sensations—holding on to his shoulders, kissing his face, feeling his hands under my shirt and his mouth on me.

"Hold on, babe," he said as he unzipped his fly and filled me to the core. I could barely speak from the pleasure of it.

"Go harder," I begged. It was pure instinct. And the farther he sank into me, the more alive I became until I was only myself and nothing else mattered. Not who saw or knew or heard me cry out, not whether I was good or right or followed the rules. When Matt and I had sex it was just him and me and the deeper he drove, the more it unleashed something inside of me—something raw and real and totally uncensored. It thrilled me beyond words and it scared the hell out of me too, but not that night. That night I was high as a kite and I didn't resist or hold back a thing.

I tugged hard on the silky, dark hair at the nape of his neck while he kissed my mouth and sucked my tongue. He pushed my shirt up and pulled aside my bra so he could take my nipple in his mouth, making me cry out again with pleasure. I grabbed his hips and pulled him hard into me. "Fuck me," I cried, "don't stop." I could feel my orgasm rising and I wanted it so bad. I was determined to have it. I closed my eyes and felt the sensation of him thrusting in and out, and his tongue, and his hands, and his hips pumping back and forth. We went at it with such vigor that even in my vaguely hallucinogenic state, I realized my thighs would be black and blue in the morning. But I didn't care. I was impelled by my need and his own, and the overwhelming magic of the mushrooms.

***

Was that really me? Drinking some stranger's mushroom tea? Trespassing at an illegal rave? Having sex in an alleyway? Looking back on my younger years, that wasn't exactly how I remembered them. I was hardworking, driven, a gunner. My parents prized academic success and succeed, I had. I was third in my high school class and accepted directly into the Honors College at UCLA. I never skipped classes or drove drunk or went home with guys I didn't know. I was choosy and careful with everything I did but Matt blew all that to pieces. He did something to me, something imperceptible, that changed everything and, for a while, I'd been different. But whatever he'd opened had closed after he left. Now, I remembered it like a half-lost word fragment, something I meant to say before I forgot what it was.

RESTLESS IN L.A.
Mommy Musings. Stupid Confessions. Life.
Posted by Anonymous

Reminiscing

I friended an old boyfriend on Facebook. I didn't actually mean to. It was like some weird body snatcher temporarily took over my right hand and clicked on that beguiling little box. I was so embarrassed, hoping he wouldn't think I was a loser the way I do about people who randomly friend me even though we haven't spoken in years and wouldn't recognize each other if our carts collided in an aisle at Marshall's.

My motto's always been, if we're not friends in real life, why be friends online? Clearly, I'm in the minority. At least he didn't seem to think I was a weird sociopathic loser because he messaged me that he's coming to town and wants to meet for dinner.

The weird thing is that my husband is away that weekend so it spares me from having to discuss it with him, not that there's anything to discuss. Just two old friends getting together for drinks and reminiscing. My best friend keeps quoting a certain TV-psychologist who swears "online flirtations" threaten to wreck the institution of marriage. I think it's overblown. Lots of people re-connect online with old friends and coworkers. It's important to get out of one's comfort zone once in a while and do something different. I haven't left my ZIP code in months. So even though I'd normally say no to the dinner invitation because I felt too weird or was too tired or didn't want to leave the neighborhood or hadn't had my roots done in months, I said yes. It's a good reminder that once—a long time ago—I was someone other than my children's mother.

CHAPTER 7: PYRAMID OF SUCCESS

Last Mother's Day, Laurie gave me a tiny stuffed bird wearing an apron and fuzzy slippers and holding a sign that read: "Raising children is like being pecked to death by chickens." At the time, we'd howled with laughter. This week, I felt locked in a chicken coop.

The morning began with Natalie's unwillingness to wake up. I lived in fear of the school's Automated Tardy Message From Hell and begged her to get out of bed.

"Please, I hate when you're late."

"Okay, Mom, I'm getting up but can't they BE QUIET?" Ryan and Ben were arguing in the kitchen and we could hear Ben squealing, "Stop it!" at the top of his lungs.

"Ryan just took his medicine. You know it riles him up for the first half hour. Let me go check—"

"Ryan, Ryan, Ryan! I hate Ryan!" She spat the word at me as if she hated the taste of it. "He gets all your attention!"

"Please, Nat."

"It's true! I know he's got problems but I have problems too!"

"Okay, what's going on? If you get dressed, I'll sit with

you and we can talk."

I sat down in her desk chair and listened to her frustration with her friend Vivian from down the street. Apparently, Vivian didn't want Nat to have any other friends but her, and it was hard on Natalie, and the sixth-grade social scene was rough. Nat sat alone at the lunch tables yesterday. As I listened, I hoped Ryan would settle down before Ben screamed the house down.

My daughter needed me. She was most comfortable unloading her upsets and frustrations with me. And as much as her attitude sometimes irked me, I was glad we could talk. When I was a kid, I was a good girl. I was an only child and my parents groomed me like a mini-adult. I was polite and pleasant, and their friends remarked on how mature I was for my age. Jason and I never mastered that style of parenting, the style where your kids behaved and never talked back or broke down, where they weren't really themselves but who cared? At least they made you look good. No, Jason and I hadn't mastered that and I wasn't sorry. I got a lot of things wrong but not that. Good, bad, or ugly, with me, Natalie was always herself.

I got the kids to school on time—barely, and returned that afternoon to attend a conference with Ryan's teacher to review his "Pyramid of Success". A former P.E. coach and avid UCLA fan, Mr. Burroughs borrowed from John Wooden to increase class harmony. He'd requested the conference to explain how my son could more effectively scale the Pyramid by refraining from flicking his seatmate during low-interest activities such as math and spelling. Paying attention to subjects that bored him was not Ryan's forte. It was hard for anybody, but for a kid with severe ADHD, it was nearly impossible.

"You know, Mrs. Hoffman, Ryan's a smart kid," the teacher said, "even though his grades don't reflect it." He handed me his latest math test marked with a large red 12/20. "If only he would pay attention, stay out of personality clashes with other students, and stay on task."

If only. If only I had a magic pill to make him a round peg to fit into your round hole—I've got to remember to ask the psychiatrist about that one. "You know he has an IEP, right? He's been evaluated through the school district. Do you have his paperwork?" I asked. "He was supposed to be in the class across the hall, you know, with the teacher whose pace is a little slower but, for some reason, they put him in here."

"Well, I think they try to spread out the, um, the—" Mr. Burroughs coughed.

"Kids with accommodations?"

"Yes, right," he said. "I'm not sure that would've changed anything anyway. He tends to get in conflicts with other students."

I sighed and nodded my head. "Well, look, I also wanted to talk to you about the check marks. I thought you were supposed to re-direct him when he gets distracted? Maybe we should have another meeting with the principal? Ryan's really upset about getting so many—"

"I've been thinking about that," Mr. Burroughs said. He pulled out a two-inch ceramic polar bear statue from his desk drawer and handed it to me. "I'm going to give this to Ryan to put on his desk as a reminder."

"A reminder?" I asked, staring at the miniature white bear in a bright red sweater.

"Yes, to remind him that he can't 'bear' to get off task."

He's got to be kidding, I thought, but he wasn't. "I don't think—" I started to say, imagining how Ryan would feel about a mini polar bear sitting on his desk but the bell in the hallway screeched and I needed to make a mad dash across campus to Ben's kindergarten class. The kindergartners had to be dismissed to a waiting parent and lateness was severely frowned upon. I tripped over my purse as I moved toward the door and stuttered that I wanted to meet again.

"Okay, Mrs. Hoffman," he agreed. "I think we should

set up a team meeting to go over all of Ryan's behavioral issues," he said in front of the open door. I saw Cyndi and several other mothers milling about outside. When I turned to leave, they averted their eyes. No wonder worry lines were etched a mile deep into my aging brow. Inside, I was upset about so many things—Ryan's issues, the teacher's lack of understanding, and the other mothers and their looks. They had no idea. Why couldn't I accept that and move on?

My cell phone buzzed. I wanted to smack it against the wall. I got emailed so many schedules, requests, rosters and reminders, it made my head ache. Sometimes I fantasized about faking my own death with a phony auto-reply:

We are sorry to inform you that Alex Hoffman has expired. She will no longer be available to attend meetings, volunteer in classrooms, bring in baked goods or paper supplies, give money, drive carpools, send checks, forward emails, or respond to Evites or invitations of any kind. Due to Ms. Hoffman's untimely demise, please delete her contact information from your address book immediately. Thank you.

What a fantasy! Then I'd abandon the family and take off for Hawaii or Mexico or some Caribbean island. Sigh.

***

The rest of the week flew by. Thursday, I took Ben to the pediatrician's office for the third time to deal with two stubborn warts and then ran to the hair salon to get a quick cut and color. I spent Friday at the orthodontist with both Ryan and Natalie—always a pleasure to be with them together—learning about teeth spacing, separators, headgear, and the home equity loan we'd need to finance it. When I got home, I helped Jason pack for Palm Springs, rescuing his professional golf grips and a slightly dusty box of Pro balls from a neat stack of sporting goods he kept on a bottom shelf. I was rifling through a pile of my own random shoes, lining them up in neat pairs like Jason did, when I came across the white and silver women's golf shoes he'd bought me for my birthday last year. I picked one up—the scent of fresh leather still clung to it—and turned it upside down, running my hand along its pristine spikes. He wanted me to take lessons. But I didn't like golf.

"Are you going to be okay left alone with the savages for the weekend?" Jason asked, stuffing his razor and toothbrush into his toiletry case. Even though he didn't go to the gym all week, a casualty of the big merger push, he looked great. I saw him grab his black workout shorts and a pair of ear buds and stuff them into his weekender as he zipped it up and rolled it toward our bed.

"I think so. You're only gone two nights," I added.

"I won't be back 'til late Sunday afternoon. Sorry to miss Family Movie Night." It was the one night Jason rarely missed, our Sunday Family Movie Nights. "What are you going to watch?" he asked as he scanned his bedside table.

"Back to the Future III, by request. They've been begging for it." I tried to meet his blue eyes but he was distracted, attempting to recall any last-minute items.

I couldn't remember the last time Jason had taken some down time. He needed to do intricate cobweb removal when he pulled out his golf clubs from the garage. When we'd first met, he was coming off three years of law school in San Diego. He loved living in La Jolla, with its famous ocean views and PGA Championship golf courses, going to the beach between classes and riding his bike around campus. But as the years went by, and our family and mortgage grew, Jason became more and more a workaholic. The merger was the culmination of years of ambition. It would secure the nice life he wanted us to have, a life like he had growing up in upscale Brentwood. I couldn't fault him but I missed the fun guy I once knew. Maybe the golf trip would inspire him to take more vacation? I followed him as he wheeled the weekender toward the family room.

"Just enjoy yourself," I said. "The chaos will be exactly where you left it when you get back." I thought about mentioning my plans for Saturday night, that I was catching up with an old friend from college, but Jason was already halfway to the family room. I watched as he approached the couch without interrupting the show the kids were watching and kissed each one on the head before darting toward the door.

He paused at the doorway, turned, and walked back to where I stood leaning against the kitchen island. In his Lakers T-shirt and jeans, he reminded me of the guy I married. I leaned over and opened my arms, prepared for him to kiss me but he reached behind me and snatched his cell phone off the counter instead. Feeling my face redden, I grabbed him by the shoulder and placed a quick kiss on his cheek, the rough hairs of his goatee scratching my skin.

"Bye, hon," he said, flashing his dimples, apparently unaware of the faux pas. He grabbed the handle of his weekender and headed out the door.

RESTLESS IN L.A.
Mommy Musings. Stupid Confessions. Life.
Posted by Anonymous

Let Them Eat Cake
I get so tired of reading about all the things I should and shouldn't do as a parent: praise the effort, not the child! Be sure your face lights up when they walk in the room! Let them be bored! Let them have freedom! Let them eat cake! Or don't let them eat cake, after all, sugar is poison, food dyes cause ADHD, and childhood obesity is a national epidemic.

I was talking to a food fanatic friend the other day. She

was complaining about the pressure she was getting from her kids for fruit snacks, Lunchables, and other *pseudo foods*, as she called them. I tried to defend the harried mother of multiple children who was trying to pack a lunch the kids would actually eat (me!) but she argued for kale salad and quinoa in mini-Tupperware containers.

"Well, I don't know about you," she said, "but *my* kids eat clean. None of that colored food dye crap for them. That shit's poison! I make my kids protein powder shakes every morning and for lunch—" Her doorbell rang and I heard her instruct the exterminator to go around to the back. "Exterminator?" I cried, thinking this may be my only chance. "Is he a green exterminator?" "Well," she hedged feebly, "I've been trying to find one..."

Aha! She won't let her kids touch an inorganic banana and yet she sprays pesticides all over her backyard. My point is less that my friend's a hypocrite, and more that we all do the best we can. So why do we have to beat each other up? If raising kids is supposed to take a village, how come I feel like I'm in a boxing ring?

CHAPTER 8: REALITY BITES

Between soccer games and birthday parties, Saturday afternoon went off remarkably well and the kids were settled when my sitter/housekeeper/all-around savior Maria arrived. She was great with them and me, too. A devout Seventh Day Adventist, whenever she found me with my head in my hands, she reassured me in her imperfect English not to worry, certain that "God will take care of the children," and "God knows the answers," and "All is well, thank God." Although I wasn't religious, I appreciated her optimism.

"Mommy look so pretty." Maria smiled, fluffing up my hair and admiring my little black dress. "You go out, Mrs. Alex. Have fun! You need it, too."

"Thank you, Maria. I'm meeting some girlfriends for dinner," I lied. I searched the kitchen for my cell phone and keys as Natalie walked by.

"Can I go to the mall if Vivian's mom takes us?" Her dark hair was pulled up in a ponytail and she wore a pair of white-rimmed glasses, even though she had perfect vision.

"Not tonight, Nat. Plus, it's late." I smiled at her.

She rolled her eyes. "Well, you're going out."

Maria and I gave each other a look. I wasn't taking the

bait. "What's with the glasses?"

"It's a look, Mom. Jeez." she rolled her eyes again and headed toward the TV.

"You don't worry about nothing," Maria said, nudging me toward the door. "I see you later."

"You're the best." I wasn't sure if it was her intense faith or her natural sweetness or the fact that she'd raised four sons by herself but Maria never flinched at my kids' shenanigans and was relentlessly cheerful.

I offered a warm goodbye to each of my children, threatening them with various punishments if they didn't behave. Ben gave me a big hug, Ryan snorted, and Natalie waved a hand in my direction. I bolted for the door.

I needed this night to myself: a little grown-up conversation, a glass of wine. This will be fun. I tried not to think about the butterflies in my stomach. Maybe it was just gas. Great. I plugged the restaurant's address into the SUV's GPS and checked the rearview mirror as I entered the freeway. Traffic was usually a nightmare on a Saturday night but tonight, of course, it was wide open and I cruised to Hollywood doing sixty-five. My hands were sweating on the steering wheel but I flipped on the radio and turned up the A/C.

I pulled down the sun visor a final time and double-checked my makeup in the mirror before handing the valet my car keys. Straightening my little black dress, I grabbed my jacket and got out of the car.

Katsuya was an ultra-modern restaurant right at Hollywood and Vine—very chic. I wedged myself behind several large parties jockeying to get a table and looked around. There was a group of young women in short party dresses, one in a white baseball cap with a veil down the back, a bachelorette party no doubt. Couples and groups crowded around the hostess stand waiting for their tables. I twisted my neck, studying the vast array of diners, wondering if I'd recognize Matt. Scanning the crowd, I wondered if maybe he wouldn't show, maybe I'd gotten the wrong night, maybe I'd misread the restaurant...but then I stopped. Even in profile, twenty years later, he was unmistakable.

Wearing dark jeans and a blue button-down shirt, he stood gazing out a window toward Vine Street. I steadied myself as I darted behind the bridesmaids and studied him in profile. Still tall and dark, but now flecks of gray dotted his unruly black hair. The gray only added a sexy, older-man appeal that he didn't have twenty years ago, not that he needed any additional sex appeal. He certainly had not let himself go. And he was just a few feet away...Matt Daniels. Maybe I should take off and let him remember me as the cute twenty-year-old I once was? I wedged myself deeper into the crowd. Maybe he could tell I was skinny-fat? I could text him from the car and say I came down with a sudden case of influenza or that flesh-eating bacteria or something.

I felt nauseous and kind of dizzy and I was slowly edging toward the door but it was too late. The crowd shifted as his head turned. I froze, uncertain what to do next. Our eyes met and, in an instantly familiar gesture, he brushed his hand through his hair. I stood immobilized and watched as his green eyes lit up and a wide smile broke out across his face.

"Alex," he called, jolting me out of my stupor and reaching a hand toward me.

"Matt," I smiled, feeling a heat in my cheeks and taking his hand.

He held me at arm's length. "You look...beautiful."

"You don't look so bad yourself," I laughed.

We stood there, smiling at each other. I felt momentarily awkward until the hostess interrupted and asked for his name.

"Reservations at eight," he said. "Daniels." He turned to me, "Is it just you? I made the reservation for three because I wasn't sure if—"

"It's just me," I nodded. "My husband Jason would've

loved to come but he's out of town on a golf trip."

"Two," he told the hostess, holding up two fingers. "I'm sorry I won't get to meet him." He gestured toward the white leather furniture and the overlarge images of dark eyes and puckered red lips that hung on the walls. "Have you been here before? I know it's popular but the sushi's fantastic and the space is incredible. I love the high ceilings and glass walls."

"It's beautiful," I answered, suppressing a smile. "I don't get to Hollywood much. I've been to Katsuya in Brentwood but it's not nearly as striking."

They seated us at a table in the corner, perfect for conversation. After our initial greetings and inquiries about each other's spouses (Heather, an interior decorator), kids (twin boys, Teddy and Reed, nine), jobs (very successful), and mutual friends (only one, Scott Riley, a cinematographer he kept in touch with from our London days), there was an awkward pause during which I ordered a watermelon cucumber mojito. He matched me with a martini. During the meal, we shared a bottle of red and shortly thereafter I felt myself relax. We talked about his work and our kids and the general trajectory of our lives over the past two decades. Eventually, we reminisced about our London days, talked about our friends from back then, our favorite bookstores, and the pubs and wine bars we frequented. As we talked, I loosened up and began to feel more like myself. The alcohol consumption didn't hurt, either.

"Do you remember the day we met?" Matt asked. "You were frantic about getting your schedule changed and you bumped right into me in the street." He took a sip of wine and smiled. "You practically knocked me over."

"Oh god, I was mortified!" I put my head in my hand for a moment and laughed, waves of embarrassment coming back to me. "You saved me with your comment about how Americans can't help bumping into each other. You were always quick on your feet."

"I was just trying to keep you from running off," he said." His hand rested across the table and lay open next to my elbow. "I could tell you were in a rush and I wanted to keep you talking so I could get your number," he added with a laugh.

I was silent for a moment, remembering that day. I literally ran headfirst into Matt on the street as I sprinted to the admin building hoping to get my schedule corrected before the day ended. I was so flustered at our collision and tried to apologize but when I looked up into his sparkling green eyes, I was mesmerized. I stood there on the sidewalk tongue-tied as he peppered me with questions until I finally remembered my schedule and dashed off. That day was vividly imprinted in my mind.

"That was a pretty memorable day," I said as the waiter laid plates of sushi rolls on the table. I caught the faint scent of cilantro.

He smiled and gestured toward the appetizers, his hand lightly bumping against my elbow. I could feel the electricity flow between us. I crossed my arms to collect myself, beginning to regret the second glass of wine that followed the watermelon cucumber cocktail.

"Tell me about your wife," I said, seeking to diffuse the layer of intensity that formed around us.

"What do you want to know?" he asked, raising his eyebrows with the question and a thousand visions of Matt raising his eyebrows at me came into my mind: dancing at wine bars, kissing in the park, saving me from my ever careful, ever appropriate self. The irony that we now sat across from each other carefully sharing a meal and making appropriate small talk wasn't lost on me.

"How did you two meet?" I asked.

"Heather just came back to Manhattan from Rhode Island where she did her undergraduate work. She and I were both working on a film that a friend of my father's was making and we just kind of hit it off. I was at the office late every night while the film was in post-production and Heather was there, too, so we started ordering in, and before we knew it, we moved in together. We got married not long after."

I took a sip of my wine. "Does she still work in the film business?"

"No, not for years. She's busy with the twins but she does interior decorating on the side, mostly helping her friends re-do their apartments and beach houses in the Hamptons."

"I love when everything looks really well chosen and pulled together but I can't say I'm very good at it. Too many decisions," I admitted.

"Well, we all have our talents, right? As I recall, you were pretty damn smart." He leaned toward me and asked, "So you're not writing?"

For some reason, I answered truthfully. "I—a little bit. I starting blogging a little while ago—it's nothing really—I write about being a mom and what it's like for me. It's sort of my take on how crazy it feels, you know, staying home with the kids. It's nothing special, just silly rants."

"Really? That's hard to believe. I read your stuff and it was good. Really good. And you worked so hard, you were an academic monster."

"Well, that was a long time ago. These last few years, I've been pre-occupied...you know, the kids and life in general. I write when I can—I post anonymously, by the way."

"Anonymously?" he asked. "Why is that?"

I shifted in my seat. I didn't mean to get into this. It was hard to explain what my anonymity meant to me. "I just—I tend to keep the way I feel about things inside—things that disturb me or make me mad. It's a really small community and I have this crazy inner dialogue that's always running—that's what I write about and it's not...it's just...if you read it, you'd understand. I'm not ready to go public yet."

"I'd love to read it someday. If you'd let me."

"I'll keep it in mind," I said, my heart pounding. I didn't know what prompted me to tell him about the blog. There was no way I'd ever let him read about my inner miseries and constant upsets. And I certainly couldn't tell him I blogged about him, about our Facebook friendship, anyway. Thankfully, the waiter appeared. He refilled both of our wine glasses.

"Tell me about your husband. How did you two meet?" Matt asked.

I told Matt the infamous story of how I met Jason at a movie theater a year after I graduated from UCLA. I showed up by myself at an unfamiliar Loews to see *Reality Bites* with Winona Ryder and Ethan Hawke and didn't know the theater was cash only. As I stood at the transparent window, cashless and clutching my rejected Visa card, a twenty-dollar bill seamlessly slipped under the glass and a handsome face said, "It's on me." The rest was history. We dated for a year, were married at the Biltmore in Santa Barbara, and had three adorable and challenging children.

"Your husband's a smart guy," he said, shaking his head and smiling. "If Heather didn't like Chinese, I'd probably still be single."

"Oh, please. I doubt you had any trouble with the ladies." I couldn't help but notice his mouth, the playful grin still teasing at the edges.

"Well..." He paused as if unsure what to say next. "You know, I didn't, uh, see anybody for a long time after, uh...London."

"What are you talking about?" I wanted to know but I was afraid to know, too. I spent a year with Matt in London and we hadn't seen or spoken to each other since. There were times over the years, particularly the first few years, that I wondered about him and if he thought about me, what he was doing, if he met someone. I built up a fantasy in my mind about what his life was like after I left, how he achieved his success in the film business, fell in love with a beautiful woman, got married, and lived a fabulously exciting life. I didn't know what actually happened. And that was the thing we weren't talking about: what actually happened. I wasn't sure I wanted to know and yet, I couldn't help but ask.

"I left England and came back to New York not long after you left," he said, fiddling with his napkin. "Everything kind of fell apart—the documentary I was working on ran out of money and I couldn't find another job. When I lost the flat in Earls Court, I came home and was lucky enough to land on a big-budget project."

I was stunned. I had no idea he'd come back to the States so soon after me. In my fantasy, he'd stayed in London for years, launching his successful filmmaking career from there. I had imagined him at our favorite pub, chatting it up with the locals who made fun of our American accents, picking up a loaf of hot bread at the small market around the corner, meeting friends at our favorite Indian restaurant down the street.

"When I got back to New York, I was focused on my career. I worked all the time. After a few years, my friends and my folks became relentless about setting me up but I didn't want it. I guess after London..." he shrugged.

I realized we were staring at each other and quickly looked away.

"When Heather and I met, it was at work and it never seemed like 'dating'. We were friends and then...it just became more." He suddenly slapped his hands on his jeans and smiled. "And my boys are terrific."

"They're nine?" I asked, taking another gulp of wine.

He nodded.

I bit my lip but asked anyway. "So how long have you been married?"

"Ten years."

I sat there silently trying to digest what he told me. Ten years. We came back from London nearly twenty years ago. I met Jason not long after graduation and married him

shortly thereafter. Matt must have been single for years—
ten years. All this time, I'd imagined his life after I left—
happily living in London, dating and having a great time,
when in actuality he was single and alone, living in New
York City. I wasn't sure if this revelation made me happy
or sad. I'd created a fantasy of his life after I left and it
became, over the years, the truth. To find out now that I
was wrong was a shock. What else had I been wrong
about?

The busboy came over to clear the table. I wondered
why I'd waited so long to look him up. Why I didn't search
for him on the Internet years ago, just to say hello? We
shared an incredible time; we had an intense connection
from the moment we met, and for nearly a year we were
inseparable. As I looked back, it was a miracle I went to
school at all. Matt's schedule was erratic, weeks of nonstop
work followed by weeks of free time. Days were spent
exploring the city and traveling—to Amsterdam, Paris,
Prague—and the nights…I blushed thinking about our
nights together. Of course, he remembered.

I suddenly realized it was late and the restaurant was
emptying out. There were a few couples left at the sushi
bar and a group of older men at a table toward the front.
The busboy cleared the remaining dishes and the waiter
approached politely. "Would you like anything else, sir?"

"Coffee?" Matt asked, turning to me with the question.

Between us, we'd polished off several rounds of sushi
rolls, a Japanese salad, grilled lamb chops, two cocktails,
and a bottle of wine.

"No, thank you. To tell you the truth, I'm drunk and
stuffed." I tried to lighten the mood. I reached for my
purse.

Matt looked at the waiter. "No, thank you. Just the
check." Then he turned back to me and said, "Thanks for
letting me take you to dinner." I hung my purse back on
the chair.

Although the waiter's interruption helped, there was a

dark veil of quiet over the table.

"Alex," he said, his sparkling green eyes looking squarely into my own.

I jumped at the sound of my name. "Yes?"

"Lost in thought?" The gentle lilt of his question brought back other nights, other questions.

"I guess I was. It was a long time ago." I couldn't help but look into his eyes. I remembered how they'd entranced me decades ago. I could see the faint lines that surrounded them now.

"Yes, it was. And life is incredibly busy," he agreed, looking back at me. I wondered if he noticed the lines around my eyes, my forehead, my smile.

"Well, I'm glad we did this," I said and meant it. "You look great and I'm happy things are going well. I always knew you'd be a big success." I turned and gathered my purse and jacket. Matt seemed to be staring at me but I couldn't think of what else to say. The solitary candle in the votive between us was nearly melted. "It was...a pleasure to reminisce." I smiled and started to get up.

"Wait," he said and reached for my arm. My awareness slowly shrank to a pinhole as the restaurant, the busboys, our table, all fell away and I was conscious only of the feel of his fingertips pressed against the skin of my upper forearm. "I'll wait outside with you while they bring your car around. I walked from my hotel."

"Oh, you don't have to do that," I said.

"I want to." He took the jacket from my arms and held it up while I slipped into it.

We stood next to each other on the sidewalk without speaking. I was so engrossed in the turmoil in my head that I was caught off guard when a short, balding man in khaki pants and a Yankees T-shirt suddenly lunged at Matt with an outstretched arm.

"No way! Matt Daniels!" A hairy arm reached across me and shook Matt's hand.

"Jerry. What a surprise," Matt said with warm smile.

"Yeah, it sure is. It's been, what? A year? How've you been?"

"I've been fine, just fine," Matt responded, unflappable. "And what about you? What brings you to L.A.?"

"I'm in town location scouting. I just had dinner—this place was fantastic!—and I'm on my way to the Redbury to meet some friends. Oh, this must be your wife," he said, looking over at me and extending a sweaty palm. "Matt and I worked together on the Russell Crowe project."

Oh shit. I'd had a lot to drink and this situation was beyond my powers of improvisation. His outstretched hand waited so I shook it. I didn't know how to respond but Matt saved me.

"Jerry, this is an old friend of mine from college, Alex Hoffman. Alex lives in L.A. and came to meet me for dinner to catch up." Matt smiled at Jerry as he introduced me. Wow, he always knew what to say, even in an awkward moment.

"Nice to meet you, Alex," Jerry beamed. "You live in L.A.? Have you been to the Redbury Hotel? I heard the new rooftop bar is amazing."

"No." I smiled. "But I heard the same thing."

"Actually, that's where I'm staying," Matt said. "It's just a block north of here." He turned and pointed in the direction of the hotel.

"You heading over there now?" Jerry asked him. "Hey, why don't we all go for a drink? The place's supposed to be swanky. It was designed by some celebrity photographer, what's his name?"

"Rolston." Matt turned to me. "I totally understand if you need to get home?"

"Oh, come on, Alex," Jerry said, sensing my hesitation. "You've got to check it out—one drink can't hurt."

"Okay," I said. "One drink."

***

Matt drove with me over to the hotel. On the way, he told me about his nine-year-old twins, Teddy and Reed. Heather came from an old New York family and insisted the boys be given family names so they were named for great uncles on their mother's side. Matt described the humor in raising twins—how they finished each other's sentences one minute and fist-fought the next. His office was in downtown Manhattan so he walked the boys to school most mornings and then hopped a cab to his office. Manhattan life was so different from L.A. We joked about how Los Angelinos drove everywhere, even around the corner—as I was doing at that very moment—and I vented about my husband's lead foot. "Jason is the only person in L.A. who can get from one end of the city to the other in twenty minutes. I have a feeling he floors it in the carpool lane but he'll never admit to it." We both laughed. I pulled in, got my ticket, and we walked into the Redbury Hotel.

The lobby was covered in black and white checkerboard tile. Heavy gold-fringed red velvet curtains pulled back to reveal English chairs and black, baroque mirrors. Jerry was waiting for us by the elevators. There was a crowd getting in and more people entered as the doors opened on the twelfth, sixteenth, and twenty-second floors. Finally, we reached the rooftop and spilled out onto the white-tiled floor of the overcrowded, all-white lounge. The walls were lined with white leather-upholstered booths and girls in mini dresses sat on white ultra-modern Barcelona chairs that dotted the space. Matt took me by the elbow and maneuvered me to the bar. Jerry ordered a martini and Matt and I each had another glass of red.

"So what do you do, Alex?" Jerry asked.

"Right now, I stay home and raise my three kids." It was hard to hear over the music and the sound of laughter, talking, and drinking. I wished I had a cigarette.

"That's hard work," Jerry said. "I've got two myself."

He was just about to launch into his biographical

information when he spotted his friends waving from the other end of the bar. He invited us to join them but we begged off, claiming we were too tired and I needed to get home. Matt told Jerry it was great to see him, I said a friendly goodbye, and off he went into the sea of hipsters.

I stood at the bar and nursed my drink as Matt settled the tab. I'd promised to take Natalie to the mall in the morning to get a gift card for a friend's birthday. I rifled through my purse and grabbed my valet ticket. I set my nearly full glass of wine down on the sparkly white countertop and rose to leave but a corner of my sandal caught on the edge of the barstool and I stumbled. Matt caught me with both hands around the waist. "You okay?" he asked.

"Oh, uh, yes…I'm fine." I was keenly aware of the pressure of his hands on the curve of my hips. He was so close I could see the flecks of brown and yellow hidden in the green of his eyes. I meant to pull away, to avert my eyes but I didn't. Maybe it was the alcohol or the music or just the weirdness of the evening. Whatever it was, I looked right back at him.

"Do you need some coffee…or a glass of water?" he finally asked.

I stepped backward, put a hand on the counter to steady myself, and quickly collected my purse. "No. Thanks. Really. I barely touched that last glass of wine. I'm just clumsy," I said, waving off the moment.

We walked to the elevator in silence and Matt pressed the down button. "I can walk you to the lobby," he offered as we stepped in.

"No, you don't have to," I said, shaking my head. "I'm really fine." At the seventeenth floor, he stepped out but turned toward me and covered the doorway with his hand to keep the elevator open.

"It was great to see you…" He held the door and it seemed like he might say something more but he didn't. He just stood there and smiled. I smiled back at him, hoping to remember the way his eyes gleamed and how his hair was just turning gray at the edges and his smile—that same smile that lit him up from the inside. But this time, I noticed something different: a shadow on his face, as if the light couldn't penetrate the deepest corners.

I leaned over the threshold and kissed him on the cheek, feeling just a hint of stubble. "It was great to see you, too." I could smell his aftershave.

He held on to the door as seconds ticked by. It was great to see you, too? That's it? That's all I had? I hadn't seen the guy in twenty years and might never see him again. But whatever else would have to remain unsaid because the elevator door kept trying to close and, if he didn't let go soon, I was sure an alarm would sound.

"Bye," I finally said. A memory floated up but I couldn't quite catch it: a reluctant Matt not wanting to say goodbye. He smiled again and let go.

I watched the elevator door close in front of me. What a night, I thought to myself, as I fished through my purse for the valet ticket. I felt this strange hollow feeling in my chest that reminded me of a dream I once had where I arrived at my own birthday party and realized I didn't know any of the guests. I was anxious to get in the car and drive—radio off, sunroof open, the cool night air to calm me down. My mind reeled from the revelations of our conversation, the accidental encounter with his colleague, and the weird and yet not-weird feeling of seeing him again after all these years. I needed time to digest the evening, to pull out singular lines and admissions and match them up against my fictionalized account of what happened since I left London. But I couldn't find the damn ticket. I must have dropped it when I stumbled upstairs. Damn! The elevator door opened at the lobby but I stayed inside and pressed Rooftop, intending to go back up to the bar and look for it. On the way, the door opened on seventeen and there stood Matt holding the valet ticket in his hand.

"Hey! I was just coming down after you," he said,

covering the doorway firmly with his hand. "You must have dropped this when we said goodbye." He held up the ticket.

"Oh! Thank you! I'm sure they'd charge me a fortune if I lost it."

He kept his hand on the door and I knew I should reach out and take the ticket. From where I stood, I could see the creamy walls of the hallway, the oversized chandelier hanging above the elevator bank, each light with its own miniature lampshade, and a pair of shiny red leather chairs leaning against the wall. The valet ticket was still in his hand. Neither one of us spoke for several seconds.

"Are you sure you don't want a glass of water?" I heard him ask.

My mind froze, the question hanging in the air between us like a thin strand of spider web barely detectable in the sunlight. I thought I didn't respond. I thought I'd pressed the Down button when I noticed my legs step out onto the floor. This was so not a good idea. Oh, relax, chimed the other side of my brain. It's harmless flirtation. He's happily married, for god's sake. Either way, my legs followed him down the hall.

CHAPTER 9: INFIDELITY 2.0

I leaned against the door and watched him insert the plastic key card into the slot. At close range, I could see the grays dotting his dark hair, the lines on his forehead, the curve of his jaw. His green eyes caught me staring and he smiled as he opened the door and gestured for me to enter.

The room was clean and stylishly attired in a cool, retro-Hollywood vibe. Burgundy walls met dark wood floors, with a modern white pedestal lamp tucked into a back corner. A queen bed covered in a black velvet duvet sat at one end of the room next to a huge window that overlooked Hollywood Boulevard. Matt took off his jacket and dropped it on a chair by a small writing desk littered with notebooks and highlighters. His suitcase laid half open in the corner with various clothes flung around it. I watched as he unbuttoned a top button of his shirt and caught a brief glimpse of the skin of his bare chest. He walked over to the cabinet where the fridge and minibar were nestled.

"Do you want something to eat?" he asked.

I followed him over. "No thanks. Just a glass of water."

He lifted two bottles of Pellegrino out of the bar and

turned to face me. The floor seemed to sway beneath my feet, either from the alcohol consumption or the sheer tension between us. I watched as he placed two miniature, green bottles on top of the open armoire. He seemed to be moving in slow motion. I couldn't think of a single thing to say so I stood silently as he unwrapped the glasses, turned them over, and filled each midway with bubbling water.

"Here you go," he said and handed me one. He stood less than a foot from me, close, but not touching.

I held the glass in my hand but didn't move. We were frozen, rooted to the spot. It seemed like time ticked by. He looked directly at me and I stared back, once again noticing the flecks of brown, yellow, and hazel that formed the green of his eyes. I leaned into the wall to steady myself. His eyes, questioning and unsure, searched mine. I hesitated, my mind raced, and I desperately wished I could pause the moment in real time to consider what was happening.

"Alex?" he said, his voice so low I could barely make out my name. He was just inches from me.

A million thoughts went through my brain at lightning speed. Is this a question? Is he asking me a question?

"Yes," I whispered.

He took the glass from my hand and set it down on the armoire. He moved toward me slowly, his eyes still questioning. I couldn't look away. His left hand gripped the wall above my head as he leaned into me, his body hovering just above mine. I could feel the heat coming off his shirt. When his soft lips and hint of late-day stubble grazed my mouth I gasped out loud—or was it just inside?—I couldn't be sure. It was an electric shock and the nerves all over my body fired wildly.

We'll just kiss. I'll just let him kiss me for old time's sake and then I'll leave. That's not cheating. My heart pounded violently beneath my dress. His mouth pressed against my lips and I caught a trace of spicy cabernet and cilantro. But it was the scent of him that undid me, that unlocked all of our nights together from decades ago. I breathed him in and I was twenty years old again and he was my lover and my body knew and remembered the promise of that scent.

Every part of me was on high alert. I reached down and linked my fingers through the back belt loops of his jeans, imprisoned them there, afraid to let them roam unimpeded. His lips on my mouth, the prickle of his stubble on my chin, and that musky scent that was unmistakably Matt threw me off balance. I knew we should stop but I couldn't seem to muster the necessary will to say anything. My body was dissolving and I wasn't sure how much longer I could remain in a solid state.

He finally pulled back and our eyes met. I wanted to say something but no words came. I felt jittery and fidgeted under his intense gaze but slowly the stillness seeped into me and I relaxed. Was this really happening or was it a dream? His chest rose and fell and my heart pounded in my ears so it had to be real. But then what was I doing here? With Matt Daniels? In a hotel room?

I leaned against the wall, considering a thousand thoughts and staring into Matt's green eyes when he suddenly reached for my face with both hands and fit his mouth hard over mine, devouring me with his tongue. Every hair on my body strained toward him, every muscle, every tendon was taut and pressed forward. He tasted like London; like being twenty years old; like being alive and unfettered; like a long time ago. My knees shook and I wrapped my arms around his back, feeling his muscles tense beneath his shirt and pressing him against me. The kiss went on and on, the feel of his mouth, the taste of his tongue, the feeling of wanting so strong inside of me. I was lost, so lost.

"Wait," I said breathlessly, pulling away. "What are we doing?" I asked, trying to make sense of what was happening. I needed to know we weren't just two drunk and horny people about to fuck up our lives. I wanted to understand how we got into this moment.

"I…I don't know," he said, still leaning into me and breathing hard. "I have no idea."

"Shit," was the only response I could think of.

He kissed me again. This time, my back melted into the wall while his mouth traveled from my lips to behind my ear. I leaned my head to the side to give him full access as one of the straps of my dress spilled over my shoulder. Matt's mouth kissed and sucked the bare space of skin and then moved to the hollow of my neck before stopping at the top of the cleavage that peeked out. His mouth seemed to be the focus of all of my sensory perception. I could feel every inch of his lips on my skin; every point of pressure as his hands searched up and down my sides, making me shiver. My little black dress was twisted and tangled in different directions. How could I stand there— clothes askew, lights on, as if exposed for an examination? He hadn't seen me in twenty years and I had three kids and needed to be at the mall in the morning. I had to get home in case my husband called to say goodnight. My husband.

"We have to stop," I groaned. "We're not the same people. We're both married."

The fog had cleared. I couldn't go through with this craziness. I needed to take control of my brain. I had to get the hell out of Hollywood and back to the Valley where I should have stayed to begin with.

He untangled himself and stepped backward. We were both panting. "You're right," he said nearly out of breath. "I should never have brought you here. I just—I just didn't want you to leave."

"What's happening?" I whispered but I remained there, staring at him while my inner voice screamed how wrong this was. I willed myself to move away from the irresistible pull of his body. Leave, Alex! Get out of there!

"It's up to you," he finally said. He didn't blink. His pressed shirt was wrinkled, his dark hair, already unruly, looked almost wind-swept, and his eyes gleamed. He stood just inches from me, holding me with his gaze. "But in another ten seconds, I won't be able to help myself." He had never, in all the time I knew him, looked more serious and he waited for my answer.

I closed my eyes and tried to make sense of the situation. It was hard to think because my brain had shut down sometime earlier in the evening, somewhere between, "Hello Matt," and, "Do you want a glass of water?" Deep inside I heard Laurie's voice, "And do you know why it's so dangerous to re-connect with an old boyfriend online?" she warned. "Because there's already something between you, something to build on..." But Laurie was far away, another universe really, and Matt was here and I couldn't string together a single coherent thought. It wasn't the alcohol or even autopilot; I simply surrendered to the raw need inside of me.

I looked into his deep green eyes and asked, "How many seconds do I have left?"

But it was too late. I ran out the clock.

Our mouths met in a rush of desire and desperation. My heart pounded as I pushed against him in an effort to get deeper into his arms, his mouth, his skin. There was no turning back. His hands stroked my hair and my face and I felt myself relax into the moment, savoring the sweet flavor of my youth. He reached around and unzipped the back of my dress, pulling the spaghetti straps to the side. The dress slipped effortlessly to the floor and I stood before him in a black strapless bra and black silk underwear.

The rest seemed to happen as if in a dream. He took my hand and led me toward the bed. My strapless bra was tossed aside as he cupped my bare breasts in his hands and moved his lips from one to the other. I moaned out loud from the pleasure of his mouth on me. My fingers trembled as I unbuttoned his shirt and slipped it off. I traced the lines of his back and ran my hands over his chest and downward. He unzipped his pants, adding to the crumpled pile already on the floor. He pulled out of his briefs and we lay there skin to skin, my silk underwear the only thing between us. I saw his hand glide across the lace edge. It was right there; one flick of the hip and I was undone.

"Alex?" he asked, and I realized he was saying my name. I was so lost in the feel of his hands and his skin but the sound of his voice called me back. It was the question without a question but this time I knew what he was asking.

"Yes."

He slipped off my underwear. I was soaked from wanting him. We lay naked and intertwined, our bodies eager and ready but he hesitated. For one moment, nothing moved. There was utter stillness in the room except for our panting and the beating of our hearts. I felt his hardness against my hip and waited, looking into his eyes, so familiar and yet foreign too. He stroked my cheek with his hand, brushed back my hair to expose my face.

I wanted it so badly. And I knew it was wrong and I shouldn't be there and yet it didn't feel wrong. It felt right, so right. Everything inside of me cried out, Yes! Yes! Oh god, oh god. What was I doing?

Our eyes met in a look that conveyed a spectrum of pent-up emotions; longing, frustration, grief, joy, and excitement.

"I had a vasectomy three years ago," he offered.

"I've had an IUD for five," I countered.

We both laughed. He traced the curve of my hip and thigh with his hand. Then he leaned down and kissed me. The kiss seemed to reverberate throughout my entire body. My heart pounded and every internal system switched into overdrive. Each imaginable sensation was magnified by a thousand; I smelled the scent of him wafting up from each of his pores, the blood raced through my veins, and my fingertips felt the texture of every molecule of his skin, his hair. I kissed him back hard, letting my tongue explore his mouth, sucking him into me.

He took me in his arms and I felt myself literally open to him. He rolled on top of me, his eyes boring into mine without blinking. What was he searching for? I remembered the hypnotic powers of those eyes. They'd always entranced me as they did still. Thoughts of the past and the present and Matt and his eyes and his smile coalesced in my mind as he entered me without friction, just one long, smooth movement.

"Ohhh," he murmured. We matched rhythms effortlessly. I buried my nose in the musky scent of his skin and clung to him, pushing him down harder onto me. Our eyes locked. He urgently plunged into me, again and again, and my hips rose to meet him. His mouth crushed against mine and we clung to each other. Matt was there, inside of me, making love to me. I let out a soft moan of pleasure and resignation as I met him, over and over again, all the while Laurie's words at the edge of my awareness: "There's already something between you….even if it was a long time ago…" Oh, shut up, Laurie.

"You feel so good," he moaned.

"Harder," I begged, lost to desire. I pulled him into me, wanting him inside the depth of me, wanting him to fill me up. He seemed to know and understand because he reached beneath my pelvis and pushed me up toward him as he hunkered down and made me cry out in satisfaction.

"Yes, oh, please, yes."

He swallowed me up until I moaned out loud, and then he came as I squeezed my eyes shut to concentrate on the release that engulfed me. A kaleidoscope of images flashed in my mind: Matt and me at the Tate Gallery; playing ultimate Frisbee in Hyde Park; at his flat in Earls Court; Jason on a bike in San Diego; the kids laughing in the pool; me, at the keyboard, in my office, Matt's profile picture flashing on the screen. There was a low humming in my head as lights and colors danced before my closed eyes and my body shook with pleasure. Finally, I returned to myself. Matt leaned over me, resting on an elbow and looked into my face with a concerned smile.

"Hey, Alexandra." He brushed loose strands of hair from my face.

"Don't. Please. No one ever calls me that."

The spell was broken. I still reverberated with the tremors of my release but my thoughts cleared. I was lost in a haze of sensations—the hunger for his skin, the scent of our lovemaking, the taste of his mouth. Now that our bodies were sated, I felt awkward and self-conscious.

"I guess I want to say, this was a surprise," I said, shaking my head. I looked at him and was struck again by his face. Aging only made him more attractive, adding a bit of mystery and maturity to his once youthful features. "I don't, I mean, I've never…done this before."

"Neither have I. Ever." He reached over and stroked my arm with his outstretched hand. "Are you all right?"

I pulled the crisp white sheet around my chest and thought about how I felt. "I don't know…this whole evening has a strange, dreamlike quality." And it did.

I truly believed meeting him for dinner had been innocent. I'd never done anything like that before, not even remotely like that. I was faithful in my marriage. It's true I wanted to see Matt, was intensely curious about him. Of course, I felt the sparks when we saw each other, but still, my intentions were pure. There was a part of me that wanted to flirt with danger, wanted to be in a situation that was unknown, wanted to feel wanted and alive and sexy. But I didn't mean to *do* anything about it. It was supposed to be a fun flirtation, a night to share with Laurie over cocktails on our next Girls' Night Out—the night I had dinner with my old flame and flirted up a storm. And yet, it somehow went awry. He'd looked at me and his eyes flashed and the scent of him and the feel of his hands…none of it seemed real. Now we were naked in his bed at the Redbury Hotel, limbs intertwined, covered in the scents of sweat and lovemaking. I couldn't understand how it happened and yet I felt a deep sense of satisfaction in my core, as if some primal itch finally was scratched. Was this a midlife crisis?

"I'm sorry if I—"

"You didn't," I said quickly. "You know how I got here? I walked." I looked up at the square shapes cut into the ceiling and blinked back tears. "You didn't drag me. You didn't make me. I knew what I was doing. And now I know."

"Now you know what?" The white sheet tucked around Matt's midriff pulled slightly as he turned toward me. In the dim light, I could make out the shadow of concern on his forehead.

"How it feels to cheat on my husband." My voice cracked.

"Hey," he said, sitting up and reaching for me. "I don't want to fuck up your life. This," he gestured between us, "it just happened. It wasn't planned. Something about being here with you; it feels right."

"Even though it isn't?"

I suddenly realized the time and panicked. It was nearly midnight and I needed to text Maria. "Look, I've got to go," I said, scooting away from him and getting off the bed. I moved quickly about the room, sliding into my black bikini underwear and pulling up my dress.

"I'm on a 9 a.m. flight out of LAX tomorrow." He grabbed his pants off the floor and slipped into them then stepped behind me.

"Thank god," I answered, lifting up my hair and facing away from him while he zipped up my dress.

"Are you sure you're okay?" He turned me around to face him.

"No. Jesus, I'm not. One evening with you and my whole life is...unhinged." I grabbed my strapless bra off the floor and shoved it into my purse. I put my foot on the desk chair and began to fasten my right sandal.

He sat down on the edge of the bed. "Are you sorry?"

"Honestly?" I paused in thought, the other sandal midway onto my foot. "No. It was inevitable—Infidelity 2.0," I mumbled under my breath.

"What?"

"Nothing, nothing," I replied as I hurriedly scanned the floor for any leftover belongings.

He watched me from where he sat. I couldn't tell what he was thinking from the look in his eyes. It was a very long time since we'd been together, and although some physical memory of us was clearly stored in my body, I couldn't read his face. I noticed the dark stubble along his chin and my fingers rose to scratch it but I smoothed down the wrinkles in my dress instead.

"I gotta go," I said as I moved toward the door.

Matt got up and walked over to me. He'd thrown on his slacks but not his shirt and I could once again feel the heat coming off his body. He gently held my face and kissed me. My arms wrapped around him and that place inside that was stirred, ignited again, and my head was filled with the sound of rushing water and I couldn't move. I simply surrendered to it and let myself be comforted temporarily from a growing sense of dread.

"Did you feel that?" he asked earnestly.

"Yes," I smiled. "It's called lust."

"I don't know..." He reached for my hand, forcing me to stop and look at him.

My mind raced. There was no air left in the room. If I didn't leave, I was going to suffocate. "I have to go."

He let go of my hand and stepped aside. "Hey," he said. "Don't disappear. Not again."

It struck me right in the chest. I couldn't breathe. I dashed out of his room, his hotel, Hollywood, in a blind panic.

What did I do? Did I ruin my marriage? Did I have to tell Jason? Could I keep it to myself? I was freaking out. But, oh, it felt so good. It. Felt. So. Good. Oh god! I was a complete mess. And now I was a cheater too. I cheated on my husband. I'd committed Infidelity 2.0. I wasn't just a cheater; I was a modern-day cliché. Maybe I'd get recruited onto the next season of *Couples Therapy* and all of our friends and family could record it. Why didn't I listen to Laurie? I needed a cigarette. Would the kids smell it if I smoked in my car? I hated Facebook. I fucking hated it. I didn't know what to do. I couldn't go home and face Maria. I thought she'd smell Matt all over me, the smell of sex. I did the only thing I could think of.

"Laurie? It's me. Are you up?"

"Hey Al, yeah, sure. What's up? Oh my god, did you have dinner with Matt?"

"Can I come over? Are your kids awake?"

"No, they've been asleep for hours and Evan's in New York until Monday, remember? What's wrong? Of course you can come over."

"Oh thank god! Can I come now?"

"Yes, of course, come. Are you all right? You sound strange."

"I'm around the corner. I'll see you in a few."

I hung up and drove directly to her house. She'd left her outdoor light on. I parked in front, opened my glove box, pulled out a hidden pack of emergency Marlboro Lights, and got out of the car. I leaned against the car and lit up a cigarette. Taking a deep breath, I inhaled, looked up at the night sky and thought about everything that happened.

Was it all a dream? Is it possible that I'll go inside and Laurie and I will giggle about my innocent, out-of-practice flirting and she'll tell me how awesome I look and we'll crack up. Maybe we'll watch an episode of one of her therapeutic shows and then I'll go home and wait for Jason to call. Jason. That's how it was supposed to go. But it didn't. Oh, why didn't it? I could still smell him, feel his hands on me, feel his mouth, what did I do?

I took a few more drags off the cigarette then stomped

it out. Scrambling up her driveway with mounting hysteria, I got to the door. Laurie was waiting.

"God, I don't know what I've done. Laurie, you can't tell anyone, not even Evan, swear to me—swear it!"

"I swear, I swear. I won't tell Evan, I won't tell anyone. Jeez, Al, come in. You're scaring me."

"You were right," I moaned, following her into the family room and throwing myself hard onto her couch. "I fucked up. I fucked up so bad. I was…I was with him."

"Him, who? Matt?" she asked.

I nodded.

"Well, what do you mean, *with*?" Laurie's eyes narrowed and for a moment I didn't think I had the courage to continue. My head ached and tears welled up but it came rushing out.

"It was like I was twenty years old and I could never think straight around him and I can't now either. I mean, I don't know what I was thinking, I wasn't thinking—" I paused to catch my breath. Laurie didn't say a word. She sat silent as a stone, listening.

"It was like inevitable, in this weird way, like I didn't know in my mind that any of this was going to happen but in another place, it all seemed planned, you know what I mean? Like that car accident I was in last spring, when I felt myself in that long, slow skid into the other car—it seemed like it was happening in slow motion but I couldn't stop it—it felt like that." I tried to slow down.

"Alex, what are you talking about?" I noticed her pink tuxedo pajamas. She wore no makeup and her cropped hair went every which way and still, she looked adorable on a night at home eating popcorn and watching housewives shows. Oh, how was I ever going to tell her? And would she understand?

"And when he asked if I wanted a glass of water, it was as easy as following a script. I didn't have to think about it because my legs kept walking, they were on autopilot—they just seemed to know where to go." I kept talking without letting myself stop. "And I left but I needed to go back and when I went to his room, it was like the dinner and the talking and the drinking was all just a prelude to the moment when he kissed me and that kiss...it just undid me." I couldn't look at her so I lowered my gaze. Her pink pajamas swam before my eyes. "I—I—can I get some tissues?" I asked, afraid I was about to start bawling. She hesitated a second then hopped off the couch and padded out of the room in her fluffy white socks with the treads on the bottom. When she came back, she handed me the tissue box but didn't sit down.

"Go on," she said.

I nodded.

She nodded back. She seemed as nervous to hear what came next as I was to tell her.

"He kissed me," I said as mascara-laced tears trailed down my face. "And that kiss, it lasted so long but it wasn't enough, not nearly enough." I pressed my hands against my temples as if the pressure could hold back the truth. "We had sex, Laurie. Desperate, passionate sex. And now I don't know what I'm doing." I buried my head in my hands and started to cry. The enormity of what I'd done hit me in the stomach and I doubled over, weeping ferociously until I shook with the effort.

Laurie put her arm around me and patted my back, comforting me as best she could in her shocked state. I could only imagine how she felt. I knew she loved Jason, and even though I was her best friend, it couldn't have been easy. But Laurie, being Laurie, got up and brought me some more tissues and mascara-removing wipes and settled herself next to me on the couch.

"You can say it if you want to," I mumbled through my tears.

"Say what?" she asked.

"Say, 'I told you so.' Say, 'I warned you.' You did, you know, warn me. But I didn't listen." My nose ran and my eyes burned. I'd cried so hard my head throbbed.

"I'm not going to say that, Al."

"Well say something." I pleaded.

"Okay, okay, let me think. First of all, WHAT THE FUCK? He invited you to his room for a glass of water? I'm sorry, but that's fucked up." She was getting more charged by the moment. "Maybe he planned this? Have you thought of that? I mean maybe he friended you just so he could see you again."

"I'm the one who friended him, remember?"

"Well, maybe he invited you to dinner because he knew your husband was out of town?"

"He didn't know. He made the reservation for three."

"Well, he invited you to his room, didn't he? What did he think was going to happen?"

"I don't know but he didn't plan it. I mean there was just no way—we said goodbye. I was leaving. I just forgot the damn ticket and then I went to his room because…"

"Because why?" she asked.

I answered without looking up. "Because I wanted to." There was silence in the room.

She got off the couch and faced me, "What were you thinking? Were you drunk? Because I mean this 'autopilot' thing is ridiculous. You had sex with him, Al. I mean, what do you want me to say?" She paced back and forth in front of the couch as if walking the length of her family room could produce a logical explanation for what happened. "Are you and Jason having problems?"

"I—I don't think so." My voice broke at the thought of my husband. "I mean, you know, he works like crazy…and it's so hard with Ryan, and the other kids and…I…I don't know." I tried to breathe through the overwhelming emotions that threatened to crush me. "I think maybe I'm having a midlife crisis. Or just a total mental breakdown."

"Oh, Al," she sighed. She sat back down on the couch and put her arm around me. "You love Jason. I know you do." She squeezed my hand with her free hand. "He adores you; you guys are great together." The arm that was around me pulled me into her until I was tucked against her side, her pink tuxedo pajamas pressed against my wrinkled black dress. "Listen to me," she said, turning toward me as I blew my nose. "I watch the shows and I know: people get overwhelmed, they do crazy things, things they don't mean. Especially with someone they used to know; it can seem like the moment was just waiting to happen."

Even though Laurie didn't mince words, even though she'd beat me up to get the truth, I knew she loved me and I knew I could trust her. I had to be honest.

"The thing I don't know is," I said, gasping for breath, "if I was waiting for this, you know, ever since we re-connected a few weeks ago—" I was having a hard time talking through the tears and intense hiccups, "or Laurie," I gulped, momentarily unable to continue, "if I've been waiting for this—" my throat constricted and I choked out the rest, "—for the last twenty years."

She held me while I uncontrollably sobbed out my guilt, confusion, and misery. I laid in the corner of her couch for what seemed like hours, my black dress wrinkled and covered in balled-up tissues, my nose running and my mind racing. Laurie sat next to me in her pink silk pajamas, silently rubbing my hands. Finally, through the involuntary trembles and sniffles, I was able to exert some control over my emotions.

"You okay?" She asked.

I nodded.

"When's Jason coming home?"

"Tomorrow night."

"Well, that gives you a little time."

"I guess so," I said, pulling myself together. I stood up and picked tiny white lint crumbs of tissues off my dress. I smoothed back my hair and went to pick up my sandals.

"Alex," Laurie said, as I bent over to slide in the silver buckle.

"Yes?" She didn't answer so I looked up. When I saw

her face, I let the shoe drop to the ground and turned to her. She moved across the room and stood directly in front of me.

"As your best friend in the entire world, I have to ask." Her large brown eyes fixed on my face. "Are you in love with him?"

It was a night of questions hanging in the air, beginning with, "Would you like a drink of water?" and ending with, "Are you in love with him?" I looked into her dark eyes, noticed the faint shadow of smile lines radiating out from the corners, the arch of her perfectly shaped eyebrows, and said the only thing I knew to be true.

"I don't know."

RESTLESS IN L.A.
Mommy Musings. Stupid Confessions. Life.
Posted by Anonymous

Stained

I got it off my chest. I confessed. But it doesn't make a difference. I'm stained and all the truth in the world won't change that. I've been teetering on an invisible brink, skirting the edge and although I didn't see it, I felt it. Can someone tell me what to want? Because all this wanting is killing me.

CHAPTER 10: HOMECOMING

I thumbed through the *Selected Poems of Rainer Maria Rilke* and stopped at a line about having faith in things not yet said. It was late Sunday night and I thought if I drank a glass of wine before Jason got home, and read a little Rilke, it would calm me down, but it was having the opposite effect. The more Rilke I read, the more agitated I became.

I couldn't help but think about all the things not said between Jason and me. I got up and poured myself yet another glass of Cabernet. But even two glasses of wine couldn't numb me up enough to feel prepared to greet my husband, who'd innocently gone away for the weekend while I had...well, I knew what I'd done.

I stared at that Rilke quote. I couldn't bear to think about it anymore. I fucking hate this book, I thought, as I grabbed it by the spine and threw it across the room. It smacked into the pale gray master bedroom wall and bounced onto the floor, the red cover staring up at me. "Thanks for nothing, Rilke," I mumbled, looking at my bedside alarm clock. Its large, backlit retro numbers blinked 10:30 p.m.

I tiptoed into my office and grabbed my journal. The pink tulips stenciled on the cover seemed to wave to me. I tiptoed back into my room, stepped over Rilke lying face down on the floor, and climbed into bed with the journal.

February 18

Matt took me to Amsterdam for the weekend. I suspected it might have something to do with sex clubs and pot cafes but I was wrong. He wanted me to see the Van Gogh museum, which was high on his list of *essential* artistic experiences not to be missed. I was so excited to see Van Gogh's irises and sunflowers but Matt hardly stopped to look, he was so enthralled by the building. It was designed by some famous modernist designer that he worships. He was so engrossed in pointing out the way the light floods the building and its curves and contradictions that he practically knocked people off the stairwell and didn't even notice. Watching him, you would've thought he was talking about a lover—their every angle burned into his mind. He is so intense about the things he loves. It's as if he studies them in detail until he knows every inch intimately.

On the way home, we wandered through the red-light district where semi-clad women posed in storefront windows. Just as we turned down a narrow cobblestone street, it started to pour so we ducked into a small shop, which sold beautiful, handmade lingerie. It was near closing time and the shop was empty but Matt insisted I try on a red lace bra, G-string and garter belt he'd picked out. The Dutch salesgirl was gorgeous and, of course, she kept eyeing him...

***

"Would you like to try it on?" she asked in heavily accented English.

"Well, um—"

"Yes, she would," said Matt, the wolfish look flashing in his eyes. He handed the salesgirl the sexy red outfit he'd chosen for me.

"You may use this room," she said, tossing her long, blond hair over a shoulder. She wore a slim black skirt, tight white blouse that strained over her large breasts, and expensive snakeskin pumps. She led us to the back of the store to a small dressing room with a heavy red velvet curtain for a door and a large mirror hung on the inside.

"Please," she gestured, reaching in and hanging the lingerie on a large brass hook on the wall.

I went in, drew the curtain behind me, and felt enveloped in the small room, with an oversized leather stool in one corner and the cold, wood floor beneath my feet. I slipped off my jeans, T-shirt, bra, and jacket. I could hear the salesgirl and Matt talking. I put the red lace G-string over my own white bikini underwear and hooked the back of the red bra. I lifted my leg onto the stool as I attempted to attach the garter belt to a pair of nude silk stockings she'd selected. I heard singsong-like laughter and pulled back a corner of the curtain to peer out. I saw the salesgirl leaning in to Matt, shaking out her blond mane and smiling.

I was used to this. Girls constantly flirted with Matt, often right in front of me. With those piercing eyes and knock-out smile, I could hardly blame them. I sighed to myself.

"May I come in?" she asked.

"Um, okay."

She entered the dressing room and pulled the curtain shut behind her. I was standing in the red lace bra and G-string with the garters running down my legs.

"This fits you nicely," she said, smoothing her fingers across the lace of the demi cup. "And these look lovely on you as well." Her hand crept along the back of my shin, behind my knee and up my hip. "You have lovely legs," she added. She lightly touched my breasts, commenting on the fit of the bra, and then ran her hand back over my legs, lingering on my thighs. Finally, she put her hands on my hips, murmured, "I find the outfit very flattering," and kissed me on the mouth.

I was completely taken off guard. "There is no one else in the store," she whispered, as she leaned in to me and kissed me again, pulling my hips toward her and this time, pushing her tongue into my waiting mouth. Her breath was sweet and minty and her full breasts pressed against my own. She squeezed my hips with her hands and ground against me, sending shivers between my legs. I relaxed into her floral perfume and the feel of her soft lips on mine when Matt suddenly opened the curtain and ducked inside. I darted backward, as if I had been caught making out in the school broom closet, and nearly fell over the stool resting in the corner.

"Having fun?" he asked with a twinkle in his eye, clearly enjoying his glimpse of me in the arms of the blonde.

"Matt! I, uh, we were—" I regained my balance quickly.

"Yes?" he asked.

"I was getting dressed," I answered, feeling my cheeks burn.

"Are you certain you don't need anything more?" the salesgirl asked coolly, her eyes wide as she turned to me and then Matt. Matt gave away nothing as he raised an eyebrow and waited for my response. I stifled the urge to fan myself from the heat in the tiny room. Finally I stuttered, "No. Thank you. It's beautiful but I, uh, I better not."

"I've got it from here, love," Matt said as he stepped forward and pulled back the edge of the curtain.

She made an exaggerated pout and kissed me on the cheek, then looked up at Matt with a sigh. *"Doe-doei,"* she waved. "Have fun." And then she left, closing the curtain firmly behind her.

Matt grinned at me. "That looked interesting," he said, raising his eyebrows.

"I…well, I…"

"Spit it out, Alexandra. Were you interested? Because I'm cool with it if you are."

"Oh shut up!" I said. "You look dreamy-eyed just thinking about it."

"I do? So how come you're the one with the pink cheeks?"

I pushed him toward the curtain. "Can you get out of here?" I felt exposed from what he'd seen and my current state of undress. I longed for my jeans and sweater.

"Hey, Alexandra," he whispered. "I'm only kidding. I'd never let her touch you, as cute as she is. I like having you all to myself." He kissed me on the mouth and slid his fingers alongside the garter belt and around the back. "Leave it on," he added. "I'll take it off myself when I take you back to the hotel and fuck you."

"Shh!" I giggled, shocked and thrilled. "She's going to hear you—"

"I don't care," he groaned. "Poor thing feels the same way. She's just jealous she isn't feeling your ass right now."

"Matt!" I yelped and jabbed him in the arm but he didn't care who saw or heard. I pushed him out of the room and jammed the curtain shut.

I got dressed while Matt paid for my new lingerie. I wondered—and not for the first time—what happened to me? I left Los Angeles a nice girl but months with Matt had corrupted me: public sex, making out with Dutch girls in dressing rooms, eating space cakes and 'shroom tea— who knew what was next? And he "liked having me all to himself?" Matt passed up a chance for a ménage because he "wanted me all to himself?" He never said much about us but I wondered…

***

Those days came flooding back to me—his hands, his eyes, his laughter—he was an addiction I couldn't quit. With him, I saw things that had been there all along and yet never noticed before. People and places just occurred differently and I couldn't explain how or why that was. It was some kind of invisible signal that he gave off and people attuned to his frequency, well, they just got it. When I was with him, I got it, too.

The sound of keys at the front door made my heart pump faster. I turned off the light, stuffed the journal under the bed, and rolled onto my side.

Act normal, I told myself. I heard Jason crisscross the house. I heard the plink of his keys tossed carefully into the silver bowl on the entry table and the beep-beep-beep of the alarm as he set it to sleep mode. I heard the creak of the doors as he entered the kids' rooms. Natalie's door was particularly in need of WD-40, and it practically shrieked as he entered her room last. I followed him in my mind and knew when he would be approaching our bedroom. I pretended to sleep.

I can't face him tonight, I thought to myself. It'll be easier in the morning. He set down his weekender on the upholstered chaise in the corner of the room and unzipped his toiletry kit. He took pains to be quiet as he brushed his teeth and slipped out of his clothes. I was turned away from his side of the bed with my face to the wall but my heart pounded as he slid in next to me.

"Al?" he whispered.

"Mmm," I mumbled as if I was half-dreaming.

"I'm back. I had a great time," he laughed quietly. "Sleep late in the morning. I'll take the kids to school. Good night, hon."

He pulled me into him and I felt his goatee tickle the back of my neck. I tried to relax against him as I had so many nights over the last sixteen years but it was hard. I kept thinking of that fucking line from Rainer Maria Rilke about "setting free my most holy feelings." My mind wandered back to the messages I'd deleted. *Call me*, Matt wrote. *We need to talk*. But I didn't need to talk. I needed to forget. Things between Jason and me weren't perfect but whose marriage was? He worked hard for our family and he loved us. Whatever was missing between us could be fixed, I was sure of it. I finally fell asleep listening to the rhythm of his even breathing and vowing to make it right.

The next morning, true to his word, Jason got up, helped Ben get dressed, gave the kids some cereal, and took them to school. I mumbled and shuffled various body parts to indicate I was still asleep and heard Jason laugh as he left, "Boy, the savages sure pulverized Mommy." When the front door closed, I finally relaxed.

Laurie called at 7:51, one minute after the kids were out the door.

"How are you?" she asked.

"I'm alive." I was in the kitchen in my fleece bathrobe looking for a light for the cigarette hidden in my pocket.

"How'd it go?"

"I haven't talked to him," I sighed. "I can't look him in the eye."

"Shit," she said. "Try not to make yourself crazy."

"Er," I corrected. "Crazi-er."

"Alex—"

"It's true and don't think I don't know it." I rummaged through the shelf with the spices but couldn't find a single pack of matches. "Can you hold on a sec?" I finally found a lighter in the utility drawer and walked out the door of the kitchen into the yard. I sat down by the pool and took a deep breath. "I've thought a lot about what you said last night…about Jason and me…and you're right. We've always been a good team. I think I'm just…confused." I choked back a sob. "I know what I did was unforgivable. But it's over now. The whole thing's behind me." My fingers shook as I lit the cigarette and inhaled.

"You sure?" she asked.

"Yes," I answered, shaking my head. "Definitely." I

exhaled in a whoosh.

"Are you smoking?"

I moved the cigarette away from the phone.

"Jesus, Al, it's eight in the morning."

"There's extenuating circumstances right now, don't you think?"

"All right, you're right." She was silent for a moment. "Do you think it's over for him too?"

"Absolutely," I said without missing a beat. I got up and wandered around the yard, noticing the grass by the pool was overwatered and that one of the ends of a purple Styrofoam swim noodle was chewed off, probably by a squirrel, and that two missing pairs of fluorescent green swim goggles were wedged beneath a lounge chair. I sat down and took another long drag off my cigarette. "Look, I have a great life. I'd be an idiot to mess it up."

"You made a mistake," she said. "It happens."

"But to me? I never thought it would happen to me," I said, my voice cracking. "But it doesn't matter—it's over and I'm not going to think about it." I inhaled and held my breath, feeling the burn in my lungs.

"All right," she said. "I'm glad to hear it...but Al, call me if you need me."

"You know I will," I said.

We hung up but not before she reminded me that she loved me, that she was there for me, and that I could always tell her anything. I knew it was true but for some reason I didn't tell her about the messages I'd deleted.

***

The next several days went by in a blur. I tried to pretend nothing had changed. My night with Matt already seemed like a dream.

At the end of the week, after the kids and Jason left, I found myself staring out the kitchen doors. I wiped up the remains of the kids' hot oatmeal and turkey bacon and contemplated working on my blog. But something inside me festered, a sense of manic energy. I wanted to get out of the house, go do something, but I didn't know what. The memory of that night tugged at me but I didn't want to go there. Forget it ever happened, I told myself. I tried to push it out of my mind but it wouldn't leave.

I walked around the house, straightening up as I went, and headed for my bathroom to take a shower. I undressed quickly and sat down at the edge of the tub to wait for the shower to heat up. I closed my eyes and allowed our night together to take shape in my mind in perfect detail: the first glimpse of him at the window in his pressed shirt, the strain of our conversation at the table, the weird reunion with his friend from New York, and the moment the elevator door opened and there he was holding my valet ticket. I sighed out loud as I relived the kiss and the way it felt when his mouth lingered on my bare shoulder. I recalled the stripping off of our clothes and his tongue sliding between my lips and the feel of him entering me, again and again. By the time I reviewed the rest of the night, I had my hand between my legs. Everything will fall apart if you don't forget this, I warned myself. But my body remembered how good it felt whether I wanted to or not. So I forced myself to remember the rest of it: how I shut the door when I fled the Redbury and I tried to shut it inside myself, too. If it wasn't regret I felt, it was something akin to it—remorse or resignation? Maybe all those things. I could see it was way too dangerous to hang around the house so I filled up my day, and that entire week, crossing things off my list. I even went to the grocery store twice.

Thankfully, Jason was swamped at work and got home well after I turned off the light and began my pretend sleep. He quietly washed up, gently nudged me a few times, then gave up and went to sleep. I lay awake next to him in fake slumber and wondered how long I could keep this up. It was going pretty well until the end of the week.

***

"Hey hon," Jason leaned over me and shook me lightly. It was after eleven.

"What is it?" I answered.

"We've barely spoken two words to each other all week. You awake?" he asked, standing by my side of the bed.

"Mmm, barely. I'm really sleepy," I mumbled.

"I'm sorry it's been such a late week. I miss you." He leaned down and kissed me on the forehead.

"You must be exhausted. Let's talk in the morning," I muttered, adding a loud yawn. I heard him undo his belt and pull off his shirt and slacks. He flung them over the side of the chaise in the corner of the room.

"I'm actually not that tired," he whispered in my ear as he slid in next to me. I felt the scratchy texture of his goatee against the skin of my chin. "You just lie there and dream."

So I lay there in my pretend dream state and felt his hands roam under the covers. He pulled down my gray, cotton pajama bottoms and began to rub my legs and stomach. His warm hands traveled over my waist as he lifted up my tank top and gently squeezed my breasts.

"I'm so tired," I pleaded with as much sleepiness in my voice as I could muster.

"It's just a dream, don't wake up," he whispered as he bent his head to my breast and began to suck while his hands descended into my beige Costco underwear. He rubbed the sweet spot with his index finger and I couldn't help but squirm. He took this as a sign of encouragement and pulled off my underwear. I was out of excuses and he was horny and determined. The only thing to do was follow his lead, so I lay still with my eyes closed as I felt my husband enter me. He knew what I liked and did his best to satisfy. He kept an even pace waiting for me to come but I couldn't get there, not even close, so I faked it as best I could. Finally, he let go with a groan as he collapsed to the side of me.

"Hon?" he whispered with a chuckle, "I hope you're having sweet dreams. Good night."

"Mmm," I replied with my eyes closed. But I knew I wouldn't sleep. My brain was in rapid fire and there was nothing I could do. Jason rolled over, tucked a pillow between his legs, and drifted off, untroubled.

What have I done? I wondered as I glanced at the sleeping face of my happily satisfied husband. But the mixture of colors in Matt's eyes came unbidden into my mind. If I thought about his eyes then maybe I wouldn't have to think about the kids and how I loved them and how they weighed me down and made me feel as if I was drowning. I wouldn't have to think about what I got right or wrong or whether Ryan's teacher would stop putting check marks next to his name, check marks that told him he was bad and further separated him from the kids he so desperately wanted to be like. Maybe if I thought about Matt's eyes I could pretend, just for a minute, that I was never naked with him inside me, that I didn't cheat on my husband who was good and who loved me and who came home with a smile and a killer pair of dimples.

Forgive me, I begged in a silent ESP message to Jason in his dreams. I imagined emailing Matt the next morning and telling him never to contact me again. I imagined getting out of bed, throwing a pair of jeans and a T-shirt in Jason's newly unpacked weekender, and heading straight to New York City to see him again. I imagined sending out my fake death auto-reply and fleeing the country. I finally fell asleep wondering how I'd gotten into such inner turmoil. I was okay. I was on stable ground before I deliberately went and stepped into quicksand. Now, I watched as it threatened to devour my entire life, including my three innocent children. I had a vivid nightmare in which Dr. Phil confronted me in front of a studio audience. Jason, the kids, and Laurie were in the front row while Matt and I sat in guest chairs on the stage.

RESTLESS IN L.A.
Mommy Musings. Stupid Confessions. Life.
Posted by Anonymous

Stop the Madness
I walk around like I know what I'm doing—like I've got this mommy thing and this marriage thing and this midlife thing all figured out. But I don't. Sometimes it's hard to make it through the day. My brief moments of happiness occur when I'm lying down alone on my living room couch eating one-hundred-calorie Snackwell cookie packs. I feel almost happy when I'm alone with my cookies and not required to do a damn thing. I actually don't know if I would call that state "happy" but at least I don't feel anxious or freaked out or overwhelmed. I do have a whole laundry list of things to accomplish and of course, the fact that I'm lying on the couch eating Snackwell cookie packs only supports my sneaking suspicion that I am, in fact, a loser because—let's face it—that's what I choose to do with my free time? Lie on the couch and eat one-hundred-calorie Snackwell cookie packs that I then run out of when it's time to make the lunches and the kids are all bummed out?

Somehow, I thought if I did something different, broke the pattern, stopped the madness—got out of my house and went somewhere other than a food market, sporting goods store, or Target—it would help, but it didn't. Because I went to the worst possible place—the one place I should never have gone. And even though I've deleted his messages, even though I've tried to purge him from my memory, that night replays itself over and over again in my mind like an endless loop. I don't know how to make it stop.

CHAPTER 11: THE PARTY

After the two messages I deleted, there was no more attempted contact from Matt. The evening of my fortieth birthday party arrived and I reminded myself to enjoy it as I carried folding chairs from the garage to the back yard.

Maria and the kids were outside arranging tables and setting up twinkly lights around the patio when I went to take a shower and slip into a brand new turquoise sundress. I sat down at my makeup table and peered silently into the mirror, trying to take an honest assessment. Still pretty, I thought to myself, maybe not the looker I once was, but still pretty. I could see why the doctor had suggested Botox—even if he was an asshole. I did have lines on my forehead and around my eyes, lines I didn't use to have, lines that told a story I almost forgot until I glimpsed my reflection in a storefront window and was vaguely surprised at the face that stared back. But still…I wasn't into injecting poison under my skin, not just yet. I thought I'd wait until my fiftieth and decide…by then, I'd probably need a lot more work than a few Botox injections.

Jason invited thirty of our closest friends to our back yard and they were crowded around several margarita machines, a jukebox, and a table piled high with fresh tacos and quesadillas. The smell of onions mixed with cinnamon wafted across the back lawn as Maria's brothers, in yellow TACO TONY T-shirts, grilled up ground beef and diced chicken on large, portable BBQs. Churros sprinkled with sugar and cinnamon rotated inside a glass display case that already had a waiting line. Natalie, Ryan, and Ben walked through the crowd, beaming with pride as friends told them what a lovely party they'd made. My heart swelled at the looks on their faces, especially Ryan. He turned to a friend's husband who'd stopped him with a hand on his shoulder. I watched from the corner of my eye as he wiped sugar from a churro onto his shirt and nodded agreeably, standing still just long enough to make eye contact before dashing off with a wave and the hint of a smile. He looked relaxed…and happy.

The kids mingled long enough to have two tacos and a churro each before Natalie announced it was time for her iMovie. Jason hung up a large, white sheet against our rear fence and we'd borrowed a friend's projector to hook up to her laptop. The guests turned their seats toward the makeshift screen. Jason grabbed two folding chairs and called out to me. I noticed he was wearing the short-sleeved, button-down shirt I'd bought him for his birthday last year. "You're gonna love this," he said, pulling my chair closer to his as the opening bars of "100 Years" by Five for Fighting echoed across our back yard.

"MOM: THEN AND NOW" swirled onto the screen and then dissolved into me in pink footy pajamas hugging a worn-out Bugs Bunny doll, riding a red Schwinn ten-speed, driving my mother's sedan for the first time. Friends laughed and hooted at pictures of me in high school: big hair, bright lips, smiling in front of the first limousine ride I'd ever taken to my senior prom. There I was in college, before I ever met Jason, book in hand and three more stacked on a nearby desk, coffee mug pressed to my lips, obviously in test prep mode. Jason put his arm around me and kissed my cheek at the shot of us at the Biltmore just before our wedding, holding hands and beaming into the camera. I looked at him on the screen and then turned to him sitting next to me, Corona in one hand, the other draped over my shoulder. He took a swig of his beer and smiled. "Remember that day, hon? Seems like a million years ago."

He squeezed me closer as shots of our honeymoon flew by, fading into us, standing amidst boxes, as we moved into our first apartment and then Jason, in sea green scrubs, cradling a newborn Natalie in his arms. The feel of his fingers caressing my bare arm and the photos whirling past and the two strawberry margaritas I'd just downed only exacerbated the pit in my stomach. I bit my lip and tried to swallow the warm bit of cinnamon churro that lodged in my throat, sweet and sugary and yet it burned. Our friends watched the screen and pointed and oohed while I sat cradled in the crook of my husband's arm, his hand endlessly rubbing small circles into my shoulder, cinnamon crumbs falling onto my dress, and tried to digest it all—the churro, the yard, my family, my beautiful life. I smiled hard and mouthed a silent prayer, *please let me be happy.*

I blinked at the screen but the memories kept coming. There was me clutching my new daughter wrapped in a pink blanket and cap but before I could wonder where I was or remember the tiny yellow and green flowers printed along the underside of the blanket, there was Natalie holding her baby brother Ryan—who was healthy and perfect in that moment—until she became a big sister again, and there was my third child, my Benny Boy, coming home from the hospital, until the three of them were skiing down a mountainside, all in helmets and different-colored striped parkas, and I was forty—and a well of emotion threatened to engulf me like a sea of sadness itself.

I wanted to stop the slideshow and shut the damn

music off. Slide after slide spun by every six seconds, expertly synchronized by Natalie, and each song seemed to fade into the next, just like my life. I wanted to crawl back inside each picture—I looked so happy then—and have each moment stretch out before me, those perfect moments. I wanted to stick my nose into Natalie's baby blanket and inhale the sweet smell of fresh diaper and fat baby thighs. I wanted to hold an infant son to my chest once more, feel him nurse, feel the wonder of being a newly-minted mother. I willed myself not to think about the photos that weren't there, the photos that didn't belong in a slide show of my family and me. I tried not to think about a different face, smiling eyes, wavy black hair caught in the breeze.

I looked over at my daughter sitting cross-legged on a blanket next to the laptop, her hazel eyes, so like mine, sparkling under her long, dark lashes as she hummed along to the tracks she'd so carefully selected...for me. "I'll be right back," I whispered to Jason as I hunched down and walked over to Natalie. We sat next to each other watching the final scene dance onto the screen—a clip of Natalie, Ryan, and Ben, interrupting each other and shouting, "Happy birthday, Mommy," from the front lawn and then Jason, in navy slacks and pressed white shirt, standing in front of the front door. "To my beautiful wife, Alex. Happy fortieth, honey. We love you.' He stood on the flagstone porch, dimples ablaze, staring into the camera. Then he turned his head to Natalie off screen and asked, "Hey, should I say 'The End'?"

"You already did, Dad!" she shrieked and the screen dissolved into the sounds of their laughter.

The yard broke into a wave of applause and compliments. "You guys are adorable," "Natalie's amazing," "What a perfect family!" Natalie and I stood up and I reached over to hug her.

"Thank you, sweetheart, it was beautiful."

She shrugged it off. "I liked doing it," she said. Then

she paused for a second before adding, "You look really pretty tonight, Mom."

She stood next to me in the short, black Brandy Melville dress she'd begged for, not yet a teenager but almost. The promise of curves emerging was as evident as the black mascara she'd brushed on and she was nearly as tall as I was. I resisted the urge to hug her again and smiled. "So do you."

"Thanks," she said, the corners of her mouth drifting upward in spite of herself. I didn't move. Her nearness was enough although it never quite lasted. The boys had changed into their pajamas and were waiting at the door, pleading to say goodbye. Maria had packed them for a sleepover and they were ready to go.

"Bye, guys, you were fantastic," I said, breaking away from Natalie and walking over to them.

"Bye Mommy," Ben said, hugging me tightly. Ryan didn't say much but I could tell from the curve of his mouth that he was content. Maria wrangled everybody into her minivan, including Natalie and her two overstuffed duffel bags. They'd return in the morning and Maria and her sister would help with the clean-up.

After the final compliments and toasts and hugs and promises to get together soon, the last guests finally left. Only Laurie and Evan hung around as TACO TONY scrubbed the grills, loaded up the margarita machines, and cleaned and folded the tables. Sounds of chuckling drifted over from the pool where Evan and Jason reclined, two shot glasses and a bottle of José Cuervo between them. From the volume of their laughter, the guys were having a good time. I knew how Jason felt about my smoking but I took a chance and sat down to have a cigarette. My thumb throbbed from flicking the lighter six times before it sparked. I blew a perfect smoke ring and watched it rise above the strands of twinkly lights strung across the yard before it disappeared into the night air. Laurie pulled over a rattan ottoman and sat down next to me.

"Here she goes again," she said, waving her hand at me in reference to my smoking habit. "Hey, won't he get pissed?" she asked, pointing toward Jason.

"Come on, it's my birthday. And he's wasted anyway."

"You've got to stop, Al" she said, pretend-coughing and waving wildly at the second-hand smoke.

"I'm going to. This is my last cigarette. I'm older and wiser now."

"Ha!" she laughed. "Well, that was some party. A bunch of middle-aged drunk people. How fun!"

"So true." I nodded, brushing some chocolate cake crumbs off my sundress.

"Natalie's movie was a real hit, huh?" she asked, laying her hand over mine. I noticed the metallic silver nail polish on her fingertips practically glowed in the moonlight.

"It was amazing," I said, taking another drag off my cigarette and carefully exhaling away from Laurie.

"Those shots of you two at your wedding—priceless! And I love the hospital pictures, can you believe our kids were ever that small?"

"I know, right?" I nodded.

"And the honeymoon shots...I loved the photos of you and Jason moving into this house and the kids skiing and—"

"Please, Laurie, stop. I'm really lucky. I get it."

"What?"

Tears filled my eyes. "I get that I have a charmed life and I have everything anybody could ever want and I have so much to be grateful for, okay?"

"Alex, I didn't mean to—"

"To what? Make me feel bad?" I tapped the ash off my cigarette, my pointer finger smacking down on the end so hard that the burning head almost fell off. I turned back to Laurie. Her eyebrows stood straight up while her mouth formed a small frown and she'd folded her hand against her cheek. "Oh, Laurie, I'm sorry," I reached out and grabbed her hand. "It's not you. You didn't make me feel bad—it's me." I clutched my heart, digging my fingers into the folds of my new dress. "I do it to myself. I'm sorry. I didn't mean to blame you."

"It's okay," she said, "forget it." She waved at the air as if she could dissolve my angry outburst like the second-hand smoke that kept creeping back in her direction. "It was a great party, Al, a great night... Try to enjoy it."

"No, you're right, you're right. It was. A great party, I mean. Really great..."

"It was," she nodded. "But listen, Evan and I better get going." She stood up and forced a smile. "I want to give you guys some alone time."

Jason and Evan apparently finished the tequila and were stretched out, legs hanging over the sides of the lounge chairs they'd crashed on. As we turned toward them, one of them burped distinctly and the other laughed out loud.

"Sheesh—" Laurie said, giggling.

"Yup. It appears our guys are pretty wasted." I nodded emphatically.

"Well, I better get my sleeping beauty home while he can still walk."

She went over to Evan and looped her arm around his waist. They hobbled together to the car while I marveled at how well she managed in her four-inch heels. I would have stumbled and probably fallen down, which was why I stuck to wedges, but not Laurie. She could have been a runway model the way she handled those shoes, even with a hammered husband draped over one shoulder. She got in the driver's seat while Evan drifted off beside her. We gave each other a solid hug through the open window.

"Happy birthday, bestie," she said. "I love you."

"I love you too," piped Evan from the passenger seat, one eye open and grinning.

"Evan!" we both chided in unison. We rolled our eyes and laughed but the comic interruption was the perfect distraction from the pall hanging over us after my snarky outburst.

I looked at her short, black hair, her deep brown eyes, her gorgeous cheekbones. Her manicured nails rested on the steering wheel and I noticed her well-chosen jewelry. Laurie was as stylish and well put-together as they came— but she was even more beautiful on the inside. "I love you, Laurie girl. I wouldn't have made it through the last two decades without you. You know that's true." I leaned in and kissed her on the cheek. "I'm sorry if I—"

"It's forgotten, Al."

"You sure?"

"Sure about what?"

"Okay." I smiled. "Drive safely."

"Will do. Talk to you tomorrow." As they drove off, I heard her call out, "Go fire up your coffeemaker."

I went back outside to find Jason dozing on the lounge chair. I looked down at his sleeping form and noticed his arms. They were strong, muscular arms from the years he spent surfing, growing up in Brentwood, not far from the beach. I smoothed back the sandy blond hair that fell into his face. He shifted. I sat at the edge of the chair and watched him. I was glad he was resting, glad he was home, and yet I felt alone.

"Jason," I whispered and shook him lightly. "Wake up. Everybody's gone and I want to talk to you." I nudged him. "Jason?" He snored softly. I gave him a less gentle shove and he opened an eye.

"Hey birfday girl," he mumbled.

"Honey, come on. Nobody's here. It's just you and me." I gave his arm a tug for encouragement.

"Oh Alex...so tired...tequila...all Evan's fault..." And he began to snore.

I remembered the last time Jason got stinking drunk on tequila. He and I were in Mazatlan, a year after our wedding with a bunch of his law school friends from San Diego. He'd downed way too many tequila shots and eaten a worm or two when we found ourselves in a bar with a mechanical bull. Jason decided he was a cowboy even though he'd never been within a mile of a stable and jumped on. After two bucking spins, he'd smacked his mouth on the metal saddle and flew off, splitting his lip in the process. We ended up in a Mexican hospital getting Jason's lip sewn up without anesthesia. He laughed at the whole mess, repeatedly saying, "You should've seen the other guy." When we made it back to the hotel, he insisted on joining our friends in the hot tub. "Don't splash the mouth," he ordered and positioned himself happily in front of one of the jets. His only complaint was that it hurt too much to kiss me.

I dragged him out of the lounge chair and into the house, making sure he collapsed safely onto our bed. I thought about getting in next to him but I was restless.

"Hey, sweetsie. Did you have a good time?" he asked as his head hit the pillow.

"I did, hon. Thank you." I leaned over and kissed him on the cheek.

"So glad. You deserve it. You really do." His eyes closed.

"Sweet dreams," I whispered. He had no idea what I deserved. And I couldn't tell him. I was too ashamed and he was drunk and tired. He was out cold before I turned off the light.

I'd wanted to review the highlights of the evening, Natalie's iMovie, the drunken antics of our guests, but he was already deep in REM sleep. Jason was gone so much of the time and I wished he was home more. But the weird thing was, when he was home, I felt lonelier. Living with him was like living with a ghost; even when he was around, he was hardly there.

I paced the lawn, picking up bottles of Corona and throwing away leftover paper plates and plastic cups. It was quiet outside with no kids home and no guests streaming in and out. I flicked on the outdoor speakers and a song I loved came pouring through. I sat down on one of the white folding chairs and listened intently as the band described a deep yearning to escape from a well-known life, a life of being who you are, stuck inside yourself—but as the song crescendoed into the tension between how things are and how they could be, I couldn't listen anymore. I switched off the speakers, left the plastic garbage bag by the door and turned off the patio lights. Before I knew it, I'd drifted to the desk in my office. I kicked off my shoes and stared out into the motionless back yard. In the faint light, a forgotten white lace wrap gleamed against the back of a lounge chair. I dug my hand into the desk drawer and carefully removed the journal.

December 17

Matt met me after class yesterday and we went to our favorite Indian restaurant for dinner and then back to his place. I was embarrassed at school today because I wore the same clothes and my friends teased about my "wardrobe of shame." Matt laughed his ass off when he found out, saying he liked them knowing he bedded me nightly and suggesting I wear the same outfit all week—he's terrible! But when I woke up this morning, he was standing by his dresser. He said he had something to show me...

***

"Morning, Al. Guess what this is?"

My eyes were barely open and I could see Matt leaning over an open drawer in the morning light, smiling at me and looking adorable in his striped boxer shorts and rumpled bed head.

"A chest of clothes?" I guessed, walking over to him.

"No, be specific. It's a drawer, dummy. It's your drawer. As much as I love advertising to your classmates that you've slept over, I respect the fact that you may not want to appear in the same clothes day after day." He picked up my hand and held it in his own. "I thought you might want to bring over some stuff so you don't have to fly out of here in the morning to go home and change. You know how I love my mornings with you."

"Yes, I know, which is why I'm frequently late for class," I answered, shaking my head and trying to hide my elation at the gesture he was making.

"And why you're going to be late again this morning, " he teased.

"Matt, come on. I know you don't have to work today, but I've got places to be." I wiggled away from him.

"Oh no you don't, not until I get my fill." He grabbed me around the waist and carried me back toward the bed. "I'm serious," he said, nuzzling my neck and pushing me onto the bed, "I want you to stay over more often. I love waking up with you."

I grabbed a goose-down pillow and hit him in the head with it. "I think you're a bad influence on my studies." He pulled the pillow out of my arms and kissed me on the mouth.

"Alexandra?" he asked, looking into my face.

"Yes?"

"This may sound totally self-serving but I just gotta say it." He rubbed his hands up and down my bare arms.

"Go ahead," I said, riveted by his twinkling green eyes.

"I absolutely love to fuck you."

"Wow, I bet you say that to all the girls, you charmer," I answered with a laugh.

He took my face in his hands, "No. Just you."

"Well…ditto."

"Ditto? Are we in high school?"

"C'mon," I said, feeling shy. "You know I feel the same way. And maybe more…"

"That's the thing I love about us, Alex. I'm just crazy attracted to you and you're busy and I'm busy and—"

"Oh, so you're saying we're just a hook up?"

"No. I'm saying I totally respect your work and it's clear you respect mine and, you know, when I left the States, it was like Noah's Ark—I'm not kidding—everyone was pairing up, two-by two. I dated this girl when I was in film school and within weeks, she was obsessed with our future. The only future I envisioned was me behind a camera."

"So you're saying—"

But I never finished the thought because he pulled me to him and kissed me again. I put my arms around his shoulders and kissed him back, my tongue tasting the sweetness of his mouth, his scent, so seductive. I loved the feel of his mouth and his tongue and his hands on my face. He kissed me like he meant it, like he was pouring himself into me. I gulped him up. He was delicious.

"All right, Miss Goodie Two-Shoes," he said, finally letting go of me. "How about I pick you up after class and we go back to your flat and get some of your stuff?" He pulled back the covers so I could get up, and smiled broadly. My heart skipped a beat. His dark, morning bed head set off his glittering eyes. And he'd thrown back the covers wide enough to reveal his bare chest and below... It made me weak at the knees just to look at him and he'd given me a drawer. Whatever we talked about—or didn't—could wait.

"Yes. Good idea," I agreed. "Then I won't have to walk around in wet underwear."

"But I like it when your underwear's wet," he countered, still grinning ear to ear.

"Argh!" I groaned. "I have to get to class!" I swatted at him playfully and collected my clothes. I was full of him: his hands, his mouth, his sweet scent were all over me. My heart nearly burst with that strange mixture of happy and alive and dangerous I felt whenever we were together. But mostly happy.

That afternoon, I packed up clothes and toiletries to bring to Matt's. He kept adding more and more stuff to my bag, ordering me to, "Bring this shirt," and, "Take another pair of jeans." He even threw me a box of tampons and demanded I bring them.

"What if you get your period?" he asked solemnly.

"For god's sake, Matt, it's not like there isn't a drug store on every corner."

He was worse than my mother packing me for a month of sleep-away camp. By the time we left, my bag was so over-stuffed, he had to hold the sides together while I forced up the zipper. He grabbed it, threw the strap over his shoulder, and carried the bulging duffel to the tube. He held my hand as we walked.

***

I closed the journal and returned it to its hiding place beneath the stack of folders in my desk drawer. The excitement of the party had worn off and a desolate feeling had taken its place. Why did I read the journal? It didn't make me feel good. It made me feel sad. I didn't want to remember the drawer or Matt or the way things were between us—not decades ago or weeks ago, either—I wanted to forget it. I resolved that tomorrow I was going to toss the journal in the trash.

RESTLESS IN L.A.
Mommy Musings. Stupid Confessions. Life.
Posted by Anonymous

Someone Else

No matter how much I want to let go of being me, it's never going to happen. I had a night like that once, where—for a moment—I didn't feel like me. I'd felt like someone else, like maybe I was back in time and young again, and beautiful, without a lined forehead and saddlebags, when the world was filled with possibilities and my life wasn't nearly as over-full as it is now. But I can hardly think about that night without the voice inside of me whispering how selfish and spoiled I am. I know it's wrong to want more. I just can't seem to help it.

The point is to focus on the present. This week marked a special birthday. I tried to talk to my husband about it, what it meant to me and how it made me feel, but what was there to say when the most important thing, the thing that must be said, remains locked deep inside me? And I can't ever tell him about it. I keep wondering how long it takes for a memory to fade from vivid to vague? How long does it take for the details to be erased and the small remnants brushed aside until you're left with just a nebulous feeling but not the instant replay of every detail? I can tell you one thing—it's longer than three weeks. I'm hoping to forget it soon, expunge it from my memory. The sooner that happens, the sooner I can get back to living the happy life I lived before any of this happened.

CHAPTER 12: DUCKING

I hated to return to the scene of the crime. In my mind's eye, yellow plastic streamers draped across the front of the hotel with "DANGER: DO NOT CROSS" printed boldly on them. Why had I agreed to meet him? A lump wedged into my throat the minute I pulled into the parking lot. I grabbed my water bottle and took a large gulp, trying to wash it away.

As the weeks passed, I began to feel safe. I thought it was possible for that night to fade into a memory. I tried not to conjure it over and over again—his mouth on mine, the sweet taste of it, and his body naked and warm, and his hands, oh god... I commanded myself to forget. In my mind, I knew there was nothing to say, nothing to do about what happened. I didn't feel Matt owed me anything and I didn't owe him anything, either. I felt good about my resolution to put the whole thing behind me until I received an unexpected voicemail on my cell phone that nearly sent me into a panic: "It's me. I have to talk to you. It's urgent. Call as soon as you can."

Had his wife found out? Was she going to expose us? What could he possibly need to tell me that was urgent enough to leave a voicemail on my cell phone? I definitely wasn't cut out for cheating; I couldn't handle the stress. I replayed the message sixteen times searching for any inflection, any pause that might give me a clue before deleting it permanently from my call log. I bit my nails all morning and the second Jason was out the door, I returned Matt's call. He answered on the first ring.

"It's me," I said. "What's going on?" I couldn't remember the last time we spoke on the phone. The sound of his voice through the speaker made me nervous. I wanted to get the conversation over as quickly as possible.

"I need to see you," was his cryptic reply.

"Did your wife find out?" I blurted out. I needed to know, to prepare.

"What? No. She has no idea."

"Oh, thank god. I—I thought—what is it?"

He was abrupt but insisted it was urgent. When I realized he wanted to meet, I tried to refuse but he staunchly insisted we talk in person. I finally gave in and agreed to meet him back at the Redbury. I could tell from his tone that he wasn't going to let up.

I thought about consulting Lark about the situation but I'd cancelled on her for the last several weeks so I wouldn't have to face her. Two nights ago, she'd emailed me out of the blue saying she received a "message" that I might need her assistance. I didn't ask whom the message was from, but knowing Lark, it was probably the Universe. I emailed her back and said all was well but the kids were sick and I had to postpone our session another week.

Only Laurie knew the truth and she was sworn to secrecy. She told me she thought of it as a momentary midlife psychotic break and encouraged me to forget the whole thing. Yeah right, if only it was that easy. I wanted to tell her about Matt's call—I used to tell her everything—but, this time, I just couldn't. I knew she wouldn't want me to see him again. Ever.

I got dressed and purposefully chose a pair of underwear from my Costco ten-pack, a pink blouse buttoned to the top, and a below-the-knee length skirt. I wasn't exactly going for "religious woman," but I wasn't going for cougar hottie, either. I got off the freeway, pulled into the parking lot, and practically threw my keys at the valet guy before darting into the hotel. It was 12:30 and I didn't want to be spotted by the lunch crowd. I walked directly to the elevator and pushed the button. I didn't look around but kept my eyes focused on the lighted numbers as the elevator made its ascent.

It was a huge mistake. We'd both drank way too much. What was it that Laurie said—there was once something between us? We got drunk and confused—that was all there was to it. I reached into my purse and my fingers closed around the comforting shape of a pack of Marlboro Lights.

The elevator doors opened and I walked slowly down the hallway, looking for the room number he'd texted. I carefully reviewed what I was going to say. Somewhere in the back of my mind, I accounted for my three children and reminded myself that Maria was picking them up from school. I had errands to run before I got home and was desperate to make this quick. It was the opposite of the night nearly three weeks earlier; this time I forced my feet toward him and used all of my breathing techniques to quell the urge to run.

I knocked lightly on the door and he opened it immediately, as if he'd been just standing there waiting on the other side. He was wearing jeans, a white shirt with a dark gray sweater, and sneakers.

"Hi," I said, noticing the flexed muscle of his outstretched arm resting on the door. I was disarmed by his physical presence. My heart pounded and I felt myself begin to sweat. Matt Daniels. He was here.

Make this quick.

"Come in," he said and stepped aside allowing me to enter. I didn't bother to look around; I already knew what the inside of a hotel room at the Redbury looked like. I

could see from the lines around his jaw that he was tense.
So was I.

"Thank you for coming," he said formally, rubbing his
hands on his jeans.

"Look, I don't have a lot of time. You said it was
urgent—"

He raised his hands, palms up and stopped me midsentence. "I have something to say and I want to say it
before you steamroll out of here. I know you didn't want
to come, but please, let me talk. When I'm done, you can
respond or leave, whatever you want. But, please, let me
finish."

I nodded in agreement and waited. I could feel the
weight of his words by the way he paced the room and
brushed his hands through his hair. I tried not to notice
the look of his body in his jeans and the curve of his cheek
as he spoke. My plan was to listen politely and leave
quickly.

"I take full responsibility," he began, "for what
happened three weeks ago." He paused and seemed to
grasp for words. "It was not my intention to ply you with
alcohol and get you back to my room. I think you know
that. It just sort of happened and once it started, I
couldn't—I didn't want it to stop. But I know you're
married, and I am too—and I should never have taken you
back to my room." He shook his head and looked at me.
"For that, I am sorry."

"Matt, I—" but he cut me off with his hands.

He was deep in concentration as he paced back and
forth on the hard wood floor. "Let me finish, *please*," he
asked.

"Okay, okay."

"That night...with you..." He reached up and gripped
his chin, rubbing his hand back and forth along the
stubble. "Something happened, something I wanted to talk
to you about but you obviously didn't—want to talk about
it—since you never responded to my emails. So I tried to

forget it but I couldn't do that, either...and I've given this a lot of thought...and I want to know why—why you left me in London—why I didn't hear from you for years—and why you contacted me out of the blue—twenty years later—and agreed to have dinner with me? And please don't tell me it was because you wanted to be Facebook friends."

He paused and took a deep breath but kept his hands up so I wouldn't speak. "I'm not done—just wait, okay?" He turned his head to look out the window and I could see the muscles in his neck stretched taut.

"You didn't talk to me then and you're not talking now. But the fact remains that three weeks ago, you met me for dinner and somehow, we ended up here, in this very hotel. And you looked so beautiful and sad, and you came back to my room—I know I didn't imagine it—and you let me take you to bed—to my bed, Alex—after twenty years! And now you don't want to speak to me? You want to forget it ever happened? That's your plan? Well, that's fucked up."

"Matt, I, I—"

"JUST LET ME FINISH," he practically roared, his eyes blazing. "I know you didn't mean for this to happen and neither did I—but it happened. And now I can hardly think of anything else. I have a life—a career, a wife, two boys—but I can't stop checking my damn phone to see if there's anything from you. And I want to talk to you. But I can't. Because you won't return my messages. And I'm fucked, Alex. I am seriously fucked."

He stopped in the center of the room and rested his head in one hand. I watched him rub across his forehead with the tips of his fingers before he raised his head to face me. He didn't say another word, didn't move or sigh. He stood unblinking in front of me, full of silent tension, as still as the moment before a leopard pounces. I was grateful that he didn't want anything of me, just to listen, but the aftermath of his honesty reverberated through the room and I was desperate to say anything to break the tension. I thought about the speech I prepared: *It was a huge mistake. We'd both drank way too much*—but couldn't force it out.

Finally, he sighed and his voice softened. "I wanted you to know, okay? I needed you to know. That's it. You can respond or leave, whatever. I won't try to contact you again." He shrugged and looked at me, his hands stuffed deep into the pockets of his jeans.

I should've left right then. I should've picked up my purse and left. I definitely shouldn't have looked into his eyes because when I did, my breath caught in my throat. And although I considered reaching for my purse, and there was a part of me that meant to, I didn't. I got off the chair, walked over to him, and looked directly into his incredibly handsome and tired face. I was prepared for battle, to defend my choice if need be. I had steeled myself for that. But I was not prepared for his vulnerability. I was not prepared for his raw need or the pain in his words. I was not prepared for the open wound he uncovered inside of me, that festering scab, ignored for years, that still bled darkly when touched. I walked over to him, put my arms around his waist, and bent my head into his chest, staring down at the dark wood floors.

"I don't know what I'm doing." The muscles in my throat constricted so tightly that it hurt to form words.

He pulled me against him and buried his face in my hair. I leaned into him and inhaled the musky scent of Matt, an irresistible aphrodisiac. Our arms wrapped around each other, clinging out of desperation and desire. Our mouths crushed together with magnetic force. I ran my hands up his neck and into his hair and leaned my head back, closing my eyes in a kind of ecstatic reverie. The feel of his mouth on my neck caused waves of electric pulses to cascade down my spine. "Oh, yes," I murmured without thinking.

He stopped suddenly and looked at me. "What do you

want?" he demanded, eyes flashing. He was tense and turned on and totally infuriated, from the look on his face. "Tell me," he said but I didn't know, I couldn't answer.

"Do you want me to fuck you?" he asked hoarsely. I could see the passion and frustration in his eyes. I nodded. He was breathing hard as he looked at me.

"Say it."

I had this desperate need to feel him inside of me, to feel the world obliterated until there was nothing left but him and me; no kids, no cheating, no twenty years before or since, nothing but Matt and me locked together. It was as if being with him was an alternate universe where time had no meaning. I could trick myself into believing I could steal that moment and not pay for it with everything I had.

"Fuck me," I said.

He lifted me onto the bed and pulled up my skirt in one swift motion. I could hardly breath as he yanked down his zipper, grabbed me around the hips and pulled me toward him. He ripped aside my underwear and entered me with such force that I gasped. He pushed himself so deep into me and I loved it and I couldn't stand it. His fury turned me into nothingness and yet I was there and alive and I loved him and I loathed him too.

"Matt, please," I begged, my nails scraping at the back of his jeans, wanting him deeper inside me, wanting that insatiable itch scratched.

"Yes," he groaned as his hips slammed into me and his hands, tucked underneath my hips, pushed me forward to meet him. He maneuvered me beneath him so that each thrust pressed upon that magic spot that engulfed me in waves and waves of pleasure. He pulled open my shirt and sucked my breasts and licked my neck while I rubbed his hips and felt him grow harder and harder inside of me. I was going to die from this, from him. I was going to explode into a thousand tiny pieces or scream out loud and bring hotel security banging furiously at the door. This had to stop. I couldn't stop. God help me, I couldn't stop.

We went at it like animals, sweating and tearing at each other. I came once, and then again with him, bucking upward in a frenzy of release, my skirt bunched up around my waist, my shirt hanging open at the arms, my underwear torn and discarded. We were bruised and battered and, at last, finally, sated.

"You feel so damn good," he murmured into my hair.

I was speechless. I lay there looking up at him, struck dumb by my own frenzied desire. "Shhh," I whispered, pulling him close and inhaling him.

I got up from the bed, grabbed my underwear, and stumbled to the bathroom. I rinsed my body, washed my face, and rearranged my clothes, fixing my make-up in the process. I looked in the mirror and didn't recognize the woman who stared back. She looked cool, satisfied, and self-contained. She didn't look like anyone I knew. I composed myself as best I could before I walked back into the room. I didn't know what to say, how to address his confession, or what just happened—again—between us. I hesitated for a moment before I turned suddenly to the left, grabbed the doorknob, and bolted. I didn't say goodbye.

I was a coward. I couldn't face Jason and I couldn't face Matt. I couldn't even go to Laurie for comfort because I couldn't face her, either. She was like my mother—one look at her and the truth would tumble out and I wasn't ready for that. I hated myself. I really loathed myself, and yet, if I hated myself so damn much, why—oh why?—did I feel so good? Could it be the Klonopin? I have to get off that shit, like, ASAP. I still felt him in me. I felt his mouth on me. I felt so, so…alive. It was like I'd been one of those cardboard cutout display people who finally became real.

Of course, there was a huge line of lunchers waiting for their cars so I stood there in my wet underwear and wrinkled skirt listening to a litany of private self-loathing. I wanted to get the hell out of there and as far away from

Matt as possible. I couldn't stand feeling this way; I was reeling inside. Why had I left him in London? How did I know? What was done was done and, like a grave, it was better left undisturbed. To go prodding around now risked resurrecting unfinished business, unfinished business that could haunt me forever. I didn't want to be haunted by this, by him, by the decisions I'd once made. Better to leave it like it was, dead and buried.

But I couldn't deny something was surfacing, something I desperately wanted to hold down, and the higher it came, the more I felt my firm grasp on the ways things were slipping away. It was like trying to hold an inflated beach ball underwater. It took so much effort to keep it submerged, and every time I saw Matt, I seemed to lose my grasp and the ball started to come to the surface. If I didn't immediately regain control, the ball would shoot straight out of the water and make an arc ten feet in the sky—in view of everyone sitting nearby. I had to keep that ball submerged. My life depended on it.

And yet deep inside, I knew I couldn't hold it down forever. I didn't have the strength nor the vigilance to ensure that I never, ever let go. And then there was Matt. As I stood in the valet line observing the ordinary moments of life—men in suits on cell phones; women in stylish jeans chatting together in groups of twos and threes; valet guys hustling back and forth between cars—I let myself think about what had just happened. I had shut out some part of the reality because the whole of it was too much to absorb. And since he came back into my life, that was what I'd done: shut it out by hating myself, by hating him, by beating myself up with my infidelity, but never—not once—did I stop to consider what it meant: I wanted this. There were so many things I had that I didn't want, and so many things I'd given up along the way. Mostly, though, I wandered into things and accepted whatever came my way.

At some point in my life, I stopped driving my bus and

took a seat somewhere in the rear. With no driver at the wheel, the bus had veered wildly off course while I stared out the window in a daze, watching the scenery go by. I don't know why this happened or when it began. I suspected, deep down, it was related to fear, but I didn't know, didn't want to think about it. What I did know with complete clarity was that I wanted Matt. I wasn't drifting into him. I wasn't drunk. I just wanted him. I could call myself disgusting and a liar, I could tell myself I didn't appreciate my life; I could even hate myself and hate him, too, but none of that mattered because there it was: I wanted this. And it was going to fuck up my life. And his, too.

I stepped out of line and walked back into the hotel. I didn't have to wait for the elevator because the doors magically opened as I approached. I hit the button for his floor and walked, trancelike, down the hallway I'd just fled. I stood outside the door and breathed. Here I go, I thought, and knocked.

He opened the door in jeans and a clean white shirt. His face was freshly washed but his eyes looked tired. He stood at the edge of his room holding the door open, looking at me in silence while I stood facing him at the threshold, with no words immediately coming to mind. If ever I needed courage, it was then. I still felt the urge to run but this time, I wouldn't.

"Are you here?" I asked.

He looked neither surprised nor upset. He stood at the door, eyebrows raised, almost as if wondering the same thing. "Yes," he finally said, nodding his head. "I'm here."

"There's no chance this is a dream?" I asked.

"Not a chance." He didn't move a muscle.

"Say something," I whispered.

"What do you want me to say?" He stood still another moment and then added, "Nothing you do surprises me, Alex, or should I say, everything you do surprises me. I have no idea which."

146

He remained in his room while I stood in the hall and although there was only a doorway between us, it felt like a million miles. It was my call. I saw that clearly. Matt had taken me places I never thought I'd go—both literally and in so many other ways—but he only opened the door. If I wanted to enter, I had to take the first step. He stood at the threshold of his hotel room, leaning against the open door but making no gesture, not even a shake of his head.

"Can I come in?" I asked.

"Are you going to run away again?" he countered. "Just thought I'd ask before—"

"Listen to me. As I was waiting for my car, thinking about what happened, again, between us, one thing became clear...all this running, it isn't helping. After all," I felt my throat tighten, "I keep running back to where I started."

He moved aside.

I walked past him into the room and closed the door.

He crossed his arms and turned to me. "I asked you this before but I'll ask again: what do you want, Alex? If it's just an afternoon fuck I would think you could find that locally."

"Okay, Matt, I deserve that. But..." I looked down at the floor trying to figure out how to tell him what the last few weeks had been like for me. "I've been tortured...thinking you might try to contact me again, or worse...that you wouldn't."

He lifted my face upward, forcing me to meet his eye. When we were together that was always his way, even when we were making love—eye to eye, refusing to let me look away or shut him out. It was that way he had of looking at me, as if he really saw me, that had undone me at twenty. No one had ever looked at me like that before or since. And when he looked at me now, nothing had changed. His eyes seemed to peer directly into my soul and there was no hiding. He could see the pain and the longing, the emptiness and the fear. He held my face in his warm hands for a long time.

I leaned forward and rested my head on his shoulder, breathed him in, and let myself feel the onslaught of emotions kept at bay for so long. Matt Daniels was here and he was holding me. I tried not to think but just to feel myself in my body, from the searing pain in my chest to the flutter in my stomach to the ache in my head and the shaking in my feet. I stood there, wrapped in his arms, and let it come. I was afraid the intensity would overwhelm me, but after a while, it subsided into a dull ache.

"What makes you tick?" he whispered, almost to himself. He stroked my hair and rested his chin on top of my head.

"What do you mean?" I asked, keeping my head pressed to his shoulder.

"Why did you come back?"

"I don't know. I'm going crazy. Can't you tell?" I nestled my head further into his shoulder, breathing him in. "I can't seem to help it."

"Well, that I understand," he said, his hand still stroking my hair. "I told myself to leave it alone, let you get on with your life, try to get on with mine." He shrugged. "But I couldn't. I had to see you. And I don't think you're crazy."

"You don't?"

"No. I don't. The Alex I knew was one of the sanest people I ever met and people don't change all that much."

"Well then, what about this?" I asked, gesturing to him and me and turning to encompass the hotel room.

"I don't know yet."

"Matt," I said, stepping back slightly so we could face each other. "What are we doing?"

"Really? You're going to make me ask you again? Because I will. What do you want, Alex? I think that's the real question." He raised his eyebrows, tilted his head, and waited.

"I—I...I want this."

"Okay," he said. "Me too." And before I knew what was happening, he'd backed me up against the wall and was kissing me, my mouth burning from the sensation of his lips and his tongue.

But something changed, something inexpressible inside. When I ran from his room, I didn't know what I was running from. But when I came back, I knew I'd crossed a line. I'd set myself on a course from which there was no turning back. I was going to have to face this no matter where it took me. I couldn't pretend or forget or cover it up with hating him or myself. I had to accept this was happening: I was having an affair and I couldn't control what would happen next.

He unbuttoned my blouse. I unzipped his jeans and slowly pushed them to the floor. He held my hand as I stepped out of my skirt and then smoothed it out and laid it on the leather chair by the desk. We stretched out beside each other on the bed. I pulled off his shirt and ran my hands over him, kissing his stomach and chest, his shoulders and neck. I met his eyes, saw the sweet smile playing at the edge of his mouth, and kissed it, sliding my tongue between his lips.

"I want you again—worse, if that's possible," he said, caressing my hip with his fingers.

"It's unrelenting," I replied.

"Yes. It's unrelenting but…"

"What?"

"I'm twenty years older, Al," he laughed, "and we just had sex a half hour ago."

"Who said anything about sex? I think sleep is underrated." I scooted next to him under the sheet and ran my hands up and down his back.

He held me and kissed me, squeezing and rubbing my backside. We lay on our sides, his mouth gently sucking my neck and breasts. I traced the line of his chest over his hip and downward. He pushed the sheet down so I lay naked facing him as he slid a hand between my thighs. The heat of his fingers against the slickness between my legs made me shudder.

We took our time nuzzling and touching until he pulled me to him, wanting and ready. I rolled on top and sat upright, easing him in and out of me, watching his eyes roam over my face and breasts. He grabbed a pillow, wedged it between the headboard and his back, and sat up too, pulling me down deeper onto him, one hand on my hip, the other arm wrapped around my back. I let go of everything at that moment, sitting astride him, moving in tandem, hip to hip, chest to chest, as we slowly made love. I let my feelings come up and be felt and I was wholly present with him in that room. No part of me was denied—not the part of me that was ugly or cheating or bitter at how much of my life had gone by. It was all there with me and I was whole and I understood for a moment why I always felt so out of balance. The real me had been half-hidden for years. And now that Matt was back in my life, she wanted to be with him. My Self was emerging and she was much more powerful than some shell of me, some half-real part with puny arms struggling to hold an inflated beach ball underwater. This was my wake-up call and I couldn't go back to sleep. Even if I wanted to.

***

"Hey, it's almost four o'clock. I have to go," I said, putting my clothes back on for the second time that afternoon. We'd been in bed for nearly two hours, exploring, re-acquainting, devouring.

"I was afraid you'd point that out sooner or later," he admitted, still lying undressed in bed. He sat up and reached an arm out to me.

I stopped smoothing down my skirt and grasped his hand. "I'm not running out on you," I said, shaking my head. "Although I don't think I can take much more of it."

"Wanna try?" he asked, pulling me toward him.

"Isn't a third time 'medically impossible'—at your age, I mean?"

He picked a rumpled white pillow off the bed and threw it at me. "Haha, smart ass. Come over here and let's see."

I smiled as I picked up the pillow and sat down next to him. He rubbed his hand back and forth over my knee while I clutched the pillow to my lap, wrapping my arms around its soft lumps and laying my cheek against the edge. My mind drifted to Jason and how he'd snap at me sometimes—usually after I'd snapped at him first—but he never immobilized me. In most of our fights, one or both of us would be doing something else simultaneously—in fact, in almost every interaction, that was the case. I was washing the dishes, or maybe he was texting his office while we bickered over the TV shows the kids watched or discussed where to go on our next family vacation. Never did we face off the way Matt and I did that day. Fuzzy remnants of other moments between Matt and me drifted through my memories. In them, we were always static, two chess pieces awaiting the other's move. The intensity of our interaction seemed to require full focus. I was out of practice from years of multi-tasking while multi-tasking, and felt uncomfortable with no distractions to hide behind.

"Where'd you go?' he asked.

"Just thinking..."

We were both quiet. I put the pillow down and reached over and took Matt's hand, noticing the glint of his silver wedding band. "I have to get going...but I want to say goodbye. I'm not gonna dash out of here like I don't know what I'm doing." I exhaled loudly and realized I'd been holding my breath. I dropped my shoulders and closed my eyes, feeling a tightness in my chest, right below the breastbone. "I know what I'm doing...and I want to see you again—very soon." I forced myself to say the truth. I'd gotten used to blowing off things that were important to me. So much so, that I barely recognized the things I wanted. I wouldn't do that now.

He waited a beat before answering. "I'll email you as soon as I know when I'll be back, and Alex, we should probably set up new Gmail accounts…so we have privacy."

"Okay," I said, understanding the implication. This was what people did when they had something to hide. "I'll do it tonight," I said, squeezing his hand and turning to get up.

"Hey," he said, pulling me back toward him.

"What—"

"I miss you already."

I leaned down, kissed him one last time before leaving, and whispered, "Me too."

RESTLESS IN L.A.
Mommy Musings. Stupid Confessions. Life.
Posted by Anonymous

Some Things You Can't Even Tell Your Best Friend

I told her what I'd done and she was shocked, maybe even horrified. But being the good friend she was, she patted my hand and rubbed my back and let me use up her entire box of tissues all the while making soothing sounds while I blew my nose and bawled until I soaked the shoulder of her pink pajama shirt clean through.

I asked for forgiveness for my ways but she didn't have it to give. As my best friend, my #1 BFF, she wanted to believe that people do things they don't mean, that mistakes are made. And it was a mistake, I was sure of it. But afterward, as I laid in my BFF's arms and recounted my misery, my guilt, the sick feeling in the pit of my stomach and my confusion about what happened, I became aware of something else: the feeling that I didn't exist before that night, not really.

And now that the one-night stand has turned into two, I can't go back and tell her that I meant it, that I'd actually wanted to do it. There are some things you can't even tell your best friend. This is definitely one of them.

CHAPTER 13: BOMBSHELL

I was home by six and faced with my usual evening detail. Jason was at a meeting with his partners and I was grateful to Maria for splitting carpool with me and making dinner but I was distracted and couldn't fall asleep. In the morning as Jason got ready to leave, he offered to drive the kids to school, but he seemed pensive and far away.

"Everything okay at the office?" I asked. I walked into the bathroom and stood at the mirror as he shaved. Did he notice something different between us? He methodically mowed vertical lines through the foam, framing his well-kept goatee. I reached for my toothbrush, avoiding his reflection. Jason studied his face, his blue eyes searching for any wayward patch of hair as he knocked his razor against the marble counter top. He grabbed a washcloth, wiped his face, and then cleaned the edge of the porcelain sink. I watched the dark blond hair fragments mixed with bits of shaving cream swirl frantically around the rim before filing neatly down the drain.

"Yeah, everything's fine," he said. "I'll take the kids to school since I'm not going in until nine." He stepped into our oversized walk-in closet. I trailed behind him.

"How're things going?" I asked. "The merger on

track?" I watched him lift a plastic bag off a newly dry-cleaned dress shirt. He pulled a pair of freshly pressed khaki slacks off a hanger and turned to me.

"It's fine," he sighed. "Just some bumps in the road, don't worry about it." He stared at his generous selection of ties.

"Wear this one," I said, pointing to a satin jacquard Armani tie with gray diamonds. I followed him into the kitchen as he poured himself a to-go mug of coffee.

"Look, I know there hasn't been a lot of time to talk lately," he said as he added a drop of milk to the silver canister. "Can you see if Maria can stay over this weekend and maybe you and I can go to Shutters for a night?" He looked at me as he screwed the lid in place. It was the first time that morning we'd actually made eye contact. I looked away.

"Um, sure, I'll talk to her about it."

"Great. And listen, I'm sorry I've been so preoccupied. You seem distracted too. How's everything at school with Ryan? Is there anything I need to know?" He unplugged his phone and slipped it into his pocket.

"His teacher said everything was 'fine' when I checked in with him last week, whatever that means. He doesn't seem so 'fine' at home."

"The doctor said it could take a while to get the medicine right. Shit, Al, that's the best report Ryan's got, well, ever." He continued to walk around the kitchen, gathering his file folders and his brief case.

I sat down at the island. "But it's like I never know what's going to happen next. A few weeks ago, the teacher was so unhappy with him and now he seems to be doing okay. What's going to happen next week? And the new medicine, it makes him miserable in the afternoons. When I pick up the kids after school, they get into it the minute they see me. They start yelling at each other and vying for my attention and it's so embarrassing. The other day—"

"I know it's tough, hon. You're doing a great job.

Listen, I gotta get out of here or we'll all be late, but talk to Maria, okay?" He pecked me on the cheek and called to the kids to get in the car.

"Love you, hon, let's talk tonight."

He whizzed out the door while our three kids grumbled behind him, still stuffing lunch boxes and books into their unzipped backpacks and carrying cream-cheesed bagels on napkins.

As soon as the door shut, I got up, grabbed my cell phone, and logged in to my new Gmail account. There was a message in my inbox. I hesitated before I opened it. I knew who it was from. I thought about deleting it. I thought about putting an end to this before it went any further. I thought about the conversation with Laurie, and Jason's face as he'd cleared the white foam from his cheeks and wiped the bathroom sink, making sure to rinse down every last bit of facial hair. I thought about his idea to go away for the weekend and how hard he worked and how sweet it was of him to take the kids to school. I thought about all of these things and then I opened the email.

I want to see you. I'll be back in ten days – and I'm counting.

I replied: *Ten days. Me too.*

He was online because he responded instantly: *Pick me up at LAX @ 4pm and stay? Please.*

I paused for a moment and thought about it. He was coming back on a Tuesday. Maria usually stayed late on Tuesdays so it would be easy to swing: *Ok, I'll be there. But don't you need a rental car? I don't know about staying...*

His reply was short and to the point: *I'll get a car in the morning. I want to see you ASAP.*

I replied in a word: *Yes.*

And there I was, eight-thirty in the morning already plotting another rendezvous. I was a disgusting person. How long would it take for ten days to pass?

***

All of these colored, lacy bras and matching panties. So many different styles. Boy shorts, thongs, bikinis, even cheekies. What the hell was a cheeky? I didn't get how anyone could get in and out of Victoria's Secret in less than two hours. Was this really what moms wore beneath their sweat pants? I guess I should've been ashamed that, except for special occasions, I'd been wearing beige Kirkland ten-pack underwear from Costco for the last three years.

"Um, excuse me," I said, stopping an attractive brunette in her early twenties walking by, holding a clipboard. "What's the difference between the Miraculous Plunge and the Bombshell?"

"Well, hon, it depends on what you're going for."

"Huh?"

"Are you looking for a subtle lift or something really eye-catching? By the way, are those real?" she asked, pointing to my chest.

"Um, yes."

"Really? Well, you've got something to work with. What are you, a 34C?

"Yes, I—"

"We can take it from subtle to extreme. Depends on what you want. If you're going for major cleavage, we have maximum lift and it comes in some super hot colors."

"Maximum lift?" I asked, imagining my breasts riding on top of my ears. "No, I just wanted something pretty...and sexy," I added.

"For you, I'd go for either the Bombshell or the Showstopper. Do you want memory fit?"

"Memory what?"

"Memory fit. It's state of the art. The bra actually molds to the shape of your breasts for maximum comfort. You haven't been in for a while, huh? Our new bras really lift you up and out, hon, really get you some awesome cleavage. I think you should go for the bombshell. It adds two full cup sizes."

She walked over to the display, opened one of the drawers, pulled out a pink leopard push-up bra, and handed it to me.

"Wow," I said. It felt like I'd stuffed my bra with four pairs of soccer socks. "Do you have something with less, um, padding?" I asked.

"Well, I think that would look really hot on you but if you want something more natural, go with the Showstopper. It comes in a demi-cup without all the padding and it comes in lots of awesome colors."

"Okay, great. Does it have matching underwear?"

"Of course," she snorted.

I tucked myself behind a huge wooden door in the dressing room and wondered what the hell I was doing at the Westfield Mall on a Friday afternoon trying on the Showstopper in both black and red lace. Red lace—it had to be red lace. I stood in front of the mirror and stared at my reflection, wondering if my face looked different, searching for signs that something had changed.

I remembered back to a Memorial Day decades ago, the night I lost my virginity. I came home afraid to look at my parents, certain that if they caught my eye, they'd know what I'd done. And now, twenty-something years later, I found myself once again peering into the mirror, wondering if it showed on my face—what I'd done and was obviously preparing to do again. It was hard for me to know how to hold my eyes, my mouth; afraid they'd give me away. I had cheated and I'd been afraid to look Jason in the eye since that night. Is that the first sign? I wondered silently. Your spouse stops making eye contact? I wanted to tell myself it was all a mistake, I hadn't mean to do it. But I knew I had.

I thanked the pretty brunette and paid in cash for the Showstopper with matching thong underwear, in both black and red lace. I went home and stowed the bag at the bottom of my closet behind some shoeboxes to wait ten days.

***

Jason came home that night earlier than he had in months. He ate dinner with us and helped get the kids to bed. I heard Ben giggling from his room.

"Good night, monkey face," he called out to him and went to our bathroom to take a shower. I was midway through my millionth reading of *Pride & Prejudice* when Jason emerged and came over to sit at the end of the couch where I was stretched out.

"I guess you spoke to Maria, huh?"

Spoke to her about what? What was he talking about? I must have given him a blank stare because he continued with a grin.

"I found my present." He smiled at me knowingly. "I already called Shutters and made the reservation."

Oh shit. I hadn't said a word to Maria. I couldn't deal with spending a night alone together right now. And what present?

"I'm glad you got on this, hon. I know it's hard for you to be away from the kids but we need this." He leaned over and stroked my thigh, adding softly, "I can't wait to see you in it."

Huh? He stroked my thigh again. "Sorry, but I was looking for my running shoes when I saw a Victoria's Secret bag in the closet. I couldn't help but peek in. What guy could resist?" he asked, chuckling.

Oh shit. "I mentioned it to Maria," I stuttered. "She didn't say for sure if she could stay over. She's supposed to let me know tomorrow," I lied. "I was just being optimistic."

"Al," Jason said, settling in at the other end of the couch and lifting my feet onto his lap. "I know it's been hard but we're gonna get through this." He was clean and warm from the shower, dressed for bed in a T-shirt and plaid pajama bottoms. He picked up my left leg and began massaging the ball of my foot through my white sock.

"Ryan's doing okay and so are we," he said as he rubbed my aching arch. His strong hands and the pressure he applied soothed the sore spots.

"What I really want is time to talk," I broke in. "There's always so much going on in this family. Sometimes I feel so lost in the shuffle..." I wasn't sure where I was going but when I looked at my husband just then, I saw him for who he'd always been to me: comforter, lover, partner, friend. It had been so long since we spent a quiet moment together and I couldn't help but want to open up, to somehow share some aspect of what I was going through. He turned toward me, his blue eyes focused on my face while his hands began massaging my other foot.

"Maybe I don't tell you enough—" His cell phone, perched on the kitchen counter, vibrated. "Hang on," he said as he dropped my foot and jumped off the couch to grab it.

"Hello? Are you serious?" He moved the phone away and spoke in my direction. "I've got to deal with this but we'll definitely talk this weekend."

***

I asked Maria to stay overnight Friday but she couldn't. Her church was having some kind of special service she couldn't miss so she asked her sister Lena to take the kids. Although my kids loved Lena and her family, I didn't feel as comfortable about Ryan staying overnight with her. With Lena's four kids and my three, it was a chaotic circus and chaotic situations weren't great for Ryan. But there was nothing I could do. Jason had made the reservation and wanted to go.

I hoped Lena would remember to give Ryan his medicine. And I hoped she'd make sure he ate and got to bed at a reasonable hour. And I hoped Benny wouldn't miss me too much and that Natalie wouldn't be in emotional turmoil about anything. But it wasn't just the kids. I knew Jason and I would be alone and there was the Victoria's Secret lingerie...I wasn't sure how I was going to handle it but I didn't have a choice.

Friday morning came and I popped the weekender onto the bed. I'd just fished out a pair of jeans and a clean blouse when my home phone rang. The Caller ID read, "Rankin, Laurie."

I glanced at the screen but hesitated. I couldn't talk to Laurie. I'd told her it was over. I'd told her it was temporary insanity. I couldn't admit it wasn't as temporary as I'd thought. At least the insanity part was true. The phone rang again. I reached for it, half expecting to see "Rankin, Laurie" again but it wasn't. It read, "Pineview Elementary."

"Hello?" I answered, hoping none of my children had fallen off the jungle gym and broke an arm.

"Mrs. Hoffman?"

"Yes."

"Everything is all right. I'm calling to talk to you about Ryan."

I recognized the principal's voice immediately. "What about him? What happened? Is something wrong?"

"Ryan and another student were involved in an altercation. The lunch aides assured me that both students were at fault, however, Ryan punched the other student in the shoulder.

"He what?"

"He punched the other student."

But he's doing so well. This wasn't supposed to happen. He was in therapy and on medication. "Do you know the details?"

"It's not entirely clear but I need to let you know that, by our school bylaws, a closed-handed punch is grounds for suspension. I let him off with a warning today but if it happens again, he'll be suspended."

"You know Ryan's on medication. He has severe hyperactivity. He doesn't read social cues well and he gets frus—"

"Mrs. Hoffman, no one's perfect. I don't want you to get too upset about this. We know Ryan has some special challenges. He hasn't been in my office for a while."

"But you said he'd be suspended."

"If it happens again. Let's hope it won't. Now let's not make too much of it. Have a nice weekend."

"Um, okay. Thank you." Oh my god—he could be suspended. And what? Have a nice weekend? Was she kidding?

I closed my eyes and pinched the bridge of my nose as an image of boys in juvenile detention centers floated into my mind. I wished I hadn't read that article about the link between ADHD and incarceration or the one about Asperger's and intense irritability. I already had a list a mile long of things I worried about and now I worried about suspension, too.

I held the blouse in my hand and stood next to the weekender lying open on my bed and wondered what happened and how he felt and if he got yelled at and if it was in front of the other kids. He was working so hard. He was on medication, saw a therapist, and was in a social skills group. He was a good boy who struggled so much. WHAT ELSE COULD I DO? Should I move him to a special school? I'd been thinking about it for months but I didn't dare bring it up to Jason again. I knew he'd go ballistic at the mere mention of another school. It wasn't that he didn't know Ryan needed help; it was just that he went into these denial moments, where he suddenly minimized all of Ryan's problems. He'd describe all the roughhousing that went on when he was a kid and the bloody noses he gave and got on his way to adulthood. "That's how boys are," he'd say.

But that wasn't true. And with today's helicopter parents, there was little enough tolerance for normal childhood conflict, let alone an impulsive kid with ADHD—which didn't excuse Ryan from punching someone. I constantly felt on edge, never knowing what was going to happen—whether the week would be rough or smooth, whether I should be optimistic or in despair—and, although we invested a small fortune in therapy, evaluations, and medication, the roller coaster never stopped. I felt like I rode it alone.

When Jason came home to pack, I recounted in detail the phone call with the principal. "She said if it happens again, he'll be suspended," I repeated, agitated.

"Al, relax. I'll tell Ryan he better make sure his hand is open the next time he slugs someone."

"Not funny, Jason."

"Oh come on. It was one time. He's doing better."

"Is he?" I asked, suddenly exhausted.

"What is that supposed to mean?" he snapped.

"I don't know." I didn't tell him about the kids from Ryan's class who were carpooling to a movie the other day; how it felt to be standing in the parking lot while Ryan counted each boy's backpack dumped into the open trunk of some mom's minivan. I didn't want to relive the sound of animated voices echoing through the open windows as the van drove off. I asked Ryan if he wanted to watch a movie at home with Ben but he turned to me, eyes red and squinted, and shouted, "No! I hate Ben!"

"What is it?" Jason asked, forcing the rolled pairs of white socks I laid out for him into his duffel. "If you're not happy with how he's doing—"

"It's not that easy and you know it. He has social issues."

"Social issues? Come on, every kid has social issues. I

didn't have it easy when I was a kid, either. My best friend moved away in the fourth grade and I had to make all new frie—"

"Please, Jason. I can't take that story again." I stopped packing and glared at him.

"Well, it's true."

"Ryan's not you. And he's never going to be. He can't make all new friends. He doesn't even have any old friends." I grabbed the red cotton pajama shirt I was about to fold and shoved it in the weekender.

"So get him a new therapist, Al. You complained about the social skills group, so find him another one. And if you don't think the medication is working, then get him back to the doctor and we'll try something else. Do it. I'm behind you all the way."

"You're behind me? Well, that's just great. That helps so much that you're 'behind me,' Jason, while I spend my life driving our son from one damn therapy appointment to another," I said, my voice rising. "And if the principal calls me and tells me my son might get suspended, I have every right to be upset. That doesn't mean I'm ready to change his entire treatment plan, it just means I'm upset." I slammed the door to our closet and faced him, clutching a pair of white flip-flops in my hands.

"Fine," he said, waving me off.

But I was just getting started.

"Don't you think I want to have a life? What do you think I do all day? Eat bon bons? Last year, my book club went to Vegas, but did I go? No. You were busy at the office and I didn't think Ryan could handle it and I didn't think anyone could handle him so I stayed home."

"Well, whose fault was that?" he exploded. "I told you to go. I told you I could handle it. You didn't want to." The veins on his neck popped out like miniature mountain ridges. Finally, he was paying attention.

"I didn't want to? Are you crazy? I wanted to, believe me, I wanted to. But you're never around and even when you are, you aren't! I didn't feel I could go."

"Well, what do you want me to do?" He asked. "I. Was. Working."

"You're always working. Who can argue with that?'

"Alex, I offered you more Maria—you didn't want it— and what do you think this is? Huh?" he asked, gesturing toward the luggage. "I wanted us to spend some time together. I thought that was what you wanted. I don't know what you want anymore."

"You don't know what I want? I'll tell you what I want. I want you to stop telling me you hear me but nothing ever changes. I'm a married single mother. That's the truth!"

"Well, I'm here now, aren't I?"

"Yes, you're here but why does every talk turn into a fight? It's like you won't listen—"

"Listen to what? How fucked up my son is? Maybe you're right, maybe I don't want to hear it. He's got problems, okay? I get it. But sitting around worrying about it all day isn't going to solve anything."

"So that's what you think I do? Sit around worrying about it all day?"

"I don't know, Al. You tell me."

"You know what? This may come as a shock but there are some problems that can't be fixed, no matter how much money you throw at them, problems that just persist and—"

"We've been over this," he said loudly.

"But nothing changes. I feel like I carry—"

"I came home early, didn't I?"

"STOP INTERRUPTING ME. You're like one of the kids—I can't even get a sentence out. And what's the point? No one listens anyway." I put my flip-flops down. I felt a throbbing in my throat. "I don't need grand gestures, Jason, nights at Shutters…You want to know what I want? I want to be by myself."

"That's fine. Go ahead, Alex." He stopped packing and pointed to the door with his open palm. "You seem like you could use some alone time."

"Fine. I will. You stay home and take care of the kids tonight on your own, like I always do."

I grabbed the suitcase and wheeled it to my car. Then I ran back into the house and into the office. I rifled through the desk drawer, grabbed the journal, and tossed it into my purse.

Shutters, here I come.

***

Later that night as I sat on the balcony looking out at the Pacific Ocean and illegally smoking Marlboro Lights, I thought about my argument with Jason. Was I really angry at him? Or just desperate to weasel out of being alone with him? How was I going to deal with him for an entire evening when I couldn't even look him in the eye? But he didn't deserve the way I acted. He tried to make light of things. I always took Ryan and everything to do with Ryan to heart. Everything.

I picked up the phone.

"It's me. I'm sorry," I said, before he could say anything. There was a brief pause and then a sigh.

"I'm sorry too."

"Do you want to come join me? It's not too late. We could still go for a drink?" I asked, honestly hopeful.

"Nah. I told Lena to forget it. I think she went to church or something."

"Do you want me to come home?"

"No. Stay. You could use a break...from all of us. I think I just felt guilty because I've hardly been around and I wanted to make it up to you but, maybe, what you really need is some time to yourself. So take it."

He felt guilty? I cringed inside. "Okay...I'll see you in the morning."

"Good night, hon. Love you."

"Love you too. And Jason?"

"Yeah?"

"Thanks."

I spent the night on the balcony with only the Pacific Ocean for company and was grateful for the time alone, time to think. My thoughts kept drifting back to when I first met Jason, how taken I was with his certainty, his confidence, his easy sense of how things should be. I let him make most of the decisions in our life together, grateful to be free of them. He always knew what to do. He seemed to revel in the role of provider and didn't demand much except that I take care of the kids and the house. Jason liked things as they were. He was a product of a traditional marriage; his mom was home every afternoon, and we duplicated that without thinking. But raising Ryan was such a challenge. It seemed like there was always a battle to fight. Maybe if I didn't have a kid who demanded so much, maybe if I didn't need Jason so much, maybe then, things would have been easier between us. And yet none of this explained why I'd cheated. I didn't know. I couldn't coherently explain it, even to myself.

I picked up the journal and poured myself a glass of wine from the bottle I'd ordered to the room. I studied the pages as if some clue might suddenly emerge, like a hidden object in a child's coloring book. I closed my eyes and relived the scene twenty years earlier when I'd bumped headfirst into Matt on a sidewalk. He'd recovered quickly and followed me through the streets of London to get my phone number. What was I wearing that day? What did it feel like when I looked up, in my surprise and embarrassment, and found his green eyes staring back at me? And why, when I looked back now, did it seem like the world had been perfectly still?

I found the spot where I'd left off in the journal and remembered my younger self furiously scribbling, as if the ink itself could indelibly capture all the thoughts and feelings that erupted out of me that year. I thought about how my relationship with Matt evolved during that time, how he became so much more than my lover. But I had been too young to understand that. So I tried to understand now the choices I'd made and the ones I was making. I lit another cigarette and probed the journal for clues.

***

April 17
'History of the British Novel' was my favorite class all semester even though the arrogant Professor Clarke could be an intimidating asshole at times (always wearing his Oxford scarf). Still, he's everybody's favorite—young and brilliant, his wild hair pulled into a ponytail—and wickedly funny. I was flattered and amazed when he offered to read my manuscript—what a total and complete idiot I was!!! Late yesterday afternoon, Matt and I walked over to his office on campus for our meeting. I was dying to hear the professor's thoughts on my book...

***

"You're an artist," Matt said, as we walked to the professor's office, housed in an ancient building in the back corner of campus. His black biker jacket, dark green wool scarf carelessly flung around his neck, and heavy, black hiking boots, matched with his natural good looks, gave him the appearance of a rugged rock star. "You don't need anyone else's approval. Besides, your story's incredible. The only thing you lack is confidence," he insisted, squeezing my hand.

I was so terrified the professor would hate my manuscript and think I sucked as a writer that I'd worked myself into a massive state of anxiety. I paced back and forth in front of the door, blowing on my hands from the cold, while Matt gave me a pep talk.

"Come on, Alex, it's just one person's opinion. Think of Hemingway or Woolf or even the great Jane Austen. Where would they be if they'd been too afraid to try?"

"Well, I'm hardly in that categ—"

"Quit making excuses. You're a great writer. The only person who doesn't believe that is you."

Matt had stayed up late a few weeks before and read through my entire manuscript with a black pen, jotting questions in the margins and underlining passages he'd found particularly moving. When he'd finished, he'd left the two-hundred-fifty page manuscript next to my side of the bed topped with a yellow sticky note that read, "Wow."

He took my hand and gave it a squeeze. "You can do this. Now, go get 'em, tiger!" He'd laughed, adding a ridiculous growl and pushing me toward the large, old-fashioned office door. I leaned onto my tiptoes and kissed him goodbye as he reminded me he'd be back to take me to dinner.

"Okay," I told him, forcing a smile. "I'm sure I'll have a huge appetite by then, after having so much praise lavished upon me."

"There you go," he said with a wink and took off toward our favorite bookshop to browse for an hour.

My hands were cold and fidgety from being outside and from being nervous. I opened the door and was grateful for the blast of warm air emanating from the heated office.

Professor Clarke, the young toast of the literary town, was dressed in a white button-down shirt, navy blazer, and jeans, his hair hanging loosely at his shoulders. He was reading one of the classics, *Crime and Punishment* by Dostoevsky. I was nervous as I approached him reclined on his leather couch. London weather was chilly for April and I wore my favorite Italian suede jacket over a ribbed gray turtleneck and jeans. He offered to take my coat but I declined, my fingers fiddling with the long strands of fringe that hung down the front.

"Your story was surprisingly charming," he said. "There were a few minor issues with the plot and, of course, the protagonist was one-dimensional, but, overall, a good start. So tell me, how are you enjoying London?" he asked, putting his book down and looking up at me.

"London's great. I love it," I answered as his comments began to sink in. Wait, what? Issues with the plot? My protagonist was one-dimensional?

"What were some of the issues?" I asked, waiting for critique.

"We'll get to that later," he said with a dismissive wave of the hand. "Would you like some tea?"

"Sure," I answered, confused. He got up and went to a corner of the office that housed a tiny kitchenette. As he poured my tea, he said with his back to me, "I think I've shared with the class on several occasions that I'm an excellent cook. Are you free tomorrow night? I'd like to cook a meal for you in my flat." He returned to the couch and sat down, patting the seat next to him.

"Me? Free? Do you mean a class dinner...or just me?" I stumbled, sitting down where he indicated.

"Just you."

"Oh, well, Professor—"

"Call me John," he said, looking at me and shaking out his long, blond hair.

"Um, John, I'm, uh, seeing someone," I stuttered, shifting in my seat

He waved his left hand in the air as he handed me the mug of Earl Grey with his right. "Yes, I know you Americans tend to get caught up in love affairs with one another but that's none of my concern," he said dismissively. "I haven't noticed you spending time with any particular classmate."

"Oh, well, Matt, he isn't a classmate. He's a filmmaker and he—"

"How is seven o'clock? We'll discuss your story in

more detail," he interrupted, scooting closer to me on the couch.

"I don't think so," I mumbled.

"Alex," he said, putting his hand on my knee and upsetting the mug carefully balanced between my thumb and forefinger. A hot spot of tea spilled onto my jeans. If he noticed, he acted like he didn't. "I think there's an obvious attraction here."

"What? No, I don't think so. I—" He lifted the mug out of my hand and placed it on a cork coaster on top of the glass coffee table. I didn't know where to look but I didn't want to make eye contact.

"Look, Professor, I came here to talk about my manuscript. I have to get going." I started to get up.

He leaned over, grasped me in mid-rise, and stuck his large, too-warm hands on either side of my face. He pulled me toward him and forcefully kissed me on the mouth. I was too stunned to pull away, which he unfortunately took as a go-ahead and his tongue invaded my mouth.

I pulled my face out of his lip-lock and recovered my powers of speech. "Professor—" I squeaked.

"John."

"John, I have to go," I said, getting off the coach. "This isn't what—"

"Now wait a minute," he ordered as he pulled me down by my jacket. He was practically sitting on top of me. He reached over and groped me over my turtleneck.

"I've admired your body all semester," he said. "I'm sure you're aware of my attention." Using the back of his palm, he pushed my hair off my shoulder and leaned in. This time I felt his lips on the bottom of my chin. I was frozen.

"Professor!" I yelped, pushing him away. "Stop!"

"John," he said. His eyebrows knit together and he seemed not to hear me.

"John! Cut it out!"

"Relax," he said, pressing me into the couch by the

sheer weight of his body. He was a tall man and heavier than he looked. I couldn't force him off me. He reached over and tugged on my shirt. I braced my hands to keep it pulled down but he gripped my two hands with his one, putting an end to our wrestling match.

"Let's make this easy, shall we?' he asked, raising his bushy, blond eyebrows. His wide cheekbones and pale, broad-set face conveyed his determination. "There's no need to play hard to get."

He yanked up my top, successfully sliding one hand underneath. I squirmed and jerked, trying to dislodge him. He pressed his full weight against me and forced me onto my back on the couch, flattening me into the black, leather cushions and lying on top of me. His hands burrowed under my bra as he grasped my breast and moaned. I felt his erection pressed against my thigh as I desperately attempted to shove him off me.

"Professor! John! Please!" I yelled into the side of his hair. His mouth was busy trying to pull up my turtleneck with his teeth.

"Shhhh." His hips grinded against me, dry-humping me through my jeans.

"Get off me!" I yelled, pushing at his waist but he was too heavy.

"You're going to like it," he said, holding both my wrists in his enormous hand and pulling them over my head. I bucked hard but he used his free hand to unzip his fly.

He was going to rape me right there on the couch in his office. And it dawned on me how secluded the building was, how it sat right at the outer perimeter of campus with nothing behind us but trees. I screamed as loud as I could.

Suddenly Matt burst through the door. It took one moment for him to assess the situation: Professor Clarke stretched out on top of me, one giant-sized paw trapping both my hands while the other gripped my hip; me, underneath him, bucking and screaming, jacket open, turtleneck pulled up.

Matt grabbed him by the back of his blazer and hauled him off me, slamming him into the wall opposite the couch. His eyes blazed as he faced him.

"What the fuck are you doing?" he roared.

"Now hold on, sir," Professor Clarke said, holding up his hands in mock surrender. He stood up and straightened himself to his full height—about an inch taller than Matt—stuck his nose in the air and wiped the dust off the arms of his blazer. I marveled at how cool he seemed, how indignant.

"I'm afraid you misunderstand the situation," he announced, still wiping at his arms. "She and I," he said, gesturing toward me, "have a mutual attraction."

He leaned down and zipped his fly. The impact of that gesture on Matt was immediate. His jaw tightened and I almost felt sorry for the professor—almost.

Matt punched him squarely in the face. Blood splattered everywhere, onto the couch, the mushroom-colored shag rug, the glass coffee table where my hot mug of Earl Grey still sat steaming. The professor slumped back onto the floor, silent and stunned, cradling his broken nose.

"Well, don't misunderstand this, you wanker," Matt spat. His fists were clenched at his sides and the veins in his neck rippled. "You ever lay a hand on her again and I will rip your fucking heart out. You got that?" Matt glowered while the professor cradled his nose with both hands.

"Stay the fuck away from her," he hissed. "Let's go." He reached for my hand. I stood up awkwardly, bumped into the table, and splashed tea onto the floor. Matt put his arm around me and opened the door.

"Are you okay?" he said, running his hands through his dark hair, traces of fury still evident on his face. "Did he hurt you?"

I started to cry. "I'm so sorry. I thought...I thought he

wanted to talk about my book. I'm such an idiot," I sobbed. "He just wanted to get me alone and attack me." I walked along the brick path as quickly as possible, head down against the cold, hurrying away from the professor's office and toward the busy street opposite the campus.

"Hey," he said, jogging to keep up with me. "It wasn't your fault." I turned suddenly and was wrapped in his arms, my nose pressed into his leather jacket.

"I was so stupid to think he cared about my work," I said, pulling away and covering my face with my hands.

Matt pried my palms from my eyes. "Alex, you're so talented. This had nothing to do with you. The guy's sick. You didn't do anything wrong. How were you supposed to know he was a fucking rapist?"

"I should have seen it coming," I sniffed.

"You're being ridiculous. He's an asshole who attacked you. You're a writer, a really good one. The two are not related. Do you hear me?" He unwrapped his scarf and, using a corner, gently brushed tears off my cheeks.

"Yeah…"

"I mean it. Say it."

"They're not related." I repeated woodenly.

"No, the whole thing: 'Professor Clarke is a twisted prick. I am a talented writer. The two are not related.'"

"Matt, come on—"

"I'm serious. You can't let this derail you. Say it."

"Do I have to?"

"Say it."

"All right, all right. He's a twisted prick."

"Go on," Matt nodded.

"I'm a talented writer."

"Mm hm," he nodded. "And the two?"

"Are not related," I finished. I felt a sense of resolve at the end of the sentence despite the bruising on my wrists and the fucked-up scene that had just played out and the adrenaline still coursing through my veins.

"Okay," he said. "Now that that's settled, do you want

to call the police?"

"Can I do it later? I just want to go home."

"Whatever you want," he said, reaching up to hail a cab. "You're safe now."

RESTLESS IN L.A.
Mommy Musings. Stupid Confessions. Life.
Posted by Anonymous

Gorging on My Own Stupid Behavior

I recently spent a night alone in a hotel. It was good to have some time to reflect on what the hell is going on. I mean, what am I doing? As I tried to take an honest emotional inventory, one thing became clear: I care way too much about what other people think of me. I've spent hours of my life wondering if this woman from my neighborhood or that woman whose daughter is in my daughter's class likes me, approves of me, or says nasty things about me when I'm not there. The worst part is I don't even like the people I'm so concerned about liking me. How stupid is that? And I'm particularly embarrassed to admit that I put myself into situations—repeatedly— where I don't feel good. It's like going on an eating binge and knowing I shouldn't and yet, getting a certain thrill out of treating myself badly and watching myself self-destruct as I stuff my face. I put myself in situations with people who I know make me feel small and I watch myself squirm, feeling unwanted and uncomfortable, and yet there's been a part of me that delights in the self-flagellation of it all.

How many years do I have to sit at PTA meetings before I accept the fact I do not fit in with the power-hungry, stay-at-home mothers who—even though they begged me to be involved—really don't want me in their closed coffee klatch? They go out to lunch, have dinner parties, spend afternoons entertaining each other's perfect children and I feel like shit because they never invite me and my flawed kids even though I know damn well that I wouldn't want to hang out with any of them, anyway. How many seasons do I have to sit in a beach chair wishing the earth would open and swallow me up as I listen to the coach publicly harangue my son for not being "coachable?" What does it take for me to realize that soccer is not a good sport for my son or for me? I am sick and tired of gorging on my own stupid behavior. I'm not sure how this relates to the affair I'm now consciously having, not by "accident," or by "alcohol," or by anything other than by choice. I know it's unacceptable and wrong and, oh my god, the looks and finger-points I'd get if I were found out—but somehow I don't fucking care.

CHAPTER 14: IT WILL RAIN

It was Tuesday. I chose my clothes carefully: the red lacy Victoria's Secret bra and matching thong underwear I'd just purchased, jeans, and casual blue blouse with sandals. I washed and conditioned my hair, took extra time putting on my makeup, and threw a clean pair of underwear, a powder compact, and mascara in my purse for later. I plugged my iPod into the car stereo and listened to Bruno Mars as I drove to LAX to pick up Matt. *It Will Rain* had been my favorite Bruno song for months but today, as I drove to the airport, the part about how nothing could "save me"—no religion, no amount of prayer—seemed to burrow into my heart.

I was way too far gone for saving and I knew it. I'd walked down this path that I knew was wrong and nothing could change that, nothing. I didn't even know if I wanted to be saved. I thought about the decision I'd made ten days ago: this affair was happening. And it dawned on me how many smaller decisions grew out of that—whether or not to pick Matt up, how much time to spend with him, what days we'd meet—decision after decision, each one an opportunity to make a different choice. Even now, I could pull away from the curb and drive off—I could leave and not go through with this. I sat in my car, eyes glued to the doors, mulling over my options, when I saw Matt stroll through the sliding glass doors pulling a black weekender and carrying a laptop in a messenger bag under his shoulder. I watched as he scanned the curb. His eyes lit up when he spotted me.

"Hey," he said, as he got into the car and slid his arm around my waist. He closed the door before he leaned over and kissed me full on the mouth. The feel of his soft lips and the scent of his skin made me edgy. I checked the rearview mirror and merged into the oncoming traffic exiting the airport.

"I was afraid you might not be here," he confessed.

"The thought did cross my mind..."

"And?"

"This isn't New York, Matt. L.A. taxi service sucks."

He laughed and his face lit up as he reached over and grabbed my hand. I found myself smiling too. The 405 was jammed so we had plenty of time to talk as we crawled toward the hotel. He told me about the action comedy he was working on. It was about two out-of-work actors who inadvertently got involved in a bank heist. As he described the convoluted storyline and the complexity of the crash scenes, he joked about the on-set antics of the cast and crew and made me laugh with his descriptions of the action stunts.

"There's nothing Hollywood likes better than a 'sure thing' and big action films draw an audience. That's why everything today feels like a sequel."

"Well, that's how you get those mega-budgets, right? I read the Entertainment section."

He shook his head and chuckled. "Yep, big budgets are good. Small films, the kind that have to be made, rarely have any money to make them." He stared out the window for a moment then added, "Car crashes definitely pay the bills."

While I kept my eyes on the freeway, edging ever closer

to the hotel, Matt told me about his boys. He described how they'd decided to build a rocket ship the previous weekend and how excited they'd been during the planning stages but their enthusiasm waned when they realized the difficulty of the task.

"Teddy freaked out when he realized they weren't going to break Earth's gravitational pull," Matt laughed. "But Reed, being one minute older, acted as if he'd known all along. I could see how heartbroken they both were and I tried to get them into building just for the sake of it, but they didn't buy it." He shook his head and added that it made him happy just to see them working together.

"I can relate to that," I agreed, thinking about the occasions when I witnessed my three kids getting along. Even if there were few, it was a great feeling watching them build a pillow fort in the family room or have a splash contest out in the pool.

I pulled into the valet while Matt went to check in. I rarely thought about Matt as a father or a husband. He seemed to exist only inside the sphere of a hotel room at the Redbury but today, he'd revealed more of himself: filmmaker, funnyman, parent. Our conversation helped normalize the afternoon—as if it were normal for me to pick up an ex-boyfriend at the airport and drive him to a hotel where I planned to, well, I knew what I planned to do—but our conversation about his work and family relaxed me and made me forget. Now that he was checking in, I suddenly felt uncomfortable. It was four o'clock on a Tuesday. What was I doing at the Redbury Hotel? I warned myself to be careful; it wouldn't be impossible to bump into someone I knew. I waited in the lobby until Matt got the key and followed without acknowledging him into the elevator. Two people entered behind us, and it wasn't until we exited on his floor and the doors closed behind us that I breathed a sigh of relief. We walked silently to his room and he opened the door. He set his luggage on the desk and kicked his shoes off then turned to me.

"You all right?" he asked, pulling off his dark blue sweatshirt and tossing it onto a chair.

"Yeah. I guess so."

"You're so quiet."

"I suddenly feel weird," I said with a shrug, sitting down awkwardly on the edge of the queen-sized bed.

"What is it? What's wrong?" He sat down next to me and reached for my hand.

"I don't know. It's just the two, or actually three, times we've...been together, they weren't...premeditated. The first time, well, you know how that happened, and the second time—I thought we were going to talk—and you know how that went..." I let out a nervous laugh.

"And you feel awkward now?" he asked, scooting closer to me and still holding my hand.

"Yes, I guess I do," I confessed. "It's like, I know you have a life outside of this room and this...uh...relationship...and yet we're driving here and I know we're going to..."

He sat on the bed and waited, letting me stutter along.

"Feel free to say something," I finally said.

"I was sitting in a meeting on the thirty-third floor of a building on the Upper East Side, just sort of staring out the window at the East River when I realized the project being pitched sounded just like every other project I'd done lately. So I started to flip through an old email—my boys download these games and I have an old email I use to make sure they aren't bleeding me dry—and what do I find?" He rubbed his thumb across my knuckles as we sat facing each other on the bed. "A message from Facebook—which I rarely use—with a friend request. It said, *Alex Hoffman wants to be friends.* Well, it only took one glance at your picture to figure out who Alex 'Hoffman' was."

"You were in a meeting?"

"Yes. A very long and boring one. Where were you?"

"I was at the soccer field. I kept looking behind me to make sure none of the soccer moms knew I'd friended my old boyfriend."

He laughed and let go of my hand. "Look, Alex, I don't know how we got here but we're here. And I think it would be pretty strange if neither one of us had any reservations. We don't have to do anything. Do you want to leave?"

"No," I said. "Do you want me to?"

"No."

He got up and walked into the bathroom. I could hear the sound of running water as he returned.

"Let's take a bath. Come here." He took me by the hand and led me to the bathroom. The main light was turned off and only the small face mirror glowed faintly from the corner.

"Why don't you undress?" he asked gently.

"Come on."

"Shh," he answered as he sat down on the edge of the tub watching me. "Just do it, Alexandra."

Oh, why did he have to call me Alexandra? And how was this supposed to make me feel less awkward? Stripping off my clothes while he watched? What was I doing? But I wasn't going to let myself go down that road because deep inside, I knew why I was there. So I stopped thinking and analyzing and second-guessing and did what he said: I slipped out of my sandals, unbuttoned my blouse, and undid the zipper of my jeans. I pulled them off very slowly, never looking away from his face. His eyes narrowed and glowed in the dim light like a hungry wolf. I will remember that look for a hundred lifetimes, I thought to myself.

"Red lace, Alexandra," he tilted his head and smiled. "Brings back memories."

"I didn't know if you'd remember," I said.

"I remember everything."

I stood there in my red lace lingerie and was

transported back to Amsterdam on a dark afternoon in a small lingerie shop: the thick curtain, the leather stool, the pretty blonde girl, and Matt and me behind a curtain.

"Go on," he said, nodding approvingly from his seat on the side of the tub.

I unhooked the red lace bra and let it drop to the floor. I carefully lowered my thong and stepped out of it until I stood naked before him. His eyes followed me up and down. Was Little Red Riding Hood really afraid of the big, bad wolf or excited by him—or both? I must have a thing for wolves because I was suddenly reminded of a favorite expression of an old college friend from Italy. "*Bocca al lupe*," she'd tell me before an exam, which literally meant, "In the wolf's mouth," and was an Italian's way of saying, good luck. She taught me to reply, "*Crepi*," which meant, "He dies," rather than *grazie* or thank you. Only killing the wolf brought good luck, I noted wryly. I caught a glimpse of myself in the bathroom mirror and silently whispered, *Bocca al lupe* to my reflection.

The tub was full and Matt reached over and turned off the faucet. He was in a shirt and jeans and I was naked and self-conscious.

"Your turn," I volunteered, wanting us to be on equal footing.

"Not yet," he said, "turn around." He gestured with his pointer finger in a circular motion. He stared at me as I slowly turned from front to back to front again, totally vulnerable and exposed.

"Matt, come on—"

"Quiet," he commanded, his eyes fixed on my body. "Come here," he said as he stood up from his seated position on the edge of the tub. He pulled me to him so we were facing each other. I thought he was going to kiss me but he didn't. He put his hands lightly on my shoulders and raised an eyebrow.

"On my knees?" I whispered, my heart pounding.

"Only if you want to." He waited.

"I—" I couldn't answer.

I knelt on the cold marble tile of the bathroom and put him in my mouth. He rocked back and forth, straining against the back of my throat. I wrapped my hand around his jeans, driving him deeper into me, tasting his salty skin. He moved slowly, deliberately until he reached down, tangled his fingers into my hair, and pushed me forward into him, forcing himself deeper and deeper into my mouth. I wanted to engulf him, swallow him whole, suck him dry until he emptied himself into me. I heard him moan and would have moaned myself if my mouth wasn't already occupied. This was what I wanted, what I needed. How did he know?

He pulled away suddenly, lifted me to my feet, and turned me around so I leaned over the vanity. He cupped my breasts with his hands and slid into me from behind. Our faces were reflected in the mirror as we stared into each other's eyes and moved back and forth toward our peak. Me, naked, breasts covered by his hands, his fingers, and Matt, T-shirt, jeans puddled at his ankles. He drove into me again and again and I took the full force and moaned out loud. I watched us in the mirror, his hands on my breasts, fingers rubbing my nipples, my hips thrusting back and forth in time with his. His green eyes never left mine. He seemed to be looking at me and into me at the same time. We kept up the pace, faster and faster. I could feel my release rising, the anticipation, the agony, the throbbing ache that longed to be satisfied. He held on to my hips with both hands and called to me, "Come on, go…"

I shook with the force of my orgasm and his.

"Oh god, that feels so good," I murmured.

He rested his head on my shoulder. I closed my eyes and felt his hair tickling my cheek. "Alex," he said, "you're incredibly beautiful. You know that, right?"

"Oh, please. I have a lot more lines than I used to." In the faint light, I pointed to my forehead and around my mouth. "I'm not the same girl."

"Have you looked at yourself lately?" He shook his head and spoke to me in the mirror, "Really looked at yourself?"

"Stop it. You're making me uncomfortable." I tried to wiggle away from him but he was pressed up behind me and wouldn't let me escape. Even though the lights were low, I was naked and he was half dressed and staring at me. It was one thing when we were having sex and under the influence of desire, but afterward, it was something else entirely. It felt like an examination.

"Stop wiggling and just look."

I looked, reluctantly at first and then with more detail. I saw the lines around my hazel eyes and the darkness underneath them. I stared at my cheeks—were they slightly hollowed out?—and my forehead. My light brown hair was a mess and my lipstick was gone but I saw a light in my eyes. Was that a trick from the lamp? Or was it something else? My eyes swept over my breasts and my stomach. I noticed the bulge that never quite went away after kid number two and, of course, there were small scar lines from a hernia repair. I saw my hips and how rounded they were and my arms—they looked way looser than I remembered—and my shoulders, and then I looked back into my eyes and into Matt's. His chin rested on my shoulder, watching me appraise myself, taking survey of everything I'd lost since the first time we were lovers.

"You're luminous," he said into the mirror.

"You're crazy," I said. "Let me go."

He turned me around and kissed me. "You don't realize who you are."

"What does that mean? God, you sound like my life coach."

"You have a life coach?" He took my hand and pulled me toward the tub.

"I do. Her name's Lark."

He climbed in first and opened his legs for me to lie

inside. I stepped over the porcelain rim and folded myself into the circle of Matt's arms, resting my back against his chest, my head perfectly relaxed on the slope of his shoulder.

"Tell me about her."

I described Lark and her sayings and her intuition and her amazing posture. He laughed as I told him about her giant breasts and her hugs, but then I explained how important she was to me and how I'd been dodging her ever since things between us heated up.

"You can't trust her?" he asked.

"No, I can. I absolutely can. It's just that...well, I haven't wanted to talk about it."

"Alex, at some point, we probably should—talk about it."

"Not now, okay?"

"Okay. But at some point, we're going to have to."

***

"I've got to get home and check on my kids," I said, sitting on the bed in the plush white terrycloth hotel robe and taking two more bites of the burger Matt ordered. After the sex and the long, luxurious soak, we both were starving. Matt had room service bring up two beers and two burgers with sides of fruit. "I should at least feed you," he'd joked.

"I am hungry," I said.

He moved toward me wearing nothing but the white towel he'd wrapped around his hips after our bath. He leaned over the bed where I sat munching my burger and kissed me on the neck. "I have meetings all day tomorrow and then a breakfast meeting in the morning. I made my flight for Friday because I was hoping you could steal away Thursday afternoon." He walked over to the balcony door and opened it. Cool air poured into the room.

The days were easy for me. Jason was at work and

Maria often picked up the kids from school when I was running errands or having school-related meetings and doctor's appointments. No one kept tabs on me during the day or knew where I was or what I was doing so I didn't have to create an elaborate lie or cover up.

"Sounds good. I'd have until maybe six o'clock," I studied his bare chest and hips wrapped in the towel.

"My meeting's at ten. Can you meet me in Santa Monica at 12:30? There's something I want to show you."

"You and I are going to hang out outside this hotel room?"

"Yes. Unless that's a problem?"

"Well...I just, you know..." I pulled on my jeans and blouse before dashing into the bathroom to check my makeup. When I returned to the bedroom to slip into my sandals, Matt was sitting at the desk.

"Look, we'll arrive separately and we won't act like...we're involved. I'm sure we won't bump into anyone you know."

"It's important?"

"To me, yes."

"Okay. Tell me where I'm going." I had no idea where in Santa Monica he wanted to take me or why but I grabbed a pen and a piece of paper and jotted down the address. I threw it into my purse and knelt down to kiss him goodbye.

He looked at me and I felt that strange synchronicity between us, as if we were wired to the same frequency. Lark once told me that people vibrated at different levels and that we're most comfortable with people whose vibrations matched our own. I couldn't say what frequency Matt was on or myself; I just knew we matched.

He held the door open for me as I started to leave but still had hold of my hand. I boomeranged back into his arms and he kissed me once more on the mouth. I lingered there in front of the door wanting the kiss to last just a second longer, wanting to stand inside the warmth of his arms for just another moment and then, finally, pried free from his grasp and left.

As I drove away, I was flying. I felt every pore of my newly-washed skin. Even though my mind immediately began to worry, I couldn't deny I was satisfied from the inside out, from deep inside my core to deep between my legs. I smiled as I listened to Bruno croon all the way home.

RESTLESS IN L.A.
Mommy Musings. Stupid Confessions. Life.
Posted by Anonymous

Unbelievable

The first time I thought I could justify it as an impetuous moment or mistake. The second time it was for sorrow. The third time, for truth. And now what? How many times could I bear to repeat the same deception?

I loved my husband, of that I was sure. He and I were determined to have a happy ending. We dealt with our kids as best we could and we looked for the good in our lives. Of course we had problems; everybody does, but we rubbed each other's backs at night as we lay together, dozing. We made a good team. Until we became strangers to each other.

I could barely think of a worse person to have an affair than me. I was already on meds for anxiety and coffee for energy. Between my coaching sessions and blogging about parenthood, I tried to find "my voice," tried to come out a little bit as myself. And now I had a secret that no one could know.

It was just unbelievable to me that I was behaving this way and yet every time I got an email to my new account, I felt the thrill. I knew it was from *him* and I could barely wait to open it. When I was alone, I'd daydream about our last time together, trying to remember every detail of how it transpired; running through the paces of the night. I don't know how I'm going to manage this or what the plan is. I just know that when I'm with him, I feel comfortable in my own skin.

CHAPTER 15: EMERGENCY CONTACT

When I walked in the door, I knew immediately something was wrong

"Where have you been?' Jason asked. He was standing in front of the kitchen island in pressed pants and a white dress shirt with staggered blue stripes. His briefcase was carelessly thrown across the entry table as if he'd hurried in from the car. I scanned the house and saw the boys watching TV out of the corner of my eye. There were no signs of Natalie or Maria. My face flushed and my heart pounded in my ears as I approached him. From the look in his eyes and the tone of his voice, it was obvious he was angry.

"I—I was at a school meeting," I said unsteadily. "What's going on? Where's Maria?" I could feel myself whither under his steely gaze.

"I've been trying to call you for over an hour," he said. "Ryan had a shitty afternoon—he got upset and shoved some kid on his team, and the coach wanted to speak to a *parent*. I kept calling you, and Maria texted you and no one could find you. Don't you check your phone? The coach wants to talk to you."

"Jason, I'm sorry," I sputtered. I reached into the brown leather purse hanging off my shoulder to search for my phone and my fingers closed around something silky. I turned my head to peer into the depths of my purse and my eyes nearly popped out of my head. A pair of silk underwear lay half-balled up next to a tube of black mascara and my leather wallet. I grabbed the phone and snapped the bag shut so quickly, I almost dropped it.

"My—my phone must have died," I said, trying to hold my voice steady and not looking at Jason. I could feel myself break into a sweat as I checked the screen. I'd put it on vibrate mode and forgotten to switch it back. "I had no idea you were looking for me." I shoved the phone into my back pocket.

"Your phone died? Why didn't you charge it? I mean, c'mon Alex, I can't be the emergency contact." He was pissed that he had to leave an urgent meeting because of the kids. He loved them, would do anything for them, but he was usually unavailable.

"I'm really sorry," I repeated, my heart still racing. I flipped my hair off my shoulders, fingering the ends to see if they were damp. I fought off the compulsion to smooth down my jeans and the creases in my blouse, to rid myself of any remnants—real or imagined—of where I had been and what I had been doing. I hadn't planned on seeing Jason for hours, and not like this. Not face to face in the middle of the kitchen. I brushed off my arms and wiped my hands on my jeans.

"I've got to be able to fi—Jesus, you're jumpy—what's wrong with you?" he asked.

"I—I—can you tell me happened? Why did he get so upset?" I glanced around and spotted Ryan splayed out on the family room floor watching *Sponge Bob* with Ben.

"Who knows?" he answered. "Call the coach. I have his number." He reached into the pocket of his slacks and slapped a business card onto the table. "Maria took Natalie to get some dinner. What time is it? Shit." He looked down and noticed a spot on the diamond pattern of his tie. He untied the knot at the neck and pulled it off roughly. "I have to get back—oh, and can you drop this off at the cleaners?" I took the tie and turned to him.

"We should talk to Ryan." As anxious as I was to regroup after the afternoon I had, I needed Jason's help. "Can't the meeting go on without you? We should talk to him together."

But Jason was already at the entryway, grabbing his briefcase. "Can you handle this, please? If we don't get these details ironed out, the deal will never close. I'm sorry, Al. I. Have. To. Go."

He stopped at the family room. "Bye, guys," he waved. I watched him walk over to Ryan. He bent over and laid one arm over the shoulder of his pajamas. "It's okay, buddy, you're working hard. You're doing okay, Ry."

"No I'm not, Dad." Ryan broke free from the pull of the TV and rolled over. He pushed his sandy blond hair out of his eyes and looked up into his father's face. I watched as their blue eyes met and Ryan kicked his heels against the white shag carpet. Jason hovered over him expectantly and then Ryan blinked a few times and said, "All of my friends hate me."

And that's how it was with Ryan. He could be so damn frustrating he'd make me want to bang my head against a wall, and then he'd break my heart with just a phrase.

"That's not true. It was a rough day. That's it, buddy," Jason said and squeezed his shoulder. Our eyes met as he walked to the door as if to say, *It's killing me, too,* and then he was gone.

The minute the door closed, Ryan melted down. He refused to talk about what happened. When I tried to broach the subject calmly, he screamed at me. After he ran off and slammed his bedroom door so hard it cracked the jamb, I made him stay in his room for the night. I knew he felt guilty. I knew he was angry with himself. I just couldn't find the right words to soothe him but I knew he treated me no worse than he treated himself. That was what cut me inside—not the altercation, not the impulsivity, but the self-loathing. Even in the middle of his meltdown, I thought about how much I loved my son. Would he ever believe it? Would he ever learn to accept himself? And how could he when Jason and I obviously didn't?

I leaned against Ryan's door, listening to the sounds of his shouting and crying and considered the endless parade of therapeutic interventions we'd attempted. I'd never give up, I'd always keep trying, but I wished—every day since he was little—that I could make his life easier, that I could somehow fix whatever wasn't right. I walked to the kitchen and poured myself a glass of Cabernet. What kind of mother can't help her own child? Maria's oft-repeated belief floated into my mind, "God never gives us more than we can handle." In my case, I couldn't help but wonder if She overestimated.

During the next hour, Maria came back and brought the boys orange chicken, their favorite. I thanked her profusely and said good night and then helped Ben finish his math and spelling pages. After he brushed his teeth and got into bed, I went to say goodnight to him. His door was half closed as I approached but I heard him talking so I peeked in and listened. He was lying in front of his big, mirrored closet doors, his blue and white racecar pillow in one hand and SpongeBob the Pillow Pet in the other. As I peered through the crack in the door I overheard racecar pillow tell SpongeBob that our neighbor's cat died last week. Then SpongeBob said, "Is that why your mom's face looks so sad?" Racecar pillow was quiet for a second then answered, "I don't like cats." I opened the door and walked straight over to Ben.

"You okay, Benny Boy?" I asked, lifting him onto his bed and tucking SpongeBob and racecar pillow in next to him.

"I'm sleepy, Mommy. G'night," he yawned, nuzzling

his head into his pillow. I gave him a kiss and turned out the light. He was sound asleep before I left the room.

As I walked into Nat's room, I noticed Maria had left her freshly folded clothes on her bed before she left. Nat was lying on top of her yellow and white polka-dotted sheets, three pillows tucked under her neck. Her dark hair was pulled into a ball on the top of her head.

"Good night, sweetie." I lifted her pile of newly washed clothes onto a desk chair and picked the turquoise-striped comforter off the floor. I shook it out and laid it over her while she ignored me and hummed along to her iPod.

"Mom," she said, popping her hot pink ear buds out of her ears and looking at me with a scowl. "All of my friends want to know what's wrong with *him*."

"Honey, you know your brother is doing the best he can. We're his family. We have to be there for him." I tucked in the edges of her comforter so it wouldn't fall off again.

"I wish my brother was normal," she said. "I hate when my friends see him freaking out. It's so embarrassing." She tossed her iPod onto her night table and began picking at a scab on her arm. When she looked up, I could see tears in her eyes. "I think they make fun of him."

"We all have challenges, Nat. Some people's may be more obvious than others but I can promise you no one is perfect—not even your friends." She looked at me and I sensed she was really listening. "Ryan is your brother and he always will be. How do you think it feels to be him?"

"I don't know."

"Do you think he feels good all the time?"

"I don't know, Mom."

"Well, what do you think?"

"I think it's…probably hard."

"Yeah," I said, smoothing down the sheets. "I think it's probably hard too." I sat down on the edge of her bed and looked at her. "He really loves you, you know."

"I love him too," she sighed. "Sometimes he's funny

and even nice, like when he gave me the Tootsie Roll bank that he won at Chuck E. Cheese. But then he's so mean and he hits Ben and slams his door and starts freaking out and it just—it just sucks!"

"I know."

"What's wrong with him? Why won't you tell me?"

"Nat, you know he has ADHD—"

"Well, some of my friends have ADHD and they don't act like that."

"Well, he's got other issues too. I don't know what you want me to say."

She started to pick at her arm scab again. I watched as her nail dug into the freshly irritated spot. "Can I tell you something?" she asked, "and you promise you won't get mad?"

I nodded and moved her hand off the reddening sore.

"I know this is really mean...and I wouldn't want anything bad to happen to him or anything...but sometimes...I just wish...Ryan wasn't part of this family." She looked up and the tears she'd been holding back came streaming down her face. "I know I'm a really bad person to say that," she continued as her eyes squinted shut and her lips puckered in a tight downward curve that quivered, "but I think that sometimes."

"Oh, Nat," I said, putting my arms around her. She laid her cheek on my shoulder and I felt her shake as a wet patch of tears collected on my blouse. "That doesn't make you a bad person, honey." I stroked the side of her face as long as she let me.

"Yes it does. You're just saying that—" She pulled away and rubbed her comforter against her eyes.

"No it doesn't. You love your brother. And it's okay to feel angry sometimes. And even to wish he wasn't here. It really is okay." She scooted beneath her comforter but I reached over and took her hand. "I know you love him, Nat. And he knows it, too." I could feel the tears gathering in my own eyes. "Sometimes, as a mom, I wish I could

196

make your life perfect—all of yours, but I can't."

She nodded.

"We all do the best we can. You, me, Daddy, Ben, and Ryan, too. Sometimes that just has to be enough. You know what I mean?" I leaned down and kissed her forehead then rested my cheek on the top of her head.

"Love you, Mom," she whispered as she rolled over and closed her eyes.

"Love you, too, sweetie."

I saved Ryan for last. The therapist advised us to let him calm down from an emotional episode in a safe space. When I walked into his room, he was tucked into bed. I could see the sleeve of his pajamas peeking out of the covers. He was nearly asleep, which was a miracle given that insomnia was a major side effect of the medication, but these episodes took a lot out of him. I noticed he'd lost more weight—another side effect. I sighed as I leaned over to kiss my boy in his dreamy state.

"Mommy? I love you."

"How you feeling, honey?"

"I'm tired."

"Okay, Ry. We'll talk in the morning. I love you, too."

"Mommy?" he asked, as I was walking out.

"Yes?"

"Do you think Trevor will ever be my friend again?"

I stood at the door and looked at Ryan cuddled under his plaid comforter. "I don't know, honey."

"Good night," he whispered. "Come check on me later."

"I will. Now go to sleep." I tiptoed out of his room and closed the door softly.

In the hallway, I stopped and listened to the hush of near silence in the house. I could make out the soft hum of the air conditioner and the low shushing of a red-eye heading east out of Los Angeles. I heard the faint rustling of covers and various yawns and chortles of three children slowly falling asleep. I stood in the hallway, one hand pressed against the wall, and was overcome with the infinite preciousness of my children. The beauty and the weight of it was staggering. There was no way I would hurt this family. My kids needed me too much. I didn't have the kind of life where I could go AWOL—anything could happen. There was too much at stake. Ryan needed me and I wasn't there. I couldn't risk that happening again. And Nat and Ben needed me, too. Not to mention that I almost got caught. Was that what I wanted? For my husband, who I loved, to discover I was having an affair? I'd almost had a heart attack tonight—the underwear in my purse—it was too much. I didn't know how but it had to stop.

***

The next day, I took Natalie to dance and Ben to karate, and then shadowed Ryan at his soccer pizza party. In those brief moments of solitude between the ringing phone, incoming texts, gardener needing a check, someone's teacher needing a permission slip signed, and the pool man wanting a new key, I tried to consider the Matt Issue. There must be a way to silence the conflicting voices in my head; I just hadn't found it yet. And it was hard to think while juggling the hundred and one tasks always on my radar. On the way to the pharmacy to pick up Ryan's medication refills, the phone rang. It was Laurie. I watched her number blink on the dash screen several times and then picked up.

"Hey Laur, I've been so busy—"

"Are you alone?" she asked.

"Yeah, I'm in the car running err—"

"What the fuck, Alex?"

"Huh?"

"Oh give me a break. You've been avoiding me. I haven't talked to you in days. You're seeing him again, aren't you?"

"I—"

"Don't lie to me. Lie to Jason. Lie to *him*, for all I care. But don't you dare lie to me. You slept with him again, didn't you? I already know you did so you might as well admit it."

She was a mind reader. Always had been, where I was concerned. Last month, I smoked a quick cigarette in the back yard and called to see when she was picking me up for a movie. All I said was, "Hello?" to which she responded, "Are you smoking again?" Maybe we were identical twins in a past life? Who knew, but it was pointless to lie to her.

"Yes."

"Yes to which part?"

"To all of it." I sighed. "What do you want me to say?"

"I don't want you to say anything. I just want to know you're okay. Are you okay?"

"I don't think so."

"What do you mean?"

"I, I—do you really want to hear this?" I wanted to respect her friendship with Jason, her devotion to us as a couple, and the fact that I was adding to secrets she now was sworn to keep from Evan. She generally told him everything, but not in this case.

"Just tell me," she said.

"I don't know where to begin but this time, it's really over."

"Oh, Alex."

I detailed my time MIA and how I'd missed the call from Ryan's coach and how upset I was with myself and how damn close I had been to getting caught. I told her about the comment Ryan made to Jason about his friends, and how Natalie confessed wishing he wasn't part of our family, and how confused I felt about what I was doing. I could feel the agony rising, but I swallowed it. I didn't expect—or want—Laurie's sympathy. I pulled into the pharmacy parking lot and searched for a space.

"Why did you let it get this far?" she asked. I could feel the severity of her stare through the phone. "Is it the sex?"

"I—I don't know. I thought I could figure it out."

"Figure what out?" she asked.

"What's going on. Look, Laurie, I don't expect you to understand—"

"Understand? Alex, listen to yourself! There is no *understanding*. You're on a crash course to disaster and I'm too invested in your family not to say something." She paused and then added in a softer voice, "Don't you get it? This can't possibly end well."

"I know. Jesus, I know. He's married, too. He's got two kids, for god's sake. I don't know how I got into this." I pulled into a spot and turned off the car, leaning my head against the steering wheel and listening to my best friend chastise me.

"Well, you've got to get yourself out of it—and fast. I'm worried about you," she said. "You're not thinking clearly."

I couldn't help but turn that over in my mind. *You're not thinking clearly.* She was right or I wouldn't be in this situation but then, why? Why did things seem clear for the first time in a long time? I sat in my car, shaking my head and wishing it made sense.

"Please, be careful." She paused and then added, "You've got a lot on the line."

"I know. I really do know. And I'm sorry to put you in this position. That's why I didn't call you back, why I ignored your messages. I know how you feel about keeping secrets."

"Stop it," she said. "You're right. I don't like keeping things from Evan, and I usually don't. But in this case, I have to. I may not like it but I'll do it. You're my best friend, Alex. You can always tell me the truth."

But the truth was that he was constantly on my mind, just beneath the surface of my thoughts. Maybe it was because we never broke up? There was never closure; our relationship was a loose end, a page left unturned. Over the years, I'd tried not to wonder what if? When those questions came knocking on the door—and from time to time, they had—I'd become a suburban home on lockdown: doors and windows shut, blinds drawn, alarm armed. But when I found the journal, all the what ifs I'd trained myself to ignore came dancing in a back door— and they paraded around me, tantalizing me with visions of roads not taken. How I wished I'd burned the journal, taken a match to it twenty years ago, and burned it to ashes. How could I have known what a Pandora's box it would become?

But I didn't tell Laurie any of this. I didn't tell her how, with one fell swoop, or click, in my case, I'd released all of my long-suffering what ifs and there was no way to lock them down now. I didn't tell her how tortured I felt, wondering what might have been, or that now, inside myself, it was like a chaotic Mardi Gras. My unfulfilled dreams paraded up and down the streets, throwing beaded necklaces from purple crepe-papered floats, and lifting their shirts, gleefully exposing themselves. I walked among them, dazed and confused, wondering, what the hell happened?

***

Thursday came and I was supposed to rendezvous with Matt in Santa Monica. Jason had an early meeting so I dropped the kids off at school and was home by eight-fifteen to meet Lark. I hadn't seen her for weeks. I didn't want to see her that morning, either, but I'd run out of excuses. Plus, she'd emailed me that she sensed I needed her.

"I've been getting strong messages about you, Alex," she said.

"I'm sorry. I'm so busy. Can we do a forty-five-minute session today?" I wanted to make it fast and didn't think I could handle my usual hour. She agreed, but only after she called in the Light, asked the Universe to guide her service, called to her spirit guides, and made me sit while we did a one-minute peace meditation. I was emotionally exhausted before we even started.

"What's your intention for our session today?" she asked.

"Clarity," I said. "I'd really like to get some clarity on some issues I've been having."

"With your writing?" she asked.

"Um, yeah, that's right," I said.

"So how's your blog going?"

"Good, it's all good…" I answered lamely.

"That's great. It sounds like you're sharing yourself."

"Sharing myself? What does that mean?" I noticed her huge rack was barely restrained by her tie-dyed tank top. I could feel my anxiety rising and tried to focus on the wood tile she wore around her neck. "What do you mean, Lark?"

"What do you think I mean?"

"I have no idea. All I know is I'm doing my best, okay? I know you want me to be authentic, you've been telling me that for months, whatever that means."

"You seem really triggered," she said.

"Well, what does it mean to be 'authentic?' I write, okay? I try to 'share my truth' but you know what? I'm not sure that's such a great idea—I mean, doesn't that depend on what your truth is? Doesn't it depend on the kind of person you are?"

All of my buttons were pushed and I could feel myself ready to explode. I needed something concrete, not her spiritual mumbo jumbo. I picked up a throw pillow from the floor and gripped it like a line thrown to a drowning man. My knuckles ached but I needed her to understand.

"Don't you see? Some truths are better left hidden— there's no point in digging too deep—don't you get it?" I was nearly shouting. "What's the point of finding yourself if you can't stand what you've found? I mean, once you start poking around, anything's possible. What if you find you're not who you thought you were? Huh? What then? What if you find you can't trust yourself and you don't know what you're doing and the only time you seem to feel anything at all is when you're fucking your ex-boyfriend in a hotel room—oh shit." I clamped my hand over my mouth but it was too late.

"The old boyfriend?" Lark asked calmly. "From Facebook?"

"Yes," I said miserably. "Please don't tell anyone."

"Of course. Our sessions are confidential. You know that. Do you want to talk about it?"

She turned to me, her curly, red hair falling over the side of her head in an escape from her off-center ponytail. I noticed a curly strand easing itself into a green spot of morning kale juice that had dripped onto the lid of her juice cup. "I think," she spoke slowly as if measuring each syllable, "this has needed to come out for a while."

"What has?" I pressed my head against the throw pillow and closed my eyes. I was spent.

"Your feelings."

"I don't know how I feel," I mumbled. "It's not like I'm miserable..." I stared out the door at the clear blue water of our freshly-skimmed pool.

"Can you describe a time that you felt happy?"

"With Matt? Or in my regular life?"

"In your regular life."

"I don't know...some mornings...after Jason and the kids are gone...I clear all the dishes and wipe down the kitchen counters..."

"Uh huh."

"And I scrub off all the pieces of cereal and grease from the turkey bacon and the sticky blotches of juice. And after I clean the entire counter and no one is home, I sit there and notice how spotless it is—there's not a single speck of dirt or food or anything on the entire counter; it just gleams. When I look at the countertop and there isn't a single crumb on it, well, that's my moment of perfection and I feel…" I took a deep breath and shrugged, "happy."

She leaned in so that the arm with the Chinese characters rubbed against me. She didn't say anything right away, just sat and breathed with a peaceful expression on her face. I breathed with her. "What does happy feel like, Alex? Go into your heart…"

Tears sprang to my eyes. "I can't trust my heart," I said. "I found something I never expected and now I don't know what to do."

"What is it?" she asked. "What did you find?"

"All this time, I thought it was me. I thought there was something wrong with me. But I found out, it isn't me. There's just something wrong. And I'm trying to figure out what it is."

She sat with her hands in her lap and nodded.

"Look, Lark, I know you're not big into advice-giving, but do you have any for me? Anything at all? And please don't say the answers are inside me."

There was silence in the room and then she said, "Sometimes, it's difficult to tune into our own Inner Knowing. Sometimes, all we can do is surrender and ask the Universe to show us the way."

"Oh, that's easy," I said, let down. "I knew you'd say that."

"The hard part," she said, polishing each word like a precious stone, "isn't the asking. It's having the courage to hear the answer."

RESTLESS IN L.A.
Mommy Musings. Stupid Confessions. Life.
Posted by Anonymous

Cosmic Restlessness
How can I find what I don't know is missing? Is there a way to treat a constant sense of restlessness? Whatever I'm

doing, I constantly feel I should be doing something else. I've known something was wrong but I haven't wanted to look too closely at it. Up until now, I thought maybe if kept my head down and kept moving—kept volunteering, kept grocery shopping, kept driving the kids all around the planet, I wouldn't have to think about it.

That's why I refuse to do Yoga or meditate. I don't like to just 'be' because questions begin to arise, questions like, what do I really want? What does that even mean? I want what everyone wants, to know who I am and why I'm here, what my purpose is on the planet. Maybe I even hoped to discover something unusual and worthwhile and exciting about myself. Somehow, I feel like I've failed but I'm not sure I ever knew what I was supposed to succeed at. I thought I'd succeeded at the family thing—husband, kids, house—but apparently not. I just feel empty inside and desperately want to feel something.

CHAPTER 16: MISSING

I jumped in and out of the shower, threw on some eyeliner, lipstick, and mascara, pulled on a pair of snug jeans, a pale yellow top, and a gray wrap, and ran out the door. And, as Lark advised, I silently asked the Universe for guidance as I drove to Santa Monica. At a red light, I turned off the radio and rehearsed explaining my feelings to Matt out loud:

Matt, there's no question that something inside me responds to you. It always has. Maybe it always will. But I'm not that person anymore. The other day my son needed me and I wasn't there. That can't happen again—ever. My husband came home and could've caught me in a lie. I can't risk that. And neither can you. I know what I said the other day but we've got to stop this now, before it goes any further.

I was anticipating his possible responses when my cell phone rang. It was my neighbor. I reluctantly answered.

"Hi, it's Sara."

"Hey, Sara, what's up?" I wanted to keep it brief. I was pulling up in five minutes and needed to review the discussion in my mind one more time. My prepared speeches didn't go well, and this time, I needed to be sure I said what needed to be said.

"Can Vivian get a ride home from Maria today when she picks up Natalie?"

"No problem," I responded quickly.

"I need to talk to you about something else." Sara paused in her dramatic way.

"Yes?" I braced myself.

Sara and her daughter Vivian lived next door. The girls had been friends since preschool and I admired Sara for raising Viv on her own since her husband had walked out on them twelve days after she was born. She was a hardworking real estate agent and a devoted mother but she made me crazy. She seemed to know every detail of the intricacies of our eleven-year-old daughters' social lives. If you wanted to know who wasn't talking to whom, or what kids had a fight, or who went to the principal's office for using foul language, forget the kids—ask Sara. She constantly shared information with me about Natalie that I was certain my daughter wouldn't want me to know. And although I asked her repeatedly to leave me out of it, I was convinced it was a compulsion she couldn't help.

"I'm not getting involved," she began, firmly involving herself, "but Viv told me Natalie hasn't eaten lunch with her for weeks. Viv keeps asking Natalie to sit with her at the lunch tables but Natalie won't. I don't think the girls are friends anymore. And Natalie sits every day with the new girl and it really hurts Viv's feelings. And did you know Natalie told Viv she looked fat in her new yellow sundress? So now Viv won't even wear it! This has got to stop—"

"She said what?" I rubbed my now-aching temples.

She was breaking up but snippets of her voice wafted out from the speaker: "Her feelings...so upset...can't believe..."

"Sara, if you can hear me, I'm really sorry. I don't know why Natalie would say something like that. Our family's kind of going through a rough patch right now. I'll definitely talk to her and…I'm really sorry."

I heard her say, "Thank…much" and hung up.

I pulled into a parking lot near the beach and sat in my car in stunned silence. Maybe Natalie was acting out because she felt the added tension in the house? God knows I wasn't myself lately, Jason was hardly ever home, poor Ben was usually with Maria, and Ryan was…well, Ryan was Ryan. Nat needed me; that much was clear. I vowed to get her to talk to me more even if it meant flushing her iPod down the toilet.

I texted Matt that I'd arrived and looked around. At the end of the parking lot there was a modern building with glass walls and a sloping roof. I didn't know where I was. I felt jittery as if I'd drunk an extra cup of coffee that morning. Sara's call weighed on my mind and I wondered why Nat would purposefully hurt her friend. I locked the car and tried to focus on the conversation I was about to have with Matt: *I'm not that person anymore…my son needed me and I wasn't there…we've got to stop this now, before it goes any further.*

As I wandered toward the building, my phone vibrated with a text:

Go inside and knock on the first door to your left. I'm alone.

I followed his directions, pulled open two double-doors and entered into a bare lobby with a small desk and a standing lamp. I turned left and knocked on a narrow door. Matt opened it and I peered inside. The room was dark and I could barely make out what looked like a four-foot disk in the center of the room.

"Hey," I said. "Where are we?" He closed the door and took my hand in the dark.

"It's a camera obscura."

"A what?" I could barely make out his face in the blackness.

"It's basically a dark room with a hole in it. Check this out." He pulled me into the center of the room and put my hand on what felt like a steering wheel. "It's physics, Alex. Light travels in a straight line and when it passes through a small hole, the rays don't scatter but re-form, upside down, on a flat surface."

"What do you mean?" I'd wanted to get the talk over with as soon as possible but I was swept away in spite of myself by the dark room and the contraption in front of me. I turned the wheel back and forth as a three hundred and sixty degree view of palm trees, the clear blue sky of Santa Monica, even the ocean came into focus on a large disc in the center of the room. As my eyes adjusted, I watched Matt grasp the edge and slowly tilt it back and forth. The image of the ocean came into sharp focus.

"The wheel rotates a lens sticking out of the roof above us. What you're seeing is the view from this building reflected on the disc. It just happens to be an incredibly clear day."

"How'd you find out about this?" I asked. "I've lived in L.A. for years and never heard of it."

"Yeah, it's pretty wild. A friend told me about it. I've only been to a camera obscura once before—in Europe—and I thought you'd like it."

I turned the wheel back and forth and watched the image shift from ocean to sky and back to ocean again. Matt moved behind me and slipped his arms around my waist. I stood in the dark, feeling the pressure of his chest leaning into my back and studied the changing perspective. He went to one in Europe? I vaguely remembered him telling me about it.

"Was it in Scotland?" I asked.

"Yes," he said. "It was."

I stopped the wheel at the image of palm trees swaying in the breeze. The world felt upside down and off balance.. Was anything ever as it seemed?

"Can we go outside and talk?" I asked.

"Now?"

"Yeah. I have to get back earlier than I thought."

We walked out of the building and around the corner to a bench facing the ocean. I squinted my eyes as they adjusted to the daylight. Matt sat down next to me and we looked over the bluff at the afternoon surfers rising and falling with the strength of the late-day waves.

He reached into his pocket and pulled out a folded piece of notebook paper, fingering it gently before holding it up. "Do you remember this?" he asked, handing it to me.

I looked at the slightly yellowed paper and slowly unfolded it. I could hear the sound of seagulls squawking and cars driving by and voices floating up from the beach below. Somehow I knew what it was even before I opened it but my stomach still clenched as I scanned the faded numbers. It was The List.

The year we'd lived in London, Matt made a list of all the places, objets d'art, and cinematic masterpieces he wanted us to see together. He'd jotted them down furiously whenever he discovered some "essential" life experience that I'd missed. "I can't believe you've never seen this," he'd mumble to himself, or, "As a writer, this will blow your mind," or even, "Come on, Alex, do you live in a bubble? You've never been to—" and then grab his spiral notebook and scrawl it onto the list. I studied the frayed page, noting he'd numbered well into the fifties and that some of the items were checked off. But we never came close to finishing. It would have taken years. Now the yellowed paper fluttered between my fingers in the breeze coming off the Pacific Ocean.

"I know it's crazy," he said, his eyes bright, "but I kept it all these years." He gazed at the ocean and shrugged.

I held the page against my thigh as it rippled in the breeze. Listed after one of the numbers, *Camera obscura— Edinburgh* swam before my eyes. So many things we thought we'd do but never did.

"Why?" I asked, my voice catching in my throat. "Why did you save it?" I swallowed hard and tried not to give in to the tangle of emotions that were brewing in my chest.

"I just…never threw it away. I don't know why. Funny thing is, if I was making a new list, I wouldn't have any of that on it."

"You wouldn't?" I asked, surprised. "Where would you want us to go?"

"Nowhere," he said. "Here is good enough."

I stared at his face and then back at the paper. I noticed that number fourteen, a quick scribble of *Van Gogh Museum—Amsterdam,* was checked off, as were *Rave* and *Tate Gallery.* I could still make out the faint lettering in number thirty-nine, *Take Alex to Madrid.* He swirled the bottom of his cursive A as he always did in the notes he left me on his kitchen table. I used to tease him that a masculine guy made such a girlish sweep at the bottom of his cursive A. After that, the sweep went from girlish to positively baroque.

I refolded the page along the crease lines and held the delicate square in my hands, my thumbs caressing the papery stiffness. I handed it back to him and felt my stomach seize again. "We have to talk," I said.

"Look, if you feel uncomfortable, we can lea—"

"No. It's not that…it's about you and me." My heart pounded in my chest. All memory of the elegant speech I composed in the car was lost as I groped for words. "I—I almost got caught."

"What?"

He'd thrown on a sweatshirt as we walked out of the building and he looked totally at ease, in his jeans and flip-flops, sitting on a bench near the beach in Santa Monica. But I couldn't relax into the sound of pigeons squawking at picnickers, or the red dragon kite flying above my head, or the surfers pulling out of wetsuits on the shore below. I wasn't there to enjoy a beach day with a friend. I wasn't on a field trip to see a camera obscura. I took a deep breath.

"Ryan got in trouble and no one could find me. My son, he needed me, and I was MIA. And Jason left a meeting—that didn't go over well—and Ryan was having such a bad night and I...I was with you. I can't afford to go missing like that again. I've told you about Ryan. And Natalie. And Ben. I can't keep hiding out in this crazy un-reality."

"What happened? Is he okay?"

"Yes, he's okay but that's not the point." I stood up, turned my back to the beach, and faced Matt. "Ryan had a hard time. He has a hard time a lot of the time. This time, it was at soccer practice—he shoved a kid on his team. The time before that it was at school—do you really want me to go on?"

"I'm sorry. It sounds hard."

"It is hard. You have no idea how hard it really is. But what makes it even harder is sneaking around—"

"Are you kidding me?"

"What?" I asked loudly.

"Are you seriously going to tell me you don't think we should see each other because your son has ADD? I already knew that. And you wanted this two days ago and Ryan had ADD then, too," he paused, his voice rising. "I don't care if your son has ADD, Alex. Life is complicated. I get it. I have two kids of my own, remember? And none of that matters—"

"Well, it matters to me. I mean, come on, what else matters? I'm sorry, but it's this," I gestured between us, "that doesn't matter. I know what I said the other day but I fucked up and that—that can't happen...god, Matt, don't look at me like that."

"So that's it?"

"It can't go any further." I lowered my voice and reached toward him. "The sex, it's so compelling, but it's nothing compared to this." I waved my hand wildly at him and me and the building behind us. "I can't keep going down memory lane with you. I've got to put my life back together."

Matt got up and stared out at the glittering expanse of sea and sky. The creases between his eyes darkened and in the fading light, I could see the stubble on his chin and the gray lines in his hair as it ruffled in the breeze. He turned to me and his eyes pinned me to the spot. Finally he said, "So that's what this is? A trip down memory lane?" He shook his head and before I knew what happened, he balled up the yellowed piece of notebook paper and tossed it out over the bluff where it was caught by a sudden gust of wind.

"Oh!" I said as we stood next to each other and watched as the list he'd made twenty years earlier in a flat in London was carried off by a breeze down toward the beach and out to the ocean. I hugged my wrap tightly around me.

He shrugged. "I'm not interested in memories, Alex. I want to know how long you're planning on hiding out? How long you're going to pretend there's nothing real here?"

"Real?" I asked, glaring at him. "I know what's real. And what's real is how hard it is to raise three kids—my three kids—which includes a child who takes up more energy than you can possibly imagine." I leaned toward him and crossed my arms. "You don't know me anymore, Matt—"

"Yes I do," he said. "I know you, Alex. And you know I do." We faced each other and he took two steps toward me. "That's why you're so pissed off."

He moved closer but I wouldn't look at him. I raised my shoulders and tucked my fists under my crossed arms to keep my wrap closed against the chilling breeze, to cover my chest from the words that were needling themselves into my heart. I already made my decision; it *had* to end. I looked out at the ocean. Wave after wave rolled in, then pulled back to reveal glittering grains of sand that were immediately swallowed up by the force of another enormous wave. It felt like every lie I told myself hid an even deeper lie, and the deeper I dug the more lies I uncovered. Matt knew me. He knew me better than maybe anyone. How that was possible, I didn't know. But it was so seductive...that feeling of being known. But still, I needed to finish what I started.

"My kids—my kids are suffering. They're acting up and I have to stay afloat so I can keep us all from sinking." I put my hand on his arm. "You have to understand—that's what a mom does. You're a dad. Not a mom. It's not the same thing."

"Fine. Maybe you're right," he said. "But I love my boys. I'd never want to hurt them. I just can't give up everything for them."

"Well, I guess that's the difference."

"Well, I guess it is. I don't believe it makes you a better parent to sacrifice yourself for your kids. But it's one hell of a way of not letting yourself feel anything."

"That's not fair," I said, blinking back tears.

"Maybe it's not fair but it's true. What do *you* want? I asked you that our first night together. You don't take yourself seriously as a writer, I mean what the fuck, Alex? You? Not a writer? I'm sorry but it's hard for me to wrap my mind around that one and don't tell me you're happy."

I covered my mouth with my hand and choked back the sobs that formed in my gut and were forcing their way up. "I—I want things...things I haven't wanted in a very long time..." My stomach shook but I forced myself to keep going. "But that doesn't...it doesn't justify what we're doing...and it's not just about *me*." I snatched my purse off the bench and turned quickly to leave, my hair whipping in the breeze.

He grabbed my arm. "Don't go."

"There's nothing left to talk about." I twisted my arm from his grasp, stepped back and lowered my voice. "I can't keep having sex with you to feel better about the things I didn't get to have—and the things I got that I didn't expect." I faced him, standing next to the bench, lines of emotion carved into his painfully familiar face.

"It's not just about sex, Alex. It never was." He looked through me as if searching for words. "Look, I want...I want...okay, fuck it, I'll say it...I want to be with you." His eyes blazed as he reached for my waist and drew me to him. "I know you have a complicated life. I won't downplay it. And you're right, you're the mom and I'm the dad and maybe it's not the same thing. But I have a family, too. I have a lot at stake that I care about. But there's something between us...something I haven't felt in a long time, something that I'm not sure I can live without...and I have to know what that is." He stopped and added, "And I think you do, too."

I could feel myself at war, screams and anguish and knives drawn inside. The part of me that made up her mind, that knew and understood how absolutely crazy—and dangerous—this was in a death match with the other part—the part that wanted this without reason or recrimination. She didn't care about logic or rightness or risk. She just wanted this. The gaping void inside me was desperate to be filled. And no matter how I'd tried to fill it over the years: marriage, motherhood, volunteering, blogging...nothing came close, not even in the ballpark, to making me feel whole. And then Matt showed up.

I took a deep breath and steadied myself. I was sick and tired of numbing out. I seemed to be less and less capable of it. I couldn't go ahead with the canned speech I'd prepared that urged us to do the "right" thing. I didn't even know what the right thing was anymore. I just knew that I was lying to Jason and the only way to remedy it was to lie to myself, to convince myself that this was over, that I wanted it to be. But it wasn't. And I didn't want it to be. The runaway train had left the station. And even though I feared for my family, it was too late to get off now.

"Okay. I can't, I won't, deny it," I said. I looked down at the intermixed swaths of dirt and patches of crab grass that thrived up on the bluff. I struck a clump with my sandal and felt something inside me leave...some resolve that I'd meant to hold on to. It slipped away. I looked at Matt standing next to me. "I hoped if I ignored it, it would go away...but it won't. I—I can't make it go."

We didn't say much after that. I followed him to his car and he opened the door for me to get in. We sat for a moment, side by side, looking out the windshield as I counted the cars, vans, and SUVs parked in perfect rows around us. I felt a crushing pressure in my chest, as if the weight of the air in the car was pressing against my breastbone and I gasped out loud for breath.

"Alex, Alex—" Matt reached across the center console and pulled me into his arms. I buried my face in his shoulder, taking deep inhales of him through his sweatshirt and squeezing my eyes shut against the tears. I felt like I was coming apart, literally tearing into two and there was nothing I could do to stop it. I breathed in and out, in and out, willing myself back together. I clung to Matt and felt his heart beat against my chest and remembered how Lark told me to look for signs, that the Universe would be my guide if I had the ears to hear. So I listened. I listened to the steady thump of his heart as he buried his head in my hair. And I smelled him, the scent of Matt, and it cut me inside because I knew this was real, as wrong as it was.

"I know you have to get back," he finally said. "I'll drive you over to your car."

He stuck the key in the ignition and then stopped and turned to me. I looked at him and thought how ageless his eyes were. They looked exactly as they had the day we met. Nothing about them changed, not their deep green color, not their shape, not the way I felt when I gazed into them. Everything else changed: Matt and me and our lives and what we wanted, it was all different now, but the way I felt when I looked into his eyes, that was exactly the same.

***

Much later in the evening, well after I said goodbye to Matt and went home to take care of my children, I found myself alone in the office. Jason texted that he was working through dinner. Relieved, I sat down at my computer to post on my blog since it had been a while. My fingers attacked the keyboard with gusto. When I sat back to read what I wrote, I was shocked.

I've really lost it, I thought, but I couldn't help it. It was as if a cork had been unplugged and there was nothing to stop the flow of truth. It wasn't pretty or polite or even socially acceptable but there it was, nonetheless. There was no way anyone could ever peg me as *RESTLESS*. I clicked "post" and went to bed.

RESTLESS IN L.A.
Mommy Musings. Stupid Confessions. Life.
Posted by Anonymous

Below the Surface
My husband isn't one of those get-drunk-and-tell-your-girlfriends-what-a-dick-he-is kind of guy. He's a good guy. So what is it that I need so badly that I lay with another man, letting him explore parts of me long since forgotten? My husband makes love to me like a beloved slipper: I fit so well and am such a comfort; he can't help but want to slip inside for the warmth and familiarity. He likes to know he's pleased me, wants me to sleep with a smile on my face, but he's never once looked for the hidden parts. I doubt he's ever considered there might be hidden parts. He loves me but he doesn't know me. And I can't blame him.

I'm the one who saw him drive away and, instead of picking up the phone and calling him, instead of following his tracks and seeing if I could catch him at a red light, I turned and walked in the opposite direction, grateful to be free from holding up my end of the conversation. I can't blame what I'm doing on my husband. If he thought he knew me well it was only because I let him think so. I showed him only the parts of me I wanted him to see. But then I met someone who pinned me down, forced me to ante up, pushed me to come forward. With that kind of intensity, I knew I couldn't help but find me. After all, I was right there below the surface, just waiting for someone to look.

ROBIN FINN

220

CHAPTER 17: LADIES' MAINTENANCE

I lived my life, avoided the grocery store, dealt with parent-teacher conferences, wrote on my anonymous blog, smiled at my husband, attempted to parent my kids, and all the while lived with the fact that I was having an affair—not a one-night stand, not even a "fling," but a true long-term extramarital affair. It might have been gentler not to think about it, but every time I found myself headed to LAX, it was hard not to remember what I was up to. When Matt was gone, I had moments of clarity where I realized the insanity of how much I was risking and I'd think about ending the relationship. My stomach knotted and my throat ached at the thought, but I told myself to have courage, that it wasn't too late to fix things between Jason and me—it had only been six weeks…two months…four months—and then I'd see him.

I'd sit in my car and watch the sliding glass doors for his stride—his dark hair, dark jeans, jacket causally thrown across his arm, eyes alight with anticipation, and there he was and any thoughts—any possible thoughts—of ending it flew out the window. His physical presence totally disarmed me, my resolve melted, and as the car door closed, I was in his arms.

So I lived with it. Even though the two parts of myself continued their death match—I could feel them wrestling inside: one side with its shoulders pinned to the mat before it slipped from underneath and then the other side on its back, and me, watching and waiting. That's what I did, watched and waited—and tried as hard as I could to ignore the ultimate outcome—either way, I lost.

Since Matt wasn't coming back for two weeks, I'd decided to put in an actual appearance at my Tuesday book club, which so often was my cover. I became so engrossed in the story of our earlier relationship that I began to carry the journal around in my purse. Even though I knew everything that happened, rereading the details I'd written as a twenty-year-old gave me a totally different perspective. Having an hour to kill before book club started, I stopped at a Starbucks for a cappuccino and read.

June 1

I can't believe my junior year is almost finished. The lease on my flat expires as soon as finals are over next week. Even though I've been practically living at Matt's, I'm totally broke and I can't ask my parents for money. My mom called last week and told me that my dad lost his job! It happened months ago but they didn't tell me because they didn't want me to worry. Now, they're panicked. My mom said they don't have any money left for my last year of school and begged me to come home right away and get a job. Our house is for sale and things are pretty desperate. I'm so lucky to have gotten a scholarship to study abroad or else I would never have come to London, never met Matt, never had this perfect year...

But I have to face reality. I can't work in London without a permit and that would take months and I have to finish school. Last week, when I told Matt about the lease, he jokingly suggested I move in with him but I'd never want him to feel responsible for me and anyway, I have to help my parents. They do so much for me and they're sick with worry. They need me to come home. I can't let them down.

***

"Maybe after your finals," Matt said, rubbing massage oil into my back, "you and I can take a trip to the south of France."

It was early in the evening and I was lying face down on Matt's bed in my underwear with a towel beneath me. Next week was final exams and I was busy studying. I hadn't stayed over in days, insisting that I needed a good eight hours of real sleep to be able to focus on my coursework, but Matt swore he wouldn't keep me up if I spent the night. He said he just wanted to help me "relax" and was giving me a heavenly back massage.

"Maybe," I said, not sure how to broach the subject of my imminent departure. I'd tried to bring it up a few times but, each time, I'd chickened out. Now, with the feel of his hands on my back and the scent of the lavender oil wafting up from my shoulders, I thought I should tell him.

"Matt, I—"

"Roll over, will you?"

I rolled over and lay on my back, noting his wolfish expression. His eyes narrowed and sparkled at my bare breasts, and the shape of his mouth shifted, almost as if he wanted to devour me. The feeling of being his prey totally disarmed me. If ever there was a willing victim, it was me.

"You go ahead and review your notes in your mind while I give you a full-service body massage."

"Oh, please—" I laughed but I stopped arguing as he slowly pulled down my underwear. He massaged oil into my breasts, rubbing and caressing each one. I could feel his tongue as he bent over and softly sucked each nipple, his mouth biting me and making me wet, so wet, between the legs. He started to massage lower into my hips and thighs. He spread my legs apart as he massaged all the way down to each toe. Slowly, he moved his hands back up and started to massage between my legs.

"Open your eyes."

I looked steadily into his as he fingered me gently.

"Does this feel good?' he asked.

"So good," I panted.

"You're so wet, Alexandra. Your sweet pussy's been lonely all week. You're such a diligent little student, studying so hard like the little scholar that you are. You need a tension break, babe. What do you think, my little Einstein?"

Sometimes he just killed me. I struggled not to laugh. He looked directly into my eyes, daring me to turn away.

"Yes, you're right, I'm so tense. I need a release."

"Okay, I'm gonna help you prepare for your finals by releasing some tension. This isn't for me, this is for you, for your grades. You know how important education is to me."

He leaned over, opened his drawer, and pulled out a wand-shaped vibrator.

"I got this for you, babe, a tension breaker for your studies."

"No way! What the hell is that thing?"

"Shhh, Alexandra, relax. It's an educational device."

And before I could squirm away, he turned on the vibrator and placed it between my legs. Instantly, I melted. I could hear the soft hum of the motor and I closed my eyes to withstand the friction.

"Yeah, doesn't that feel so good?" he asked.

He rubbed the vibrator in a circular motion between my legs, slowly moving it onto and away from the sweet spot so that I could barely stand it. The tension was building inside of me so badly, I was panting. Just when I wanted to scream, he inserted the tip of the vibrator inside of me. I gasped. He gently moved it in and out, my hips arching to the rhythm he was setting.

"Oh god, don't stop," I moaned as I came again and again until I pushed the buzzing wand away because the sensations were overpowering.

He unzipped his jeans, tore off his underwear, and climbed on top of me, already rock solid. He entered me effortlessly. I was drenched.

"Alexandra...you...are...the...sexiest... bookworm...I've...ever...met... Oh god, hold on, babe."

And he thrust in and out of me hard and fast. His face was a mask of concentration and pleasure. His dark hair fell over his forehead and he bent his head to kiss me and suck my neck. I laid open to him, feeling his hips, pushing my pelvis up to meet him. He broke into a wide grin as I came again and gritted my teeth to let him finish.

"Matt, you're crazy, so crazy...wow."

"Yup," he grinned.

"Listen, I have to talk to you about some—" But my confession was interrupted by a knock at the door.

"It's just Ev dropping off some work stuff. I'll be right back. Oh, and you can thank me later when you get straight As," he said, smacking me hard on the backside as he threw on a pair of jeans and a shirt and went to greet Evelyn.

He closed his bedroom door and I could hear the two of them talking in the next room. Evelyn and Matt worked together and, although I was pretty sure they'd had a fling early on, they were good friends. I didn't know what came over me but I strained my ears to eavesdrop on their conversation.

"Here's your stuff, dude. Wow, Alex isn't here?"

"Yeah, she's in the bedroom studying. What?"

"What, what?" I heard her say.

"I don't know, Ev, what's the face?" I wished I could

see through the walls.

"It's nothing. I'm happy for you—I can't believe it, but I'm happy for you."

"Huh?" he said. "What're you talking about?"

"Really, Matt? Are you that stupid?"

"I have no idea wh—"

"You're in love, dumbass."

"What? I am not. I'm in like, I told you. I really like this girl."

"You keep telling yourself that, dude. But you're in love. It's obvious to everyone but you." I could hear her shuffling papers. "Go figure. Matt Daniels in love. Who would've guessed?" She laughed out loud. "Well, if it can happen to you, there's hope for the rest of us. See ya, dude."

I heard the door close and slipped into my shirt and hurried into the bathroom. I turned on the water and pretended to wash my hands, feeling the pressure of the cold water run over my fingers. What did Evelyn know? She barely knew me. He even said he was *in like*. In like, that was what he'd said. Not *in love*. I dried my hands and walked over to the bedroom door. Leaning against it, I waited and wondered what he was doing. When I finally opened the door and peeked out, Matt was sitting on his leather couch, staring into space.

"Hey," I said.

"Hey."

We looked at each other and I wondered for a moment if he knew I'd been eavesdropping.

But he just smiled and asked, "Now where were we? Oh yeah, study break massage." He grabbed my hand and led me back toward the bed. "So what were you saying?"

"Me? Nothing. I should get back to work."

***

I closed the journal and buried it in my purse, pushing it

226

below my wallet, a wayward maxi pad, and a tube of clear lip-gloss encrusted with old gum particles. I'd desperately wanted to stay in London, but every Sunday my mother called and begged and pleaded and cried and called it a family emergency and an absolute necessity that I return to L.A. and earn money for school. I didn't tell her about Matt. I didn't want her to feel guilty. I knew how ashamed my parents were about losing whatever money they'd saved for me. I strung them along as long as I could, not wanting to make a decision. Months later, I found myself alone in Los Angeles, working for an insurance company and saving money for my senior year of college.

Looking back, it seemed impossible that Matt and I had never discussed our feelings. Hard to believe given the hours I spent writing in this journal in the tiniest of lines, filling it with the details of our every moment together, barely being able to tear myself away from him long enough to attend classes, that we never, not once, talked seriously about us or the future. Whatever Evelyn believed, Matt never said a word. And me? I was too afraid to bring it up.

***

I was so lost in reading that I was late to book club and Cheryl, our book club leader, and the rest of the group were deep in discussion when I arrived.

I'd been invited to join the book club a few years earlier through Laurie, who'd come to one session before dropping out due to a conflict with her Pilates class. Even though she'd quit, I'd remained and still put in the occasional appearance. That day, they were analyzing the latest novel they'd read and comparing it to the film adaptation they'd taken a "field trip" to see the week before. It was easy enough for me to follow the plotline of the novel and I'd made sure to go to a lunchtime viewing of the movie two days earlier.

Cheryl was clearly passionate about the superiority of the movie over the book. "Well, I, for one, think the movie was way better for several reasons: first of all, that scene where he first sees her...I practically sobbed my heart out. I mean, there they were, face to face, and she's so strong and lonely and he's so intense and devoted to her." She took a giant swig out of her bottle of coconut water and continued without missing a beat. "The book was good but it didn't have that smokin' shower scene! I mean, whew, how hot was that?" she asked, fanning herself. "And can you believe how that kid has grown up? I remember him from those teeny-bopper flicks and, wow, has he become a man."

"Gross," chimed in Emily, a neighbor of Cheryl's from down the street. "Who knew you were a pedophile? He barely has any hair on his chest."

"Well, honestly, Em, who wants a man with a hairy chest, anyway?" Cheryl asked. "That's so 1980s. My husband shaves his entire undercarriage. Does anyone have ungroomed body hair anymore—pubic or otherwise? I don't think so!" She banged her hand on the coffee table in support of her point.

Wait, what? No one has ungroomed pubic hair? What were they talking about? How come nobody told me?

Cheryl's friend Stacie agreed. "Pubic hair's disgusting. I'm so glad it's out. Women have been taking it off for years and it's about time men started doing it—straight men, that is. There's just no excuse for guys not to shave their, uh, undercarriages."

What the hell were they talking about? Men shaving their undercarriages? What's an "undercarriage" anyway?

"Um, ladies, don't you think it's a little creepy for grown women to make themselves look like pre-pubescent girls?" I chimed in, trying to snatch the conversation back from the bizarre abyss it was teetering on. "I mean, come on. We're women, not little girls, and women have pubic hair."

"No offense, Alex, but you're one to talk. Look at those hairy legs." Cheryl pointed open-mouthed at my bare legs that admittedly hadn't been shaved in over a week. "I certainly hope the rest of you isn't in that wild, native state," she hooted.

"I'm sure Alex waxes her bikini," defended Emily.

I don't know what came over me. I was thinking about all the sex I'd had the last several months and how good it was and the fact that I never got a complaint and I definitely had pubic hair.

"Hey, you know what they say, ladies: it's not the size of the wave—or how hairy it is—but the motion of the ocean."

I stood up, unzipped my jeans, and lowered them enough that my natural, unwaxed hairline sprang into vision. Emily, Cheryl, and Stacie leaned over, took one look at the kinky hair, and gasped.

"Oh my god!" Cheryl screeched.

My unshaven public hair rendered the group temporarily speechless, which for this group, was a miracle in and of itself.

"That's just wrong," Emily finally said, shaking her head in disgust.

"I agree. That's so rude to Jason," muttered Cheryl. "You're like a native, Alex, it's disgusting. Please, for the love of god, pull up your pants."

The three of them looked at me like I just revealed a third breast. "I don't like to wax," I stuttered. "It's painful. I do trim up the sides—"

"So shave," retorted Stacie. "Anything, Alex, but you simply can't go around like that anymore." This was a statement of fact.

"You know," said Cheryl, looking brighter, "I think the problem is you haven't gone to the right place. I have to send you to my girl, Oxana. She's Russian. She'll hold your hand. You have nothing to be afraid of. You could start with a Brazilian. She'll leave you with a nice little landing strip. Please Alex, you've just got to get rid of all that...that...hair," she said, waving her hand at me, her nose wrinkling in distaste.

Suddenly the room erupted.

"Minka's amazing, she does custom work. I think you really ought to go for a Hollywood," Stacie shouted

"A Hollywood?" gasped Emily. "That's way too shocking. For god's sake, Stacie, she'll faint when she sees there's not a shred of hair left." She turned to me and put her hand on mine. "Go to Gloria, she'll clean you up. She's the best, she even does vajazzling—"

Wait, what? Vajazzling? What the hell was that?

"Oh, great idea," piped Stacie. "You'll love it. She'll put Swarovski crystals on your freshly waxed skin, right above your—your—uh—"

"Vagina?" I finished for her. Jeez, all this talk about pubic hair and she couldn't even say vagina?

"Yes, right," she said. "I got an awesome butterfly there for Valentine's Day. The waxologists are so professional and Dave went crazy the night I showed it to him." Stacie continued with such passion that little droplets of spit shot out of her mouth like saliva grenades. "You'll love it," she gushed.

Swarovski crystals? Waxologists? I felt like I'd wandered into some weird surreal universe where everyone decorated their vaginas for the holidays. Nevertheless, I felt my phone abuzz with contacts being shared.

Emily continued undeterred. "I suggest you start with a good waxing. Either the Love Triangle or the Power Strip will give you a nice, well-groomed appearance."

Cheryl turned to me and said, "Honestly, hon, you'll love a Brazilian. It feels sooo good when you—you know—have sex and there's no friction. You're as smooth as a baby's butt," she giggled.

I couldn't tell her this, I couldn't shout it out over the raucous conversation of the group, but I thought to myself: I like friction. I don't want smooth and hairless; I liked it hard and deep and rough. The friction made it more real, more compelling. I felt like a woman, not a little girl, and I liked it that way.

Cheryl turned to the others and nodded my way, "C'mon you guys, Alex is like Samson over here. We don't want her to go bald or she'll, she'll," she could barely continue, she was giggling so hard, "she'll lose all her powers." They collapsed in a fit of laughter. Emily, who was in the middle of taking a sip out of her Evian bottle, spurted water all over her jeans. Cheryl held on to her sides for dear life and Stacie was practically rolling on the floor. I just sat there, laughing too, and flicking all three of them the finger, which only made them roar harder. I thought Cheryl might pee in her pants. Emily brushed off her jeans and said to herself, "Maybe the Power Strip would be perfect."

RESTLESS IN L.A.
Mommy Musings. Stupid Confessions. Life.
Posted by Anonymous

Bottomless Abyss

I hate ladies' maintenance and the waxing, peeling, painting, pinching, spraying, plucking, tweezing, twisting of it all. I can't stand having my nails done, baring my feet for strangers, when I know within three days, the polish will chip or crack or split and my nails will look like shit again. I hate doing anything that requires me to do the same thing a week later. Washing the car, shaving my legs, driving back and forth to dance rehearsals. It's like falling into a bottomless abyss. No matter how far down I go, I never seem to reach the end.

ROBIN FINN

CHAPTER 18: WTF

I picked up Matt on a Thursday. He'd come in for a week to wrap things up. His project was nearly complete, which meant there would be no further reason for his frequent trips to Los Angeles. I sat at the arrivals terminal, eyes glued to the glass doors, and waited. I couldn't miss him as he strode through the exit. His eyes were hidden behind mirrored Ray-Bans, but his smile was unmistakable.

As was our custom, he opened the trunk, deposited his suitcase, got in the passenger side, and firmly closed the door before he greeted me.

"God, I missed you." He leaned over and kissed me softly on the lips but I could sense tension in his body.

"What's wrong?" I asked.

"Let's just go, babe, we can talk on the way."

"Matt, come on, what's wrong?" I repeated as I pulled away from the curb and headed toward the freeway.

"I think we should wait until we get to the hotel." I watched as he ran his hand through his hair. He was tense.

"What is it?" I asked nervously, my heart pounding in my chest.

"Heather knows," he said simply.

And there it was. The two words I most dreaded and

yet, deep down, anticipated.

"She what?" I turned my head to look at him full on.

"Look, she knows. Hey, watch the road, okay? We don't have to talk about this right now."

"Yes, we do." I turned off the radio and pulled off Sepulveda into a sprawling plaza parking lot. It was too hard to drive and listen at the same time. I switched off the ignition and looked at Matt.

"What happened?" It was hot in the car even though I had the A/C on. I lowered the windows and a cool breeze suddenly wafted through. L.A. weather was unpredictable this time of year and Matt dressed for it in a white T-shirt under a navy collared shirt and slacks. He'd thrown his jacket in the trunk with his luggage.

"She doesn't know who or when but she knows. She asked me last night if I'd been screwing around."

"Oh god."

"I denied it, but it sucked. I don't want to lie to her." He glanced out the rearview mirror, checking the cars that lined the parking lot. "At the very least, she deserves better than that from me..." he trailed off, looking out the window.

"What did she say?"

"Look, Alex, does it really matter? I've been distant for months. We barely have sex. Most of the time I try to avoid it, make excuses, or just come to bed late. She knows something's wrong and it is. I didn't confirm her suspicions but she knows. And I don't want to keep lying to her."

"So how are you going to handle this?" I tried to keep my voice steady to hide the creeping hysteria.

"How do you think?" he answered with lightning precision.

"I don't know. Why are you mad at me?"

"Because," he stopped and took my hand in his, "you know what I want to do. I want to tell her the truth—that I've met someone."

"I—I don't know what you want me to say."

"I was hoping you'd give me the go-ahead."

"The go-ahead for what?"

He took off his sunglasses and turned to me. "Come on, Alex. How long do you think we can keep this up?"

"I can't do this right now. Let's just get to the hotel." I gripped the steering wheel and switched the ignition back on.

"Hey," he said, holding onto the wheel so I couldn't reverse out of the parking spot. "We both knew this might happen. We both knew we might be found out. Maybe it's time to come clean, not just with Heather and Jason, but with each other." Just then, I heard the double honk of a shopper locking up her car and watched her walk into an El Pollo Loco.

"Okay, okay, just let me drive." I pushed his hand off the wheel and resumed course to the Redbury. "We'll talk when we get there."

I dropped him off to check in while I valeted my car and waited for his text. I felt this crazy urge to drive away from him, Jason, the kids, Laurie, everyone I ever knew in Los Angeles, straight to the Mexican border. But I didn't. I checked my phone for the text with his room number and got into the elevator. My heart pounded as I walked to the door. Matt was sitting at the desk, his bag unopened on the floor.

"Talk to me," he said.

I froze. I could feel how much I wanted to retreat—from the truth, from him, from further fucking up my life. But as I stood there, I observed rather than directed my arms to wrap around him. I felt my cheek rest against his shoulder and I could feel the matching rhythm of our heartbeats.

"I know you're freaked out," he whispered. "It's going to be okay." My mind raced as I breathed in the singular scent of Matt, a salve to my anxiety. I breathed him in and out and a calmness settled over me. As the minutes ticked by, our embrace moved from comfort to desire and soon his hands were roving up and down my body, tracing the curves of my hips. I pushed against him eagerly and felt his hardness through his jeans.

He pulled my shirt over my head, followed by his own. We could barely stand the moment of separation. My lace bra pressed against his bare chest. He reached behind me, unhooked it, and devoured me like a starving man. With a moan, he pulled me toward the bed.

"Matt, wait, this isn't going to solve anything."

He raised an eyebrow and looked at me. "You sure?" he said, and tugged.

I fell onto the bed and there were shoes kicked off and zippers unzipped, jeans thrown out of the way, and then nothing but his naked body and mine. I thought fleetingly how funny it was that we made love during the day. He always had a daytime fetish. I didn't know what suddenly crossed his mind, but he rolled off me so we were lying side by side. He kissed me and rubbed my body from shoulder to hip and downward, relaxing me like a jockey patting down a skittish horse. His hand lightly stroked between my legs. I was excited despite myself. His fingers found the sweet spot and circled it, teased me, made me wet with desire.

"You scare me," I whispered. "I don't know how to respond to you. I don't have the courage you do. I'm so afraid of getting it wrong." It was difficult to carry on the conversation while being made love to but I tried.

"Alexandra, you're so sweet and wet and warm," he murmured.

Oh god, why did the sound of his voice make me so crazy?

"Let's talk later. You're so ready." His fingers expertly moved in and out of me while my hips grinded into his hand. I gave up thinking until he suddenly stopped and moved lower on the bed. I felt his tongue on me with a jolt.

"Watch me," he said, lifting his head momentarily and tossing me a pillow.

I tucked the overstuffed pillow behind my neck so I was slightly elevated and, with the daylight streaming through the sheer curtains, I watched him go down on me with a determined joyfulness. I put my hands in his dark hair and gazed at my trembling knees as his tongue explored and drank me in. I felt my orgasm burst forth and I moved my hips as his hands snaked under me and held firm to my thighs. He moved his mouth back and forth and held me down while I bucked and moaned and came hard into his open mouth. He sat up and mounted me, setting a slow and deep rhythm. I thought I'd explode with sensation overload, but he came with a moan and rested on top of me. We were both covered in sweat and all manner of bodily fluids.

"Oh god, you make me feel so good," I purred as I stroked up and down his back, relishing the feel of his weight resting on me.

"I want you," he said, shifting onto an elbow.

"You just had me," I laughed, reaching out to rub his thigh but he blocked my hand.

He leaned over and brushed my hair away from my face. The smile faded from his lips and the usual playful glint in his eye was replaced by something darker. "I don't mean now...I mean on a regular basis."

"Matt." I started to get up, but he grabbed my waist and held me next to him.

He turned me to him and his eyes flashed. "I have to say this. And you're going to have to hear it—I'm in love with you."

I'd waited twenty years to hear him say it—ever since I'd crashed into him on a London street decades earlier and then we'd been friends and lovers and so much more, and then nothing at all until we'd re-connected on the Internet, of all places. And now, twenty years and two full lives later, he'd finally said it: *I'm in love with you.* All I could think of was, why now?

When I didn't respond, he asked, "What are you thinking?"

"Truthfully?"

"Yes, please—truthfully."

"I'm asking myself, why, now, of all times? Now, when we have five children between us, when we have full, complicated lives in cities across the country from each other; when we have spouses—spouses who love us, and families, our families...why now? I'm tortured." I gripped the sheet in my fist, feeling the soft cotton between my fingers and knowing no amount of squeezing could untangle the knots we'd made.

"You don't have to be."

I sat up. "What exactly are you suggesting?"

"I'm suggesting I go back to New York and tell Heather the truth." He hesitated for the briefest second and then said, "And I'm suggesting you go home and do the same."

His words hung heavy in the room. It was as if we were paused in the middle of a movie scene. Neither of us spoke or moved. The room was completely still save the quiet hum of the air conditioner. Minutes ticked by and still neither of us broke the silence. I figured since he spoke last, it was probably my turn.

"I don't know what's going to come out of my mouth right now."

"Say you'll do it. Say you want to be with me, not like this, not hiding in hotel rooms, not lying and sneaking and fooling around behind other people's backs—other people we both know deserve better than this."

"But what about our kids?" I thought about my three and his two and now, on top of everything else, I'd be a home-wrecker: two homes, five kids.

"They'll be okay," he said, the lines in his forehead deepening. "It'll be hard, very hard, but they'll survive." He seemed certain of it as he moved closer to me and pulled my hand off the sheet clutched to my breast. "Listen to me." I looked at him and felt that now-familiar sense of agony, of wanting something so badly and knowing it wasn't mine. It was longing, I realized with a start. When I looked at him, my heart ached with longing. "It happens every day," he continued, "it does. People change and they make different choices and their kids survive. Our kids will too."

"I don't know," I said, thinking that he didn't know my kids.

"I'm talking about our lives, Alex, yours and mine. I'm talking about giving us a real chance."

Giving us a real chance? The day I left him replayed in my mind with detailed precision.

***

There was a downpour for days. Matt was on a long shoot and we hadn't seen each other all week. He was filming in London, so he didn't have to travel, but he was gone from dawn to dusk. He begged me to come over and sleep in his bed so that when he came home, exhausted and overworked, he could collapse next to me. For a few nights after final exams, I gave in, but that last night I stayed in my own place. I didn't tell him that my parents had sent me a ticket from London to LAX. I didn't tell him my flight was leaving in five hours. I meant to. I kept trying but I couldn't get the words out.

I took the tube to Earl's Court and walked up the steps to his door and buzzed. No one answered. I didn't expect anyone to since I knew he was working all weekend. I took his key out of my backpack and let myself in. I sat down at his desk and took out a pen and a piece of paper:

June 17
Dear Matt,
   I came to say goodbye. My dad lost his job and I

have to go home and get a job for the summer if I ever plan to graduate from college. I've been meaning to tell you for a while now but it never seemed like the right moment. By the time you get this, I'll be gone. Please understand that I didn't want to ruin a minute of our time together. I wish I could have stayed but I just can't.

I want you to know that this year has been the best of my life. You make me feel like a different version of myself, one I like much better. The time I spent with you changed me on the inside and that will always be with me. You are amazing and I know you will be a huge success. Please don't be mad that I had to go. I don't have a choice. I can't let my parents down. They really need me right now.

I'll miss you—every day.
Alexandra

I left the note on his bed and took a final look around the large, one-room flat. His bed and dresser were in one corner, the farm table and chairs sat next to the kitchen. I surveyed the brown leather couch, the TV unit, his big wooden desk and chair. I looked once more at his queen-sized bed and the gray print duvet that had kept me warm so many nights. I opened "my drawer" and emptied my clothes, socks, tampons, a beat-up copy of *Pride & Prejudice*, and a brand new tube of mascara into my backpack. Ghosts of us making love were everywhere—on the couch, the bed, even the kitchen table. I saw us reading the paper, cooking pasta dinners, cuddling by the TV.

Goodbye, Matt. I can't believe I'm leaving you. I can't believe I won't see your scruffy cheeks and sparkling green eyes tomorrow. I won't hold you or touch you or...

I couldn't stand to be there another minute. I closed the door behind me, opened my black umbrella, and placed his key under the mat.

***

I got out of bed, threw on my clothes, opened the sliding glass door, and walked out onto the balcony. Matt slipped into his jeans and followed behind me. He walked over to the white iron rail and leaned against it, taking in the view. Over his shoulder, I could see the wide, curved awnings of the Capitol Records Tower on Hollywood Boulevard and the spike at the top. It was an overcast day but I could feel the sun beating down on me, making me sweat beneath my hair.

"What if I don't have the strength for this?" I whispered to his bare back.

"That's bullshit," he said, not turning around.

"No, it's not." He turned to face me then, the back of his jeans pressed against the railing.

"I don't want to be the kind of person who does this," I whispered.

"We're already doing it."

"But we can still undo it—"

"Really? You can? Because I can't." He cupped his forehead with his hand to block the glare. "I haven't enjoyed lying to my wife for months. But I did it because I had to know... And now I do. And I don't have a choice. I've got to tell her the truth. What about you? Do you have a choice?"

"Don't pressure me," I said, forcing out the words. "I don't know if I can live with myself. My kids, my husband...they deserve better."

"So you're willing to live like this?" he asked. "What about what you deserve?" He let go and turned back toward the view. We were both silent for what felt like hours. Finally he said, without turning around, as if asking the city itself, "Why did you leave me in London?"

When I didn't respond, he spun around and his dark

241

jeans went black against the midday sun. He fixed me with his stare and I wanted to look away—away from the blinding light, away from the view, away from him—but I couldn't.

"I want to know." He paused as if to survey the balcony; the two modern white patio chairs, the sleek silver cocktail table, the open slider leading to the room, and the potted fern perched in the corner, as if he needed to get his bearings. His voice was low but deliberate. "Well?"

I stood up straight and took his hands in my own. "I—I didn't leave because I didn't care."

"Then why? Why did you leave?"

"Why is this important? I don't know, I don't remember. I was twenty years old and my parents were going through a bankruptcy and...and...you know all this." I folded my arms. "There was a lot of pressure on me and I was scared."

"Scared of what?"

"Scared of what? Come on, Matt, really? I can't remember what I did a month ago, how am I supposed to remember—"

"Just think. What were you scared of?"

"Look, when I left for England, I wanted to be a writer and I thought I'd finish my novel but then I met you and everything changed. I did things I'd never done before and our attraction—it was so intense—and I loved being with you but I also felt something...more. But you never brought it up. And any time it came up, you told me you loved to fuck me. So I let myself be content with that. I was too afraid to know that, maybe, that was all there was. And meanwhile my parents had no money and that wasn't supposed to happen—not to me, not to someone who always followed the rules, so I went home. I felt like I had to. I felt like it was time to come back to reality and let go of whatever fantasy I created about you and me."

"What do you mean, fantasy?"

"I overheard you and Evelyn talking once. She said you

were in love with me and do you remember what you said? You said you were 'in like.'"

"In like? Shit, Alex, that was wishful thinking. That's all that was. I was crazy about you. I just didn't want to be."

"Well, I believed it—it was 'like.' So I went home and tried to do the right thing, like I always did."

"So that's why you left? Because you didn't know how I felt about you? I had no idea you gave up so easily. That brainy, controlled exterior of yours was like a magnet for me and I could tell there was something inside, something that wanted to be freed and I had to know what it was. The whole sexy bookworm thing made me crazy. Don't laugh because I don't think I ever wanted anyone as much as I wanted you—but later, it was like I couldn't get enough of you. And before I realized what was happening, I was changing and we were traveling together and practically living together and you fit so perfectly in my life and, well…it felt like you were meant to be in it."

"You never told me, Matt."

"I never told myself, either," he said with a shrug. "That doesn't mean it wasn't true. I was just too blind to see it. I knew you were following your own dreams and this voice kept telling me there was something special there but I didn't want something 'special.' So I hid behind the sex, telling myself it was the chemistry and we kept pushing the envelope, and every time your cheeks blushed and you leaped outside your comfort zone, well, I wanted you more. But I don't think I was ready for how I felt—or I didn't think I was. I moved to London to avoid commitments and before I met you, it had worked perfectly."

I knew what he meant. I had just re-read the journal in detail and remembered every moment, the fear, the excitement, the overwhelming insecurity. "Matt, I was too scared to tell you I was leaving because I didn't know if you'd let me go…or if you wouldn't. Either way, I couldn't handle it so I—I didn't handle it at all." I paused. "I left because I was afraid to find out how you really felt about me."

"Are you sure?" He leaned over the balcony and then turned back to me. "Because it sounds to me like it's the other way around, you left because you were afraid of how *you* really felt about *me*."

"Why does it matter?" I asked. "You could have come after me if you wanted to."

"Come after you? It was impossible. I tried calling and even mailing letters. The phone was disconnected and the letters came back. I even called the registrar at UCLA but they wouldn't confirm you were enrolled. Those were the days before the Internet, Alex, I couldn't find you. Believe me, I tried. I even thought about flying to L.A. and wandering around UCLA looking for you but I figured if you wanted to talk to me, you'd call. And you never did," he said, shaking his head. "I waited a long time, hoping."

"God, Matt, I…I didn't want to trap you into being with me."

"I should have been given the choice. It never occurred to me that you would just take off." His eyebrows drew together. After a minute, he shook his head. I came over and leaned against the balcony next to him as he stared out at the city.

"I went back to New York to try to recover my equilibrium, to throw myself back into filmmaking and to forget you," he said. "And for a couple of years, it seemed to work. And then Heather and I got together and she moved in, and before we knew it, she was pregnant. I figured it was a sign, you know? I was thirty-five years old; it was time to grow up. The funny thing is, when the boys came, being a dad was so much better than I ever imagined. I thought maybe that could be enough."

I nodded slowly, lost in the view and the story Matt was telling. Our elbows pressed together as we leaned out over the balcony. "I'd already been married for years by then," I trailed off.

"Tell me about him."

"Jason? Jason was—well, he was so *solid*. He was smart and driven and he wanted everything I wanted—kids, a family...I thought I'd found my footing."

He nodded.

"Why are we rehashing this?" I asked suddenly, shaking my head and wrapping my arms protectively around myself. "What's done is done and neither one of us can change the past."

"The point is, Alex, I'm not going to repeat it." He took my face in his hands, brushing my hair back behind my ears. "I realize it's late, so fucking late, but I can't do anything about that. I'm in love with you." He lifted his shoulder in a half-shrug. "And now that I know, I can't pretend that I don't."

I looked into his deep green eyes, noticed the stubble along his cheeks and jaw, and felt the honesty in his words. The last layers of defense around my heart gave way and I felt myself drawn into his orbit, helpless to pull away.

"When I'm with you, I feel..."

I listened to him with my ears and my heart and I understood what he meant more than he knew. He gestured with his hands as he struggled to explain his feelings. I noticed the streaks of gray in his hair and the gentle creases around his eyes. I watched the muscles in his arms as he gestured around the patio, trying to articulate how he felt about me. But the words didn't matter because I felt it deep inside.

"And I don't think I ever stopped missing you," he said. "Not really."

I was aware of the chill that ran up my arms and the feel of his chest so close to the flimsy blouse I'd thrown on. A hard, painful lump lodged in my throat, whether from joy or terror, or both, I couldn't tell. I leaned over and kissed him firmly on the mouth, sucking his upper lip and barely resisting the urge to bite down hard and sink my teeth into him. I knew what he meant, I felt it in my core. I knew all about longing and loneliness and the need for something that wasn't there, something so elusive I couldn't define it no matter how hard I tried. He pulled me into his arms, seeming to sense the need in me. His kiss was deep and full of emotion.

"Alexandra," he said, rubbing his hands up and down my forearms, "I want to wake up with you in the morning. I'm forty-five years old. I can't wait much longer."

"Oh, I—"

"Just think about it, okay?"

I nodded. "I will."

RESTLESS IN L.A.
Mommy Musings. Stupid Confessions. Life.
Posted by Anonymous

You Can't Always Get What You Want

I'm often reminded of the great Stones song, *You Can't Always Get What You Want*. But if you try, the song promises, you might get what you need. What do I need? I wish I knew. And what I do I want? Well, I know what I don't want: I don't want to be in the situation I'm in. For me, knowing what I want has never been easy. Sometimes I try to find it acquiring stuff, even though I know, deep down, that no outer thing can provide the feeling I'm hoping to sustain.

Retail therapy is the perfect example. When I go to the mall to do some shopping, I feel like I just had a grande cappuccino with a double espresso shot. I walk around smiling and loving all of my fellow human beings and beaming at everyone while I try on the latest summer dress, or a great pair of suede boots, or a hip new purse with fringe that makes me feel cool and bohemian. But when I buy it—the boots or the purse, whatever—I'm only thrilled with life until the low hits. Then I wonder why I squandered my money. Do I really need it? Do I even really like it? The high was there but it was so fleeting and then I crash back to reality. Getting what I think I want is like retail therapy, the high just doesn't last that long. And getting what I need? I'm too scared to figure it out.

ROBIN FINN

CHAPTER 19: SUDDEN OBSERVATION

The elevator doors opened in the lobby and I stepped out lost in a million thoughts...*I'm in love with you, Alex...and now that I know, I can't pretend that I don't...I'm forty-five years old...think about it, okay?*

"Hey, Al."

I nearly jumped out of my skin. "Jason—what—what—what are you doing here?" My heart banged against my chest and my mouth went dry. I began brushing off my blouse as if I could palm off with my bare hands what I'd been doing.

"The merger meeting went bust—the whole thing went to hell. I tried calling you but you never answer your phone anymore so I used Find Your Phone—it's amazing I found you." He was wearing his navy blue power suit with a crisp white shirt and a red tie. His dark blond hair was slicked back with gel and he looked very lawyerly. "What are you doing in Hollywood at four in the afternoon, anyway?"

Today was the big merger meeting? How did I forget? "Where—where are the kids?"

"Maria's got them." He flashed his dimples at me. "I thought if I found you, I'd take you to dinner."

My mind was a blank. "Oh."

"I've never been to the Redbury," he said casually, looking around the lobby. "Nice vibe. So what're you doing here?"

I wiped my hands on my blouse again. I had to come up with something—fast.

"You know...I—I have book club on Tuesdays," I said, trying to sound matter-of-fact and not meeting his eye. I looked down and noticed a small, white goose-down feather clinging to my jeans. I quickly flicked it onto the floor.

He walked over to the seating area near the entrance and I trailed behind him. He turned and regarded the street through the glass door of the hotel entrance. He'd stuck his hands into his suit pockets as he walked and I faintly heard the clatter of coins through the intense thump-thump that reverberated from my chest into my eardrums. I stood behind a high-backed wing chair and he stood next to another.

He cleared his throat and turned to me. "Alex, I texted Cheryl when I couldn't reach you. She told me you couldn't make it today. And she hopes you feel better."

He turned his gaze away from the street and studied me for the first time in months. His eyes lingered on my face and then dropped to my cream blouse, my ripped jeans, my gold sandals, and back to my face. Did he notice my eyes refused to look directly into his? Was there a blush to my cheeks or a protective stance to my shoulders? Could a primitive sense deep within him have recognized the scent of another man on me? That freshly fucked scent of sweat and body fluids. Of course, I'd showered, carefully dried my hair, and cleaned and arranged myself before I'd left Matt but still, I carried him on me and inside me. I didn't expect to see Jason for hours, and then not in the lobby of the hotel, with Matt in a room just floors above us.

My heart pounded violently. I was caught in a lie. I stood silently, not knowing what to say. Part of me was shocked he'd looked for me. If I missed a book club or a PTA meeting, he didn't know. What made him search for me today? Didn't he assume I was doing mommy errands: doctor appointments, teacher meetings, child emergencies? But another voice in my head asked, *Does it matter? You're caught. Tell him the truth. Do it now. Tell him.*

"I'm sorry, Jason. I'm sorry." I stumbled on my words, felt my throat constrict, choked back the sentences, the consonants and vowels that would tear our family apart.

The quiet in the lobby was deafening. Not a single sound could be heard, not the constant stream of guests, nor the ringing of cell phones, not even the sounds of diners drifting over from the lobby restaurant.

I stood with my hand on the back of the armchair, steadying myself as I tried to formulate the explanation that wouldn't come. Jason stood across from me, facing me. I realized he'd recently gotten a haircut. His sideburns were neat and trim. I stared at his face, his blue eyes, his dark golden hair, his well-kept goatee. He looked polished in his business suit.

"For what?" he asked.

I couldn't form the words, couldn't make my mouth enunciate the appropriate sounds—how do you tell your husband, "I've been having an affair?"

"I...was meeting someone."

"Meeting someone? Who?" he asked, evenly.

"You don't know him," I answered, purposefully evading the question to buy more time.

"Him?" There must have been a full two-second silence before that one syllable hit him like a truck: *Him.* "Him, who? What are you talking about?" He was eerily calm given where the conversation was headed.

"Matt Daniels," I answered, my heart going a million miles a minute.

"Matt Daniels? Who's Matt Daniels?" Jason reverted

into lawyer-mode. He calmly collected information, pieced together details, made amazingly accurate inferences.

"He's an old boyfriend...from college, my junior year abroad."

"Okay, so you weren't at book club because you were meeting an old boyfriend for lunch?" His tone was measured but I could feel the force behind his words. He looked around. "Where is he?"

"I...he..." Jason must have first spotted me in the lobby and not seen me walk out of the elevator. I could just nod—just a slight movement of my head to confirm: Yes, I met him for lunch; yes, I was sorry I'd lied—but I couldn't do it. He noticed my hesitation because I could see the implication taking shape in his mind.

"Did you meet him for lunch, Alex?" he asked slowly.

I shook my head. My hands clasped together in front of my chest. I dug the fingernail of my right thumb into the palm of my left hand and steadied myself. I would have given my life for a cigarette.

"Drinks?' he asked, gripping the back of the opposite chair.

Oh, how am I going to do this? "No, Jason—"

His eyes bore into me. "You're only leaving me one other option."

The seconds ticked by. I prayed for a large group of people to burst into the lobby, a cleaning crew, a wedding entourage, anything to postpone the inevitable. But none of that happened. It was just Jason and me facing each other in the lobby of the Redbury Hotel. There was no bolt of lightning to save me.

He stood perfectly still and asked, "Did you fuck him?"

There was nothing else to say. Just one syllable, three little letters, that's all it took to unravel a marriage. It astounded me to think of the endless effort required to make it thrive, and yet it unraveled in only a syllable.

"Yes," I said quietly.

"Yes?" he repeated louder, his eyebrows intersecting in

disbelief. He stood still as a statue behind the chair, gripping the back of it white-knuckled and looking at me like an archer taking aim. There was still a tiny bit of hope attached to his response, as if he wasn't sure he heard me correctly. That one word—yes—floated in the air between us and then laid at my feet. There was nothing left for me to do but dispose of any ambiguity and break my husband's heart.

"Yes."

He flinched visibly but continued the line of questioning undeterred. "Was it the first time?"

"Jason, we should talk about this at home—"

"Just answer the question—was it the first time?"

"No."

"So you've been having an affair?" he asked.

"Yes."

"How long?"

"Jason, we should—"

"Shut up and answer the question, Alex."

"Okay."

"How long?"

"About six months," I squeaked.

He pulled out the high-backed chair and slumped down into it. He didn't say another word and I could feel his heart break and I could feel my own break, too. It wasn't just a sick feeling in my chest; it was as if the world somehow shifted and I watched Jason and me from afar: his blue eyes, the smile lines at the corners of his lips, hands in the pockets of his well-tailored suit, even his leather loafers—and yet that couldn't be us—Jason and me—poised between two wing-backed chairs in a hotel lobby, torn apart by my deception. That wasn't our story.

Jason looked past me through the glass doors and out into the street, still shaking his head and speaking softly to himself. At this point, I didn't think the conversation could get any more crippling, but it did.

"What an ass I've been," he said, staring outside. "All

this time I knew you were going through something…and I thought if I gave you some space, you'd work it out…I actually thought you seemed better lately, more like yourself, and now you're telling me you were here all afternoon…fucking some guy from college…"

"I—I didn't mean for it to happen. It just started and I—I couldn't stop it and I know I've lied and—"

He stood up and looked directly at me.

"Are you in love with him?"

I took a quick intake of breath to barrel forward in my explanation but found speech suddenly failed me. Tears rolled down my cheeks, my face flushed with heat, and I felt a wave of nausea like I might throw up.

"I don't know," I finally whispered, shaking my head.

"You don't know? You've been fucking some guy behind my back for six months—and you *don't know* if you're in love with him?"

"I—I don't know how I feel."

"Well, that's great because I know how I feel—sick to my fucking stomach."

He turned and stormed out of the lobby. He didn't say another word, didn't glance or nod in my direction. He stalked out of the hotel as I stood immobile and watched, knowing I'd been warned, knowing I'd been well aware of the risks the whole time—and I'd done it anyway.

RESTLESS IN L.A.
Mommy Musings. Stupid Confessions. Life.
Posted by Anonymous

Lies I Tell Myself

I keep telling myself that everything's okay even though I know it's not. And maybe it won't ever be again. I've exerted a lot of effort over the years to keep down the feelings that have threatened to engulf me, feelings of misery and isolation and a sense of being really lost. But the truth is, in some weird way, I've been attached to my own misery and overwhelm, they've been my default settings. And I've been way too tired and complacent to do anything about them except try to keep my head above water. I thought if I slowed down and tried to find some landmark to hold on to or a sign to orient myself by, I just might drown. But I can't avoid it anymore because I'm pulling all the people I love right down with me. I've got to find a way to come up for air.

ROBIN FINN

CHAPTER 20: ALONE TIME

I sat in my empty house and paced like a caged animal. I always longed for alone time and now I had it. The kids were with Maria, and Jason was, well, Jason was gone. I didn't know where he was or when or if he was coming home.

I thought back on how this all started. Where did I go off course? Was it the day my finger sent the friend request? Or was I still safe then? There were a number of different ways this could have gone so where was the point of no return? Was it when I agreed to meet him for dinner? Or was it the moment I followed him to his room? Even when I found myself in his bed that first time—even then—there was time to turn back. When was the moment of my undoing? It seemed critical that I pinpoint it.

But in my heart, I knew when it was. It was that day, three weeks later, when I returned to the Redbury to tell him it was a mistake. That day, we had sex again and I ran—I ran fast—but I ended up right back at his door. That was the moment that I gave it all away, everything I had. Because I knew that it would inevitably end in a moment like this. Now was I happy? Was I free? I felt exhausted, miserable and sick. Maybe I was a train wreck?

Maybe I wanted to screw up my happy life? I picked up the phone.

"Laurie?"

"Alex Hoffman. To what do I owe the pleasure of this call?"

"Will you meet me?" I asked, biting down on the inside of my bottom lip.

She paused for a full thirty seconds. I wasn't sure if she hung up. "Are you all right?" she finally asked.

"No. Not even a little."

"Evan will be home in a half-hour. Where?"

"The Diner?"

"Okay. I'll be there by seven-thirty."

"Thank you—"

She hung up.

I got a booth in the back and slid into the black vinyl seat. I stared out the window at the cars driving down Ventura Boulevard and thought about all the times we'd been there over the years—high chairs stuck at the end of tables, booster seats propped onto benches, crayons and coloring pages spread out between Chinese chicken salads, baskets of French fries, and club sandwiches. My skin crawled and I thought about dashing into the alleyway behind the restaurant for a quick cigarette but I couldn't afford to piss off Laurie any more than I already had.

"Hi," I said as she slid in across from me. She looked gorgeous in a pair of skinny jeans and a yellow peasant blouse.

"What's going on?" she asked.

"I—I need to talk to you."

"Go ahead," she said, her eyes wide and her mouth a well-glossed perfection of a straight line.

"I don't know where to start." I looked down at the grain in the shiny wood-like Formica and then forced myself to meet her eye. "I never ended the Matt thing."

"Yeah, I figured as much."

I shook my head. "I guess I knew you knew…"

"Come on, Al, I've been your friend for twenty-two years. No offense, but you're no Mata Hari. And I made it pretty clear how I felt about what you were doing."

"I couldn't lie to you, Laurie so I—"

"Look, I told you to tell me the truth. I figured, when I didn't hear from you, that you didn't want to talk about it. I knew when you did—and I assumed you eventually would—you'd call."

"Do you hate me? I wouldn't blame you if you did, if you never even wanted to speak to me again."

"Of course I don't hate you. If anything," she leaned over, squeezed my hand, and her voice softened, "I'm worried about you. I know you've been tortured."

"Oh, Laurie." I finally let myself crumble. I didn't deserve her compassion. If anything, I deserved to be shunned and treated like the scum that I was. But she didn't recoil. She sat across from me, holding my hand and waiting for me to continue.

"Tell me what's going on," she said, one elbow on the table, her head tilting toward mine.

"I told Jason tonight. About Matt. Well, I didn't exactly 'tell' him, he caught me and I admitted to it."

"Holy shit. What happened?"

"He used that Find Your Phone app and he found me, only I was in the lobby of the hotel just leaving Matt. He wanted to know what I was doing there and I told him the truth. He was stunned. Just stunned. And then he left me. But not before asking how long it was going on and..." I choked out the last part. "If I was in love with him."

"And you said?"

"I told him the truth—that it's been going on for about six months and that I don't know how I feel. It would have been kinder if I'd just stabbed him; you should have seen his face." I dabbed my eyes with the orange linen napkin.

"Jeez," she said, looking out the window and back at me. "Look, what did you expect him to say? At least you were honest."

"Honest? There is nothing about me that's honest." I pressed my hand against my mouth, trying to hold back a sob. "I'm a cheater and a liar and I know it. And the thing is, this whole time I knew it, but when I came to a crossroads and I had to make a decision, I kept going. Even knowing how low and shitty I was." I looked down at my cream blouse and could not believe it was still the same day, that I'd chosen that blouse and slipped it off the hanger that very morning.

Laurie rubbed my arm across the table.

"You're the only person I can tell, Laurie. I'm so ashamed. I did try to end it—but my heart was never in it. And even though I knew it was wrong, I—I didn't stop." I squeezed my napkin, trying to swallow the deep groans of sorrow that wanted to come bellowing out. "And even now, I'm not sure what's going to happen. I don't want to lose Jason, I know that's a completely fucked up thing to say but I don't. And yet, and yet—" I buried my face in my hands and bit down on my lip, trying to compose myself. Even though we were hidden in the back of the restaurant I knew I had to keep it together.

"I hate myself and I know I'm a really awful person, but I can't help it. I can't go back to the way things were. Matt makes me feel things. I mean really *feel* things. And frankly, I'm too old and tired and weak to fight it. It is what it is—I love him."

And there it was. The thing I'd been too afraid to say. I loved him. I loved him then, I loved him now.

Laurie looked shocked but to her credit, her grip on my hand never wavered. "What does he want? Matt. Has he told his wife?"

"He's wanted to tell her for a while. She has her suspicions and he wants to come clean. He wants to be with me."

"What about your kids? And his?"

I clutched my blouse as my heart constricted inside my

chest. "He thinks we can work it out. Somehow. He loves me, Laurie, and he doesn't want to let this go."

"Oh my god," was all she could say. We sat in a back booth of The Diner, holding hands across the table as the world spun out of control.

"Alex," she gripped my hand in both of hers, "are you sure about this? I mean, really sure? Because I've watched you and Jason together for years and you've always seemed happy. You've been through a lot together. I mean—come on—sixteen years of marriage." She leaned in more. "How do you know this isn't just physical? Maybe it will pass? Having sex with an old boyfriend in a hotel room is not the same, at all, as weathering life's storms. You know this. Maybe you two won't even get along outside a bedroom? It's been decades since you were in a real relationship. I mean, honestly, you have no idea."

"No, I guess I don't," I admitted.

"Are you telling me you don't love Jason? Because it seemed like you loved him last year and at your party and, and—"

"I'm not telling you that. I know the whole thing's fucked up."

She waved away the waitress trying to refill our water glasses and leaned over the table until we were practically nose to nose. "Have you considered that you might be having a mid-life crisis?" Her brown eyes widened and she nodded her head in emphasis.

"Of course I've considered a mid-life crisis," I blurted out. "Believe me, Laurie. As well as the possibility of a Klonopin-induced psychotic break, nervous breakdown, prolonged anxiety attack, and adult onset bipolar disorder. I just don't think what ails me can be found in the DSM-IV." I squeezed her hand back and looked out the window. How could I hope to explain to her what I barely understood myself? "I don't think I'm going crazy," I said, "even though it might seem like it."

I just couldn't explain to her the unshakable feeling that

plagued me, the feeling that somehow I'd drifted into a weird alternate reality where I'd failed to become the person I was meant to be—that deep inside, I was sure I missed my boat. A string of decisions, or rather non-decisions, that took place after a cowardly escape from London twenty years earlier resulted in a life where very little resembled the things I wanted, a life in which I ultimately felt like a stranger—until the sudden reappearance of Matt Daniels. He was the only thing I recognized, the magnet to which I was unalterably drawn. I didn't know how to describe that to Laurie. And I knew full well it didn't make sense and there was no way to logically explain it—not to Laurie, not to Jason, not even to myself. Matt stood in front of me that very afternoon struggling to describe the exact same phenomenon. The only difference was, I didn't need to rationally understand it because I experienced it whenever we were together.

RESTLESS IN L.A.
Mommy Musings. Stupid Confessions. Life.
Posted by Anonymous

The Truth

When my affair first started and I confessed it to my best friend, I told her it was hard for me to look in the mirror and that was true. But there are many truths and that wasn't the only one. What I didn't tell her, what I was unwilling to admit even to myself, were the feelings beneath the shame: the elation of soaring above all the constraints of my daily life, soaring above the grocery store and the kids' school, and the two Targets—the one in North Hollywood and the one in Van Nuys—and the Rite Aid and the drycleaner and the donut shop. I didn't tell my BFF about the bonfire lit in my bones or about the loneliness that died that night. How could I? She loved my husband, she loved us as a couple, she loved our Saturday-night-outs and our family barbeques. How could I possibly tell her the truth? That I had a repetitive loop playing in my brain of my lover and me together and, when we were apart, all I wanted to do was shut my eyes and remember. I could barely stand the minutes between the feel of his mouth on mine and getting out of my clothes—skin hunger, we used to call it in high school. Skin hunger. Yes, I was confused and torn and totally guilt-ridden but somewhere deep down I knew why I kept coming back.

CHAPTER 21: MRS. DOUBTFIRE

"Jason, it's me. I'm sure you don't want to talk to me but we need to make a plan about the kids. I know you told them you were out of town but they're wondering when you're coming back. Can you please call me or email me or something when you get this message? Jason…I'm so sorry."

Jason left a week ago. He called Natalie's cell phone in the evenings and the kids passed it around and said good night to him. He told them he was on a business trip and didn't know exactly when he was coming back. It was Sunday night and the kids wanted to know where he was. They were settled in watching *Mrs. Doubtfire* and were disappointed he wasn't there to make the stovetop popcorn. My cell phone rang.

"Hello?"

"Hello Alex."

"Jason. How are you?"

"I'm at the Beverly Wilshire. I got your voicemail about the kids."

I remained silent.

"I'll be here for a while…until I figure out my next move."

"I understand," I said. "Is it possible for us to talk?"

"Are the kids watching a movie?" he asked.

"Yes," I answered. My heart hurt thinking about past Family Movie Nights.

"What movie?" he asked.

"*Mrs. Doubtfire*," I answered.

"I love that movie," he sighed. "Text me when it's over and I'll come by and say goodnight to them and we can talk. I'm going to tell them they won't see me in the morning because I have an early trial."

"Okay, Jason. Thank you."

I hung up and sat thinking. Everything felt painful these days, even simple matters, like the movie the kids watched. Everything was loaded with meaning, with memories. I didn't talk to Matt for two days after Jason left and, even then, I didn't tell him what had happened. Finally, almost a week later, I called him.

"You told him? Five days ago? What happened?"

"It's been hard, really hard. After I admitted to the affair, Jason didn't say much, except that he was leaving." I didn't describe the stab wound I'd inflicted or how small and dirty it made me feel. I didn't mention that he'd asked if I was in love with Matt. "It was as difficult and as painful as you can imagine."

"Do you need anything?"

"No. Please. I have to figure this out on my own." It was the most stilted and unnatural conversation we'd ever had. We had a physical relationship, the first time around and this time, too. The solidity of his body, the scent of him, the feel of his arms and hands seemed to ground me. The artificial sound of his voice through the phone didn't have the calming effect that being in his presence did. If anything, the phone call made me more anxious and uncomfortable.

"I don't have any expectations about how this is going to go. I just want you to talk to me."

Matt seemed so far away and it made what we'd done

seem all the more crazy and selfish. His life was in New York and mine was in L.A. Or at least I'd had a life in L.A. before I blew it all up. I didn't know what I needed. I just wanted to get through the day.

"Do me a favor and please don't tell Heather yet. I know you've been waiting but I think one relationship blowing apart at a time is best."

There was silence for several seconds and I wondered if I dropped the call but then he said, "Okay, I'll wait a little longer."

"Thank you. I've got to go but we'll talk tomorrow."

"Alex?"

"Yes?"

"I'm here."

***

As the credits to *Mrs. Doubtfire* rolled onto the screen, Jason walked in. He brought each of the kids a gift from his "trip." Ben squealed with delight at his new pillow pet, Ryan was thrilled with his Lego Star Wars set, and Natalie eyed her dad sweetly after receiving a large gift card to the mall. After Jason piggybacked Ben to his bed, he sat in Natalie's room and listened to the dramas of her week, then built Lego with Ryan for a half hour. Finally, everyone's lights were out and we met at the kitchen table.

I opened a bottle of Merlot and poured us both a glass. We sat down in opposite tan leather dining chairs.

"I missed them," he said quietly. He was wearing dark jeans and a blue striped golf shirt. Must have been a business casual day, I thought to myself.

"Not half as much as they missed you," I said. Our conversation was awkward, what with land mines littered around every subject such as our kids, our marriage, my affair, but we managed to navigate through it as best we could.

"Look, I have to figure some things out but I can't

without more information from you," he said steadily.

"I'll tell you whatever you want to know."

The room was quiet. I could hear the soft hum of the refrigerator and the swish of the dishwasher on Dry Mode. Other than that, there was silence. Jason looked at me and I could see the red rims of his eyes. His face was heartbreakingly familiar, his blue eyes, his dimpled cheeks. I once again felt like I watched two people who looked like us but couldn't be.

"Are you still seeing him?" he asked, moving his eyes from his wine glass to my face.

"Yes."

"So you intend to have a…relationship with him?"

"I don't know what's going to happen."

"So it wasn't just about the fucking, I assume."

He had a right to his anger. He had a right to feel betrayed, that's what I'd done, betrayed him.

"Alex!" He shouted as he banged his hand on the kitchen table. "Wake up! Do you know what the fuck you're doing? We have three kids, for Christ's sake. Do you really want to rip this family apart?"

"Jason, please. They'll hear you," I panicked. The kids would be devastated enough when they found out we'd separated. I didn't want them to find out this way.

He pressed his fist firmly against the kitchen table over and over again making soft little thumps as he squeezed his eyes shut. "I know things haven't been great with us. There's been a lot of stress around here and I know I've hardly been around, but still, how could you? God damn it, Alex. How could you?" He lowered his voice. "I haven't been able to think about anything for the last seven days but the image of my *wife* taking her clothes off in a hotel room and getting fucked by some guy," he choked out. "I just don't get it. I don't know who you are anymore."

My lips trembled as I tried to swallow over the golf ball-sized lump lodged in my throat. "I'm sorry."

"But not so sorry that you aren't seeing him anymore."

"I can't make any decisions right now," I said. "I know that's not fair. But, I just—can we please, for now, talk about the kids—please."

He shook his head and sat silent. Finally, he asked what I thought was best and we agreed to tell the kids we were taking some time to live separately. He didn't mention the affair, or even raise it as an issue for our kids' information. He would never put his own desire for revenge or righteousness over our children's wellbeing. I knew that implicitly. Jason was distracted, preoccupied, a workaholic, certainly, but he wasn't small or cruel. He was coping with what I'd done to the best of his ability and seeing that made me feel grateful to him and sick to my stomach all at the same time. After we ironed out the details of what and when we'd talk to our children, I walked him down the hallway to our front door. He looked at me and I could see the tears welled up in his eyes.

"I don't know what to say to you. We've been married a long time. I don't know how to hate you. I've spent most of my adult life trying to make you happy, wanting the best for you, for us. It's not easy treating you like my enemy."

A runaway tear streaked down my cheek. He put his finger to it and stopped it in its tracks. His hand opened and cupped the side of my face. I peered into his blue eyes and saw the faint shadow of dimples below his cheekbones and the rough-hewn hair of his goatee. I put my hand over his and pressed it against my face.

"I never meant to hurt you," I said, leaning against the front door for support. "I know it's lame but it's true. I want you to know, what I'm going through, what I've done—it really isn't about you." The dam finally burst and I sobbed fervently through my burning throat. "I know it sounds like total bullshit but it isn't." I held his hand against my throbbing cheek while my nose ran and I hiccupped violently. I barely got the words out but I had to. I didn't know if I'd get another chance.

Without warning, he let go and his powerful hands

clasped me by both shoulders. "What did I do wrong? What did I miss?" he demanded.

I shook my head, wordlessly, tears openly streaming down my face.

He stood still for a minute looking at me. I had this crazy idea he might take me in his arms and hug me but he didn't. He opened the door and left.

RESTLESS IN L.A.
Mommy Musings. Stupid Confessions. Life.
Posted by Anonymous

Friends Hanging Out

I went on Facebook recently, scrolled through my newsfeed and hoped to take my mind off my current situation. I paused at a picture posted of a group of boys from my son's class. I could see from the dark cabinets and flowered rug that they were at the house of my son's former friend. His mom titled the photo, *Friends hanging out*. The boys sat around her kitchen table, big slices of pizza balanced on paper plates in front of them. I stared at the picture. *Friends hanging out*. Friends, I thought to myself. His mother was once a friend of mine. Whatever. I clicked, "Like," logged off, and got ready for bed.

As I tossed and turned, I thought about a conversation I recently overheard between a mother of one of the boys in the picture and another parent. She said her son had a hard time paying attention, "But he's a good kid, you know. It's not like he has any behavior problems." I barely resisted the urge to butt into the middle of the conversation, just poke my head between her and the other woman and ask, "But what if he did—have behavior problems? Would that mean he wasn't a good kid?"

Kids aren't produce. They aren't bad because they have a

soft spot or a bruise or some other kind of outer imperfection that makes them look not quite as perfect as the others. Kids are human beings and they are all good— even if they don't always look like it, even if they have bruises, even if they occasionally bump up against each another. Why isn't that obvious? I reached toward my night table to pull out a tissue and stopped my hand midway. I will not cry over this, I told myself. I had so much to cry over, I vowed not to shed another tear over this.

CHAPTER 22: ALTITUDE

"One cannot know another human being completely. Even less so, ourselves," Lark said to me.

I'd finally admitted to Lark the whole truth of what I'd been doing for months. I'd blurted out that I'd had sex with Matt weeks earlier and alluded to struggling and being confused. But I didn't tell her the truth of what was really going on: that I was having an affair with him, that I spent hours in his bed reveling in his body and feeling like I was twenty years younger. I didn't tell her the excruciatingly fucked-up details of what went on in my deranged mind. I was a mother of three and a grown woman and yet...and yet...there was still so much I wanted. So damn much. I didn't know how to make it go away.

Lark encouraged me to ask for guidance and look for "signs" from the Universe. And I did. But still, I must have needed the remedial message because I couldn't interpret any spiritual signals telling me what to do next. I needed a text message or an oversized billboard, I was so lost in a sea of my own longing and fucking and lying and feeling like shit that I had no real idea how to sort it all out. So I told her the truth. She didn't flinch or even look surprised or horrified or judgmental. She looked serene, like she

273

always did.

"Just tell me what to do," I practically groveled. "Please. Ask the Universe or something. Jason's walked out on me. I told him the truth and he left. I have to make a decision about where to go from here and yet nothing seems to make sense anymore."

"So it sounds like you're confused?"

"Yes, Lark. I'm confused—totally at a loss. I feel like I'm losing my mind."

"Have you considered the possibility that the answer isn't in your mind?"

"Okay, so? What are you saying? The answer is in my heart?

"That might be a good place to start," she answered, nodding her head in encouragement.

"There's nothing in my heart right now except anger and grief and a huge sense of failure. Sixteen years of marriage and I've failed—I've failed Jason and myself and my kids. You should have seen their faces last night when we told them we were separating. Natalie burst into tears, Ryan was screaming at me that he wouldn't live in the house if his father wasn't there and Ben, well, Ben didn't know what to make of it."

Ben actually threw his arms around me and told me not to worry if Dad didn't live there anymore because he would live with me forever. Just thinking about it wracked me with guilt.

"I feel like—like I'm on a mountaintop and I can see the village beneath me and the people scurrying around living their lives but I can't get down. I've got this lofty perspective and no legs to hike. I can see in every direction but I'm stuck up here, immobilized on a mountaintop. What good is this? I've got to make some decisions."

"Is it possible," she said gently, "that you're not ready to make any decisions just yet? That the altitude you describe is all you need right now? Perhaps there is an opportunity to take things in, to process them, to just be?"

Lark continued. "Sometimes scurrying around keeps us so busy we don't have time to process our feelings—our *feelings*, Alex. Maybe immobilized on a mountaintop is right where you need to be. Maybe where you are is perfect."

That's what killed me. Just when I was certain Lark was the most obtuse creature on the planet, she'd come out with something so raw, so true, that it hit me right in the gut.

"I invite you to take no action. Let things unfold. Consider that you don't need to 'do' anything. I think you'll know when you're ready."

I was grateful she'd come. Slowly, surely, I was starting to piece this together. I looked down at my sweatpants and said, "You're right, Lark. I know I have decisions to make but I can't seem to make them come. I feel like I should hurry up and figure this out but I can't. The truth is, I spend my whole life rushing around—getting the kids here or there—always trying not to be late, not to make anyone wait, not to forget or screw up anything. But right now, I just can't follow anyone else's timetable—not even Jason's." I looked up and took a deep breath.

Lark pressed her small, birdlike palms together and pointed them at me. "Keep checking in with yourself, Alex. Keep asking for guidance."

She blew out her homemade patchouli candle and leaned in for our one-minute bone-crushing, goddess embrace with which she always ended our sessions.

"Give what you can, take what you need," she whispered.

I clung to her, felt her large breasts squash into mine, smelled her organic laundry detergent and the remnants of the patchouli candle. I hugged her so hard and didn't let up for the full minute, understanding finally what she meant: "Give what you can, take what you need." I took and took and took, my arms wrapped around her full figure, my body pressed against her, trying to absorb some of the comfort she offered. I felt so desperately alone. I burrowed my head into her shoulder and let myself be cradled in her arms. Laurie was right about Lark; she had great energy and was incredibly intuitive. In spite of myself, I said a silent prayer of gratitude and handed her a hundred to "keep the balance."

***

Later that afternoon, I received a call from Simone Hills. Her son, Miles, the boy Ryan punched in the shoulder last month, told his therapist that he couldn't have a good day unless Ryan had a good day. Apparently Miles' therapist thought it would be a good idea for Ryan to attend one of his therapy sessions to "explore their enmeshment." Simone called to ask if I was willing.

"And, honestly, Alex, it does seem like the least you could do after the incident. Miles was so upset about what happened and I think it would be therapeutic for both boys."

"Um, Simone, you know Miles and Ryan play handball together at recess? I think they're kind of over it. Why doesn't Miles just come over after school and the boys can talk and have some one-on-one time. I'll be here to supervise," I offered.

"I'll talk to Miles's psychologist, Alex, but I think meeting in a therapeutic environment is best," she said, hanging up.

I felt like saying, "Well, why don't you have your son's therapist call my son's therapist." What a world. As I walked to my car, Jason called. I took a deep breath and picked up.

"I'll pick you up tonight—seven sharp."

"Seven sharp?"

"Yes, for Dr. Ross. Or did you forget?" And then his tone changed and he added, "You've obviously been juggling quite a few things lately. No wonder your son's psychiatrist appointment skipped your mind."

"I didn't forget, Jason, I just—listen…" I started to bounce off him Simone's suggestion but I'd hardly gotten through it before he went ballistic.

"You've got to be kidding," he exploded on the phone. "Her kid's therapy's not our problem. God knows we have enough of our own. I'll be at the house at seven sharp. Goodbye."

"Jason—" But he hung up. There was no point arguing that I wanted to drive myself, that I didn't know how we'd bear a twenty-minute car ride together but we were able to talk about the kids and I wanted to keep that up.

Ryan had been seeing Dr. Ross weekly for months but we only checked in with him sporadically. Tonight, we were meeting for an update on Ryan's progress and I was anxious to hear the doctor's perspective. At times, Ryan seemed better, more balanced on the medication and at others, I just couldn't be sure. Living with anxiety and ADHD was a continual roller coaster: days, and sometimes weeks, spent at a manageable plateau, and then—boom!— without warning, the teacher called about another "incident." Ryan's teacher, that very morning, had spent twenty minutes enumerating his difficulty working with others and how often he shouted out. I tried to listen and respond thoughtfully but it was hard. The teacher didn't know, of course, that now, we were in the midst of a family crisis that didn't directly relate to Ryan.

Promptly at seven o'clock, Jason arrived wearing slacks and a dress shirt, his suit jacket laid out carefully in the back seat. I slid into the passenger seat and we headed over to the doctor's office. Since he'd insisted on driving me, I thought he might want to talk but he studied the road. I followed his lead and hit a Favorite button on his car stereo. We drove in silence, listening to Natalie's favorite XM radio station as Chris Daughtry belted out the complexities of "Home." As I listened to Daughtry pour his soul out on the radio, I wondered, not for the first time, if the song was speaking directly to me? Was *home* where I belonged? Where was *home* anyway? I looked over at Jason to see what effect, if any, the song had on him but his eyes were glued to the road.

I reached over and turned off the radio. I never heard the song before and I definitely couldn't take it right then. Music had a way of finding me and expressing exactly what was going on in my mind. This wasn't what I needed now—not with Jason in the car, not on the way to my son's psychiatry appointment, not when I needed to steel myself to be cool and in control.

Jason parked the car and we walked silently into the building. He kept his eyes on the floor and then to the lighted numbers as the elevator made its ascent. I didn't know what to say to my husband. The tension between us was as heavy as if we'd sunk together to the bottom of our swimming pool, suspended near each other but not touching, not relating in any way. I couldn't help but think of the look on Natalie's face as she burst into tears at the news of our separation. She'd said, "Great, now I'm from a broken family." A broken family, where did she hear that expression? Is that what we were now? A broken family. It felt like a knife wound and I wished I could bleed right there in the elevator just to let out the dark red drops of guilt dripping from my gut onto my black flip-flops, announcing, *this is my fault.*

I opened the door and pressed the square button next to the nameplate J.T. Ross, M.D, Ph.D., to indicate we were there. Dr. Ross appeared almost immediately and invited us into the office. We sat down at either end of his tweed coach.

"Overall, Ryan's impulsivity seems to be improving," Dr. Ross began, getting right to the point. At $450 per hour, we were glad he didn't waste time on pleasantries. "But, as you know, pills without skills won't work. Ryan needs to continue our weekly sessions and work on anger management." He went on to share his concern about the school disciplinary system and the fact that Ryan needed clear boundaries and consequences.

"Children with ADHD need very specific routines. Predictability and stability are key," he said calmly. "I understand, Mrs. Hoffman, that you're engaged in an extra-marital affair. Your husband explained the situation to me, confidentially, of course. I would feel remiss not to underscore that, for kids with ADHD, change is particularly challenging. The medication will only take you so far, Mrs. Hoffman. Ryan needs stability in order to thrive."

What the hell? How dare Jason blindside me like this. I had no idea Dr. Ross knew about my personal life. I was mortified. Jason could've at least given me a heads up.

I focused on picking lint off my jeans as Dr. J.T. Ross, in his corduroy pants and plaid jacket, told me how selfish I was and how I sucked as a mother and what low morals I must have and how my behavior was going to fuck up Ryan—and my other children—way more than they already were. Even though he didn't actually say those words, I knew he meant them. But I moved on to another subject that been gnawing at me for months.

"Dr. Ross. I've been thinking for a while now that Ryan might be better served at a different school. Pineview's great and my other two love it, but, for Ryan, well, the teachers just don't get him, and socially...it's been very difficult—have you heard of North Roads? Because I've read a lot about these ADHD schools and—"

"What?" Jason looked as me accusingly. "We never talked about this."

"I've been talking about it for months—"

"We agreed we'd give it more time, Alex. We'd give the medication time."

"No. You agreed. I've been wanting to look for a new scho—"

"It hasn't even been a year. You said," he pointed to Dr. Ross, "that it could take a year to find the right dosing."

"That's true," Dr. Ross answered, adjusting his plaid jacket. "Ryan is responding nicely but it can take time to work out the kinks."

"Fine," Jason said, crossing his arms, "then it's settled. We'll wait."

"No, it's not settled." I said, sitting forward on the couch and addressing both my husband and the doctor. "I believe Ryan would do much better at a school that addresses his particular needs, where he could get the support he deserves, without me constantly having to beg for it. And maybe, he'd find some friends there, too—"

"Is this about that kid who wants him to go to his therapy session? I mean, give me a break."

"Can you please stop interrupting me? I can barely get a sentence out."

"Excuse me, Mrs. Hoffman," Dr. Ross chimed in. "But I do think Mr. Hoffman has a point. Your family is going through a difficult transition right now. I'm not sure I can recommend more changes." He ended our discussion by saying he was concerned about all the members of our family and hoped our struggles would resolve shortly *for our children's sake.*

Since Jason insisted on driving together to the appointment, I asked him to stop at 7-Eleven on the way home so I could buy a new pack of cigarettes. I was seething inside but I couldn't unload on him, not when I was really the one to blame. Either way, after that meeting, I needed a carton. Jason looked surprised but didn't say a word. I knew how he felt about my smoking but I couldn't help it. I bought a pack and a blue Zippo lighter and returned to the parking lot to light up. I leaned against the side of his car and put the cigarette to my mouth, but Jason took the lighter from my hand and lit it for me. I leaned in and took a huge drag, feeling the toxic smoke fill my lungs. To my surprise, Jason took a cigarette out of the pack and lit one for himself.

"How do you think the kids are doing?" he asked,

inhaling.

"As well as they possibly can," I said, "given the circumstances."

He exhaled and leaned against the car. "Yeah, their reactions were pretty much in line with their personalities: Nat's pissed off, Ryan's freaking out, and Ben's, well, Ben's Ben."

"Ryan won't talk to me."

He raised his eyebrows in surprise. "Really?"

"He's so angry at me. After we told them, when I put him to bed, he said, 'Mom, I know you made Dad leave. I know you did.' And then he turned away from me and wouldn't let me kiss him goodnight. He's barely spoken two words to me since."

"I didn't say a thing to him, Alex." He turned away and flicked his ash into the parking lot.

"I know," I said. "But somehow he knows it's all my fault." A blue Honda Pilot pulled into the lot and three teenagers in short shorts and oversized sweatshirts jumped out. I watched as they walked into the store. "It won't be long till Natalie's a teenager," I mused out loud.

"Are you still seeing him?" Jason suddenly asked. He held his cigarette in his left hand and I watched the glowing ember at the tip. I will not cry, I told myself.

"I don't want to talk about this now," I sighed. It wasn't going to get any easier.

"Look, Alex, here's the thing. Do you think you made a mistake? Because I think we owe it to ourselves to try. We have a family. Our kids need us. And, to be honest, I need us too." He raised his cigarette to his lips and took another drag then looked out into the near-empty lot. "I still don't understand how this happened. I wish you'd talk to me."

"I don't know what to say, Jason," I said, buying time by exhaling out of the right corner of my mouth. I watched the smoke slowly dissipate into the night air before I turned to him and answered. I still couldn't look him in the face. "I had an affair."

"Are still having," he corrected.

"I haven't seen him in weeks, but it's true. I haven't ended it." I couldn't bring myself to say his name. "I told you I don't know what's going on with me and I can't be more honest than that. Something is wrong—very, very wrong—and I'm attempting to figure it out but it's slow. I can't make it go any faster."

"Well, that's just great but we have three kids to consider," he answered angrily. "While you're enjoying your afternoon fuck, our kids are really suffering. Didn't you hear what Dr. Ross said?"

"Yes, I heard. I heard every word. Can you take me home now?" I'd had enough. I didn't have answers and I definitely didn't want to fight. I flicked my cigarette into the lot and gripped the door handle on the passenger side of his car, waiting for him to unlock it.

"Wait, just wait, this isn't what I planned," he said, facing me. "I wanted to talk to you, not yell at you. I'm just so—so angry. But that's not what I wanted to say. I wanted to say..." He stepped closer to me and lowered his voice. "This isn't easy for me, Alex. But I was there with you when all our kids were born, and I held on to you when they told us about Ryan and his ADHD and his anxiety and his moods. It was me, Alex, whose shoulder you cried on and maybe I didn't cry too, but I wanted to. And I was there when we moved into the house and when we celebrated all the birthdays and when the goddamn back yard flooded—I've been there. And maybe I haven't been around as much as I should and maybe you've tried to tell me and I didn't hear, but still, that doesn't give you the right to go and fuck it all up."

He dropped his cigarette onto the pavement and crushed it with his leather loafer. I could see his eyes shining in the dimly lit parking lot. "You know, you're not the only one who didn't get exactly what you wanted. I didn't want this—my wife cheating on me—that's not what I wanted or expected. Ever."

"Jason, you're right, you're—"

He held up his hand. "But still. I want to try. I spoke to a friend of mine who does family law. He gave me a recommendation for a marriage counselor."

I heard Dr. Ross's accusations reverberating through my mind: *Ryan needs a stable home environment. This back and forth is very damaging for kids with ADHD.* I thought about the way Dr. Ross looked at me, as if to say, "You owe this to your kids." And I did. I owed it to all of us.

"I think we should work at it…for the kids' sakes…and for ours," Jason said as he took another step closer to me. "I don't know where it went wrong but I want to know. I think I deserve to know…I don't want to lose my family." I was sandwiched between his Porsche and him, fumbling for another cigarette and quickly lighting it before he took my free hand in his. "And we can't do that, Alex, we can't even begin to do that unless…you cut him loose." He finished, took a deep breath and looked directly at me.

I inhaled the carcinogenic smoke and exhaled, inhaled and exhaled, pressing the cigarette to my lips. A "broken" family, she said. Broken. I didn't reply. I just stood there gripping the cigarette and taking slow drags until I smoked it down to the filter. I tapped the box for another so I could continue chain smoking but I couldn't pop one out because my hands trembled so badly. Jason looked over, took the box, tapped out a cigarette, and put it to his lips. He lit it and handed it to me. "Think about it," he said and got in the car. I finished my cigarette and we drove home in silence.

***

Maria reported that the kids were asleep and wished me good night as she left. I watched her blow a kiss to Jason as he pulled away from the curb. I locked the door, put my purse down next to the silver bowl in our entryway, and kicked off my shoes. It was always Jason's job to do our nightly lockdown, but since he moved out, I walked the hallways at night and made sure all the windows and doors were closed and locked. I saved the kids' rooms for last. Benny was asleep in his Pokémon pajamas, his small body wrapped around his racecar pillow. I kissed him softly on the forehead and went to Ryan's room. He was snoring softly with two Marvel comic books peeking out from under his pillow. I put them on his night table and kissed him on the cheek. Finally, I went into Natalie's room. I opened her door slowly but it still creaked loudly from the effort. I've got to oil that thing, I reminded myself, as I checked in on my sleeping daughter. Her face was smooth and unlined and in her slumber state, with no rolling eyes or scowls, I could see the little baby she'd once been. "Good night, sweet girl," I whispered as I tiptoed out of her room.

I walked slowly to my office, the images of my sleeping children fresh in my mind, and sat down in front of the computer screen. There were two new voicemails on my cell phone but I didn't listen. I sat down at my computer and logged in to my email.

Matt,

Things have been very difficult here, as you can imagine. I'm glad you waited to talk to Heather. I can only suggest that you really think this through. Matt, my kids miss their father. And Jason wants to try counseling. He wants to keep our family together. I owe it to all of them to try. Even though I know what happened between us caused a lot of pain, I am not sorry. I could never be. Somehow, I know it had to happen. But I have to do the right thing now for my family. Please understand. This is how it has to be.
Alex

I stared at the note, re-read it twice, and pressed Send.

***

The day flew by and it wasn't until I collapsed in bed at ten o'clock, exhausted and alone, that I let myself think about the email I'd sent. Relief washed over me like the cool sweat I'd been in all day. I didn't hear from Matt and I figured he was dealing with things in his own way. Maybe he, too, realized it was for the best. I started to breathe again. I got the kids to school on time that morning, made dinner, served it, and cleaned up. I checked homework, made lunches for the next day, and read to Benny before bed. I thought about the fact that, in many ways, nothing really changed. Jason moved out and I continued to man the fort alone, as I had for years. It was true that some days Jason put in an early appearance and that, on the weekends, he sometimes helped with soccer game duty, but mostly, things continued as usual. I took a sleeping pill and finally fell into a disturbed sleep.

At twelve-thirty, my cell phone rang.

"Hello?"

"It's me."

"What? What time is it?" I glanced at my phone. "It's three-thirty in New York. What are you—"

"I'm outside."

"Outside? Outside where?"

"Outside your front door."

"What?"

I tiptoed down the hall and opened the front door. There was Matt standing on the flagstone walkway beside my potted begonia. From the glow of the porch light, he looked disheveled in a faded pair of Levi's, a relaxed tan T-shirt, and a rumpled black blazer. He carried a messenger bag over one shoulder.

"Are you crazy?" I asked. "What are you doing here? My kids are asleep."

"Then I guess you better invite me in."

I gestured for him to follow me to the back of the house, into my office. We circled each other over the Oriental carpet. He seemed so out of place here: Matt

Daniels, in my office, in my house in Los Angeles. It was as if he had popped out, whole and alive, from the pages of my journal hidden in the desk drawer. But he wasn't a memory, he was real and he was standing in my house where I lived with my husband. Even though Jason was gone, I felt my betrayal even more keenly, if that was possible.

"What are you doing here?" I repeated.

"I got on a flight as soon as I got your email. My first impulse was to call but I decided to wait and talk to you face to face. I know Jason moved out and I'm sorry if I'm intruding but I had to see you."

"It's disorienting, okay?"

"You didn't leave me any other choice." He sat down on the old glider in the corner of the room and laid the messenger bag at his feet. I sat in the chair at my desk. The distance between us seemed to pulsate. I was drawn to him and yet I was surprised and upset by his presence in my house.

"You could have called," I finally said.

"You wouldn't answer."

"Okay, okay." I couldn't argue the point.

"Look, Alex, on the flight over, I tried to convince myself I was lucky that I didn't come clean with Heather yet, lucky that I escaped a painful episode in my marriage. I asked myself if maybe this wasn't for the best." He took a deep breath and looked at me. I shifted in my chair.

"And then I realized I was full of shit. And it dawned on me—don't you see? We're doing this whole thing again. You said you left twenty years ago because you didn't know how I really felt about you. But that was bullshit. It was bullshit, Alex. That wasn't why you left and it wasn't why I let you go. You knew I loved you and I knew it, too." He stood up and his eyes gleamed. "I think we were both scared."

The force of his words hit me like a blow.

"When you ran off, I let you go. I blamed you, but the

truth is, I let you go."

He paced back and forth as he spoke, looking down at the carpet and concentrating. I knew the look of tension in his body, the pacing, the hand running through his hair, the tightening of his shoulders. I didn't interrupt.

"Maybe there was a part of me that was relieved—I was twenty-five years old and I was afraid you were going to change my life. And tonight as I was thirty thousand feet above the ground, I thought, if I was scared then, I should be terrified now. We both have kids and marriages. Our decisions have consequences not just for us, but for the people we love most in the world. But I'm not scared. You know why? Because, back then, I had no idea what I was giving up. I was too young and arrogant and stupid to get that this would never, ever, happen to me again."

He came over to my chair and looked down at me.

"I'm just not that stupid anymore. I'm not that young anymore, either. And I am definitely not scared. Not about ruining my life or my kids' lives or your life. These things happen; I can live with that. There's just one thing that terrifies me...do you know what that is?" He paused and lifted my chin with his hand so I couldn't avoid his eyes. "You. That you won't take the chance."

I felt like I was standing at the edge of a thirty-foot diving board, looking down. I knew if I jumped, I'd be okay. I knew I could do it and my heart leapt at the thought. The only problem was, my feet were planted on that board. My mind was plotting the number of backward steps it would take to retreat down the ladder. I couldn't do it.

"I told you I won't make the same mistake twice," Matt said. "This time, I chased you to L.A. like I should've done the first time. I love you—have loved you—from the moment I first saw you standing in the middle of the street. You're 'The One.'" I apologize if it's late and fucked up and messy, so messy," he said, running his hands through his hair and pacing back and forth in front of the desk.

"But I can't deny it. And I'm willing to turn my life upside down. I won't pretend it's going to be easy. Given your situation and mine, it's probably going to be hard as hell, but I'm willing to," he said, clearing his throat as he turned to look at me. "What about you?"

I sat in the swivel chair and he stood in front of me. He reached out his hands and pulled me up so we stood facing each other.

"Do you realize what you're asking me to do?" I whispered. "I've betrayed my husband in every possible way. He deserves——" But the words wouldn't keep coming. Tears streamed down my face. The howling of coyotes that lived in the hills behind my house echoed through the glass doors and into the room. I took a deep breath and tried to continue, "He deserves—he's earned— a second chance. He loves me. He's devoted himself to me for the last sixteen years and it was good even if——" I clamped a hand over my mouth as if holding back the words could change anything.

"Even if what?" he asked.

"Even if it never felt like it does with you." I put my head in my hands and a giant sob escaped. "Please Matt, I want you to go."

He reached out to touch me but I stepped back out of his grasp. His hand hung in mid-air, stretched out toward me. "Why did you come looking for me?" he asked.

Tears rolled down my cheeks and I felt like I was choking. I reached across the desk and snatched up a box of tissues. I pressed it against my chest and stared at the blue geometric pattern on the side of the box. "I don't know. But if you love me, if you really love me, you'll let this go."

"I can't," he practically shouted.

"Don't you see," I pleaded, putting the box down and moving closer to him, "we missed our chance. We missed it." I felt it viscerally. We had the opportunity once, a long time ago, but we squandered it. It wouldn't come around again.

He gripped my arm at the elbow. "No. We can start over."

"There's no such thing," I said sadly, shaking my head. My temples throbbed and my throat burned. Tears streamed down my cheeks and I blew my nose. I had a sick feeling inside and desperately wanted to lie down, curl up in a ball, and forget—forget that Matt was in my house, that my kids were asleep across the hall, that my husband was living in a hotel.

"Please," I said. "Let it go."

"You can ask me anything—anything—but don't ask me that."

"I have nothing left to ask." My legs hardly supported me but I forced myself to remain standing. "I can't ask for things to be the way they were, or for me to be a different person or to feel a different way. It's too late for that. It's all I have left to ask. Please. If you love me, you'll let it go."

We stood together in the office and I thought about the old Matt, the one from the journal, and the new Matt, the one I'd been seeing in the afternoons behind Jason's back. And I wanted to hate him and part of me did. Part of me blamed him for turning me into someone who wasn't satisfied with what she had. And I didn't want to be that person. I wanted to be Alex Hoffman, happy and content mother of three. Why couldn't I accept things for what they were and be grateful? Why couldn't I accept Jason for who he was? Why did I think I deserved more than I was already lucky enough to have? I didn't want to be in this position; I didn't want any of it. I wanted to return to a simpler time—before I had dinner with Matt, before he reminded me of all the things I once wanted.

He approached me slowly. He reached out and smoothed back my hair, gathering it in one hand at the nape of my neck and tilting my face up toward his. His eyes were so incredibly green, the color of the hillside I used to tumble down when I was a kid. He was scruffy and disheveled and gorgeous, so gorgeous it hurt to look at him. I noticed every detail of his face, his glowing eyes, his perfect nose, his dark afternoon stubble. Just then, he leaned over and kissed me, crushing his lips to mine, searching my mouth urgently with his tongue. The room began to spin and all I felt was him, his lips, his mouth, his tongue, the desire to devour him inside of me. I pressed my mouth against his, tasted him, imprinted the feel of his kiss in my mind.

Finally, we separated. He walked over to the glider, picked up his messenger bag, and looked at me. "I'm heading over to the Redbury. I have a few things to finalize and then I'm off to New York. He spoke softly and deliberately, gently offering up each word. "You should know, Heather and I are separating. It isn't fair to her or me. I have to face it. I want something more."

"Matt, I'm sorry."

He walked over and stood in front of me. "Me, too, Alex. But we both have to do what we have to do. I understand that now."

RESTLESS IN L.A.
Mommy Musings. Stupid Confessions. Life.
Posted by Anonymous

My Story
When I woke up this morning, alone in my bed, I wished I could stop time or move it backward. The quiet of my house hunkered down inside me like one of my babies forming in my womb. I just wanted to sit with myself and not feel the searing sense of guilt and shame and confusion.

My lover once asked me why I left him the first time

around—twenty years ago. I went into my story: my parents were going bankrupt, I had no money, I had to go home and get a job, I wanted to graduate from college, blah, blah, blah. I had this weird urge to shout, "That's my story and I'm sticking to it!" but I finally realized he was right—it was total bullshit. All of these things did, in fact, happen but not one of them had any bearing on why I left him. I left him for one reason, and one reason only: I was totally fucking terrified.

And all these years I secretly nursed my sorrow—if only my parents didn't pressure me, if only I got a job in London, if only he came looking for me, if only…if only…always blaming my parents, him, or outer circumstances until I suddenly realized—as I stood there spewing my reasons which got me through the last two decades—that it was all made up. I'd lied to myself for twenty years. And he was right about this too: I did come looking for him. I typed his name into Facebook and voilà. It took me twenty years, one marriage, and three children to have the courage to look for him and, every step of the way, I was in denial—it was my finger that sent the request, my feet that walked to his room, my body that wanted him so badly. It was always something other than "me." And even when I acknowledged that it was my true self that wanted him, I still wavered. I've been wavering for months.

CHAPTER 23: EMERGENCY SESSION

I called an emergency session with Lark and, thank god, she was available. I could barely sit still as she lit her patchouli candle, called in the light, and settled herself Indian-style on the glider.

"Alex, what's coming forward for you right now?" she asked in her sweet, singsong voice.

"I finally made a decision. I broke it off with Matt. Jason wants to try to work this out, and god knows I'm lucky he wants to after what I've done."

"You must feel relieved," she said.

"I thought I would...but I don't. I feel like I'm being ripped apart. Jason deserves this from me and my kids need their dad. But Matt flew in from New York and came to my house and got into all this stuff about repeating the past, and how he wasn't going to make the same mistake twice, and how we're doing it all over again and now he knows and he can't pretend, crazy things like that. But it isn't the same. We're both married. We have five children between us. Five, Lark."

Lark leaned forward. "I understand," she nodded. "Tell me about you're 'doing it all over again?' What does that mean to you? You know, when there's a lesson to be

293

learned, the Universe provides continued opportunities to learn it."

"I don't know. I think for Matt it means he's not going to let me walk out on him *again,* like he thinks he did twenty years ago. He came to L.A. this time. He wants me to know he loves me and he wants to be with me. He's leaving his wife."

"I didn't mean for Matt. I meant for you, Alex. He sounds like he knows what he wants. Do you?"

"Huh?" I asked, feeling my hands shake. "If you've got some direct line to my 'inner knowing,' please, Lark, tell me—what do I want? Because I've been trying to figure it out for months and I'm no closer to understanding a fucking thing. All I know is what I don't want—I don't want to feel like this." My eyes watered and my head felt hot and my fists were clenched in my lap.

"You seem triggered," she said calmly.

"Everyone keeps telling me what they want—Dr. Ross wants me to get this family back together, the kids want their dad back, Jason wants to work things out, and Matt? Matt wants to talk about the past. There's nothing to talk about—I didn't walk out on him twenty years ago, I ran! And I'm running this time too!"

Lark nodded and sat as still as the pot-bellied Buddha on the shelf.

"When we met, it was my junior year abroad—one year—with a beginning and an end. So I gave myself the year to be with him, to experiment, to take risks—to be someone more than I really was. It was like I woke up. But I couldn't sustain it and I couldn't bear for him to know. So I left. My parents and their whole financial wreckage gave me the perfect opportunity. The things is...I didn't plan for the aftermath. I didn't plan to grieve for him for the rest of my life. I thought I'd move on. You know, go back to sleep in my comfy chair. When I met Jason, he made me feel cherished. And safe. And I told myself; this is love. And I've been telling myself that every day for the last sixteen years."

I wrapped my arms around myself and rocked back and forth in my chair, my eyes shut tight, remembering. Lark didn't say a word but I knew she was there even with my eyes closed. I felt safe in the space she held for me.

"Our outer experience is the perfect mirror for our inner reality."

"Huh?' I asked. "What does that mean?"

She took my hand. "It means we create the situation on the outside that we experience on the inside. It means I'm not sure Jason is the only one you've been unfaithful to."

I was stunned. Unrestrained agony festered beneath my sternum and around my heart, but the awareness taking shape wouldn't quit. My thoughts flew by in a giant maelstrom, each one whizzing through my brain before I could clearly understand its significance—a wannabe writer, a phony friend, a cheating wife… It finally clicked. "There's nothing about me that's authentic—nothing at all." I felt a searing pain swirling inside of me as if all the tiny pinpricks of hurt that were disbursed throughout my body were being called home into the center of my chest.

Lark sat with me and raised her palms in my direction. Her long, red hair cascaded out of the ponytail on top of her head and down around her shoulders. She sat upright, legs folded, palms directed upward and curved toward me, as if she were holding out an apple in each hand. She didn't comment or comfort, she just sat with me as I grieved. Finally, the tears subsided and I shook and snorted from the effort.

"I've lied to myself for years. Ever since I left Matt. All these years, I've let myself believe I ran away from him but it wasn't him I was running from…it was me. And that's what I've being doing ever since—running. I never asked myself what I wanted—I didn't want to know. It was easier to do what's expected, you know, follow the program, and Jason laid it all out so well. And it was good—I could just keep shopping and volunteering and wiping my fucking counters and driving my kids all over the place and I didn't have to try anything and fail. But things didn't turn out so neatly. Ryan doesn't fit in the box, no matter what Jason wants to believe. He's different. He's needed so much for me to see that and I have and I haven't. I shook my head and looked out the office door. "I tried to force myself to forget who I was. It was just so painful to remember because I—I didn't turn out to be anything like the person I'd hoped to be. Matt tried to tell me; he tried to make me own up to what *I* wanted but I've trained myself to forget. Sleepwalking as a defense? Pathetic, huh?"

"No, not at all," Lark said. She leaned over and rubbed my hand.

"When I'm with Matt, he sees me." I wiped my eyes, leaving dark jagged lines of what was left of my mascara across the back of my hand. "And that's what's been so irresistible. I'm forty years old and I'm so freaking tired of feeling like a phony." I squeezed her hand and finally, truly, understood. "I get it. It's me I've been searching for all along."

Lark reached out and hugged me. I buried my head in her chest and wept while she held me and patted my hair. Finally, I understood. Finally, I knew. I couldn't find me in Jason and I couldn't find me in Matt, either. Not really. Somehow Matt saw through all of my façades, my bullshit and confusion and resistance and fear, and when I looked at him, I saw myself reflected back. And I wanted to see me. I wanted to see me so badly that I'd given up nearly everything for it—nearly. But how could I live only seeing myself as a reflection in someone else's eyes? That wasn't what I was after; that wasn't why I'd fucked up my whole life.

RESTLESS IN L.A.
Mommy Musings. Stupid Confessions. Life.

Posted by Anonymous

Alternate Me

This morning, I got up and got dressed, right down to the earrings, until I realized I wasn't in the mood for the outfit and had to change the entire ensemble so I felt right. What is that feeling? Discontent? Discomfort? A fantasy about a different look, a different life?

I remembered the piece on Quantum Mechanics I watched on The Science Channel. It described the "Many Worlds Theory," the idea that there are an infinite number of universes, each of which contain a different version of ourselves living every possible alternative life, a sort of cosmic *The Road Not Taken*. I wondered what Alternate-me, living in some parallel universe, was wearing that day. Alternate-me had no husband and no kids, just a colorful assortment of some-time lovers. She sat outside a cafe in Manhattan, working on her seventh novel on her MacBook (she's very prolific), drinking a latte, and occasionally reaching down to stroke the mottled neck of her Lab/Shepherd mix Rex.

Alternate-me doesn't have to rush home to make dinner, doesn't get yelled at if she eats all the one hundred-calorie Snackwell cookie packs. She doesn't even know what a hundred-calorie Snackwell cookie pack is. Alternate-me doesn't do other people's laundry or drive carpool or take anyone to therapy appointments. Alternate-me is free.

I stood at my closet, rifling through my clothes, trying to figure out what outfit to wear that would fit my "mood,' listening to my kids bicker in the other room over what TV show to watch and sent out a cosmic stink-eye to Alternate-me, that prolific, latte-drinking, childless, single version of myself living it up in Manhattan.

CHAPTER 24: COMING CLEAN

I dropped my purse on the entry table and surveyed the living room. How often in the last eleven years did I come home to a quiet house with nothing immediately to do? No dirty dishes to be washed, no misplaced homework to find, no fighting to referee, no one calling my name. Maria was there yesterday to straighten up and since the kids were with Jason at the new apartment he was renting in Beverly Hills, the house was spotless and silent. How weird.

I sat down at the kitchen island and let my mind drift to the one subject I did my best to avoid: Matt. I hadn't spoken to him since he'd come to the house weeks ago. There was nothing to say. He was starting a new life and I'd made my choice. I wanted to repair the damage between Jason and me. I was going to be authentic. I was going to get in touch with myself. And my kids needed their father. It was that simple.

My cell phone rang and Jason's name flashed across the screen.

"Hello?" I answered.

"It's me. I'd like to stop by tonight and pick up a few more things. Maria will be at my place so, if it's okay with you, can I come by the house around nine?"

"Sure, that sounds fine," I said.

"Okay, thanks," he paused. "Will you be there?"

"Yes, I mean, I wasn't planning on going anywhere, unless…you want me to."

"No, no that's fine. I'll see you later then."

"See you later," I said and hung up.

I spent the evening straightening up my office. I organized the family bulletin board pinned with a zillion reminders, invitations, and schedules and input everything—finally—into the calendar on my phone. I paused at the events Jason and I were invited to: a friend's son's Bar Mitzvah, a fortieth birthday party, a housewarming soiree. These were the little details that made up our life together. Once it was all mundane and taken for granted; now, I just stared at the front of one of the envelopes: "Jason and Alex Hoffman." Jason and Alex. Jason and Alex. Did "Jason and Alex" exist anymore? Were we possible to repair? I was just getting ready to tackle the file cabinet when the doorbell chimed.

"Hi," Jason said, standing awkwardly on the walkway.

"Come in," I gestured to the entry. "It's your house."

"I just wanted to…be polite, I guess."

We laughed for a second. I followed him down the hallway as he approached our bedroom. The pale gray walls and white lacquer furniture was professionally chosen. Our bed was neatly made and I laid out a few items I thought he might want: his brown leather belt, two pairs of dress shoes, and half a dozen black socks balled together in pairs. I sat on the edge of the chaise as he rummaged through his drawers collecting undershirts and shorts.

I watched him fold several shirts and neatly stack them inside the weekender he'd brought with him. He was wearing black sweatpants with a white stripe down each side and an LA Fitness shirt.

"Looks like you restarted your gym membership," I

said.

"Yeah," he responded. "I thought it was about time I started working out again."

He grabbed a bottle of cologne off the top of the dresser and a pair of black enamel cufflinks I'd given him for law school graduation and then stopped short. I saw him lift the silver picture frame off the dresser before it registered. It was our favorite wedding photo: me, in my simple white gown sitting on a chair in front of a dressing table. The back of my gown was draped over the back of the chair to prevent wrinkling and Jason was kneeling beside me, placing a kiss on my cheek. Jason held the silver frame and stared at the image blankly. I looked over and remembered the moment vividly: after the wedding, before we'd emerged into the ballroom, I'd sat down in the bridal suite for a final re-application of make-up when Jason knelt down and suddenly kissed the side of my face. Somehow the photographer captured the moment perfectly.

"I wasn't going to do this," he said, "but I can't help it." He replaced the photo on the dresser and turned to me, his eyes damp. "You know how you always say the radio's speaking directly to you? That whatever's on captures the exact feelings you're having?"

"Yes, that still happens to me all the time."

"Well, I had that experience tonight," he said shrugging, "on my way over here." He pulled out his cell phone and scrolled through his music. "I downloaded it after I heard it," he said, and the clear voice of Jason Mraz rang out, singing, "I Won't Give Up."

I knew it was a love song, I'd heard it many times before, but I never really paid attention to the lyrics before tonight. So I sat on the chaise while Jason leaned against the dresser and we listened together to the song—the searching and waiting and believing in a love worth holding on to—without speaking. It was beautiful and heartbreaking and sad and sweet all at the same time. By the time it ended, Jason was sitting next to me on the bed.

"I feel like I've gone about this wrong. Not that there's a right way to react when your wife's had an affair." His face contorted for a moment but he quickly regained his composure. "I've yelled at you and pushed you because I've been so hurt and angry. I'm still not clear on where things stand, you know, with you and him—"

"It's over," I said. "It has been for a while."

He leaned over and sighed. I didn't know what to say. He took my hands in his and absently rubbed them before he continued, "I've asked myself over and over again why this happened, how you drifted away from me..." He swallowed and then began again, "I know it's not all your fault. I know it's partly mine, too."

"Jason, don't. I—"

"Shh," he said as he leaned in and kissed me. At first, I hesitated but then I felt it deep inside, beneath the brittle layers of disappointment and bitterness and resentment, the lit spark of love for Jason, my husband. And I remembered the shine in his blue eyes as he held our babies and the scratchy feel of his goatee in the morning and the half-laugh he'd let out at times of stress. I remembered how he used to leave toothpaste on my toothbrush in the morning before he ran out the door and how he sang "Happy Birthday" over and over again to my pregnant belly, and all the little moments of our life together. Somehow, in the flood of memories, I connected with the love I'd once felt for him so effortlessly. He pulled me up higher onto the bed and we wrapped our arms around each other as he kissed me on the mouth, on the neck, on the shoulders.

"Al," he said, breathing hard.

I paused for a moment as he pulled off his shirt. It had been such a long time since we'd made love. The lyrics of the song echoed through my mind and I pulled my shirt off, too, and wiggled out of my jeans. The feel of his body against mine was infinitely familiar and yet strange too. I'd spent so much time in bed with Matt over the last six months, losing myself in his smell and his skin and the way we fit so effortlessly together that I'd grown accustomed to his form. And Jason and I had been having quickies for years. But I didn't want to think about that now; I wanted to be there, in my bedroom with my husband, stretched out and taking our time. He kissed me again and again and caressed my thighs and stomach. I rubbed his sides and felt his chest hair tickle my breasts as he got on top of me and entered me. I struggled to hold my emotions in check as he gazed down at me. We didn't speak, we just rocked slowly back and forth until my tears finally gave way for all the things I'd lost and all the things I'd given away, and all the things I still longed for but knew could never be. We clung to each other and I tried to connect to the "us" that once was and to follow it to the place that was once as familiar as my own breath, but became less and less recognizable as the years went by. Was return possible? Could I find another way in? Could he? He put his hand behind my neck, pulled me up to meet him, and wiped the tears off my cheek with the back of his hand. "Shhh," he murmured again as he moved inside of me. We didn't speak. We just moved back and forth together, aching and thrusting, trying our best to hold on.

I must have drifted off because when I woke up he was dressed. He came over to me and said, "It's late. I better get back. I don't want Maria to have to make excuses to the kids about where I am. They're confused enough as it is."

I agreed, noting his concern for their reactions. He hesitated and then said, "I'd like to make an appointment with the marriage counselor, if that's okay with you."

"Yes," I replied.

***

Over the next three months, Jason and I met with a

marriage counselor "weekly." At least, it started weekly for the first month or so until Jason started missing sessions. I was torn between expressing how eerily familiar this felt and letting him off the hook. After all, who was I to judge? We were making slow progress and learning to communicate more openly. We didn't go to bed together again, although he wanted to; he asked a few times, but it never felt right. Meanwhile, I was making my own adjustments. I had no contact with Matt even though I still thought about him every day. I hoped, in time, that would fade. I took down my Facebook profile at the counselor's suggestion and felt good about it.

"Is that okay with you, Alex?" Lark asked me last week, "that Jason hasn't shown up to some of your sessions?"

"Yeah, I guess."

"Well, that's interesting," she said looking at me.

"What do you mean?"

"I don't know, Alex. What do you mean, 'you guess?'"

"I just meant that...that..."

"That you're really okay with him working instead of going to marriage counseling? Or that you're falling back into old patterns of not communicating your needs?'"

She was good, I had to give her that. "Okay, you're right," I told her. "I don't know why it's so hard for me. I'm going to talk to him today."

"Good," she said. "Stay with your feelings, okay?"

"Okay," I said, shaking my head up and down. "I will."

We leaned in for our goddess hug and I thought about what we'd gone over. No matter how committed I was to me, it was so easy to fall back into 'old patterns.' But I knew where this led and I didn't want to go back down that road. As I brushed curly red strands of hair out of my mouth, I realized I had to get moving. I had a long-overdue meeting that afternoon and I didn't want to be late.

I pulled up to the office, signed in, and stuck a yellow VISITOR sticker on my pale blue sweater. The principal, a small, pleasant-faced woman in her early fifties, took me on a tour of the elementary classrooms and the gym and, as we walked the track, she explained the school's emphasis on experiential education and how physical fitness was a large part of that. Just as she was explaining the school's mission, I was surprised to see Jason, in a gray suit with a baseball cap crushed onto his head, crisscrossing the lawn toward me.

"Excuse me," I said. "That's my husband, Jason. I'm not sure what he's doing here."

"Oh, I didn't realize he'd be joining us for the tour."

"Neither did I."

Jason walked across the track and stood next to me. "What are you doing here, Alex?"

"I'm touring North Roads."

"Why?" he asked.

"Hello. You must be Mr. Hoffman. I've heard all about your son Ryan. I was just explaining to your wife our school's philosophy and our emphasis on experiential learning."

"Experiential learning? Doesn't that take away from academics?"

"Mr. Hoffman, kids with certain challenges don't do well in the traditional classroom-based lecture model—"

"Well, my son's needs are being met at his *traditional* school."

"Jason—"

The principal looked at me and then at Jason and assessed the situation perfectly. She turned to me and said with a smile, "I'm going to let you folks talk. If you have any questions, please feel free to contact me. It was nice to meet you both."

As she walked away, I turned and looked at Jason. "Seriously, what are you doing here?"

"I tried calling you a few times but you didn't answer."

"I put my phone on vibrate," I said, taking it out of my purse and checking the setting. "How did—"

"You didn't answer, Alex. So I used Find Your Phone. I wanted to know where you were."

"Oh, Jason…"

"Well, you're still hiding things. I mean, come on, Al, North Roads? I thought we'd talked about this."

"No. You talked about it. I still think it needs to be considered."

"Fine. If it will make you happy, I'll consider it."

"Happy? This school is not about making me happy."

"Then what *is* about making you happy? Huh? Because whatever I'm doing clearly isn't working—even the marriage counseling. You barely let me touch you and even now, I'm trying to compromise."

"Is this a compromise? Because it doesn't feel like one. It feels like a battle between you and me over what's right for Ryan. And I don't want to fight. I've thought a lot about this. And I've spent hours at teacher conferences going over goal-setting and redirecting, and you know what I've learned from all these meetings? Ryan needs something else—something different."

"I think you're jumping the gun, Alex. I think we should wait."

"Wait? For what?"

"Give him more time. Don't force this big change on him."

"More time? He doesn't need more time. Don't you see it isn't working? He can't keep it up—not even for you. He needs help, Jase, and I know how hard that is for you. I know how much you want to believe it'll be okay and time will fix everything but sometimes it doesn't—it just can't— and sometimes, you have to make a fresh start—you have to stop pretending and face the fact that—oh god…"

I leaned against a palm tree and felt the roughness of the bark underneath my hand. I gripped the trunk, waiting for my heart to stop pounding, waiting for the words to form. It was time. It was unavoidably time.

"Fine. If it's that important to you, I'll consider it."

"I can't do this."

"What are you talking about? I said, I'll consider it."

"Not Ryan, Jason. Us. I can't fix us. And I can't keep pretending—not again—not even for your sake, not even for the kids. I can't keep hiding out in this marriage. I won't do it."

"What are you talking about?"

"Us, Jason. I am talking about us. We can't pretend we 'fit' when we both know we don't.

"Are you seeing him again?"

"What? No! Is that what you think this is about? Haven't you heard anything I've said in counseling?"

"Yes, Alex I've heard it all but I don't get it. I don't get any of it. You said you were so lonely without the kids, that you missed them so much when they were with me. I thought you wanted to be a family again."

I gazed at the ground and considered my response. I noticed that Jason's leather loafers sank slightly into the damp grass. I pictured him leaning against our white doorframe and wiping them clean with an old cloth, front to back. But some things couldn't be wiped clean, made shiny and new again, no matter how much you might want them to.

I lifted my head and finally looked him in the eye. "It's a different kind of loneliness, Jason, to be lonely when you're alone than to be lonely when you're with another person."

We stood silently next to each other. I noticed people walking to the parking lot and wondered if the bell was going to ring soon signifying the end of the school day.

"We'd better get going," I said finally. "We can talk at the house." I drove slowly, watching Jason following me through the rearview window. I pulled up to the curb and got out of the car. Jason came and stood next to me.

"Can I ask you something?" he asked.

"Yes," I said. We walked up the path together and I sat down on the front step of our walkway. He didn't say anything at first.

We sat side by side looking out over our professionally landscaped front yard. The gardenias were in bloom and the sweet perfume of their white flowers pervaded the lawn.

"Why can't we fix things?" He winced with the pain of the words. "Because, for a while there, I thought, maybe, we still had a chance."

The fact was we tried, didn't we? Or did we? We spent a few months going through the motions of counseling and attempting to re-connect but something wouldn't click. I couldn't connect to myself when I was with Jason no matter how much I wanted to. I was so used to hiding myself away so that our marriage could survive that I only knew how to pretend to be someone else, someone who was happy with the way things were, so I didn't rock the boat, with myself or with him. But I wasn't happy and I wasn't myself. Matt's words came to mind, "I won't make the same mistake twice." I wouldn't either. I already pretended my way through our marriage once; I wasn't going to pretend my way into a reconciliation. Whether we gave it three months or three years, I couldn't do it. Lark encouraged me to stay tuned in to what I was feeling and I was. No matter how guilty I felt, I had to be honest with myself, and Jason too. We didn't fit. I had to let go of my belief that getting back together would absolve me of my sins. My sins were what they were. I'd have to learn to forgive myself one day.

He sat down next to me, took his car keys out of his pocket, and began to scratch at a remnant of gum stuck to the walkway. I could feel the words inside me take shape.

"You love him, don't you?"

I looked around our front lawn at the garden bench Jason repaired last year, at the birdhouse Natalie painted years ago that still clung to our Elm tree.

"Jason, it's over. It has been for months."

"But it's true. Is that why?"

"I know you want an answer but I'm not sure I have one that will satisfy you." I shifted uncomfortably on the step. "I'm in terrain I barely recognize. It's like somehow when I hit rock bottom, it wasn't just the bottom I discovered, it was my core. I sank to my core. I didn't mean to, I didn't plan it. But over the years all the superficial layers of my happiness, of my identity got stripped away. I've sunk down as low as I can go but what I realize is that I'm not going to drown, I just don't have any fantasies left to cling to. All I have left is me, the heart of me. And I have to see what's there. I have to." This was the hardest part to admit, "And I have to look there on my own. Do you understand that at all?"

He looked at me and wordlessly shook his head. "No," he said. "I don't. I don't get why we can't keep trying."

"I can't be who you want; god knows, I'm not even who I want. But I can't do it anymore. I just can't." I took a deep breath and reached for his hand. "I'm sorry, Jason. I really, truly am sorry."

We sat there on the front steps of the house we paid the jumbo-mortgage on every month for the last seven years and watched the sky turn black. The walkway lights flicked on and I noticed that one of the bulbs was dark and I'd have to remember to change it myself. I held Jason's hand and our fingers slipped effortlessly into place and there were no words for the sorrow I felt for having betrayed my husband or how it felt to be sorry and free at the same time.

RESTLESS IN L.A.
Mommy Musings. Stupid Confessions. Life.
Posted by Anonymous

That Still, Small Voice

You'd think I'd be an expert at lying to myself by now. I had done it so often, about so many things for so many years that it was pretty much, a way of life. And yet, it still wasn't easy to drown out that Still, Small Voice. I tried to keep my life as noisy and busy as possible to try to block it out but the damn thing persisted. I tried to medicate it away both with prescription drugs and alcohol but that didn't work either because in the silence, which there still occasionally was, I could hear the whisper.

I imagined myself plugging my fingers into my ears and singing, "Twinkle, Twinkle Little Star," at the top of my lungs like my daughter did when my son refused to stop talking about his latest Pokémon battles. I figured if I belted out "Twinkle, Twinkle" long enough, that fucking Voice would finally give up and leave me alone. I didn't know what it said and I didn't want to know. I just knew it was a threat to the way things were so I did my best to ignore it.

But it just wouldn't quit. And as my life coach so often said, "What we resist, persists." And so it did. It persisted until it was no longer a whisper but an ear-splitting shriek that no amount of alcohol, drugs, or mind-numbing grocery shopping could block out.

EPILOGUE: SIX MONTHS LATER

I opened the door to my house, balancing two bags of groceries on one hip and maneuvered the key into the lock with the handles of another bag wrapped around my elbow. It was a long day. Dr. Ross and I disagreed about Ryan getting an Xbox. He wanted Ryan to have it as part of a reward system he thought we should implement. I didn't like the idea. Jason and I discussed it and we both agreed that the last thing Ryan needed was another screen to play on. We already had screaming matches whenever I tried to unhook him from the TV or the computer. I couldn't deal with another screen to fight about.

I unpacked my eight bags of groceries and thought about how things were going. Natalie had started middle school and it was okay. Some days she begged not to go, crying, "This is the worst school ever!" and other days, she skipped out the door with a smile. She had several meltdowns claiming either, "My math teacher hates me!" or "No one likes me! I don't have a single friend!" but between the friendship dramas and teacher traumas, she seemed to be doing pretty well, considering. Ben was Ben—happy, playful, silly. He took Jason's moving out the best of the three, seeming to delight in having, two rooms, two houses, two TVs.

"You don't get it, Benny, " Natalie shouted at Ben one day last week, his unfazed attitude driving her crazy. "Mom and Dad are getting a divorce! They don't love each other anymore. Soon we are going to have to live in an apartment like Vivian!" Ben cried for three days after that, satisfying Natalie's pre-teen angst immensely.

It was hardest on Ryan. He was adjusting to a new school and the myriad of other changes in our lives, and even though I felt close to him again, he seemed to yearn for the strong presence of his father. Although Jason and I agreed on an equitable share of custody, Ryan chose to spend the majority of his nights at his dad's. That hurt, that somehow Ryan needed Jason more than he needed me, but I tried to understand and accept his feelings. Ryan was a complicated kid and his dad made him feel safe in a way I could appreciate. Still, it hurt when he suddenly announced, "I'm ready to go to Dad's" right in the middle of the four of us watching a movie or playing a game. To Jason's credit, whenever I called him, he came. He didn't tell me what meeting he was missing or what case he was preparing for, he just came and got his son.

I tried not to entertain the voice that told me what a failure I was, not just at the parenting thing but at my marriage as well. Lark and I still met weekly and if there was one thing I'd learned, it was that it was my choice to listen to that voice—or not. I wasn't perfect, not even close, but at least the world would have to turn with one less phony.

***

After Jason and I legally separated, I started looking for a job. Several weeks went by with me perusing the Internet for job listings when I received an email through my blog. I was so caught up in all the drama of my life that I failed to notice how popular my blog had become. I was surprised to find an email from a literary agent asking if I was interested in discussing a blog-to-book project. She wrote that her sister-in-law turned her on to *RESTLESS IN L.A.* and she was a huge fan. "Re-connecting with old lovers online is the biggest threat to modern marriage," the agent wrote in her email. "People are intrigued by your story." I asked myself if this was the opportunity I was waiting for. It was clear writing was my passion but the blog had been anonymous.

I had a story to tell, a story I wanted to tell as myself, a story about a woman who reconnected with an old lover on Facebook and how that connection fucked up her whole life and then gave her a new, different, and unexpected life. I clicked on my blog and thought about how it all started—the journal and the photograph and Laurie's urgent warnings against the Facebook search. I reread a few posts and then logged off—for good. I didn't want to hide behind *RESTLESS* anymore. I pulled up a new Word document and started the first writing project I'd embarked on in twenty years—as me: *I didn't mean to friend him. I don't even like Facebook. Other people's perfect lives annoy me and put me in a bad mood. I have this fantasy of starting "Real Book," an online site where people post their truth...*

***

A week later, I met Laurie for lunch at the W Hotel in Santa Monica. Every few months she liked to make a special trip to her favorite purse outlet on Wilshire Boulevard and I'd agreed to meet her there for some girl time. We shared a chopped salad and a half carafe of chardonnay and settled in for a heart-to-heart.

"So, how's the job search going, Al?" she asked. She had her short brown hair blown out straight that morning and it looked trés chic, as usual.

"Actually I am working on a...book." I paused and waited for her reaction.

"Oh my god, Alex. That's wonderful. Tell me."

So I came clean again to my best friend and told her about the first real project I had started since college.

"And I don't know if it will amount to anything," I said, not wanting to get her—or my—hopes up, "but I'm writing again and I'm really happy."

We sat there for a moment silently staring at each other. She'd been there for me through everything. I reached over and took her hand.

"Thank you, Laurie, for your friendship." I could see tears pooling in her eyes as she picked up her white linen napkin and carefully dabbed at the corners so as not to smear her mascara. "You'll never know what it's meant to me," I said.

"You're my best friend," she said simply. "You always will be."

I reached for my glass of water and took a deep drink, hoping to reverse the tightening in my throat. It had been a roller coaster of a year. I don't think I would have survived it without her.

"Speaking of *friends*, can I give your number to Evan's chiropractor?' she asked. "He's a really sweet guy, divorced, two kids, lotsa hair." She laughed, lightening the mood.

"Oh Laur, no," I chuckled from her description. "He sounds great but I don't want to complicate things, and, well, I'm not up for it yet." I shook my head firmly, hoping to de-rail her train of thought.

"You don't want to start getting out there?" she asked, motioning around at the booths of well-heeled lunchers.

"I will—eventually. But it's barely been six months since Jason and I formalized the separation and...I need more time." I reached for the menu the waitress dropped off, thinking maybe dessert would distract her. "How about we share a slice of carrot cake?"

"The only time is now," she retorted.

"Come on. Now you sound like Lark."

"Well, I take that as a compliment," she said, lowering her voice. "Look, I know this year's been extremely difficult and I worry about the hermit lifestyle you're adopting." She craned her neck behind her and whispered loudly, "Besides, there's probably a hot guy in this very hotel who's dying to go out with you."

"Oh Laurie," I shook my head, squeezing her hand across the table. "It has been hard—totally excruciating, really—but I'm working things out for myself and spending a lot of time with the kids and...well, I'm okay. The truth is, I'm on my own and I'm okay. I really am." Our eyes met and she dabbed hers again with her napkin.

"All right," she nodded. "I believe you. Now let's eat cake."

We talked and laughed and clanked our glasses of chardonnay over our carrot cake until we noticed, through the oversized glass windows that lined the restaurant, that the sky darkened.

"Shit, I'm so bummed," Laurie said. "Wouldn't you know it: the one day I get my hair blown out, it rains in L.A. It rains, what? Twice a year?"

"I think I saw umbrellas for sale in the gift shop," I said. "Why don't you hurry over to the valet and give him your tickets before it turns into a downpour? I'll run over and buy you an umbrella."

"Great," she beamed. "I want to preserve my beautiful, straight tresses for as long as possible. Not everyone has gorgeous smooth locks naturally, Al. Some of us have to pay for it." She winked as she collected her things and headed out toward the lobby.

I rushed over to the gift shop and grabbed a purple polka-dotted, fold-up umbrella, bought it quickly, and hurried out. I unwrapped it from the plastic packaging as I strode toward the exit and was so engrossed in trying to open the damn thing that I collided headfirst into another hotel guest. I was knocked backward and would have fallen down flat had he not grabbed my arm and steadied me. When I looked up, I was so completely taken off guard, I fumbled the umbrella and nearly jabbed him in the stomach.

Matt Daniels gasped when he saw my face. It was ten months, three weeks, and four days since we'd last seen each other.

"Matt! What—what are you doing here?" I blurted out as I righted myself and stared at him. His deep green eyes opened wide at the sight of me and I could tell he was as caught off guard as I was.

"Alex," was all he could say. He had grabbed my right arm above the wrist to steady me and still held tightly to it. We stood there, immobile, staring at each other. Finally he responded, "I'm, uh, I'm...looking at a project in L.A.," he finished, still gripping my arm.

"Oh," I said.

"How—how have you been?" he asked, his eyes still pinned on mine.

I noticed the shadow of afternoon stubble across his jaw but quickly averted my gaze. "Good, I've been good. What about you? How have you been?"

"Going through a lot of changes but things are good," he said. His hair was a little longer than I remembered and maybe a little grayer, too. He was wearing jeans and a dark blue sweater with a black-and-white checkered messenger bag thrown over one shoulder. He looked slightly bohemian and as striking as ever.

I suddenly noticed a young, dark-haired beauty standing at his side. Why didn't I spot her before? Matt followed my gaze and stepped back, finally releasing my arm and including her in our conversation.

"Alex, this is my assistant, Jane McAdams; Jane, this is my, uh, friend, Alex Hoffman." Jane took a step closer to Matt and shook her head to the right, flipping her long, dark hair over one shoulder as she offered me her hand. No wonder things are good, I thought to myself, as I clasped it.

"Nice to meet you, Jane," I said as graciously as I could. My heart was seized in a vice-like grip and the squeezing sensation nearly knocked the wind out of me. I inhaled deeply and met Matt's eyes. "It was nice to see you," I said. "It really was." The weight of his gaze jangled my nerves but I held steady before I turned away. "Take good care."

I hurried out of the hotel as fast as my feet would carry me, not as if I was fleeing a burning building but feeling that same sort of urgency. I clutched the fold-up umbrella to my chest to disguise the loud pounding in my heart and was surprised the white plastered walls of the hotel didn't reverberate with the force of it.

"What took you so long?" Laurie asked, crowded up against the other rain-phobic patrons huddled under the skimpy hotel awning. "What's wrong? You look like you've seen a ghost." She reached over and pulled me closer. "Are you okay?"

Before I could open my mouth to answer, we heard someone calling my name.

"Alex, Alex—"

We both turned our heads to see where it was coming from but I already knew. Matt skirted the long line of people waiting for their cars and approached me huddled under the awning, Laurie's hand still gripping my elbow.

"Alex," he said. "I—"

I cut him off. "I'm happy for you, Matt. I hope you found what you were looking for."

"What?"

"Jane," I said. "She's beautiful."

"What are you talking about? She's my assistant." He ran his hand through his hair.

Suddenly Laurie interjected, "Matt Daniels, I'm guessing?"

"Yes. Sorry," he answered, reaching out his hand.

"Laurie Rankin. Alex's best friend." She gripped his palm, looking from him to me and back again.

"Nice to finally meet you," he said, bouncing slightly on his heels. "Would you excuse us for a moment?"

"Of course," she answered.

He put his arm around my back and we stepped off the curb into a corner away from the awning and the people waiting there. The rain drizzled down on my hair and jacket.

"I didn't contact you. You made it clear you didn't want me to and I didn't." He looked away for a moment and shook his head at the gray mist that blanketed the Pacific Ocean to our left. "But now that you're here, I have to know—how are you, really?"

"I'm all right," I said. I really, truly am." The valet guys pulled up Laurie's car and behind it, my white SUV and were waving the keys at the open door.

"So you two, you worked it out?"

Everything froze: the valet guy stopped waving; Laurie, craning her neck to watch us as she slipped into her car was stuck mid-stare, even the raindrops seemed to pulse in place for the brief moment while I considered my answer. I could say yes and that would be that. He would move on and I would move on and we would finally have an ending:

After more than twenty-one years, it ended on a rainy Thursday afternoon in Santa Monica when, nearly a year after the affair ended, Matt and I collided in a hotel lobby. He chased me down, asked if I worked things out with my husband, and I told him I had. He wished me well, and then he, and his beautiful assistant Jane, disappeared into the valet line. The End. "No." I answered. "We didn't make it."

He looked stunned. The valet guys resumed waving, the other guests in line began to grumble, and I stood in the rain staring into his eyes.

"I'm sorry Alex," he finally said.

I nodded.

"Why didn't you call?" he asked, shaking his head.

"So much happened," I said, thinking of everything

that went on in the last year and a half. "I couldn't."

The valet guy reached into the driver's seat of my car and honked the horn twice.

I looked at Matt and made a split second decision. "Take a ride with me?"

He followed me to my car, dumped his bag on the passenger-side floor, and sat down, wiping raindrops off his sweater. We drove to the beach in silence. The rain was coming down hard so we sat in the parked car with the heat on.

"Will you tell me what happened?" he asked.

I dug the nail of my right thumb deep into my left palm as I looked through the wind shield and summed up the last ten months. "Jason and I went through the motions of marriage counseling but after a while we both knew it wasn't going to work. He didn't want to change and I couldn't stop changing. There just wasn't any place for us to go. It's been hard, especially on the kids."

I didn't tell him that I thought about him every day. I didn't tell him how hard I tried not to. He didn't ask me, either way. He just waited for me to continue.

"The weird thing is, Matt, even though I'm alone, for the first time in a very long time, I feel whole. And it's the most amazing feeling. It's not like I know what I'm doing or that I have anything figured out, but I'm asking myself how I feel. And I'm trusting the answers."

The temperature in the car seemed to rise and I reached over and flicked off the heat. I avoided his gaze as I spoke but I caught his eye for a moment and was struck, once again, by their sameness. I looked out the window at the rain pelting the sand.

"It took me so long to get here. You asked why I didn't contact you. It's not that I didn't want to, that I didn't think about it—every day. But I couldn't risk losing myself again, even in you. And the desire to do that was so powerful." His eyes never left mine as it all tumbled out. "For me, the line between us was blurry." I reached over and took his hand. An electric current ran up my arm, making me shudder.

"Are you cold?" he asked. He pulled on his sweatshirt with his free hand while the other held firmly to mine.

"No, no, I'm fine," I answered, thinking if he pulled off his sweatshirt, I'd be toast. "It was actually you, " I said, "who showed me how easy it was to make the same mistake twice. I wasn't going to do that again, either."

His nodded as he digested my words. We stared out the window without speaking and watched the storm roll by. I felt the thumb of his right hand slide back and forth across the knuckles of my left. "Go on," he finally said.

I looked down at the floorboards, noticed the crisscross pattern of my brown, leather boots, and summoned the truth. "I didn't want to be with you out of desperation or compulsion or the need to feel something, anything." I exhaled and looked up at his now stubbly cheek. "I had to find me, the real me, and I couldn't do that if I was lost in you."

He turned his head and peered out the window at the sidewalk. Die-hard beachgoers wandered by, umbrella-less and unperturbed. As the minutes passed, I waited and wondered what he was thinking.

"I better get back," he finally said.

I nodded before I started the car and headed toward the hotel. I dropped him off at the entrance and noticed it finally stopped raining. He opened the passenger door, got out, and then turned to me before he closed the door. "Well, did you find her?"

"Who?" I asked confused.

"You."

"Oh," I laughed. "Yes. I did. I am."

He leaned in and I moved toward him for a peck on the cheek but his lips brushed against my ear. He whispered, "It was the real you I was after all along. Oh, and, by the way, I'm a very patient man."

I pulled back and our eyes met.

"Can we be friends?" I asked.

He held on to the passenger-side door and peered into the car at me. Neither one of us spoke. I gazed at his unmistakable face, the lines around his eyes, the way he held his head, slightly cocked to one side. I already knew the answer I was hoping for.

"Sure," he said as he smiled at me. "Friends."

***

We talked on the phone every day after that. As the months went by, a different relationship emerged in the space where our physical connection had once been.

The morning he landed in L.A., I picked him up and we spent the day bike riding in Venice Beach. We had an early dinner and then walked back to his hotel hand-in-hand. He kissed me good night in the lobby.

"Aren't you going to invite me up?" I asked, gesturing down the corridor.

"What?" he asked, eyebrows raised, green eyes sparkling.

"Let's go," I answered, striding toward the elevator.

"Wait, hold on. Now? Tonight? Are you sure?" He jogged slightly to keep up with me.

We got out on his floor and walked to his room. He opened the door, still peppering me with questions.

"Alex, Alex, what are you thinking?" he asked, planting himself firmly in front of the queen-sized bed. His dark hair was tousled from the wind and a crease of concern formed between his eyebrows. "We should talk about this," he said.

"Really? I haven't been in your bed in over a year and that's what you want to do right now—talk?" I kicked off my sandals.

"Actually, it's been fourteen months, three weeks, and two days but who's counting?" He laughed. "Hey, are you sure about this?"

"I was waiting until I was ready," I said. "I'm ready."

He looked at the bed and then back at me. "Alex, I think you know this but, as much as I have, uh…" he cleared his throat, "thought about this, I don't want to do anything that might, you know, spook you."

"Are you worried I might run away?"

"The thought had crossed my mind."

I took his hands, they were warm and strong and yet soft, too. "I'm ready. I really am. And I'm not going anywhere. What about you? Are you ready?" I pulled him toward the bed.

His answer was swift and fierce. He gathered me in his arms, pulling his sweatshirt over his head as we fell onto the bed. He slid down next to me and pulled me close. His kiss was electric, the sensation of his skin against mine set off alarm bells throughout my body. We kissed and touched and undressed what was left of our clothes with the urgency of newlyweds alone in an empty house. Shoes, jeans, underwear, everything was thrown aside. I gazed at Matt's face, his dark, graying hair and hypnotic green eyes. He looked at me with his wolfish grin and something inside of me bloomed.

Bocca al lupe, I thought as I rolled on top of him.

"I want you so bad, Alexandra," he said, cupping my breasts with his hands. "I can hardly wait." He sat up and we folded into each other as I moved up and down and he kissed my mouth, my shoulders, my breasts. "When we wake up in the morning, I promise to make love to you again, slowly," he laughed, holding onto my hips and pulling me down onto him over and over again. I looked into his eyes and saw my own light shining back. I let go of the guilt and the self-recriminations and the why and the wherefore of it all, and for the moment, gave in to the excruciating pleasure of making love to Matt Daniels.

The next day, after he fulfilled his promise, I reveled in our unhurried morning. I watched as he opened an aluminum packet of coffee grounds, popped open the lid of the coffeemaker, and unwrapped two recyclable cups. Just as I was thinking how incredibly sexy he was in his blue boxers and tousled bed head, he looked up and caught me smiling.

"It's amazing how something so mundane can give me so much pleasure," he said.

"Oh, so making love to me has already become mundane?" I asked, laughing.

"I don't know about that," he said. "But I've waited one hell of a long time to make your morning coffee."

I reached my arms out to him. "One cream. Now come back to bed."

***

It was noon before we got dressed. Jason and I had put the house on the market and since it was his weekend with the kids, I planned to spend the day tackling the garage.

"I hate to eat and run," I laughed, "but I promised myself I'd clean out the garage today and I'm committed." I leaned down and stroked his smooth stomach, planting a kiss firmly in the center. "I've got to get home and get started."

He nuzzled his face in my hair and asked, "Want some help? I'm pretty talented with a broom."

Together we made our way home. As we pulled up to the curb, a knot of bitter-sweetness settled in my stomach. I got out and leaned against the passenger door, surveying the pretty picture before me: charming picket fence, huge elm tree, leaves scattered along the flagstone path. My eyes rested on the loose screen on Natalie's window and the rain gutters that needed to be cleared of leaves and twigs lodged there from last week's rain. I made a mental note to talk to the gardener as an image of Jason and me walking down that path for the very first time flashed into my mind: there was Nat, a chubby toddler, clutching a pink blanket and running ahead, and Ryan, a sleepy infant strapped securely to Jason's chest. My Benny boy was only a bubble of hope floating above us.

"You okay?" Matt asked.

"I was just thinking…" I said, squinting again at the house and letting the flood of memories wash over me. "It's funny how things can be happy and sad at the same time. You know what I mean?"

"Yes," he said, nodding. "I am intimately familiar with that feeling."

We stood quietly for another moment and then I reached for his hand and said, "I'm glad you're here. Now let's get to work."

I went through the house, opened the garage door, and went out onto the driveway, armed with an industrial-size box of double-strength garbage bags. Within an hour, five bulging bags were stuffed to the hilt with old toys, broken umbrellas, discarded shoes, and ruined paint brushes and rollers left over from the previous owner. Matt carried the bags to the curb and set them down next to the mini-dumpster I'd rented for the day. I suddenly heard the roar of a familiar car engine and glanced over to see Jason pulling up behind my SUV. Matt stood beside me holding a clear plastic box of well-worn clothes. "Hang on a minute," I said, my heart racing, as Jason and Ryan made their way up the driveway toward us.

"Hi Mom!" Ryan said, running ahead into the garage to greet me. "Benny and Nat went to get pizza with Maria, and Dad and I are going to build my Lego Death Star today!"

"That's great," I answered, leaning forward to get a quick hug. He stood next to me and looked up at Matt.

"Ryan, this is my friend, Matt," I said. Matt balanced the box on one hip, leaned over, and said, "Hey, Ryan."

Ryan nodded at him and ran into the house to look for his Lego Star Wars kit. Jason approached slowly up the driveway and stood at the entrance to the garage. Matt put the plastic box down and came to stand beside me. The two men sized each other up. They were about the same height, but where Jason was dark blond and goateed, Matt was dark and peppered, his face scruffy with weekend stubble. Jason was wearing a baseball cap and cargo shorts. Matt was in jeans and a T-shirt. They were both wearing flip-flops. If ever there was an uncomfortable moment, this was it. There I was in the garage—I'd always suspected it was my own private hellhole—standing between my lover and my husband.

"Jason, this is Matt Daniels. Matt, Jason Hoffman."

They nodded curtly at each other. No hands were outstretched. The air was heavy with grime, sweat, and lemon Endust fumes. The seconds ticked by as they regarded each other while I remained soundly in the center. Jason was poised at the threshold of the garage facing Matt and me. The two of us stood side by side looking toward him and out onto the driveway, where the sun's rays shone through the basketball hoop. Together, we formed a weird isosceles triangle of pain, loss, and love.

Finally, Jason adjusted his baseball cap and turned his head toward me. "So you're seeing him again?" he asked, flipping his chin toward Matt.

"Yes." I answered.

He looked at Matt and said, "Weird, meeting the guy who stole my wife."

Matt didn't reply. He stood silently looking back at Jason. Another infinite second ticked by until he said, "I'm going to take a walk."

"That was awkward," I said to Jason after Matt left. Granted, it was over a year and, granted, it was nearly formalized but still, it was his house—our house. "I'm sorry. I didn't know you were coming by."

"Hey, don't get all concerned about me now," he said.

"Jason, you should have told me."

"I didn't think I needed to." I could see an angry blush creeping over his face. "It's pretty fucked up that your boyfriend is helping you throw away all of our family mementos," he said, gesturing toward the overstuffed trash bags. "That's classic, Alex. Even for you. I guess it's all garbage to you now."

"That's not true," I said. "You know that."

"I can't even stop by my own house without finding *him* here." He said, his voice cracking. "But don't worry, the papers are being drawn up. You can fuck him in our bed after I leave."

"Jesus, Jason! He's hasn't stepped a foot in our house."

"Spare me the details," he said flicking his hand to the side. "I'm happy you found the love of your life. Given that I'm still your husband, it kind of sucks for me." He turned away and looked down the driveway. I reached out and grabbed him by the wrist.

"What?" he asked.

"I, I—"

"What is it?"

"I don't want you to hate me."

"You should have thought about that a year and a half ago," he answered coolly, "before you decided to break up our family and hop in bed with your old boyfriend."

I had to live with the consequences of my decisions. I couldn't make that any easier, not for me and not for Jason, either. "Okay, enough. You're right," I said, pulling out a tissue from the back pocket of my jeans and dabbing my eyes.

Jason looked over at the table of odds and ends I'd sorted for the Salvation Army. He reached across and picked up a stuffed brown teddy bear in a green shirt from the top of a box of giveaways. I remembered how dearly Ben had begged for that bear as a souvenir from our first trip to Legoland. He'd slept with it for months.

"I don't hate you," he said softly, staring into the bear's smiling face and rubbing his fur. "It would be a hell of a lot easier if I did." He looked up and I saw his Adam's apple bob up and down.

I gazed steadily at Jason and really saw him. Our

separation had forced him to spend more time out of the office. He looked good in his khaki cargo shorts and T-shirt. He looked like the Jason I remembered. It had been months since we'd actually talked without gritting our teeth. I looked at his hair poking out from under his cap, his pale blue eyes, his well-trimmed goatee. I couldn't help but remember the feel of it scratching my cheek. He loved me once and maybe he still did. And I loved him, too, and I was sure I always would. Maybe I'd never forgive myself or maybe I would. But I made a choice for me. And it took tremendous courage for me not to turn away from the things I most wanted, one of which just returned from a walk and was waiting for me at the end of the driveway.

Just then, Ryan burst through the garage door carrying a large box. He flew by me and came to rest in front of Jason. "Dad! I found it!" he shouted. "Let's build the Death Star!"

"Great job," Jason said, tousling Ryan's hair. "Go get in my car, buddy. I'll be right there after I say goodbye to Mom."

"Okay. Bye, Mom," Ryan yelled and gave me a half-wave as he ran down the driveway toward the car.

Jason stood for a moment longer, his eyes lingering on my face. He walked slowly down the driveway toward his car, then turned and looked over his shoulder.

"Goodbye Alex," he said, and walked away.

***

That night, Matt and I made a dinner in my kitchen. Matt loved to cook and I made good sous chef. I excused myself and went into my office and came back to surprise him with the journal. He took one look at the pale blue cover and jumped. Although I told him I found it and explained its role in the Facebook search and our subsequent contact, still, when he saw the blue silk cover and the stenciled pink tulips, his mouth dropped.

"I remember having to pry that thing out of your hands at night. My rival—you wrote in it endlessly. I always wondered what you wrote about me but you would never tell."

"Well, now's your chance. What do you want to hear about? Our Amsterdam adventure? Or the rave? What about the time I brought all my stuff over to your apartment?" I asked, bouncing on my heels in my excitement to see what excerpt he'd choose.

He slid back his chair and pulled me onto his lap. "Read to me about our first date," he said, wrapping his arms around my waist and leaning his head against my back.

I read aloud about the way my heart beat that first night when he showed up at my flat and took me to dinner. I read about how it was the first time I had tiramisu for dessert and how he told me it meant, "Cheer me up" in Italian and how I loved the sweet flavor and lightness of it. I read about how I went to the bathroom and sat on the cold, tile floor to get hold of the spinning in my head from the bottle of Chianti and the chemistry between us. When I got to the part about how he made my knees go weak at the front door when he kissed me good night and how close he actually was to scoring that very night, he laughed out loud. But I remembered how I barely had the strength to untangle from him and fumble through the doorway, weak and desperately wanting.

"I have to tell you something," he said when I finished reading, still wrapped in his arms. I turned to look at him as he ran his hand through his hair. His green eyes were pensive. "There was truth in what Jason said to me," he said, taking a breath. "I know I told you from the beginning that I didn't want to fuck up your life, but that wasn't exactly true. Once I saw you again...I didn't want to let you go." He looked troubled and a bit tense. "I kept hoping you'd come back. And when we collided in the hotel, well, I knew you were meant to be in my life. But how do you feel, Alex? Are you happy?"

I thought carefully about the answer. "Am I happy? I've got a son on medication who'd rather be with his father most of the time, a daughter in middle school whose moods are unpredictable at best, and a six-year-old who took a walk around the block by himself last week. Not to mention I'm going through a divorce, my ex-PTA friends give me the stink eye whenever they see me, and I drink excessive amounts of coffee and cheap wine. My life is complicated—very complicated," I stopped and looked at him, "with no signs of becoming any simpler."

He raised his eyebrows and listened as I continued. "But, on the up side, I recently got off Klonopin and cigarettes, and, well, I've got me. My life isn't perfect, not by any stretch, but it feels right, it feels real, it feels...like me. And I'm hoping, one day, a book might appear in this world with my name on it. You never know." I smiled at the thought.

"So are you telling me you're happy?" he asked.

I got up and sat across from him. "It's not your job to make me happy, Matt. The only person who can do that for me is me. You didn't steal me and I can see that it's weighed on you but you didn't. I left. Nobody can take the blame for that but me. It's what I wanted. So am I happy? Well, let's just say I'm working on it. And what about you? Are you happy?"

He handed the journal back to me and grabbed the two silver salad tongs. "I'll go with, 'I'm working on it,'" he said, his eyes sparkling and a huge grin breaking out across his face, "but I'm pretty sure I'm getting close."

ACKNOWLEDGEMENTS

Special thanks to: the University of Santa Monica where I found myself and the courage to write after a very long hiatus; my dear angel-mentor Michelle Bauman; my beloved teacher Bella Mahaya Carter and my classmates all of whom deeply influenced my writing journey; the Ladies Who Lit: Melissa Gould, Courtney Crane, and Megan Austin Oberle; my beta reader and mother Vicki Finn; and my Year 3 project team: Kimberly Barclay, Julie Casey, and Maya Atzlan. Thanks to all my dear friends and cheerleaders at "book club," and to Lesley Hyatt, Ellen Finn and Carrie Kneitel, and to Lorelle Taras Schirn who always knew. My deepest love and gratitude to my three extraordinary children: Miranda, Eli, and Nina, and to Michael, for our life together. Finally, gratitude to the Universe for the 'divine download' that became this novel. I don't know from where the story came, I just know it had to be told.

ROBIN FINN

ABOUT THE AUTHOR

Robin Finn is an author, essayist, and advocate for children with ADHD/2e. Her work has appeared in *The Washington Post, The Los Angeles Times, The Huffington Post, BuzzFeed,* Disney's *Babble.com, ADDitude Magazine,* and elsewhere. She has master's degrees in public health from Columbia University and in spiritual psychology from the University of Santa Monica. Robin lives in Los Angeles with her husband and family.

www.robinfinn.com